RUSH

ALSO BY LISA PATTON

Whistlin' Dixie in a Nor'easter

Yankee Doodle Dixie

Southern as a Second Language

RUSH

LISA PATTON

ST. MARTIN'S PRESS

NEW YORK

RUSH. Copyright © 2018 by Lisa Patton. All rights reserved.
Printed in the United States of America. For information, address
St. Martin's Press, 175 Fifth Avenue, New York, N.Y. 10010.

www.stmartins.com

The Library of Congress Cataloging-in-Publication Data is available upon request.

ISBN 978-1-250-02066-6 (hardcover)
ISBN 978-1-250-02274-5 (ebook)

Our books may be purchased in bulk for promotional, educational, or business use. Please contact your local bookseller or the Macmillan Corporate and Premium Sales Department at 1-800-221-7945, extension 5442, or by email at MacmillanSpecialMarkets@macmillan.com.

First Edition: August 2018

10 9 8 7 6 5 4

For Julia Black, Devonia Crawford, and Christine King,
the three most selfless ladies I've ever known.
Although each has "passed into Glory," their memories are alive.
All three etched indelible imprints into my heart.
I'm a much better person for having been a part of their motherhoods.

And for all the ladies and gentlemen who have worked tirelessly in
sorority and fraternity houses all over the South. Thank you.

Life's most persistent and urgent question is,
"What are you doing for others?"
—Dr. Martin Luther King, Jr.

ONE

MISS PEARL

I work for four hundred and thirty-eight white ladies in a three-story mansion, not a one of them over the age of twenty-two. When I took this job, nearly twenty-five years ago, I did it out of necessity. Things in my life had . . . well, let's just say they had jumped the track. All of the women in my family, as far back as any of us knew, had worked as domestics. I had been determined to do something different—graduate from college—and make a name for myself. Yet here I am following along in their footsteps.

I clean toilets, I mop floors, I polish fancy furniture, and I shine the sterling silver. I do a whole lot more, unrelated to housekeeping, but I'll get to that later. Even though things may not have turned out the way I planned, I like to think I've made the best of it. My people always told me, "When the praises go up the blessings come down, even if they are found in the most unlikely places."

Now, let's get back to the young ladies. Only sixty-six of them actually stay in the mansion. The other four hundred or so stay in dormitories or apartments and come over for meals, to do their homework, attend chapter meetings, and just be together. They're sisters. Not by blood. Sorority sisters. Alpha Delta Beta sorority sisters. It's considered one of the oldest and finest sororities on the University of Mississippi campus. And that mansion I mentioned? We all call it "the House."

In a way, it reminds me of that Downton Abbey house on PBS. Not as spectacular on the outside, but with every bit of drama on the inside. Like Downton, there's a staff of people cooking and cleaning at the Alpha Delt House, plus a whole lot of wealth, gossip, pretty clothes, and tears.

Until it went off the air, the sisters living in the House used to pack into the TV room and watch that show every Sunday night. Made it into a party, too, bringing in cheese plates, dips, and desserts. Always had an adult beverage—*or two*—to go along with their hors d'oeuvres. They'd have to be sneaky about it, though. No alcohol allowed in the House, even if the drinker is twenty-one.

Looks to me like some things haven't changed all that much in a hundred years. Yet other times I know they have, for the better. Last year, the Alpha Delts let in their first black sister. I see the positive in that—I'm not denying it—but truth is I'm curious. I'm trying to get up my nerve to ask her why she wanted to join a white sorority in the first place when there are three black sororities on campus. Seems like she'd feel a whole lot more comfortable over there, rather than sticking out like a black swan over here. I know it's not my business. But, like I said, I'm curious. Every time we pass each other in the House, me in my navy work scrubs, she in her fancy designer dresses, I can't help but wonder what it is she's thinking when she looks at me.

Wouldn't it be nice if all the black and white sororities combined? I ask myself that sometimes. But that has about as much of a chance as all the black and white churches coming together. Personally, I think that's the way the Lord meant for it to be, but it would be easier for the Delta State Statesmen to beat the Ole Miss Rebels than it would be to fully integrate Mississippi.

We—that's the rest of the staff and me—have been working like mules for a solid week now trying to get this House ready for the new school year. It's been closed up all summer long and the cobwebs—thick as bagworms—have found a home in every nook and cranny. I've been wearing myself out ten hours a day, washing down the baseboards, cleaning the dust off all the mahogany dining room tables and the hundreds of matching Chippendale chairs. Vacuuming the draperies. Vacuuming the upholstery. Polishing the silver. *Woo.* Makes me tired just talking about it.

I finished scrubbing the bathrooms on all three floors yesterday, and today I've still got the composites. It's my job to make sure they are dust and fingerprint–free; we've got one for every year clear back to 1912. I have to laugh when I look at them all lined up and down the halls and in the chapter room with tiny oval pictures of all the members. It looks like white is the only race. Except for last year's composite with that little black head on the end. That's Alberta Williams, our pretty black swan.

Seems like I'm doing nothing but murmuring and complaining. God hates a complainer. I know that full well. Scripture says so. I do it, and I might do it more often than I should, but the truth is nobody's twisting my arm to work at the Alpha Delta Beta House. There isn't but one thing tethering me to a job where after twenty-five years of loyal service, I don't get but $11.50 an hour.

That one thing, the *only* thing, keeping me working here is the girls. I love them like they are my own daughters. And most of them love me right back. Sure, there's a few with their noses stuck up in the air who don't want much to do with me or the rest of the staff, but that's anywhere. The vast majority are twenty-four-karat gold. They're my babies. Whether it's my advice, a shoulder to cry on, my prayers, or my unquestionable love, they always seem to be in need of Miss Pearl.

"Miss Pearl!"

I hear someone squealing my name and the scurry of flip-flops on hard-wood clapping in my direction. Today is move-in day and I'm inside my hall maintenance closet searching for a spare bottle of Windex with my backside poking out the door. When I straighten up, look behind me, Elizabeth Jennings is standing there with that pearly white smile of hers spread clear across her pageant-perfect face. Mississippi is the beauty queen capital of the world and all it takes is one glance inside the Alpha Delt House to understand why.

An armload of clothes on hangers falls, *kerplunk*, onto the floor, and Eliza-beth jumps in the closet with me. She throws her arms around my neck, squeezes me like I'm family. "I missed you, Miss Pearl."

"Welcome back, sweetheart. I missed you, too."

I have to keep from laughing at her tiny self. That backpack she's wearing is bigger than she is and it's bulging at the zipper like a tight dress. She's wearing

Lululemon shorts with an oversize white Alpha Delt T-shirt and leather flip-flops. Why all the girls want to wear those big T-shirts, hiding the prettiest parts of themselves, is something I'll never understand. Her legs are dark, like caramel candy, and well toned.

"Woo-whee, baby, your skin looks like mine," I say, busting out laughing.

"I just got back from Seaside four days ago." She holds her arm up to mine. "Our family goes every summer. Did you go anywhere fun?"

I'm thinking to myself, *Me? Go on a vacation?* I'm laid off three months every summer. Best I can do is collect an unemployment check, and that's not enough to fill a sugar jar. Some might wonder why I don't look for temp work. I do. Aside from a babysitting job or two, there's not much left. Oxford is a college town. Things scale way back in the summer. But that's not Lizzie's problem, nor her fault. "No, baby, I had too much going on right here in Oxford."

The crease between her eyebrows deepens. "I'm sorry, Miss Pearl." She closes her eyes, pokes out her bottom lip. It's genuine. I know Lizzie's heart.

"I'm not worried about it. And you shouldn't be, either. What room are you moving into?"

"I don't know yet. I was on the way to Mama Carla's apartment to get my key, but there was a big line. So I came to find you." She hugs me again.

Mama Carla is our housemother, although these days people say House Director. On move-in day she checks out room keys to each girl and has them sign a contract swearing to obey all the House rules.

After a few minutes of catching up, Lizzie sighs and says, "I guess I better get in that line." She leans down, scoops up half the clothes into a messy pile, high as her chin. Any ironing done before today was a big waste of time.

I lean down, pick up the rest. "I'ma help you with your things. Come on, let's use the back steps."

"You're sweet to offer, but my dad's around here somewhere. Just stick the rest on top." She laughs. "If you don't mind."

I plop the remainder of her clothes on top of the pile, mash them down so she can see. "Be careful now."

"I will." She takes a few steps toward Mama Carla's apartment, turns back around. "I've got a lot to tell you—when you get a minute."

"You know I'm here for you. My office is always open." All the girls know they can stop by my office, also known as my maintenance closet, for counseling any time they choose. I've got two stools inside exactly for that reason. Alpha Delt In-House Counselor is another of my unofficial titles.

She steps forward to hug me once more, remembers the load in her arms, and kisses my cheek instead. "Thanks, Miss Pearl. You're the best."

Lizzie has always been one of my favorites. Oh, Lizzie is what most everyone calls her. She's a senior this year and I've known her since she was a pledge. She's also this year's Recruitment Chairman and that is one heck of a job. I've never met her dad, but her mother's real nice. She's always polite and tells me she's relieved I'm working here. Last year when Lizzie came down with that kissing disease, mono-something-or-other, and almost had to leave school, her mother must have called me every other day for three months asking would I please check on her baby.

"Pearl," she'd start, like my name had two syllables, "it's me again." There was no reason for her to tell me who "me" was. She knew I had her name in my phone. I have almost all the mamas' numbers in my phone.

Most of the rest of the mamas are good to me, too. Whenever I meet one for the first time they say, "Miss Pearl, I've heard so much about you." That lets me know their daughters have been talking well about me. Somehow or another, they all find out my cell phone number and a week doesn't go by without one or two of them calling to ask me to take care of their daughters. They are well past the age of needing taking care of, but tell that to some of these mamas.

Last year, I had Genna Ferguson's mother call and ask if I would drive over to the Walgreens and pick up a neti pot, a bottle of Advil, one of zinc, and a six-pack of Sprite for her sick daughter. After I left there, she wanted me to drive to Simpson's Deli, clear across town, to get an order of their chicken soup because it was Genna's favorite.

Another mama asked me to make sure her girl's dress was ironed for a big date she had that evening. Said he came from one of the finest families in Jackson and she couldn't make it to town in time to ensure her daughter looked all right.

Still another mama called one morning and asked if I'd go up to her daughter Liza's room and calm her down. Said her boyfriend had cheated on her with "a Chi Theta whore" and asked if I could put my arm around her and make sure she had a "mama-like" shoulder to cry on. I never turn any of them down. I'm happy to do it. I feel like the girls are half mine, anyway.

Several of the mamas bless me with nice things for taking care of their girls. I've got a collection of scarves and throws, decor pillows and candles. Sometimes it's bubble bath or a nice bar of soap. Other times it's a gift certificate to a restaurant or Macy's. And oftentimes it's plain ol' cash. Last year I got a letter from one of my girls telling me, "You are a special person. I don't know what I'd do without you. I love you, Miss Pearl." She left it for me outside my closet. Put a candle with it, too. One of those good-smelling kinds. But something about that note, the I-love-you-Miss-Pearl part, tugged at the deepest part of me.

Before I can get out of my closet, here come Scarlett McDonald and Clemé Barkley rapping on the door. When they see me, they both throw their arms around me. Caitlin Ishee slips in between. They've been rooming together in a three-person room for the last two years, and are as tight as the lid on a honey jar. That's the best thing about joining a sorority; once a friendship is formed, that bond is so thick it would take a thousand soldiers to knock down their bulwark.

"Excuse me, Miss Pearl," Clemé says, "Mama Carla needs your help. The line to check in is pretty backed up and Amelia Williamson is upstairs sick." Amelia is this year's House Manager and is in charge of room assignments. It's her job to sit with Mama Carla all day handing out keys.

"Well, okay then. Tell her I'll be on soon as I lock up." The girls scurry off in front of me as I pull out my key. "Tell her not to worry," I holler. "Help's on the way." It's not uncommon for Mama Carla to ask for my help. She gives me plenty of extra responsibilities around the House. There is nothing she can't trust me with and she knows it. Trustworthiness is paramount in this job. Without it I'd be out on the street faster than cotton catches fire.

I shut and lock the door behind me, then make my way to her apartment. It's in the front of the House near the door, so she can see who's coming and going. *Lord.* I look down, let out a big sigh. This morning I could see my face in these floors. Now, after folks been tracking in dust all day long, they are some kind of filthy all over again.

Right before walking into Mama Carla's apartment I notice the front door standing wide open, letting every bit of the cold air out. I reach out to shut it and a rush of heat hits me in the face like I've opened the oven. August is sure enough showing off today. Weatherman said Oxford is predicted to tie the record at 106.

When I do make it in, four sisters are clustered together. Arms are swinging, hands are dancing. When they see me, they stop talking and get to squealing, "Miss Pearl!" Reunion is what I love most about move-in day. When Mama Carla sees me, she rolls her eyes. Beads of sweat have collected all over her forehead and it's running down the sides of her cheeks. Her face looks like a giant ripe tomato.

"Lord have mercy," I say to her. "Are you sick?" The poor thing's hair is wringing wet and she's fanning herself with a magazine.

"This is what happens when you stop taking hormones. Is the front door open?"

"It was. I pulled it to. But it won't stay that way long. Too many people runnin' in and out of here." I grab another magazine off the table and sit down next to her.

She blows a long puff of air. "Enjoy your youth, Pearl. Once you hit menopause the party's over."

"I'm not that far away," I say, fanning her from the side.

"You've got plenty of time. Oh, to be forty-four again." She runs her fingers through her hair in an attempt to restyle. Bless her heart. There is no use.

I help her with the keys and contracts and hand each girl her welcome back gift. Every sister staying in the House this year gets her own copy of *The Southern Belle's Bible,* courtesy of the Jackson Alums. One of them self-published the handbook and to show their support the alums have bought sixty-six copies. Word is the lady spent over twenty thousand dollars of her own money on publishing costs five years ago, and she'll have to sell fifteen hundred copies to ever turn a profit.

"I'll be right back," Mama Carla says, standing up. "If I don't dunk my head in an ice bucket I'll keel over and die."

"For real?"

"Not really, but I think I'll spend a few hours in the walk-in cooler." She laughs. "I'll bring you a Coke if I live that long." She knows Co-Cola's my drink. "Will you watch Trudy for me?"

"Of course. Here, Trudy." I snap my fingers, pat my hip. But that tiny shih tzu never looks my way, just follows Mama Carla right on out the door.

I've been at the table ten minutes when Sarah Mason walks in. When she eyes me, she screams, "Oh. My. Gosh. When did you get extensions?" Then she knocks ten of the handbooks off the table trying to put her arms around my neck. "You look so pretty."

"Thank you, baby." I turn around, let her inspect the back.

"I've been thinking of getting them myself. Who did yours?"

"You know my friend, Shirley? The beautician?"

She nods. "I met her that time she came over here to meet you after work."

"That's right. Sure did. She did it for me."

Sarah eyes my hair with interest. "How long did it take?"

"Took her five hours."

She wrinkles her nose. "Forget that." Sarah's like all the other young ladies in this House. None of them like to wait for things.

"It wasn't that bad," I say with a chuckle.

"How much did it cost?"

A few moments pass before I answer her. "We do it differently than y'all do. It wouldn't cost the same," is all I say. There are some things I like to keep to myself.

"You look hot." She turns around and asks Shannon Harris and Emily Leonard, who have both just arrived, if they agree. Now everybody's talking about my hair.

Once we're alone Sarah takes Mama Carla's chair. "Wait till you hear about my summer." She pulls one foot up on the seat and props her chin on her knee. "A lot has happened."

"I hope it's good."

"It's not." Pain creeps all over her little ol' face.

I reach over, take her by the hand. "Are you okay, Sarah?"

She squeezes my fingers, shakes her head. By the way she's biting down on her bottom lip I can tell she's fighting back tears. "I'm okay. I just wish my life could go back to the way it was."

"Come here, baby." I wrap my arm around her, pull her in tight. Her parents divorced last year and it about broke her heart. Mine, too, watching the way it tore her up inside. Sarah and I are close. We've spent hours talking about everything from Alpha Delt to grades and female friends to boyfriends, even more serious subjects like faith, dying, and the afterlife. It makes me feel good to know I can soothe her.

"My dad insisted on helping me move in today. He's around here somewhere. Asshole."

I pull back, look her in the eye. "What makes you say that?"

She lowers her voice. "The truth finally came out. He's been cheating on my mom with a girl only five years older than me."

"Lord have mercy."

"I'm so embarrassed." Tears flood her eyelashes.

"Sarah. I know that's hard on you. But listen to me. Your daddy's actions do not define who you are. You may come from him, but you are your own person."

"I know, I just don't want people gossiping about me." She's right about that. Gossip is a favorite pastime in sorority houses.

"Let them talk. They aren't talking about you; they're talking about your daddy."

She nods. But only slightly. A tear streaks down the side of her nose.

Jenna Dole and Liz Lemley bounce in the door for their keys. When Sarah sees them she looks off, wipes her tears away with her fingers.

"You just remember who you are and whose you are," I whisper. "Will you do that for me?"

A shy smile builds. "You always make me feel better."

"That's what I'm here for."

What is it with these men who would sooner wreck their kids' lives than deny that urge hanging between their legs?

TWO

MISS PEARL

Once Mama Carla has returned, I figure I better see what's happening in the kitchen. As I'm making my way there, trying to dodge the dollies and rolling suitcases, I see a lady with her face down in her cell phone. Her blond hair is twisted up on top of her head like she's one of the sisters, and she's wearing light blue pedal-pushers with a white Alpha Delt T-shirt, our official sorority colors.

I try sidestepping her, but as I do she turns and—*whack*—hits me in the nose with her cell phone. I steady myself against the wall. My nose is throbbing and I'm...dizzy. Burying my face in my hands, I count to ten. When I open my eyes Miss Lilith Whitmore, the new Alpha Delt House Corp President, is standing right in front of me. Her eyes are bulging like Mama Carla's shih tzu.

"Pearl! Excuse me. That was an accident."

"It's no bother." Pinching the bridge of my nose helps to stop the pain. But even with my nose aching I still notice her scent. It's sweet, but extra loud, like a pasture full of gardenias.

"I hope I didn't hurt you."

"Nothing more than a broken nose," I say, and get to laughing.

The look on her face says she didn't think my joke was funny. "Shall we take you to the hospital?"

"I'm all right." I smile, let her know it's all good. But my nose is stopped up, hard to get air through.

I'm moving along when she tugs on my arm. "I'm glad I bumped into you, Pearl." Both hands fly to her mouth. "Oh gosh. Pun *not* intended."

I force another smile. Lord, I really am in pain.

"My daughter, Annie Laurie, is coming through Recruitment this year."

"We'll be happy to have her right here at Alpha Delt." This lady is right pretty. Her face is real smooth, but something tells me she's not as young as the other mamas. Folds and creases circle her neck, like a basset hound's.

"Alpha Delta Beta were practically her first words. If she doesn't pick us first I'll kill her," she says with a wink. "I have high aspirations for that girl." Miss Lilith took office as House Corp President in May after serving on the Recruitment Advisory Board for a year. We haven't had much interaction before today.

From the corner of my eye I see Mama Carla strolling toward us from her apartment. She's got that little smushed-face Trudy in the crook of her arm. Don't get me wrong—I like dogs, but I've had to clean up after Trudy more times than I can count. When Mama Carla sees who it is I'm talking to she rushes over to where we're standing. "Don't you look like a collegiate today!" she says to Miss Lilith. "I almost mistook you for one of the girls." Why Mama Carla's gushing over her so has me perplexed. It's not her normal, but then I remember Lilith Whitmore is her boss.

This pleases Miss Lilith. She bats her eyes. "I try."

My eye is drawn to the Alpha Delt jeweled pin fastened to her left breast. Normally I don't see many of the alums wearing them unless there's a formal occasion.

"Bet you're getting excited about Annie Laurie going through Rush, I mean Recruitment," Mama Carla says. "I'm not sure I'll ever get that right." A few years back, Rush became Recruitment. She's right. It'll take a month of Sundays for that to stick. At least for us old folks.

"I'm telling you, we've spent our entire summer sending out rec packets," Miss Lilith says. "All we had time for was one week of vacation."

Both Mama Carla and I just look at her.

"We took Annie Laurie and her friend Kate on a diving trip to Cayman." She leans toward us, lowers her voice. "We own a home."

"How lovely," Mama Carla remarks. But I know what she's really thinking.

"It's pretty dreamy, if I do say so. We could have used three weeks down there, but with Recruitment so close I was afraid to be out of the country that long. My darling husband, Gage, said, 'Not to worry. We'll go again over Christmas.'"

After forcing a grin Mama Carla adds, "Of course."

"But as long as she pledges Alpha Delt that's all that matters." Miss Lilith presses her pale pink manicured hand over her heart. "I can't stop myself from dreaming she becomes president."

Mama Carla puts a hand to her hip. "Following in her mama's footsteps."

Miss Lilith beams. "Of course I want her to have a good Rush. With all the recs and letters we've managed to amass this summer, surely she'll be a top PNM. I told her, 'Have all the fun you want, but you must pledge Alpha Delta Beta!'" PNM, by the way, is the new term for rushee—potential new member.

Although Mama Carla opens her mouth to comment, Miss Lilith keeps on gabbing. "Annie Laurie spent her entire summer working out and dieting—she practically starved herself in Cayman. And her Rush wardrobe... her daddy nearly had a stroke when he got the bill."

I'd really like to make an exit out of this conversation. My nose is still throbbing and well, I don't have much to add.

"She'll be living in Martin, didn't you tell me that?" Mama Carla asks.

"Yes, Martin is the 'it dorm' this year. All her friends will be living there, too."

"Good for her," Mama Carla says. "When does she move in?"

"Next week with the other freshmen. But we're paying a little extra for her to move in a day early. Gage wants to avoid the masses."

All our Alpha Delt girls are required to move into the House a week before incoming freshmen. It's called Spirit Week and it's their time to attend pre-Rush workshops to familiarize themselves with all the girls who'll be rushing in the fall.

I've had enough so I say my good-byes. As I'm walking off it seems Miss Lilith has something else she wants to tell me, a postscript to our initial conversation. "Pearl. May I ask you a personal favor?"

Whipping back around, I smile at her. "Yes, ma'am."

"Will you please look after her? She's never been away from home."

"Of course I will. That's my job."

"Don't misunderstand me. Annie Laurie is well traveled. Her father and I made sure of that. She went to summer camp in North Carolina practically every summer of her life, but she's never been totally on her own. I wouldn't want her to be in need of something and not be able to get it."

"Miss Pearl has been taking care of these girls for twenty-five years. You don't need to worry a bit," Mama Carla is quick to say.

"Yes, I've heard." Her eyes meet mine. "And I trust you implicitly. You'll be her third mother. Between Rosetta and me, Annie Laurie Whitmore has had it made. You don't even want to know how rotten she's become." She places a hand aside her mouth. "She's my only."

I was an only. My mother's pride and joy. But I decide to keep that to myself.

"How long has Rosetta been taking care of your family?" Mama Carla asks.

"Ten years. At least."

"She's a part of your family, huh?"

"Absolutely. That woman is captain of our ship. We couldn't exist without Rosetta."

Mama Carla turns to me and smiles, gently touching me on the shoulder. "And we couldn't exist without you."

The beeping sound of a phone interrupts our conversation. Miss Lilith yanks hers from her back pocket. "Oops. I better scoot. We have our first Recruitment meeting tonight. So many last-minute recs have come in and I need to give them the once-over. If I have anything to do with it, we'll have our best pledge class in years. No trash will slip through the cracks on my watch. Only top-notch, A-list girls. See y'all."

The second she turns around Mama Carla rolls her eyes.

"I thought she gave up her seat on the Rush Board," I say. "Since when does the House Corp President get involved in Rush?"

"Lilith Whitmore is involving herself in every single facet of Alpha Delta Beta. Something tells me we all better watch out."

THREE

MISS PEARL

The smell of catfish frying wafts from the kitchen into the dining room, setting my taste buds on fire. After busting through the swinging door, I clap my hands together and shimmy on into the kitchen, put a little dance move I learned at the club the other night into my step. Welcome back dinner is always something special.

Aunt Fee sees me and gets to laughing. "What's got you doing the happy dance?" She's Aunt Fee to me but everybody else calls her Miss Ophelia. She's our head cook. Been serving up fine feasts to the Alpha Delt girls for the last thirty-two years.

"You know exactly why I'm dancing," I say, then sing, "Celebrate good times, come on."

Catfish is not only one of my favorites, it's one of everybody's favorites around here. Most of the fish comes from Indianola, down in the Delta—pond raised and di*vine*. It tastes delicious on its own, but you put Miss Ophelia's cornmeal buttermilk coating on it, *woo-whee,* you've got yourself something fine. Put hushpuppies with it—hush your mouth. I like mine with a little chow-chow on the side.

"Got a hundred thirty pounds; forty-four of 'em already fried," Aunt Fee says. She's standing in front of the stove with a pair of long tongs in her hand, moving filets from the deep-fryer to a large cookie sheet lined with paper towels.

"Makin' enough hushpuppies for me?" Mr. Marvelle—our House Man— yells from inside the pantry.

"Got six set aside for a Mr. Marvelle Jones," Fee hollers.

"Is 'at all?" he hollers back, with his happy face poking out the pantry door. "What you think this is, an all-you-can-eat contest?"

Mr. Marvelle steps out laughing. Slaps his knee and rears his head back. "You got that right."

I walk up to Latonya, Fee's sous chef, and peek inside the pots she's stirring. Black-eyed peas in one, collards in the other. If Jesus comes back tonight, we will have had one fine final meal.

There are six of us on staff. Besides Marvelle, Aunt Fee, Latonya, and myself, we have two kitchen aides, Kadeesha and Helen. Kadeesha also helps me with the housekeeping. That is . . . when she decides to earn her check.

The radio is turned up loud, set on a gospel station. Aunt Fee is singing like she's part of the choir. Nobody's watching Mr. Marvelle but me. I notice that smile on his face reshape; then the rascal shows up. He sneaks up to the old boom box then switches off the power. The music stops abruptly and Fee's voice is the only sound in the room. She looks up in time to see his backside dashing out the door.

Zipping out from behind the stove, Fee blasts by me like a rocket, with her tongs held high in the air. "Marvelle Jones! I know that was you. You better stay out of here." Then she turns back on the radio. Even louder this time.

The Five Blind Boys of Mississippi ring out loud and clear, "What a fellowship, what a joy divine, leaning on the everlasting arms."

"And *you* better learn to lean on Him, too, if you know what's good for you. You hear me, Marvelle Jones?" Then back to the stove she stomps after throwing a subtle wink my way.

Those two have a lot of fun together. They should, after twenty years of working side by side. She teases him. He teases her. It boosts the morale in the kitchen, helping us all to forget the cares of life. I believe they're the same age. Aunt Fee's sixty-four and if I'm not mistaken he is, too. "Medicare is just around our corner," she often tells him.

Not five minutes later, the music switches off a second time. Everybody but Aunt Fee turns around to see what that man's up to now. Only it's not Mr. Marvelle. It's Miss Lilith. She must have slipped in without anyone noticing. Like a cat.

"You better turn that box back on," Fee hollers from the fryer. "This is my kitchen. I make the rules."

"Actually," Miss Lilith says with a forced chuckle, "I make the rules." Now everybody, including Aunt Fee, stops what they're doing and stares her way. Not a one of us is happy she's in here. "Hi. I'm Lilith Whitmore. The new House Corp President. It's sure smelling good in here."

"Thank you, Miss Lilith," I say after a long pause, because somebody needs to acknowledge her and no one else has.

She walks around roving her big eyes into nooks and crannies that are none of her concern—even steps inside the walk-in cooler. Once the door clicks behind her and she's back in the kitchen she props one hand on the Hobart dishwasher, uses the other to punctuate her words. "Aren't y'all lucky to have this job? Where else in Oxford could you get a fabulous free dinner every night of the week?"

I steal a look at Aunt Fee and notice she's back to frying fish. Looks like the cat's got her tongue.

"*And* paid vacations." Now she's running two fingers against the edge of the chrome counter, like she's checking for dust. "You must be the envy of all of your friends."

Latonya flashes a cool smile when Miss Lilith walks in front of her. Helen gives her a real one, but only because she's sweet. Kadeesha? *Woo.* Her face looks like a stone.

"My daughter is coming through Recruitment in October. I know once Annie Laurie tastes one of your home-cooked meals, she'll think she's never left home or our Rosetta."

When no one responds I go ahead and say, "Tell her we're waiting on her."

"I sure will. Y'all save a plate for me tonight now." Then she struts out as quietly as she came in.

Once she's gone I change the subject because if I know Aunt Fee, she is boiling inside. There's no telling what she might spew herself. "All right, y'all. Listen up. Let's start this school year off right. Who wants to participate in my I-vow-to-exercise challenge?"

Latonya is the only one who looks up. Everybody else keeps their head down. "Come on, now," I say. "We can walk this campus together. If we want to keep eating all of Aunt Fee's choice cuisine, we need to make sure we stay healthy. Who's in?"

"Me," Latonya says. "I've been thinking about doing that myself."

With an encouraging smile I say, "Good, Latonya. Who else?"

"I suppose I need to," says Helen. "My hips is bigger than they was a year ago."

"All right, Helen. Proud of you." That cat still has Aunt Fee's tongue. "This includes you, Auntie. I'm getting you moving this year."

I hear a faint "*Hmmph*" out of her then.

"I'ma take that as a yes," I tell her, playfully nudging her with my elbow.

"All right. If Miss O does it, I guess I will, too," Mr. Marvelle says.

I raise my voice so everyone can hear me over the fryer. "That's everybody but you, Kadeesha. You in or out?"

"I already exercise," comes a faint voice. That's all she says. And for the record, no she does not.

"Mmm-hmm. And I bet you get a plenty of it, too," Auntie mutters under her breath. "In the bedroom."

FOUR

MISS PEARL

On my way out after supper, once the rest of the staff has clocked out and gone—without a single lap around campus, I might add—I find Fee in one of the folding break chairs outside the back door. I plop down beside her, put my pocketbook down next to hers. Then I strip off my hairnet, stuff it inside the pocket of my scrub pants.

She's already got a wad of tobacco in her cheek and I can tell she's whooped by the look on her face. The legs on her chair are tipped up, and she's using the back wall to support her head.

"You look tired," I say.

"I am tired. Been a looong day."

"I know that's right."

Something I said must have triggered something else because she gets a sudden burst of energy. She sits straight up and leans in toward me. Outrage is oozing from every pore on her face. "What about that lady? Strutting into my kitchen, telling us all how *lucky* we are."

"I ran into her earlier. Actually it was the other way around. She ran into me. For real. Whacked my nose with her cell phone." I reach up to massage it. "Still sore."

"She gone be trouble. You mark my word."

"You think so?"

"I know so. Talking about us being the *envy* of all our friends. It's a nice job. But we don't even have benefits." She settles back against the wall, crosses her arms over her chest. "Shoot."

I reach for my pocketbook.

"Where you headed?"

"Home. I've got bills to pay." I sigh at the thought of all that work, then change my mind. I'm more tired than I thought.

"You got enough this month?"

"Not really." I lean my head back on the wall next to hers. "Now that school's back things will get better, though. How 'bout you?"

"I'm all right." She folds her hands tightly on top of her big middle, like she's feeling what's on the inside. "I don't buy much no more. Don't even get my hair done." She glances at my new weave with disapproving eyes. *"Hmmph."*

I ignore her. It's my head, not hers. "Summertime, I tend to fall behind. I haven't made a payment on my college fund since April."

She looks at me like she just heard a dog say hello. "You still doing that?"

"Every chance I get."

"How much you got in there now?"

"Close to eight thousand, I believe."

"What?" Fee rears back, bumps her head on the wall. Her eyes are big and round, like full moons. "You got *eight thousand dollars!*"

I nod. "You'd be surprised how interest compounds over twenty-five years."

"You never touched it? Not even once?"

"No, ma'am. Not mine to touch."

Fee relaxes her shoulders, then sucks in a big breath of air. "That's a beautiful thing you're doing, baby." She reaches over to rub my thigh. "Your mama would be proud."

"I know she would. She's the one who suggested it."

Right about then music blasts from the back terrace and through the spaces in the fence we see several sisters pouring out of the double set of French doors, laughing and carrying on like it's the most fun day of their lives. We can't make out anything they're saying; the music is too loud. Rush meeting must have let out early.

"Lord, I never thought I'd see the day," I say. "White girls in love with rap."

"Mmm-hmm," Fee replies. "I know that's right."

"Usher yes, but hard rap? That tickles me."

Neither of us talks for a while. We simply sit and listen to the laughter.

"What must that be like?" Aunt Fee says after a few minutes have passed.

"What's what like?"

"To laugh like you don't have a care in the world." There's no resentment in her tone. Seems like she's just curious. Then she leans down, picks up her pocketbook. Now she's ready to go.

"Might seem that way tonight," I tell her. "But it's not always smooth sailing over there. That I know. They tell me their secrets."

Fee stands up, slings her pocketbook over her shoulder. "I hear what you're sayin'. Just makes that voyage a whole lot smoother when you've got the money to take a big ship. See you tomorrow, baby."

"Why don't you take a lap around campus with me?"

She peers at me like I'm crazy.

"You better get your butt moving," I say with a chuckle. "If you plan to live long."

"*Hmmph.*" She leans down, picks up the Gatorade bottle she uses as a spittoon, and spits inside.

FIVE

MISS PEARL

The lines on this county road are starting to blur. It's just past dusk and these bones of mine are weary. Move-in day wears me out like I've been chopping wood—something I've not done and have no plans of ever doing, but God gave me an imagination. I know how to use it, too, even if it does get me in trouble sometimes. Like now, when it drifts back onto— Uh-oh, Pearl, look out for that deer.

A few feet ahead there's a multipoint buck poking his big head out from the right side of the road. Here he comes, leaping out in front of me. I slam on the brakes, hear the sound of squealing tires on pavement. Before I know it I'm skidding in circles all over the road. My hands grip the steering wheel so hard, my knuckles turn pale. My head jerks with every spin. People talk about their life flashing before their eyes. Lord Jesus, I think I just saw mine.

When I finally regain control and pull off onto the shoulder, I hear loose rocks biting at my tires. I stop the car and slump over the steering wheel. My heart is pumping faster than an oil jack. With every pound inside my chest I'm praising God and crying at the same time, *Thank You, Jesus. Thank You, Jesus.* If there had been a car coming in the opposite direction I would be *dead.* I listen to myself breathe, in and out, in and out. Feeling my chest rise and fall, a hundred miles an hour. I can hear the steady, hard, thump-thump of my heart. My mind gets going again and before long I get angry. Now I am furious. And that fury is directed at nobody but myself. There's not but a fraction of tread left on my tires. Instead of buying new ones I spent my savings on my damn hair.

After looking over my shoulder, I pull back out onto the road. There aren't but a few miles left between here and home. So I drive well under the speed limit the rest of the way and, before I know it, my mind wanders off again to something that makes me almost as angry, but I can't do a thing about: All the low-income folks have been forced to the outskirts of town into Yalobusha and Panola Counties.

It takes thirty to forty minutes now to drive in to work. I read in the *Oxford Eagle* last week that people are calling it gentrification. I called on an apartment in Oxford last year and the lady said she wanted nine hundred dollars a month for *a room*. Sharing both a kitchen and a den. "Thank you anyway," I told her, then hung up the phone. I don't know what they think we're going to do. Spending so much of our money on gas when the minimum wage in Mississippi isn't but $7.25 an hour. Thankfully I'm making more than that.

When I finally open the door to my apartment, it's pitch black inside. I flick on the overhead light, look around, and let out the breath it seems I've been holding since that deer ran out in front of me. My place is spotless and smells sweet thanks to the diffuser Kate Farley's mama gave me last year.

In anticipation of what's to come, I had scrubbed both my kitchen and my bathroom two days ago, and vacuumed the carpet and dusted everything— including the light bulbs—the day before that. I had to do a master clean before school starts back and all the mamas start calling me. From now till winter break my extra time will be swallowed up whole.

I drop my pocketbook down on the sofa where I always keep it. As I head toward the bathroom something dark and dingy catches my eye; the one thing I ran out of time to clean. Mama would not be pleased, in fact, if she could see it, she would be downright ashamed. The tarnish is thick. I can't even make out the pretty garden of roses swirling through each piece.

I walk over to where it stays and pick up the small cream pitcher. It once belonged to Mrs. McKinney. She willed it to Mama when she died. Said Mama always kept it looking magnificent, the way an heirloom silver service should look, and that she deserved to have it for her own.

Mama said it was hard when Mrs. McKinney's daughter, Daphne, learned of her mother's wishes because she had had her eye on it. Mama tried giving it back, but Mrs. McKinney's oldest son, William, said no. He said his mother meant for Ruby to have it and that it was going to her house, period.

When Mama left it to me she made me promise I'd never sell it. She wanted it kept in the family, and asked me to pass it down to my own child. But that didn't work out. Several times now, I've wanted to thank William for his generosity. But Aunt Fee says it's always best to let sleeping dogs lie.

There are five pieces—all sterling silver, except the nice big tray it sits on, and that's silver plate. I brought it in to show Mama Carla one day and she told me it's probably worth close to seven thousand dollars. By now, she said, it may be worth more than that, and I need to have it insured. Maybe one day, after I get my health insured, we can give thought to that.

SIX

WILDA

Let me start by getting something out of the way. I am one of those women who compares herself to others. Yes, I'm well aware of what healthy people think about that, and I agree, it's exhausting. Trust me, if I could do something about it I would. I'm constantly worried I'm not good enough, smart enough, or attractive enough. Lord knows I weigh too much, but at fifty-eight, I've come to accept that malady.

As long as I'm baring my soul, I may as well make a second confession. This is somewhat confidential because I don't want every Kim, Jane, and Mary to know my personal business, nor can I afford the judgment. I tend to believe I'm dying. As the saying goes, I'm always waiting on the other shoe to drop. If I even hear the word "cancer," any joy I may be experiencing at the moment screeches to a halt; my mind flips a 180 and I imagine I'm lying in a hospital bed with a chemo drip attached to my chest.

Likewise, if I read an article about someone who has recently contracted, say, Lyme disease, I'm off to my laptop frantically googling the early symptoms. For the next few days, I'm certain I'm experiencing headaches, fatigue, and joint pain. I have Hysterical Lyme Disease.

I wasn't like this in my early years. It didn't happen until my mid-thirties.

The best I can figure is that my later-in-life infertility was the catalyst for my fear of doom. Sometimes—well, all the time—I can't help but wonder what the heck went wrong down there. Because I wasn't infertile to begin with. I had given birth to two perfectly healthy little boys before I turned twenty-eight.

Ironically I grew up not knowing the first thing about boys. I was the eldest of two girls, with no brothers or male cousins, and I attended an all-girls school. Daddy died when I was eight and my only uncle lived seven hours away from Memphis in Gulfport, Mississippi. My entire childhood revolved around periods and panties. Once I became a wife, not giving birth to a daughter had never once crossed my mind. Until I became infertile.

To make matters worse, my own mother, Eleanor Dyson, dubbed my womb "the hostile uterus." That happened after she had the boys for an entire weekend. Mama, who lived less than three miles away, had invited the boys to "Mimi Camp," an entire weekend full of fun with their grandmother. Only five hours into camp, Jackson, age four, had scribbled on Mama's brand-new yellow couch with a fresh tube of lipstick he had found in her purse. When she called with a camp report later that evening, after the boys were in bed, she declared my uterus "hostile." "Little girls," she added, "would never do something that destructive."

The good Lord must know what He's doing, was the only thought that gave me comfort while Haynes and I raised our two little mischief-makers. I was twenty-six when Cooper was born and twenty-eight when Jackson came along. By the time I was thirty-nine, despite not having used birth control for eleven years, I threw in the towel and flat gave up all hope of ever dressing a little girl in hand-smocked batiste dresses from Memphis's finest children's store, The Women's Exchange. Like my mother had said time and time again, "I guess girls aren't in the cards for you, Wilda."

What's more remarkable? I wasn't that sad about it. Curious as to the reason why—most definitely—but not sad. Beside the fact that I rarely got a break, a weekend away from the boy-grind every now and then, there was nothing to be sad about. Haynes and I had two perfectly healthy, albeit strong-willed, beautiful boys. Their athleticism rivaled that of any other boys in their classes. Haynes swore they were each destined to be Ole Miss football players, which suited me just fine since that was our alma mater.

A few years later, still not using birth control but having a much-better-than-average sex life, I accidentally brought up my infertility while on a phone call to Mama. I say "accidentally" because I knew better. "I had my pap this morning," I began. "Dr. Patterson still can't find anything wrong with me. Don't you find it curious I got pregnant with Cooper and Jackson no problem at all?"

"Why Wilda," Mama said with a *tsk*. "I don't know why you're still bringing this up, dear. You're in early menopause."

"Early menopause!" Oh dear God, I thought, there goes my body, my sleep, our sex life. "I hadn't thought about that."

"Well. Even if it's not, it's too late, honey. You're thirty-nine years old, for heaven's sake."

"That's not too—"

"It's downright dangerous for a woman your age to have a child. Your chances of Down syndrome skyrocketed once you turned thirty-five."

I tried to object. "That's a rarity, Mother. All kinds of women are having healthy babies later in life. Look at Julianne Moore and Christie Brink—"

"*In vitro*. They all had in vitro. I read all about it in *People*. Don't tell me you're thinking of taking that route. It's ten thousand dollahs a pop." Mama knew full well that Haynes and I couldn't afford IVF—not that I would even consider it after two healthy children.

"Never mind, Mother. I just thought you'd want to know that there is something wrong with me down there."

"Oh for gosh sakes, Wilda. I didn't raise you to be a prophet of doom."

I was dying to slam the phone down and scream, "Look who the kettle learned it from!" But I was raised never to talk back to my mother, so I bit my tongue. And faked a reason to hang up. *Oh dear God,* I thought in horror, *like mother like daughter.*

Wilda, by the way, is not pronounced Wild-uh. It's *Will*-duh. And I'm not wild about it if that's what you're wondering.

"Things can turn on a dime" was another of the clichés Mama often used as if it were a proverb I needed to live by. One week to the day after my pap smear, Dr. Patterson's nurse left a message on my answering machine to please call her back. Upon hearing her voice, I slumped into the chair beside the phone in the kitchen and spiraled down a hundred-foot well of despair. There it was. The Big C. Why hadn't I eaten better and exercised more often? It was my own fault. How I managed to pick up the phone and dial Haynes's number was beyond me.

"I'll be dead in six months!" I shrieked the minute he picked up his office line. I didn't even wait for his hello.

"Oh no," he said wryly, no concern in his voice whatsoever. This was not my first near-death experience.

"Haynes! At least *act* like you're concerned."

"I am concerned, Wilda. But we've been here before. What's wrong now?" I could envision him—elbow propped on the desk, thumb and two fingers supporting his forehead, eyes rolling.

"Is someone in your office?"

"No."

"Are you sure?" I half believed Frank could be sitting across from him.

"Of course I'm sure. What's the problem?"

"The nurse from Dr. Patterson's office left a message on our answering machine. I just got home from picking up the boys from football practice and there it was."

"And?"

"She said I needed to call her back."

"Then call her back."

"I can't just *call her back*. I have to be mentally prepared."

In his calmest Haynes voice he said, "Didn't you have that female test recently?"

"Yes."

"She just wants to give you the results. Call her back."

I was the opposite of calm. "Don't you know anything? They don't call you with a good result. They mail you a card. The only time they call you is when it's bad." My voice cracked. "Our boys will grow up without a mother. Poor things."

"Wilda."

"Will you call her for me?"

"Oh for the love of—" There was a long, annoyed pause. "What's the number?"

I let out a sigh of relief. "Thank you. I owe you," I said after giving him the number.

"It might take awhile to get her, but I'll call you as soon as I hear. Everything is going to be fine."

"I'll be right by the phone." I could hear him readying to hang up. "But you don't know it's fine," I added just in time. "I might need to call Frank and warn him. You'll need the emotional support once you hear the news." Haynes's law partner was always good in a crisis. He had stepped in when Sam Leatherberry's wife of twenty-eight years told him she had met another woman.

"You are fine." He hung up without a good-bye.

After fifteen minutes of staring at the phone and no Haynes, my mind raced. I flew into our bedroom. Internet searching was becoming popular back then, but I was never far from my *Mayo Clinic Family Health Book*. I opened the drawer on my nightstand, used all my forearm strength to remove it. With shaking hands, I lowered myself onto the edge of our bed and flipped the pages of the monster 1,500-page manual back to the index. My pointer finger scanned the listings until I landed on it. Cancer, cervical, page 943. As my pulse banged in my ears, I read the entire listing. Hysterectomy, good survival rate if caught in time, causes, symptoms, risk factors, complications, treatments—*chemotherapy,* questions to ask the doctor.

Clutching the heavy manual to my chest, I rose slowly from the bed and death-marched down the hall toward the kitchen, glancing through the French doors at my boys throwing a football in the backyard. I finally had the answer to my infertility. If only I could have a redo. I'd go to the gym five days a week. I'd never let another candy bar pass my lips.

A solid thirty minutes passed with no Haynes. Before hyperventilation had a chance to set in, I picked up the phone to call him and happened to glance out the front kitchen window. My life passed before my eyes at that very moment. Haynes's white SUV pulled slowly into the driveway, like a hearse arriving for its corpse. I mentally calculated that if the nurse had given Haynes the bad news within the first few minutes of the phone call, he'd had enough time to dash out of his office in tears, run to his car, and make it home that fast.

My first instinct was to run out to meet him in the driveway, but I was struck with the need to live cancer-free for a precious few more moments. Instead, I moved in slo-mo, out to the backyard to watch the boys. They should have started their homework by now, but what did it matter? In six months they would be motherless. Like I had been fatherless. "Cooper...Jackson..."

I wanted to scream and envelop them in my arms, but thought better of it, opting to relish their stellar athleticism from an iron chair on the patio.

When I saw Haynes open the French doors, I held up my hand. "I do not want to see the look on your face. Don't raise your eyebrows. Don't purse your lips. And above all do not furrow that brow."

He walked toward me, expressionless, before bending down to scoop me up in his arms. I went completely limp in his embrace. "You don't have cancer," he said, slowly, no affect in his voice. I opened my mouth to speak but he placed a gentle hand atop my mouth. "We're pregnant."

Eight months later, when Dr. Patterson announced, "It's a girl!" my world went from bugs and balls to dollies and tea sets, overnight.

SEVEN

WILDA

Now here we are in Oxford, eighteen years later, moving our baby girl into Martin Hall at Ole Miss. I welcome back the flood of nostalgia, like finding an old pair of bell-bottoms in my mother's attic. I lived in Martin when I was a freshman. Haynes picked me up for our first date in the lobby. Lisa Murphey, my college roommate, and I had a garage sale in our room trying to raise money for our spring break trip to Fort Lauderdale. Hiding boys, skipping class to sleep in, prank phone calls, late-night room parties, flip-flops in the shower—now Ellie would get to experience it all.

Finding a parking spot is worse than I thought. It's like trying to park at the mall the weekend before Christmas, only it's August and the hottest day of the year. Even though we're moving Ellie in a day early, before most of the students, it still looks like a parking lot for crazies. All the SUVs and trucks are parked at careless angles, blocking one another in.

The one bright spot is: Ellie will never have to search for a parking spot. Haynes told her she couldn't take her car to college. I was totally in favor of her having it, but there are some things I need to let go and let my husband win. When I see all the brand-new Range Rovers, BMWs, and Lexus SUVs parked erratically, I'm glad Ellie left her 2005 Jeep Cherokee in our driveway.

Once we finally find a spot, a football field away from the dorm, Haynes turns to Ellie in the backseat. "You sure you don't want to change your mind? There's still time to register at Shelby State, *for free*."

Dramatically, as if she's onstage, she rolls her eyes. Haynes's teasing drives her up a wall. Southwest Tennessee Community College used to be Shelby State in our day. Even though Tennessee kids go free for the first two years, Ellie Woodcock wants nothing to do with it. She's hell-bent on the SEC experience.

"Daaad." Her tone is pure frustration. I see her struggling with the door handle. "Open my door. You've got the child locks on again. Hurry. Open."

He turns to me. "Damn thing. It happens every time I turn on the engine."

The locks click and Ellie bursts out of the backseat. Her long blond ponytail swings as she lifts her chin and gazes up at her new ten-story home. Her arms are stretched out wide, like she wants to give the world a hug.

I roll the window down and turtle my head out toward her. "Honey!" My voice is shrill, full of jollity. "You're having your Mary Tyler Moore moment. All you need is a tam."

Two freshmen are unloading right next to us. Both look up and stare. Ellie notices, whips back around, curling her top lip. "I'm having my what?"

I lower my voice. "Your Mary Tyler Moore moment. Didn't you ever see *The Mary Tyler Moore Show*?"

"Uhhh, *nooo*."

Now I'm at a loud whisper. "Mary raises her arms and throws her tam in the air. She's celebrating her independence."

Ellie's murdering me with her eyes. Both hands are dug into her hips.

"Never mind." I retreat back inside, rolling the window up as fast as it will go.

Not two minutes later, she opens the back door, leans across the seat, and mutters, "Please try not to embarrass me four hundred more times today." After another eye roll, she grabs her backpack, slings it across one shoulder, and dashes away from our SUV. She's wearing Lulu shorts and that oversize Rolling Stones T-shirt. We had taken her to Nashville to see them last summer, and she insisted on buying an extra large. She is so much prettier than I ever was. Thank You, God.

"Are *you* ready for this?" Haynes reaches over to caress my knee.

"I suppose," I say with a loud sigh.

"Let's do it." He jumps out of the driver's seat.

I just sit there. Truth is, I am not ready for this. As happy as I am for Ellie, I'm dying inside. The thought of empty-nesterness spells misery to me. Most of my friends have been empty-nesters for years. Lilith Whitmore, from Natchez, Mississippi, an Alpha Delt sorority sister of mine—actually more of an acquaintance—is the only older mother I know. When she learned through a mutual friend that Ellie was going to Ole Miss, she called and suggested that her Annie Laurie and my Ellie room together. At the time I thought that would be great. I still do, I suppose, but it's obvious the Whitmores are extremely well-to-do. That, of course, makes me feel inferior, but my biggest concern is for Ellie. I hope it doesn't cause her any unnecessary jealousy.

By the time I step outside, Ellie is waiting impatiently at the back of our Expedition, ready to unload. Haynes opens the tailgate. "Hang on. Let's not get started with all this yet. Why don't we go inside and get you checked in first?"

"I'll go," Miss Independence says. "You and Mom wait here."

Obligingly, Haynes and I stand at the truck and watch our daughter disappear inside the front door of Martin.

Between the blazing hot temperature and the high humidity, I can actually feel the halo of frizz hovering over my head. A quick touch proves I'm right. I extend a hand toward Haynes. "Give me your keys, please."

He peers at me, confused.

"If you think I'm standing out here in this steam bath you have another thing coming." That's another thing: I am a slave to my hair. It's naturally curly, and I'm not talking cute curly. I'm talking gross curly. It takes me thirty minutes to blow it out straight, and when the barometric pressure drops I might as well stay home. You would never know I had touched a blow dryer.

On top of that, I'm staying away from hot-flash triggers. I'm not having all that many anymore, but I'm not taking chances. I hop back inside, reach over, and start the engine. Pressing the high button on the AC, I point all four vents directly at my face.

Glancing out the window I see Haynes talking with another dad. Lord have mercy, he looks half our age. When his wife comes up, I know they're half our age. She looks like she could be a student. Without realizing it, I'm pushing up my cheeks with my thumbs and lifting my forehead with two fingers. I look down at my wrinkled knees and dream, just for a moment, of another day. When my legs were my best asset—at least that's what I was told.

Thirty minutes later, Ellie finally comes back with a report that we have to stand in line to get the key, but there are helpers from the University ready to "make our move-in hassle free." So the three of us begin the unloading. Considering what most people have to haul in on move-in day, we have it easy. Someone else is meeting us here with the furniture and bed linens. Lilith put us in charge of the microwave and the coffeepot. All in all, between her clothes, shoes, toiletries, and God knows whatever else, there are a total of ten boxes and suitcases. Haynes had rented a dolly before we left—smart man—and loads a tower of boxes atop. I have Ellie's Vera Bradley weekender bag on one shoulder, and the handle of a roll-away suitcase in my hand. Ellie is rolling two more suitcases behind her.

When we finally make it to the lobby, I'm floored by how little Martin has changed. The chairs have been updated and there's a new coat of paint on the walls, but other than that, it's circa 1976. It even smells the same—a mélange of dirty laundry and the scent of dirt after a rainfall.

Lines to each of the three elevators have been taped off, and once Ellie finally gets her room card—no such thing as keys anymore—we learn that her and Annie Laurie's room is all the way up on the ninth floor. We're left with no choice but to wait in line for the elevator. Lilith was the one who insisted we pay a one-hundred-dollar up-charge and move in a day early. But by the looks of the place, many others have done the same thing.

"Can you imagine what tomorrow will be like if it's this crowded today?" Haynes asks. "Best hundred bucks we've ever spent."

"I agree," I tell him.

Looping an arm through his, Ellie sidles in closer. "Thanks, Dad."

"I wonder if Annie Laurie's here yet?" I say as we peer up at the floor indicators above the elevators.

Ellie looks at her phone. "I just texted her. She and her parents got here an hour and a half ago."

Haynes clears his throat, looks straight at her. "They didn't have as far to travel."

"Dad," Ellie retorts, "Memphis is way closer than Natchez."

"Not by air. I'm sure they flew in on their private helicopter and landed on the roof."

"Stop, Dad."

I shoot Haynes my *not now* look. He shrugs and pulls on the bill of his Memphis Grizzlies ball cap.

Evidently, Lilith and Gage Whitmore are loaded. One of the wealthiest families in Natchez, from what I hear—possibly one of the wealthiest in the state. Even though we're the same age, she pledged Alpha Delt as a transfer from Randolph Macon a year behind me, and I vaguely remember rumblings about her family fortune. The word is her husband is a trust-fund baby himself. From our telephone conversations, I gather he's usually at home during the day, "managing their portfolios."

It takes a full hour for our turn on an elevator to arrive, despite the fact that our move-in times were staggered. The whole way down to Ole Miss I'd been thinking about what Haynes would say when he saw Ellie's dorm room. He was usually oblivious to such things, but there was no hiding this one.

Just thinking about that phone message I received back in June has me frozen in fear. I had just finished my water aerobics class when I checked my phone for missed calls. Sure enough there was one from a 601 area code. Mississippi. When I checked the recording I had a voice message from someone named Rhonda Taylor from Chic Small Spaces. She said she needed my address to send me an invoice. I remember thinking, *An invoice? And who the heck is Rhonda Taylor?*

I pushed redial.

She answered on the first ring. "Rhonda Taylor. Hotty Toddy."

"Hi Rhonda, this is Wilda Woodcock. You left a message on—"

"Hey, Wilda, how are you?" She definitely thought she had the right person.

"Fine, thank you."

"Great. I need your address, girl. To send you an invoice."

I put on my best semi-confrontational tone. "You mentioned that in your voice mail, but I think there's been a mistake. You must have the wrong Wilda Woodcock."

"Aren't you Lilith Whitmore's friend?"

An ultra-big pit constricted my stomach, near one of my sphincter muscles right under my breastbone. "Yes."

"I'm her dorm-room designer."

Silence. Shock. *Shit.* Every inch of me, every tiny pore of mine was dying to scream, *"Lilith Whitmore has a dorm-room designer? Are you freaking kidding me?"* But I am well versed in the art of polite Southern-speak. So I told a little white lie. "Of course," I said, in a breathy tone. "Now I remember."

"See, I do have the right Wilda Woodcock." She giggled, and I couldn't blame her. "Now. We need to talk install. What date is your daughter moving into Martin?"

"August sixteenth." I had that date branded into my heart. The day I would become an empty nester.

"Lilith told me she'd be happy to pay me an up-charge to get the exact move-in date y'all want. I'm assuming you're good with that?"

Oh great, I thought. *Lilith wants me to pay yet another up-charge.* "How much is that? Out of curiosity."

"Two-fifty."

I took a deep breath, tried to remain calm. "Oh . . . well, okay."

"I assume the girls have been chatting about their colors and designs."

"Yes, I think so."

"Great, because I'm running out of time. If y'all want a move-in-ready dorm room I'll need y'all to pick out your fabrics and decide on your room design by next Thursday."

That pit in my stomach had grown into a boulder. "Okay."

"I sent Lilith several fabric samples. Have you not seen them?"

"That must have been what she was calling me about." Lilith had left a message from the Cayman Islands wanting to talk about the design of the girls' room. Never once had it crossed my mind she had hired a dorm-room designer. Heck, I never even knew they existed. "We haven't connected yet, but I told Ellie to call Annie Laurie." I paused. "To be honest, I wasn't planning on getting all that involved. I like to let Ellie make her own decisions."

"Some moms are like that."

"So, Rhonda. You said you have an invoice. I assume you charge a design fee?" My voice was interlaced with trepidation.

A long pause followed. "Is the Pope Catholic?" She laughed out loud. "So far I haven't figured out how to volunteer for a living." Her voice was strong, snappy, ultra confident.

"Oh no, I . . . wasn't suggesting you'd do it for free. I hope I haven't offended you."

"Girrrl. No offense taken. My business has gone through the roof. My phone has beeped twice during this conversation. I don't know if I need to thank Panhellenic or Obama."

"Gosh. Congratulations. I wish I'd thought of it." My mind floated off to the job I would have to get. To pay for Ellie's *unexpected* expenses.

"I've always been ahead of the curve. It's a gift." She laughed again.

"Good for you. I'm assuming you have a total for all this?"

"I have your invoice right here in my hot little hand."

"Great. How much is it?"

"Ten K."

I was positive I had misunderstood her. "Excuse me?"

"Ten thousand."

"Apiece?"

"Yes, honey, yes. But that includes the furniture, the comforter and mono-grammed shams, the extra pillows, bed skirt, draperies, the throws. Wait, what am I forgetting?" She paused. "Oh yeah, the woven blinds, the rugs and mirrors, the art, the desk toppers and chair covers. And a dorm-warming gift. It's turnkey."

I was utterly gobsmacked. Heart palpitations kick-started into motion. I broke out in a cold sweat and if she said something else, then I never heard her. All I could think about was Haynes and what he was going to say when I told him we owed *ten thousand dollars* to Ellie's dorm-room designer.

It had taken me a week to convince him she should move in early—to the tune of one hundred dollars—another of Lilith's suggestions. But at this point, I couldn't disappoint our daughter. I'd cooked that goose last February when I encouraged her to room with Annie Laurie Whitmore in the first place.

"One more important thing before I let you go," Rhonda said, snapping me away from my thoughts. "Y'all are in charge of the fridge, the coffeemaker, the TV, and the microwave. Those are the only things I don't include . . . unless you want to pay extra. Heck, I'll buy the girl's toothbrushes if you want me to."

"Oh no," I said, quickly. "We'll bring the appliances. And the toothbrushes."

"Alrighty then." There was laughter in her voice, like she knew perfectly well she had stepped into a goldmine. "If you'll send me a deposit check of six thousand, we can get this started. Lilith's already sent me hers, so don't worry, I've got your install date on the calendar in ink."

Oh sweet Jesus. A sudden surge of overwhelming panic griped my chest as I hung up the phone. *Bump-bump-bump*—I could hear the banging of my heart. I felt nauseous. I couldn't breathe. I was either dying or going crazy. A vision sprung to mind of me, lying in my coffin, with my family peering sadly over the side. Then another replaced it with me, at Bolivar, our West Tennessee mental institution, with a drool cup dangling from my neck.

EIGHT

WILDA

When we finally make it up to the ninth floor, an hour and a half after our arrival, the door to Ellie's room is half open. "Knock, knock," I say, poking my head inside, "Woodcocks are here."

The first person I see is a woman, whom I assume to be Rhonda Taylor, giving instructions to an older African American gentleman about centering an oil painting over a gorgeous gray-and-white floral couch. The Whitmores are off to the side, seated in Lucite chairs watching them work.

"Hey, y'all!" Lilith exclaims, popping up to hug me. Gage Whitmore stands up, too. He puts his breakfast sandwich down and shakes Haynes's hand. Annie Laurie is nowhere to be found.

Ellie scans the room, wide-eyed. I can tell she is both in shock and in awe. I certainly am.

Rhonda looks over her shoulder while hanging yet another oil painting over Annie Laurie's bed. She's holding a drill. I read somewhere only peel-and-stick picture hangers were allowed, but obviously I was wrong.

"Hang on, y'all; I'll be *riiight* there." She lays the drill on the bed, straightens the painting. After wiping her hands on her pants, she shakes all of ours. "Hey, I'm Rhonda. Don't mind me, I'm a little cray-cray today. I usually look a whole lot better than this." She looks fantastic to me. Blue jeans and a cold-shoulder top. Gorgeous jewelry. A nice, shoulder-length hairdo. She's a beautiful woman.

Haynes tells her hello, but offers no small talk. Instead he walks right over to the man who's helping her. "Here, let me help you with that, man." Haynes holds the right end of the oversize painting while the man slips the picture wire over the hook.

"Thank you, sir," the man says. "Now you and your family sit down and relax. I'ma do this."

"No relaxing for me today. I'm here to work," Haynes says, rubbing his hands together. "I'm Haynes Woodcock." He shakes the gentleman's hand.

"Maurice Robinson. All right." Mr. Robinson's dark, curly hair is streaked with gray. Deep lines wrinkle his forehead. His jowls droop, and at first glance he appears to be in his seventies, but when he smiles straight white teeth make him appear much younger. Haynes turns and introduces him to Ellie and me. I notice Lilith and Gage exchange a look.

"I'm texting Annie Laurie," Lilith announces. "She's down the hall playing."

Within sixty seconds, Annie Laurie bursts through the door. "Hey!" She rushes over to hug Ellie.

I can tell it's a bit awkward for our daughter. Most of the time she's an extrovert, but there are times when shyness takes over. This is one of those times.

Ellie hugs her back, tells her hello, but simply gives her a coy smile. She looks around, taking it all in. Annie Laurie's bed has already been lofted and made. It looks like one on display in a specialty linen store.

"Ellie, I'm gonna tell you what I told Annie Laurie," Rhonda says. "Y'all wait to unpack till I'm done. Just go around the floor visiting for now; meet new friends. And when you come back you'll be walking inside Ole Miss Dorm Room of the Year. Y'all scoot." She makes a brushing motion with her hands and the girls leave.

Their room is at the end of the hall. A corner room meant for three—another of Lilith's suggestions—but the University turned it into a double, charging the occupants a premium.

Gage, now back on the couch, offers us the other half of his breakfast sandwich, but we politely decline. His feet are propped up on an upholstered ottoman. It's then that I notice his loafers: Ferragamo with no socks. Together with his pink Bermuda shorts, linen shirt, and Smathers & Branson Ole Miss needlepoint belt, he's utterly Palm Beach. Haynes has on a well-worn pair of khaki shorts, one of his Ole Miss golf shirts, and his old tennis shoes. It's moving day.

Rhonda gets back to work and Haynes jumps in to assist Mr. Robinson with lofting Ellie's bed.

Lilith was Lily in college, and ever since we've been reacquainted I've had to stop myself from calling her by that name. I know there are women who go back to their given names after a while, but it's terribly confusing if you ask me. She takes me by the hand and points out the detailing on the furnishings. "Would you look at these headboards," she says, running her hand lightly over the gray linen fabric with pink piping. They were custom cut, rounded at the edges, and have been turned to face each other, as if they are daybeds. "The girls can use them as queens when they move into their apartment next year."

This makes me feel a tiny bit better, I suppose.

Two large Euro shams are made of matching pink linen, ruched on the edges, with Annie Laurie's monogram swirled in a white linen fabric. Coordinating throw pillows, pink and white, are piled on top of the bed and a white leather step stool sits underneath a cascading throw. A large round bolster made of silk appliqués takes up half the bed, and two iron sconces flank the headboard on the wall. Lilith points to a white quilted coverlet and what appears to be a white chinchilla throw. "Doesn't this fabulous fake look real?"

"Sure does," I say, meaning it.

Lilith bends down to show me the bed skirt. It's gray linen, matching the headboard, with a wide ribbon of pink an inch from the bottom. And it's on a sliding rod so the girls can pull it back to access whatever they plan to store underneath. A mirrored chest serves as a bedside table between the two beds and two lamps made of ceramic pitchers swirled with colorful designs are on either side. Their shades are trimmed with silk, matching the color in the pitchers.

I reach out and touch one of the lamps, feeling the coolness of the pottery against my fingertips. "These are beautiful."

"They're maiolica," Lilith says. "Aren't they fabulous?"

"Real majolica?"

"You're thinking of Victorian majolica pottery you see in every antique store. This is Italian maiolica. With an I instead of a J. Very different."

"I didn't know there was a difference," I say sheepishly, as my heart lurches in shame.

"Oh yeah," Rhonda says without turning around. "Big difference."

The little couch has more coordinating velvet pillows and another fur throw. There's a tall floor lamp next to the door. A round upholstered ottoman with a large tray on top serves as a coffee table. There are not one, but two, windows in the room and the window coverings are nicer than anything we have in our entire house. Two woven bamboo shades are underneath gorgeous linen draperies that puddle on the floor.

Across from the couch are two study desks, which have been converted into vanities. The desk chairs have monogrammed covers. Custom-cut mirrors top the surfaces and white linen covers have been made to hide the content stored underneath. Each vanity is topped with two lamps that flank matching jewelry boxes and lighted makeup mirrors. Framed mirrors are above each vanity and a flat-screen TV hangs over the door, attached to a swivel for easy viewing.

The room actually has three closets, all of them in a row. Instead of closet doors, curtains that match the ones on the windows hang over the openings. They are topped by pink linen valances trimmed in velvet to match the velvet throw pillows on the sofa and the pink linen band around the dust ruffle. I can't help noticing the third closet is already three quarters of the way full of Annie Laurie's dresses.

Finally, there is a luscious gray-and-white wool rug patterned in an Alhambra motif and another small animal skin rug under the coffee table. *Please tell me that's fake,* I keep thinking, because at this point nothing would surprise me. Towel racks are hung behind the dorm-room door and fluffy towels bearing each of the girls' monograms, are already in place. The only thing left to do is make up Ellie's bed.

Until I saw it in person, it was hard to imagine just how glorious it would be. Truth is, Ellie's dorm room is nicer than any room in our entire house, including our formal living room. Mama's house isn't even this nice. Well, yes it is. It's just old.

I am scared to death to comment. If I gloat Haynes is sure to pick up on how much it all cost and well, frankly, he doesn't know yet. So I smile. And try to act as if it's just another day in the life of Haynes and Wilda Woodcock.

"Y'all must have been here for hours," Haynes says, crawling out from underneath Ellie's bed, "This room seems about perfect to me."

"We started yesterday," Rhonda replies, from a stepstool. She's adjusting the valance over Ellie's closet. "The rest of my team's already moved on to another room."

Haynes glances at me, then at Maurice. "I'll get you paid for your work, Mr. Robinson. Please leave me your address and I'll send you a check."

"Oh no, that's part of it," Rhonda says, before Mr. Robinson can speak, adding, "I run a turnkey business."

I freeze. *Here it is. My undoing. She's bound to say something about the cost.* But she never says another word. Just goes back to primping and fluffing the closet curtain. More importantly, Haynes doesn't ask.

Rhonda won't let us lift a finger. I guess not, for all the money we've spent. So Lilith and I just chitchat. Despite her extravagant taste, I have to admit I'm excited about reacquainting. We never really hit it off in college, but now that our daughters are roommates I'm hopeful our friendship will grow and we'll make up for lost time. She was our sorority president, for goodness sakes.

A knock on the door interrupts our conversation. The door is half open and a man pokes his head inside. "Is this room 918?"

Simultaneously we all answer. "Yes."

"I have a safe for an Annie Laurie Whitmore?"

Haynes's head turns slowly toward the door. His eyebrows are knitted tightly together and his lips are flat-lined. "Did you say, 'a safe'?"

The deliveryman nods.

"For what?" Haynes asks in a dubious tone.

The guy shrugs and Gage, ignoring Haynes's question, puts down his coffee and swallows in a hurry. "You're in the right place." He turns to Lilith. "Where does the safe go, darling?"

Lilith turns to Rhonda with a raised palm.

Rhonda jumps—literally jumps—over Gage's foot and stands in a small spot next to the sofa. "It's twenty-one by nineteen by thirty-seven, right?"

The fellow shrugs. "I couldn't tell ya."

"Hang on." Rhonda whips out a measuring tape clipped to her belt. Then measures and gives him a thumbs-up. "Put it right here, please."

The deliveryman maneuvers his dolly around the boxes and places the safe down with a loud thud. The floor jolts. I glance up at Haynes, whose face is void of any expression whatsoever, which, under different circumstances, would have cracked me up. Gage gives the guy a check and slips the receipt into his pocket. We all watch as he closes the door behind him.

Rhonda moves over to the closet, squats down, and pulls something out of her bag. "Looky here!" Now she's waving that something high in the air. On my word of honor, Rhonda Taylor has made Annie Laurie Whitmore a custom safe cover.

"We can hide it with this," she says while wrapping and Velcroing it around the safe. "And," she's back to the closet, "I had a piece of granite cut. That way . . ." We all watch her place the square on top of the safe. "It can easily double as an entertaining station." Patting the top, she asks, "Who brought the Keurig?"

"We did," I say, happy to make a contribution and cut through the tension. I don't need to look at Haynes to know there's steam shooting out of his ears.

"Get ya a sugar jar, a cream pitcher, and a little bowl for your stevia. Then run out to Williams Sonoma and buy an ice bucket, a pair of tongs, maybe even a wine opener." She winks. "You'll be all set."

"The safe is our treat," Lilith says. "Ellie is more than welcome to use it anytime she wants. Annie Laurie will give her the code."

"I told Annie Laurie she ought to put her Jimmy Choos in it," Gage says, with a shrug. "God knows between her and her mother I should have bought stock in that company a long time ago."

Haynes Woodcock is irate. I know him so well. He's biting his bottom lip, the way he does when he's trying to hold his tongue. The very idea that Annie Laurie has brought enough valuables to require a safe, *to college,* is making him crazy. I just know it. He steps out of the room in silence without telling any of us where he's going.

When the install is finally over, around two o'clock, and the girls—and Haynes—have returned to see Ole Miss Dorm Room of the Year, it truly looks like it belongs on the pages of *Town & Country* or *House Beautiful.* Ellie's eyes look like shiny new half-dollars and her smile belongs to a camera. I can't say Annie Laurie's expression matches Ellie's, but I can tell she's happy. The two of them hug excitedly when they see it, then crawl up on their beds, using their footstools.

"Hang on, y'all. Let me get my camera." Rhonda reaches into her back pocket for her phone and snaps a picture of the girls. "I'm gonna tweet, Instagram, and Facebook this out riiight now." Her thumbs are typing frantically. "So cute, y'all."

It takes her another couple of minutes to finish her tweeting and such and I'm reminded of how utterly deficient I am in that area. Rhonda then slips her phone inside her back pocket while strolling over to the closet. We all watch as she digs inside a large bag and pulls out a clipboard with paper attached. I see her scanning the room, making check marks. "By the way, the shades are blackout. Just like you wanted, Annie Laurie. You can sleep all day if you want to."

"Okay, thanks," Annie Laurie responds, climbing down from her bed.

"Ellie Woodcock," Haynes says. "Don't be getting any ideas."

"I won't, Dad." This time Ellie doesn't sneer, she gleams. And looks around her new room with a mixture of shock and wonder.

"I'd put my sunglasses in that safe if I were you." Rhonda touches the logo on Annie Laurie's Coco Chanels, which are holding back her hair on top of her head. "Those babies are not cheap. Okay, y'all. I think that's it. Except for"—she returns to her treasure chest, also known as Ellie's closet, and pulls out a basket—"your dorm-warming gift!"

It's large, wrapped in red cellophane, with several gems inside. "I won't tell you everything that's in it, but I will say...y'all know there are no candles allowed in the dorm rooms, right?" She looks at the girls and they both nod. "There's a diffuser in here with the most luscious scent you'll ever smell." Bending down, she places the basket on the ottoman in front of the sofa. "And all kinds of other little happies. Y'all enjoy." She takes a step toward the door then turns around. "And if you get tired of all this by next year, you know where to find me."

"Thanks for your help today, Miss Rhonda. Mighty nice of you." Haynes walks over and shakes her hand.

"No worries. It's all part of it." My heart stops. *Please don't mention the cost, Rhonda. Please.* "Come on, Maurice. Let's let these girls unpack."

Everyone thanks them and they slip out the door. She comes right back, though, before we can take another breath. "Just checking something." She scoots over to the refrigerator, opens it. "Yep. Fuji's in the fridge. See y'all." And she's gone.

For a long moment, the only sound in the room is the soft hum of the small refrigerator.

Lilith breaks the silence, saying, "Isn't this dreamy? Can you imagine if we had had this when we were in school?" She puts her arm around her daughter's shoulder. "I keep telling Annie Laurie how lucky she is." Annie Laurie tilts her head toward her mother and shrugs with a confident smile.

Gage says, "I think I'm jealous. I wish I'd had something this nice when I was living in the frat house."

I look over at Haynes. The crease between his eyebrows could hold a tube of lipstick, it's so deep. "If a guy had had a room like this in my frat house he'd have had his ass kicked."

NINE

WILDA

When it's time to leave, I feel a familiar lump in my throat. It had been there with Cooper and Jackson when we left them at their Ole Miss dorms, and it's bigger the third and final go-round. I excuse myself, step out into the hall so Ellie won't see me, and fan my eyes frantically. No tears, Wilda. Stay calm. You can do this.

I try psyching myself up by thinking about the times she had been really mean and hurt my feelings. But it doesn't work. I try telling myself that this is a rite of passage and the best thing that could ever happen to her. No good either. So I take a long, ultra-deep breath, count to ten, and move back into their room, biting the insides of my cheeks.

"Okay, let's go." I tug on Haynes's arm.

He and Ellie both turn around, surprised by my eagerness.

"Ellie's ready for this. And so are we. I love you, baby. Call us anytime." I kiss her on the cheek, trying to downplay my emotions.

A surprising tenderness creeps into her voice. "I'm not that far away, Mom. I'm sure I'll be home soon. Probably Labor Day."

Not wanting to embarrass her again, I suck in my right cheek, biting down full force.

"Of course, I'll have to find a riiiide." She draws out the word and leans in toward Haynes.

"My poor little underprivileged child." He scoops her into the crook of his arm, nestles her to his side. "No car her freshman year. No searching all night for a parking spot in a silver satellite lot miles away. No thousand-dollar parking fines. You'll thank me later when you haven't gained the freshmen fifteen because you've had to use those good legs of yours."

"You are *embarrassing* me," I hear Ellie whisper through gritted teeth. Still holding her in the crook of his arm, Haynes swings his other behind her knees and scoops her up like he used to when she was little. She puts her arms around his neck, says, "I love you, Daddy."

"I love *you,* Punkin." Haynes kisses her forehead. Then puts her down, pats her on the back. "Don't do anything I wouldn't do."

Not one to ever let him get away with a wily remark, Ellie makes a mischievous face. "Gee, thanks, Dad. Now I can be really wild."

Haynes narrows his eyes, points a threatening finger her way.

Then, to my surprise, she throws her arms around my neck and kisses me. "I love you, too, Mommy." Ellie only calls me Mommy when she needs me, like when she was little. But this is sincere. She's vulnerable, and loving, and doesn't care who sees her. All of a sudden, she's seven again and can't get enough of me. With my arms tightly wrapped around her shoulders, a tear that I had been desperately trying to hold back slides down my cheek and melts into the sleeve of her T-shirt.

"I love you, Heart. I love you so much," I whisper directly into her ear. "And I'm ultra proud of you. You are an incredible human being."

"Thanks, Mommy," she whispers back. "You're pretty incredible yourself."

None of us are paying attention to what the Whitmores are doing. Nor do we care. We're having an impenetrable family moment. Finally Haynes touches me on the shoulder and says, "Let's go, honey. The girls have a lot of unpacking to do."

Ellie and I peel away from each other, but I can't take my eyes off her.

From somewhere else in the room I hear Gage say, "We won't be far behind you."

Lilith taps me on the arm. "Before you go, I have something to talk to you about." She turns. "Hang on, Haynes. This won't take but a minute." She motions me out the door, and I follow her down the hall, away from the hustle. I suspect this must have something to do with the safe, or Rhonda Taylor, or perhaps she wants to get together for lunch.

"You know I'm House Corp President now, right?" Lilith says after stopping a few rooms down.

House Corp President means she's head of all sorority relations and represents Alpha Delt to the University. She makes all the operational House decisions and manages the housemother, all on a volunteer basis. I don't know much more about it, nor do I care. It sounds like a ton of work to me.

"No, I didn't. Congratulations?" This is meant to be a question. Like I said, it sounds like a full-time job. With no compensation.

She clasps both hands to her chest. "Yes, thank you. I'm thrilled. I was a Rush Advisor last year, but I wanted to be more involved. I've been needing something like this for years. Since I became a sustainer in the League."

With my head tilted curiously I ask, "The Junior League has a chapter in Natchez?" Jackson is the only town in Mississippi with a chapter—at least that's what I'd been told.

"I affiliated in Jackson. And I'm glad I did. I know so many Jackson people now."

It takes two hours to get from Natchez to Jackson. That must have been quite a commitment, I think without commenting.

"I love my garden club, don't get me wrong, it's just"—she looks off, like she's choosing her words—"frankly, I feel like this will keep me young. Plus I'll have a bird's-eye view into Annie Laurie–world for the next four years. That's if she decides to pledge Alpha Delt, which, in my mind, is not up for discussion."

Hearing her say Annie Laurie had to be an Alpha Delt takes me aback, but I don't comment. "So you'll be around the entire time she's in school? I assumed House Corp President would only be a one-year position."

"It's for as long as I want the job, girlfriend. Not everyone wants a full-time job with a volunteer's pay." She snickers nervously.

I sure wouldn't, but to each his own.

"Anyway. Back to what I wanted to talk with you about. I think you should be a Rush Advisor. Anne Marie Norton had to leave the board unexpectedly and we need someone to take her place."

Hmm. I shrug, contemplating her offer. "What exactly would I be doing?"

"Acting as a mentor. Helping out with Recruitment." Her hand cups the side of her mouth. "*Spying*," she whispers conspiratorially. "You could know what Ellie's doing without her knowing you know what she's doing. Does that make sense?"

"Ahhh," I say with a nod. Now it's making perfect sense.

"Honestly. It's a way to see her more often. Plus I really enjoyed my work as a Rush Advisor. I think you will, too. It's fun."

The thought of getting to see Ellie lessens the sadness I felt before we left the room. Maybe this is my answer. I'd never spy on her, never in a million years. But I'd certainly love to peek in on her every now and then. "Where do I sign up?"

Her eyes pop like she's surprised by my answer, and then she grins impishly. "All you do is tell me you want to do it and that's it. We had Recruitment meetings at the House every day last week. Even though it doesn't start till October now, we did all the normal pre-Rush stuff. It's not much different than when we were in school."

"Learning about all the girls and deciding which ones are and aren't *'Alpha Delt Material'*?" I say, with a chuckle. That's the way we used to put it when we were in the sorority. Hearing my words makes me cringe to think how narrow-minded and snobby we once were. Maybe as Rush Advisor I can help with that.

"Exactly. We have one more meeting tomorrow. Why don't you stay tonight?"

"Darn. I can't. Haynes and I rode together. I wouldn't have a way home."

"Can't you borrow Ellie's car?"

"She didn't bring one this semester, remember?"

Lilith's top lip curls.

"Haynes is old-fashioned that way."

"That is sure gonna be tough on Ellie."

"I know. But he's not budging." I'm shrinking down, feeling as small as a sparrow. Maybe I should have put my foot down with Haynes. "Besides, I don't have any extra clothes with me."

"Memphis isn't far. Come back tomorrow."

It occurs to me that I cannot ask Haynes to pay for a hotel room every time I come to Oxford for a meeting. "Where do the advisors stay? Hotels?"

"Several people have condos here in Oxford. Gage and I have one. You're welcome to stay with us."

"That's really sweet of you. Thanks."

"Okay, so you're in?"

"I'm in."

"Fantastic! There are two other great women on the Recruitment Advisory Board. Sallie Wallace has been on it for five years. You remember her, don't you?"

"Sure I do. Wasn't she Miss Tennessee?"

"Yes indeed." From the smirk on Lilith's face, and the rapid way she's nodding, I'm not sure if she's proud or jealous. "And Gwen Lambuth has been on the board two years. She's a lot younger than us. You'll see them both tomorrow."

"Sounds great." I wonder if Lilith knows how much this board appointment means to me. Our conversations over the summer never included our thoughts on becoming empty nesters so late in life. Surely she feels the same melancholy I do. Annie Laurie is her only child.

Ellie pokes her head out of their door. "Mom, do you have any scissors?"

"I think we packed some. Check your Vera Bradley bag."

She taps the doorframe. "Thanks."

"Our girls are gonna be best friends. I can already tell," Lilith says.

I think back to Lisa. We were definitely best friends. "I sure hope so. That'll certainly make college more fun."

"So you'll come back tomorrow?"

"I'll be here."

"We have plenty of food and wine at the condo. So don't feel like you have to bring anything."

"Oh, well, I can't show up empty-handed."

"Of course you can." She shoos away my offer. "Our pantry is stocked. Plus I've got several bottles of thank-you wine left over."

"Thank-you wine?"

"You know . . . for all the recs my friends wrote for Annie Laurie. What'd you send?"

She may as well have asked me which trailer park I grew up in. Ellie sent thank-you notes to all the ladies who wrote her recs, but I didn't think to include a gift. I'd like to melt into a shame puddle at her feet. Lilith is a force of nature. One minute she's got me convinced I'm her new best friend, and the next she's trapped me inside a sticky web of humiliation.

Right then, as if his instincts had fired up to save me, Haynes steps out of Ellie's room. His hands are stuffed inside his pockets. "Ready?"

"I guess so," I say, nauseous at the mere thought of my oversight.

Lilith reaches out to hug me from the side. "You go on. We'll probably hang around a few more minutes. I want to absorb this dreaminess a little while longer."

Haynes and I go back into the room, give our final good-byes to all, and I slink out the door behind him.

On the way home, Haynes is uncharacteristically quiet for the first several minutes of our drive. He turns on our Memphis classic rock station, and sings along with the Stones, but without the normal zeal for his favorite band. I notice his hands gripping the steering wheel. When he finally opens his mouth he says, "What's a Jimmy Choo?"

I can't help it, but that strikes me as hilarious. And knowing he's dead serious makes it even funnier. I laugh so hard I snort. "Jimmy . . . Choo is . . . a . . . *shoe*." I can barely get the words out between gasps for air. And hearing the rhyme I made makes it worse. Now I am truly about to wet my pants.

One of the best things about us is we can't watch the other laugh for too long without the other cracking up. I see Haynes grin. Then his eyebrows wiggle. And pretty soon he's laughing. Now we're both cackling and holding our stomachs. I drum my feet against the floorboard. He bangs his head against the steering wheel. We both have tears streaming down our cheeks.

"Jimmy Choo is a shooooe," Haynes repeats, and we fall to our sides against the windows, heehawing our brains out. He whips into a rural gas station and screeches to a halt. We both run for the toilets holding ourselves.

When we get back into the car and have settled down, about five minutes down the road, he confesses he's skeptical about Ellie rooming with Annie Laurie. He goes on and on about what a milquetoast Gage Whitmore is and calls Lilith a "bulldozer control freak," but the only thing he says having to do with Rhonda Taylor is, "I assume Gage paid Mr. Robinson. But we could have done all that stuff ourselves."

"I know."

"I mean that's pretty ridiculous. Did you know they were hiring someone?"

"No." My half-truth. I had no idea Rhonda Taylor employed an installation team.

"Lifestyles of the rich and very rich," he says, shaking his head. But he looks over at me with a twinkle in his eye. Thank goodness.

I tell him about my conversation with Lilith and how she's asked me to be a Rush Advisor. Once he sees how happy I am about seeing Ellie more often he's very supportive, despite his concerns about the Whitmores.

But the fun I was having moments ago is replaced with a gut-wrenching fear of doom. All I can think about, while watching the hot Highway 78 pavement stretch out in front of us, is the money I borrowed from Mama to pay Rhonda Taylor. The loan I'm hiding from Haynes, with no clue how to make the first payment.

TEN

WILDA

When I drag myself out to the coffeepot the next morning, before I'm awake enough to know my own name, Haynes, who is usually long gone by this time, is sitting at the kitchen counter reading the paper. The sound of him snapping it shut as soon as he sees me is my first indication that there may be a bump in our morning. Even so, I calmly pour myself a cup of the coffee he's already brewed and sit down on the stool next to him. From the corner of my eye I watch him take a long sip of his, then put his cup down softly. "I don't know, Wilda."

Alarmed by his tone, I meet his eyes.

"I'm—" He looks off, as though searching for the right words, then drums his fingers on the counter. "I'm *concerned* about our daughter."

I reach over and place my hand on top of his. "Is this about the Jimmy Choos?" My desperate attempt to add a little levity into his mood.

It doesn't work.

Haynes rubs the back of his neck, while stretching out his shoulders. Then he looks me in the eye. "Children learn from their parents. Later, when they go out on their own, parents hope and pray their children remember the values they've been taught." He gets up and paces from one end of the room to the other. He's in the courtroom.

"But..." He points a finger high in the air. "Teenagers are heavily influenced by the company they keep. Ellie is living with a girl who has two whack jobs for parents. Who the hell sends their kid off to college with enough valuables that require *a safe*? They have locks on their doors, for God's sake."

I let out a sigh. "I don't know. But I agree with you. Taking a safe to college is way over the top."

He stops pacing, moves back to where I'm sitting. "Where did you find this girl?"

"I've told you this already. Lilith called *me* when she heard we had daughters the same age."

Leaning down, he grips the counter. The veins in his hands look like planting mounds in a garden. "I get it. But didn't you research the family before you committed our daughter?"

"Haynes. I'm not a lawyer. I don't research."

Instead of commenting he just peers at me over his glasses.

Now *I'm* getting confused about our decision. "At the time, I thought it made sense. So did you. We talked about it."

He sighs, releases a heavy breath. "Maybe I'm overreacting. But she's our baby, Wilda. My little Punkin. I can't help it if I still want to protect her."

"Me, too." He's not the only one who wants to protect Ellie.

"If it's not the right situation for her surely she'll figure that out and move out next year," he says with another sigh.

"Of course she will. Our daughter has a good head on her shoulders, Haynes. She knows right from wrong and she can spot a phony a mile away. If Annie Laurie Whitmore turns out to be an insensitive princess, Ellie won't stand for it."

With a purposeful snicker he sits back down. "You're right about that."

"Of course I am. But I don't think that'll happen. When we visited the Whitmores in Natchez they were a gracious, loving family."

After a long pause and a blatant disregard for my comment he changes the subject. "That dorm room. I didn't want to embarrass Ellie so I didn't say anything, but holy crap. How much did that cost us?"

Gulp. "Three thousand." I say the lie softly, hoping he'll shrug it off.

A loud screech from his stool as it is pushed away from the counter tells me he won't. *"Three. Thousand. Dollars?"*

"All of this dorm room stuff costs a fortune. I'm telling you, we're in the wrong business." My pulse is beating so loudly I'm sure he can hear it.

For a full minute he keeps his mouth shut. Once my pounding pulse has turned into bona fide heart palpitations he surprises me. "She does have a beautiful room. And it made her happy. Did you see her face when she walked in?"

I nod. And seize the opportunity to show excitement over every inch of my face.

"That made me happy, too. Seeing how much she loves it." If there's one thing I know about Haynes, Ellie is his Achilles' heel. He slurps the last bit of coffee and stands up. "Okay, enough of this. Let's move on."

Feeling immense relief, I turn his way. "Hope the rest of your day is better." We lean in to kiss and I wrap my fingers around his forearm. "Don't forget I'm driving back down to Oxford today ... for the last Rush Workshop meeting. But I'll be back tonight after dinner. I've decided not to spend the night with Lilith. My to-do list is ten miles long."

With a tap of his forehead he says, "Ah. The new Rush Advisor. Go steer those Alpha Delts in the right direction."

"That's my plan."

"You'll be a great role model." Thank God, there's a smile on his face.

"You mean it?"

"Of course I mean it. Be careful of the traffic, though. It's move-in day for the rest of Mississippi." He grabs his briefcase off the bench, moves toward the door. Then he turns back around. "Babe."

I look up.

"I'm not pissed at you. I'm just worried for Ellie. I'm sorry if it came out like this is your fault. It's not."

I kiss the air to let him know I'm okay. But I'm not. I'm rotting on the inside. No way around it, I've out-and-out lied to my husband. The clanging of the door shutting behind him is the last sound I hear. Wallowing inside my cesspool, I sit another moment in silence before pouring myself another cup of black coffee.

ELEVEN

CALI

"Papaw," I call over the side of his pickup truck when I see him squinting his eyes and gritting his teeth, "that's too heavy. Let me help you." I shut the truck door and run back as he's maneuvering the heaviest box onto the tailgate. "Be careful, please." He pulled a muscle in his back a few weeks ago and I don't want him reinjuring himself.

He turns. "Young lady. Don't you know you're not supposed to put heavy things in big boxes? What's in here?" While he's heaving the box toward himself a small grunt escapes.

"Almost every book I own. With a few shoes and boots on top." As the two of us lower the box onto our rented dolly I can feel my arms straining.

"All these books. Well, what else could I expect from our first lady governor." After a wink, I see that familiar grin.

"That's a lot of pressure, you know."

He reaches for the next box. "You tell me how many of these pretty little girls moving in today are class valedictorians with all Honors and AP courses?"

"Papaw, shh. I don't want that broadcast all over campus."

"And why not?"

"Because I'm not a bragger," I whisper.

He stops, nuzzles me into his side. "I'm just proud of you, you hear? You've given an old man a happy heart."

"Aw, thanks, Papaw. But you're not that old."

"Since when is seventy not that old?"

"I heard it's the new fifty."

"Hogwash," he says, reaching for the next box.

"What about Dolly Parton? You're always talking about what a beauty she is. Y'all are the same age."

"Ha. She took a dip in that fountain of youth."

"She certainly did. And it cost her a fortune." Mamaw has stepped out of the truck, but left it running. The poor woman doesn't do well in the August heat.

Papaw and I continue to stack boxes on the dolly. "The only problem this old man has," Papaw says with a glance at Mamaw, "is thinking about how much your grandmother and I will miss you."

"It's not like I'm off to New York City. I'm only down the road." My high school guidance counselor had encouraged me to apply for scholarships at more prestigious universities much farther away. As much as I wanted to get away from Blue Mountain—*Population 650*—I didn't want to be that far away from my grandparents. They're the only family I have. And I'm all they have. Besides, I've been wanting to be an Ole Miss Rebel since I was a little girl. "I'm sure I'll be home all the time."

Papaw turns to face me, puts his hands on my shoulders. "You listen here. We don't want you doing that. This is your time, Cali baby. You need to soar like that ol' eagle. We'll be just fine."

I feel a lump in my throat. I've always been a protector, never wanting harm to come their way. "Thanks, Papaw." I bite my lip before grabbing a couple of bags from the truck bed. I do not want to cry today.

Mamaw looks up at my new multistory home. "Wonder what floor you'll be on?"

"I don't know; let's go find out."

Since I'd been accepted into the Barksdale Honors College, I could have lived in a nicer dorm with bigger rooms, but I chose Martin. Because Martin is primarily a sorority dorm. Most every girl who lives here will be going through Rush. That's another dream of mine. Not only have I longed to be an Ole Miss Rebel, I've had my heart set on sorority life. But one of my obstacles—and there are many—is that I don't know anyone who belongs to a sorority. Blue Mountain girls do not Rush.

As we walk the long stretch toward the dorm, amidst an army of luxury cars and SUVs parked every which way, I can't help noticing how most of the girls are dressed—extra-large T-shirts and workout shorts with fluorescent Nike tennis shoes. Why do they dress like this, and how do they all know to do it? I have on a pair of cut-offs and a cute top. I look down at my Nike tennis shoes with gratitude that I had found them on sale only a week ago. But those T-shirts. They look so . . . big.

The line to check in is out the door and down the sidewalk. Girls, accompanied by their parents, brothers, and boyfriends, are standing in the extreme heat with all their personal belongings. It strikes me as funny as I eye the crowd. Couches, headboards, chairs, rugs, boxes, suitcases. It looks like a long line of high-class refugees.

I can tell this tries Mamaw's patience. There are no lines in Blue Mountain, Mississippi, and she's lived there her whole life. As for me, I couldn't care less. Nothing about this experience is going to rob me of an ounce of happiness. Papaw suggests that she go inside and sit down while he stays in line with me. He escorts her in and I hold our place. As hot as it is, I'm still getting chills at the thought of which girls will become my friends and possibly sorority sisters.

While waiting for Papaw to return, I text Jasmine for an update. Originally, she had planned to be here by now, but her last text said she was still a couple of hours out. We've been texting all week and I can't wait to finally meet my new roommate. Jasmine won't be going out for Rush. But I understand why.

Papaw and I while away the time, talking with the other girls and parents. Mothers seem to be in charge, barking orders like military sergeants. Dads, waiting patiently for their next assignments, are talking to one another in line. Two girls in front of us see each other and scream at the top of their lungs. They throw their arms around each other and dance out their hug. Papaw

rears his head back and holds his ears. He does stuff like that to be funny. My
grandfather has never met a stranger.

When we finally open the door to my room, three scorching hours later, all the
way up on the ninth floor, a tidal wave of excitement floods through my veins,
out my pores, and pops into goose bumps all over my arms and legs. Standing
in my own dorm room, looking around at the khaki-colored walls, linoleum
floor, even the tiny closets, exhilarates me beyond my wildest dreams.

I dash over to the bare window to peek at my view. With my hands gripping the sill I can't help but gawk at the gargantuan sorority houses directly
across the street, imagining myself walking up to one of the front doors as a
member. But when I remember something that happened last fall I retreat
back, slumping my shoulders. It was a Saturday afternoon. The Daisy Tree
gift shop where I work was super slow that day. Two ladies from Memphis had
stopped in to look around. They were passing through Blue Mountain on what
they called "an antique treasure hunt." While I was checking them out I
overheard them discussing Ole Miss Rush. So I perked up my head and eaves-
dropped on their conversation.

One lady asked the other if a certain girl had a pedigree. The other re-
plied, "Of course she does. She wouldn't be able to rush without one."

I wanted to stop her right then and there and ask her to please tell me what
she meant. Because I had no idea you needed a "pedigree" to belong to a sorority. And to be perfectly honest, I had no idea a pedigree had anything to
do with a person. I consider myself an intelligent human being, but this was
news to me. My best friend Rachel's mom always bragged about having a
"purebred *pedigreed* Pom." And she took it for granted that everyone in America knew that Pom was short for Pomeranian.

Try saying it out loud. Purebred pedigreed pom. How's that for a tongue
twister? That's exactly how Mrs. Smith referred to PomPom. "PomPom, my
purebred pedigreed Pom." PomPom's American Kennel Club certificate was
framed, like it was a college diploma, and hung in their den. That's how I knew
it was true.

When I looked "pedigree" up in the dictionary that night the third definition read: "distinguished, excellent, or pure ancestry." That's when I got it. My birth-right does not include a pedigree. For the first seventeen years of my life, it didn't mean doodly squat. But now I'm not so sure. My family is not, well, we're certainly not prominent or even conventional. That's for darn sure.

After a minute or so I pull away, climb up on one of the beds, and lie down on my back. Pushing away worry, I close my eyes, tasting sweet freedom and independence for the first time. When I blink my eyes open, my grandparents are standing side by side, gazing down at me.

"You are a picture, Cali Watkins," Papaw says. "Look at our pretty baby, Marge. She'll be president of the student government one day. You wait and see if I'm not right."

"Well she certainly has the potential." Mamaw's bitterness, that sour pill she swallowed when my mother ran amok, gets the best of her sometimes. "Let's get started, Charlie. We don't have all day."

I see him close his eyes and slump over slightly. He never says anything back, just chooses to forgive every snarky comment she ever makes.

Mamaw gets right to work. As a going-away present, she bought all my college linens. It was especially meaningful because she wanted to save the money and sew everything herself. If it had been up to her, she would have made the curtains, the pillow shams, the duvet covers, and the throw pillows, for both Jasmine and me.

I didn't want to hurt her feelings so I thought about how to break it to her for weeks. Jasmine and I had talked about it over the phone and both of us loved the pink-and-gray linens from dormitup.com. They had everything we needed to have the cutest room in Martin, all in one box. A comforter, sham, matching sheets and towels. A curtain, a throw pillow, a hamper, a shower caddy, a desk lamp, and a trash can—every single thing coordinated perfectly.

In great detail Jasmine and I had discussed all of the other things we would need for our room and divided all the extras between us. A friend of hers was giving away a futon sofa. It was a little soiled, Jasmine said, but we had planned to throw quilts on top to hide the stains. She also found matching desk chairs and I found a microwave, a full-length mirror for the door, and a small re-frigerator on Craigslist.

The rug we ordered through the University is already in the room. Al-though we could have chosen from a variety of colors, we chose gray to make sure it coordinated with our bedding. It's fairly small, so it doesn't take long for the three of us to roll it out in between the beds and desks.

An hour later, we hear voices in the hall. "Here it is, Mama," a girl says, followed by a loud knock.

I nearly trip over a large box hurrying to the door. Because of Instagram, I recognize her the second she walks in. "Jasmine!"

"Cali Watkins! I finally get to meet you."

"In the flesh," I say, and we embrace. There's no awkwardness at all. We'd talked many times over the summer after learning the University had matched us together.

Jasmine puts her hands on her hips, looks around. "This room is not bad. Is it, Mama?"

"Unh-uh. I like it." Jasmine's mother, who, I have to say, is rather plump, plops right down on the other bed. The sound of a screeching frame fills the room.

"Y'all, meet my grandparents." I squeeze in between them and put my arms around their shoulders. "Charles and Margaret Watkins."

"Nice to meet you, Mr. and Mrs. Watkins," Jasmine says. "And this is my mama, Devonia Crawford." Everyone shakes hands, but Mrs. Crawford keeps her seat. I get the idea it's too hard for her to move once she sits down.

Jasmine glances around. "It's small, but it'll do. You've already made it look nice, Cali."

"It's all my grandmother." I grin, gesturing toward Mamaw.

"You have the touch, Mrs. Watkins."

"Why, thank you, Jasmine." When Mamaw smiles it's nice to see.

Papaw slides over and wraps his arm around her shoulder. "You should see our home. My Marge is quite the decorator."

"Oh, Charles, stop. I'm not, either."

Jasmine laughs. "You're just being modest, Mrs. Watkins. Cali, I like the way you've got your bed up high, by the way."

"It was already lofted when we walked in," Papaw says. "I'd be happy to loft yours. We wanted to let you decide."

About that time, a guy walks in carrying a box with dormitup.com printed on the outside. Jasmine, who I'm sure notices him, continues talking to my grandparents and doesn't interrupt their conversation.

"Ahem," the guy says after a couple minutes. "Will I have to stand here all day or are you gonna tell me where to put this box?"

"I'm sorry, baby. Put it down over there." Jasmine points to an empty spot in front of the closet. "I'll take that closet. Okay with you, Cali?"

"Sure," I say with a shrug.

He obligingly puts down the box, turns to my grandparents and me. "Don't mind Jasmine." He stretches out his hand. "I'm Carl Joyner. It's a pleasure to make y'all's acquaintance."

"I'm sorry," she says. "That's Carl."

"I need help with the futon. Are you okay to help me with it, Mr. Watkins? It's down in the lobby."

"Why sure, son. I've been waiting for something else to do. I'm ready when you are."

"Do you need to wait on the elevator or are you okay to take the stairs?"

"He can take them down, but not up," Mamaw says, rather sternly, while peeking around from the closet door.

Carl doesn't seem to mind. "No problem. We'll take the elevator." Before leaving he taps Jasmine's mother on the shoulder. "Can I bring you anything from downstairs, Miss Devonia?"

"I'd think I'd like some lunch, please, Carl. Soon as you get a chance."

We have a C-store in the lobby, but Mamaw had packed sandwiches, enough for a small army. She steps toward Mrs. Crawford. "I packed plenty of sandwiches for all of us. Chicken salad, egg salad, and ham and cheese. Do you have a preference?"

Mrs. Crawford raises a hand to her chest. "No, ma'am. I'll be happy with anything you give me."

"We have plenty of drinks, too." Mamaw moves over to the cooler and lifts the top. "May I hand you one?"

"Why thank you, ma'am. I'd love a Co-Cola. If you have one."

"Sure I do." Mamaw hands her both a sandwich and a Coke and offers one to Jasmine, who declines. Then she turns to Carl. "How about you, son?"

"No, ma'am. I'll wait till I get back. Then I might want two or three," he says, making a silly face. Crossing his arms, Carl surveys the room. "Now, ladies, I want to see this place perfect by the time we get back." I watch him give an exaggerated wink behind Jasmine's back.

"I'll show you perfect," Jasmine says, spinning around to face him. She strikes a pose with her hip cocked and chin lifted.

"Mmm-hmm," Carl responds. "Perfect in *every* way."

"Go on with your bad self." Jasmine pushes him out the door and Papaw follows behind.

Jasmine is tall. Must be close to six feet. And since I'm only five two, we look like Kanga and Roo standing side by side. She had told me she had been a high school basketball player in Greenville, but had not been offered a scholarship on the Ole Miss team. That's one of the things we have in common. We're both athletes. I was on our high school cross-country team all four years.

For the next couple of hours we unpack a little and talk a lot. It's fun for all of us to get to know one another. Mamaw and Mrs. Crawford seem to be getting along famously, talking about growing up in Mississippi. Even though the Crawfords are from the Delta, it seems things aren't that much different from Blue Mountain. Small town life in Mississippi appears to be the same no matter where you live.

The only thing left to do, besides unpacking the rest of Jasmine's boxes and suitcases, is hang the curtains. With Carl's help, Papaw installs the rods, on the window and closets, with the peel and stick strips that are allowed. Mamaw had packed her steamer and expertly steams away any wrinkles once the curtains have been hung. Sweet Mrs. Crawford, who moved over to the chair once Jasmine's bed was lifted, has been slowly folding Jasmine's clothes into neat piles.

Around four o'clock Papaw backs up to the door and lifts his arms, taking it all in. "Well, girls, it looks like we're finished."

Mamaw crosses her arms, nods her head. "This has to be the best-looking, most stylish room in Martin Hall. Even if I didn't make it all myself. You girls should be proud."

"I am very proud," I say, hiking up on my bed. "We only need one more thing. Stepstools."

Jasmine pats the top of her mattress. "Speak for yourself, shorty." She hops up with ease and turns around, jutting her chest toward me. "Our room is dope. I guarantee you nobody has our sense of style. What do you think, Cali?"

Before I can answer, Carl scoots over, puts a casual arm around her shoulder. "My baby has excellent taste." Then he winks and laughs at himself.

Jasmine looks at us, shrugs her shoulders. "I'm no dummy."

"And neither am I," Papaw says. "Cali, I think I better get your Mamaw home. I can tell she's pretty tuckered out."

When we get down to Papaw's truck, I can tell he's the one who's tuckered out. His Blue Mountain College T-shirt is damp and wrinkled. He reaches into his pocket for a handkerchief and wipes his brow, then offers it to Mamaw. Her temples are moist and her blouse is stuck to her plump middle.

Papaw is about to cry. I can tell by the way he's sucking his bottom lip. Whenever I see him cry, even at a movie, it breaks my heart. Mamaw, on the other hand, rarely gets emotional, but I still know she cares. My mother has caused them enough pain for three lifetimes. That's probably why I was always such a good girl and stayed away from trouble.

Leaning over the side, he peeks into the truck bed. "Well. She's empty." My grandfather is stalling. I know him so well.

"Come on, Charles," Mamaw responds in a frustrated voice. "I'm hot and ready to get on the road."

Never one to react, he ignores her, then turns to me. "Cali. Have I told you how proud of you I am?"

"Only a hundred times." I grin, bat my eyelashes.

"Well, that was number one hundred and one and I suspect I'll get to a thousand before I kick the bucket."

"Here we go." Mamaw rolls her eyes. "The ol' death bit again."

Papaw plays like he didn't hear her, but I know he did. He simply keeps his eyes focused on me.

"Why don't you save the other nine hundred until I become governor?" I say.

"I'll try, but don't count on it," he says. "Got your prayer stone?"

I dig inside my pocket, pull it out to show him. "Right here."

With her eyes on the stone, Mamaw wraps her arms around me, pulls me in tight. When she lets go she manages a smile. "I'm proud of you, too. You know that, don't you?" She rarely hands out compliments, so I know she means it. But she raises a cautionary finger. "Make sure you stay out of trouble. You've worked hard to earn your big scholarship and you don't want to do anything to jeopardize it."

I take a step back. No one knows this more than me.

"I'm expecting nothing less than a four point." Piercing eyes lock on to mine.

Her expectations ruin the process. I'm the one wanting to make the Dean's List. I don't need her telling me to do it. The massive expectations I've put on myself are enough to kill any kind of social life I might have in mind, much less sorority life. But I am determined to do both. And find a job on campus to pay for it.

As if he's reading my mind, Papaw says, "She doesn't need you hassling her, Marge. Our Cali will be running our state soon. She knows what she needs to do." Before Mamaw can object, he beckons us with both hands. "Come here, you two." He puts his arms around both of us and my grandmother does the same.

I know what's coming.

"Your Mamaw and I want to pray over you, Cali." They bow their heads.

I freeze. Not here. Not in front of all these people. "Will … will y'all pray for me on the way home? It's just … there are tons of people around." The sight of all of us huddled together would draw tons of attention. And there's no one else doing it.

Papaw's face droops. Mamaw looks up with narrowed eyes, but she holds her tongue. Immediately I want to take it back. But I can't help the discomfort I feel. So I hug and kiss them both and watch as Papaw opens the door for my grandmother. He pushes it to with a gentle hand, making sure she's safely tucked inside. That's who he is. Gentle, kind, protective.

I watch him stroll around to his side. Before he opens the door he glances up, then points to his right eye. He makes a gentle fist with both hands, crosses them over his heart, then points at me. I mimic his gesture, as I've done hundreds of times before, and watch him duck into the truck. My heart is stinging and I feel awful about not letting them pray for me. It was such a little thing, yet it meant the world to them. But I'm bound and determined to keep a low profile. Then no one will care enough to pry into my past.

Papaw backs out of his parking spot. Through the glass I watch him turning the steering wheel. He waves before moving his truck forward, then slowly drives out of the Martin lot. Resisting the urge to run after them, I stare blankly at the taillights of the truck while my grandfather makes a left onto Rebel Drive in the direction of home.

TWELVE

WILDA

How many times have I made this drive to Oxford? Two hundred? Three hundred? The only thing different from when Haynes and I were in school is Highway 78. Back then passing was nearly impossible. Widening the road from two to four lanes has cut the drive down by twenty minutes. I have no doubt that decision has saved the lives of many college kids.

I while away my time following up on phone calls and catching up on worry. About the boys and their jobs. And the possibility of Ellie getting cut from Rush. I'm not the only mother who's concerned. Stories of girls getting cut from Ole Miss Rush are legendary, and that's a legitimate reason to fret.

Haynes's concern is not about Ellie getting cut from Rush. It's the abundance of wealth some of these girls come from. It's not only Annie Laurie, there are plenty more. We get by fine—I'm not suggesting that we don't—but we are certainly not wealthy. Ole Miss gives a significant discount to students from Memphis and the surrounding area. The tuition is not all that much more than the cost for in-state students. And after three kids, that's a big relief.

Rush aside, the prevailing worry I've been obsessing over since Haynes left the house this morning is this grand mess I've gotten myself into. First and foremost: the lie. And second: how in the world I'll ever pay Mama back.

Both have the potential to turn into a panic attack at any moment. So I do what I always do: pull a Scarlett O'Hara and worry about something else. I pick … Lily. Well, Lilith, and the contrast between our families.

Back in June, she invited Ellie and me down to Natchez. When we saw their historic Greek Revival mansion, surrounded by azaleas and gardenias on several acres of land, it should have been my first clue: Haynes and I would be spending many more dollars on Ellie's education than we ever dreamed.

An old patina bronze mermaid fountain with water spilling out of her tail, lily pads and white blossoms, along with koi in the pond beneath, greeted us when we pulled in the driveway. Probably one of the most spectacular pieces of art I've ever seen. The magnolias were as tall and wide as our house in Memphis and Ellie and I could smell their blooms the minute we got out of the car.

When we walked up to the columned front porch, where two planted antique urns, belonging in an antique-and-garden show, were set on either side of the front door, I think the two of us knew, right then and there, we were way out of our league. But the real kicker came when Rosetta, Lilith's maid, greeted us at the door wearing a white uniform. I truly felt like I had stepped back in time.

Once we entered the foyer, Ellie and I both were mesmerized by their massive staircase, which rose to a landing with an enormous stained-glass window. There was even an old ballroom on the third floor, which Gage now uses as an office. Opulence aside, the weekend was lovely, and both Lilith and Annie Laurie were gracious hosts. Annie Laurie even gave Ellie a graduation gift—a terrycloth towel wrap and a set of bath towels, both monogrammed with her initials. The only thing remotely negative Ellie had to say on the ride home was about Annie Laurie's hair. "She spends more time than you do, Mom. Why does she care so much?"

There is no traffic to speak of until I roll onto campus. Then I remember Haynes's warning. It's move-in day for most people. The move-in day without an up-charge. Finding a parking spot is downright stressful, but when I finally walk onto the porch of the Alpha Delta Beta House, a warm feeling grows inside and I'm breathless with joy. I am home. Some of the best friendships and memories of my life were made in this House.

As soon as I open the front door and breathe in the familiar scent, I'm transported back to a time when life wasn't jaded—a four-year vacation, when I think about it. Happy, fun, and for the most part, effortless—notwithstanding tests and a minor heartache or two. Of course, I didn't appreciate it at the time. Looking back now, I marvel at my naivety. The stress over tests and grades, even the decision to switch my major from History to Journalism all seems incredibly trivial now. Even the angst I felt on Pref, over whether to join Alpha Delt or Tri Delt, is equally mild in comparison.

Speaking of which, I truly don't care which sorority Ellie ends up pledging as long as she's happy, but I can't help thinking about how special it would be if it were Alpha Delt. I could be here for her initiation and be the one to pin her, something I never experienced with Mama. Several of my sorority sisters were pinned by their mothers. I remember well my feeling of envy as I watched the ceremony. Mothers dressed in white robes, placing their own Alpha Delt pins over their daughter's hearts.

When I step into the foyer, the dead quiet in the House is as jarring as clanging cymbals. It's twelve thirty. Shouldn't the clamor of lunchroom voices be resounding through the halls? The only person around is the Alpha Delt housekeeper, the one who's been working here umpteen years. She's pushing a dust mop across the hardwood in front of the winding staircase. An ear-to-ear smile is on her face—while she's doing housework. I could learn a thing or two from this lady.

Waving her down, I hurry over. "Excuse me, I'm here for the Rush Workshop. Where is everybody?" My eyes scan the foyer and the adjacent dining room.

"Downstairs in the chapter room," she says, with such kindness in her voice. She reminds me of Annie Mae, the lady who worked for our family while I was growing up. The one I considered my second mother—and sometimes my only mother, if truth be told. Sadly, she passed away five years ago.

"Already? I thought I was early."

"I'm pretty sure it's already started."

"Well, darn." After a quick glance at my watch I say, "I thought it started at one."

"Uh-oh. I believe it started at noon. But don't quote me on that. I could be wrong."

"Uh-oh is right. I'm in big trouble."

The sound of her laughter fills the empty foyer. I can't help picturing Lilith. Something tells me she was right on time.

"I'm Wilda Woodcock, by the way. The new Rush Advisor."

"Well welcome home, Miss Wilda. I'm Pearl."

"Thank you. It's good to be home. And nice to see you, Pearl." When I reach out to hug her I notice her scent. "You sure smell good."

"Why, thank you. It's Ralph Lauren. One of my babies gave it to me."

"Have you seen Lilith Whitmore? I'm supposed to meet her here."

"Yes, ma'am. She's down there."

"Okay, let me run. Have a nice day, Pearl."

"You, too, Miss Wilda. Good to see you."

What a nice lady, I think. *Attractive, too.*

I hurry downstairs to the basement. The chapter room door is shut. Tight. The sight of that ominous entryway transports me back in time when I was late—always late—to Monday night chapter meetings. That same hot flash I felt back then courses through me now as I turn the doorknob and quietly inch my way into the back of the room and grab an empty seat against the wall.

A young lady, whom I presume to be the Rush Chairman, is speaking to the girls about their top rushees. Actually she's calling them potential new members. I suppose I'll have to pick up the lingo if I'm to be a good advisor.

Rush Workshop meetings have not changed all that much. There's still a large screen and photos of the PNMs are projected with their names and hometowns off to the side. Each member is required to learn their faces, where the girls are from, and something about each of them. That's so every girl will be recognized the moment she enters the House and graced with familiar conversation. I glance around and each collegian is holding a bundle of papers with what appears to be additional information on each rushee.

When she sees me, Lilith, who is seated across the room, creeps over and hands me a bundle so I, too, can follow along with the slide show, PowerPoint, or whatever they call it now. She's wearing her ADB pin. The old-fashioned kind with the little gold chain hanging from a tiny gold quill—on top of her left bosom, over her heart. I'm sure it belonged to her mother. But no one else is wearing one. They're supposed to be worn for formal occasions only.

The meeting goes on for a long time with comments about each girl, kind and not so kind. I hadn't anticipated this. When they discuss Ellie will I be asked to leave the room? Maybe they've already discussed her and it's a good thing I'm late. It looks like more than three hundred girls are here today, all with opinions about my daughter. I'm jittery just thinking about it.

On the other side of the room, closer to Lilith, I notice the other Rush Advisors. Right away I recognize Sallie. She was funny and well liked—only a year ahead of me. I'm looking forward to working with her. Presumably the other lady is Gwen. She looks much younger than me—by at least twenty-five years. I'm happy to know they're here. I'd hate to be the only one making critical decisions.

While looking around, I notice the room is littered with half-eaten sandwiches, chips, apple cores, and Coke cans. When I spy a tray of leftover sandwiches in the corner, my stomach responds with a loud, embarrassing growl. I'm starving and all I can think about is getting my hands on one of those sandwiches.

Should I take one? *Why not?* I finally decide, but the second I start to stand Annie Laurie's picture pops onto the screen. Lilith jumps up before the Rush Chairman, Lizzie Jennings—I've now learned her name—has a chance to speak.

"Okay, y'all, I have to tell you what Annie Laurie and I talked about yesterday," Lilith begins in a booming voice. "I've told her there's no way she can pledge any other sorority. *But,* like any mother, I do want her to have a good Rush. She's got dozens of rec letters to all the other houses, but I don't want anyone to be alarmed." She pauses, scanning the faces of every girl to make sure they're listening. "She wants to be an Alpha Delt."

Now I'm the one scanning the girls' faces. Some of them have obligatory grins. Others have sneers. Because what Lilith just did is so very awkward. Honestly, my toes are curling in my sandals.

One girl seated near me leans toward another and whispers, "She's acting like she's in charge of whom we choose and she's *so not.*" Then the other girl whispers back, "She's not a Rush Advisor anymore. Why's she down here?" They both look at each other and shrug.

Then, as if she's overheard their comment from across the room, Lilith adds, "Oh, by the way, I want to introduce y'all to our new Rush Advisor. Stand up, Wilda." She points at me, then flicks her right palm.

All the girls whip their heads around. I stand up and wave timidly.

"Meet Wilda Woodcock, everybody," Lilith says. "Sallie and I were Alpha Delts with her a hundred years ago." She laughs at her comment before continuing. "And her daughter, Ellie Woodcock—whom you all know by now—is Annie Laurie's roommate. We can't break those two up. So we have to show Ellie as much love as we do Annie Laurie."

I am amazed by Lilith's confidence. The way she tilts her head back and grins in a way that implies secret knowledge of anyone and everyone who's fit to be an Alpha Delt. But her comments have embarrassed me to death. I wasn't planning on mentioning Ellie. For goodness sakes, I would never assume she would get an automatic bid simply because I'm a Rush Advisor.

Before sitting down, I grab a lull in the conversation. "I'm really excited about getting to know you girls, and I want to help out in any way I can. Watching the love you have for one another has been really sweet. It reminds me of my pledge class and how close we all were."

Most of the girls are smiling at me.

"I don't want to take up much time, so I'll end by saying: I come from a loyal Ole Miss family and this campus is one of our favorite places on earth. My husband and I met at Ole Miss, both of our sons went here, and now Ellie." Before sitting down, in a bashful voice, I add, "And I hope you like her when you get to know her."

"Hi, Mrs. Woodcock." I look around and see Katherine Johnson, a sweet girl from Ellie's high school track team who graduated the previous year.

"Well, hey, Katherine," I say with a wave.

She smiles and waves back. "I can't wait for everyone to meet Ellie. I've been telling them how great she is ever since I heard she was coming to Ole Miss."

I blow her a kiss. It's not the right time to make a big deal about it, but I vow to find her after the meeting and whisper my thanks.

Ellie's future sorority life had taken over our summer at one point. Our dining room table was turned into an assembly line. Putting together what must have been one hundred Rush packets with her résumé, transcript, two color pictures, and a thank-you note—all in a glossy white binder—took hours and hours of our time. We had to secure recs for each of the thirteen sororities and on top of that, we had to find even more alums willing to write reference letters.

"Listen up," Lilith blurts, even though it had appeared Lizzie had regained control of the meeting. "September fifth is the official cutoff date, but we're bound to get in a few more recs after that. Let's make sure we only consider girls who are truly Alpha Delt material. Trust me, I've seen recs from girls we'd rather not pledge. Also, we need to make darn sure all the PNMs we plan to Rush can afford Alpha Delta Beta."

She's right about that. Sorority life is not cheap. It costs somewhere around five thousand dollars per year and that doesn't include all the Rush outfits, pictures, T-shirts, parties, etc. Fraternities are even higher. As crazy as it gets inside those Houses, someone has to pay the liability. Haynes nearly passed out when he got Jackson's first Sigma Nu bill.

After several more announcements and admonishments from Lizzie and other officers, the meeting finally adjourns at five o'clock. "Pick up your trash," Lizzie yells as a last minute reminder. But it's too late. The girls have already filed out of the room and left most of it behind. Bless Miss Pearl's heart. I'm sure it's her problem now.

After finding Katherine to thank her for what she's doing for Ellie, meeting Gwen, and giving Sallie a big hug, I head over to Martin. Lilith, whom I last saw talking with Selma James, the Alpha Delt president, made six o'clock reservations for all four of us at City Grocery. It can't come soon enough, as my stomach won't let me think of anything else besides dinner. After Lilith's mortifying performance in the Rush meeting, though, I can't help wondering how anyone can stomach her.

THIRTEEN

CALI

Later in the afternoon, once most of the parents have left and the hustle from move-in day has died down, I look up from arranging my clothes in the smallest closet in the universe to see a girl with a long blond ponytail in my doorway, wearing the friendliest smile I've seen all day. We had passed each other in the hall earlier so I recognize her right away. She has a spray of freckles across her nose, and I'm struck by how much we favor. Although my hair is red, we both have blue eyes, freckles, and similar turned-up noses.

"Hi there," she says. "I'm Ellie. I live next door." She points in the direction of her room.

I stand up and step toward her. "I'm Cali. Come on in."

She steps inside and glances around. "Your room looks so nice. I love your comforter." She walks over to my bed, runs her hand across the top. "Pink and gray are my favorite colors, too." I see her eyes stop at Jasmine's unmade bed and unpacked boxes. "Where's your roommate?"

"She left with her boyfriend to walk around campus. I don't think she's in a big hurry to get her stuff unpacked." I can't help the nervous giggle that follows. It's not that I care much that Jasmine is waiting to get settled, but I had hoped to see our room finished, like, before the sun goes down.

Ellie plops down on our futon. "I couldn't wait to get unpacked." I love that she seems to feel comfortable in my room.

"Where are you from?" I ask, sitting down next to her.

"Memphis. How 'bout you?"

"Blue Mountain."

Her brows knit together. "I'm not sure I know where that is. Is it in Mississippi?"

I nod. "It's a teeny-tiny town. Like, forty-five minutes north. Not many people know where it is."

Something about Ellie is nice and genuine and I feel comfortable around her already. I have a strong sense we will be instant friends.

"Are you as excited to be here as I am?" I ask. "I've been, like, counting down the days all summer."

"Oh my gosh. Totally. I've been waiting on this day for years." She twists her ponytail into a bun on top of her head, secures it with her ponytail holder. "Are you gonna rush?"

"That's my plan. What about you?"

"Yes!" When she smiles, I notice her dimples.

"Do you know which sorority you want?" I ask.

"Not really. My roommate's mom and my mom were Alpha Delts together, like, way back when." She pulls her legs up, sits cross-legged. "Anyway, her mother says she can't pledge if she doesn't choose Alpha Delt." Ellie snickers when she says it.

My eyes grow wide.

"Right?"

"Yikes." We both grimace at the same time.

"My mom doesn't care which one I join. She just wants me to be happy." She makes little quote marks when she says "happy."

"Your mom sounds awesome." *What must that be like,* I wonder.

"She is. My parents are, like, older than most of my friends' parents, but they're awesome."

"I totally get that. I live with my grandparents, and—" I stop abruptly. *Don't go there. No need to overexplain.* "So, what about you? Do you wanna be an Alpha Delt?"

She shakes her head, shrugs. "I don't care all that much. I'm open. But I am getting a little freaked out about it. Some of the girls from my high school who are sophomores this year are, like, 'Stay out of the Grove. Don't go to bars. Don't do anything that someone in a sorority might hold against you. Don't even go to a fraternity house till Rush is over.'"

"Oh, wow, I had no idea. Thanks for telling me." This information is super helpful. Any information about pledging a sorority is super helpful.

"Yeah. I hear it's getting much harder to get the House you want. With so many girls rushing and all. My mom heard there are, like, over two thousand rushees this year. And that even legacies will be cut. Are you a legacy?"

I knew legacy meant kinship to someone in a particular sorority. That's one of the things I learned when I thoroughly researched all the Ole Miss sorority websites last year. I shake my head, purse my lips together. "Unfortunately not."

"Oh, no big deal." She swipes her hand through the air. "I'm sure you'll be fine. Is there a certain sorority you want to be in?"

"Not really," I say. "Alpha Delt would be nice. Or Chi O, Pi Phi, Kappa, maybe." The last three were a few of the Houses I had been able to secure recs for. But at this point I know every sorority by heart and something about all of them. "Any of them really. I'm open, too."

About that time another girl pokes her head inside my room. Ellie waves her in. She's super pretty. Another blond with hair hanging down her back. Her makeup is thick—lots of base, eyeliner, and eye shadow—and she's wearing what I now assume to be the official Ole Miss uniform: black workout shorts, a big T-shirt, and Nike tennis shoes. Ellie's wearing the same thing, but she's not wearing makeup.

Ellie hops up, hooks her arm through the girl's arm. "Annie Laurie Whitmore, meet Cali... what's your last name?"

"Watkins. Nice to meet you, Annie Laurie."

"You, too," she says with a stark white, toothy grin. For some reason I can't tell if her expression is real or not. Probably because she's got wandering eyeballs, studying every inch of my room like she's the Inspector General. When she touches my comforter I can't help but notice the beautiful ring on her right hand and the one on her left, similar, yet with different color gemstones. The same style jewelry is around her neck. *And* on her wrists.

"I love your jewelry," I say. "It all matches."

Annie Laurie glances at Ellie, smiles that smile again. "Thanks. It's Yurman."

"I can't say I know what... *Yurman* is, but it sure is pretty."

"Yurman is the designer," Annie Laurie explains. "*David* Yurman." I catch her looking at my bare fingers before she touches her earlobes. I shrink.

"You have matching earrings, too?" I say. "That's so cool."

"Thanks," she says again, and continues looking around. "Did y'all move in today?"

I nod. "After waiting three hours. How about that line? Wasn't that crazy?"

Annie Laurie's eyes dart over to Ellie then back at me. "I don't know. We didn't move in today." Then she pulls out her phone to answer a text.

About that time, Jasmine and Carl return. After introductions, I add, "Annie Laurie and Ellie live next door."

"Wait," Carl says. "Is that y'all's room at the end of the hall? The big one on the corner?"

Annie Laurie looks up from her phone. "Yes."

"Y'all's daddies must be *rolling* in it," he says, with a chuckle.

Jasmine narrows her eyes, shoots him daggers. "Y'all don't mind my man. He says things he shouldn't sometimes."

Carl shrugs. "It's true. Their room looks like it belongs in the White House, not Martin Hall." When he chuckles at his own quip I have to suppress a laugh of my own.

Jasmine digs her hands into her hips. "Now I gotta see it. Y'all gonna invite us over?"

"Of course, y'all can come now if you want," Ellie says.

When we walk inside their room, I'm... well, I'm happy my grandmother didn't see it. All of the pride I had in our room vanishes in a nanosecond, as fast as a rabbit in a magician's trick. Their room looks like it belongs on the cover of a magazine. Carl is right. It should be in the White House.

As I look around, taking it all in, a familiar shroud of shame creeps in, making me queasy and a little mournful. Staring me in the face is this beautiful, brand-new, gray-and-white floral couch with throw pillows that actually match their *gray-and-pink* bedding. Their beds have matching upholstered headboards with extra-long dust ruffles and crisp white duvets. There are fine draperies on both—*both*—of their windows and not two but three closets, and their desks have been turned into vanities with linen draping to hide whatever they want to store underneath. My God, there's even artwork on the walls. And a wall-to-wall patterned carpet with an animal skin throw rug on top.

The chest between their beds is mirrored, like the one I saw on the cover of a magazine just last week. They have makeup mirrors with lights and a flat-screen TV. I am blown away, utterly flabbergasted, and I feel like falling apart because until five minutes ago I thought we had a perfect room. But I can't fall apart. So, I hold it together and ask, "Did y'all do all this today?"

"No," Ellie says, sitting down on the sofa. "We moved in yesterday." She pats the space next to her, motioning for me to take a seat. I do.

Annie Laurie climbs up on her bed, via a white leather step stool, and pushes back a multitude of pillows to relax into her monogrammed shams.

Jasmine and Carl sit down on slipcovered desk chairs.

I have a feeling my face must be giving me away, because I can feel my eyes theatrically bulging out of their sockets. "I didn't know we could move in before today," I finally say.

Annie Laurie crosses her legs. "Our parents paid extra."

Jasmine, who I've learned in the short time we've known each other always has something to say, says nothing. But Carl, under his breath, mutters, "Mmm-hmm."

Ellie points to their Keurig coffeemaker next to the couch. "You won't believe what's under there."

"Under the coffeemaker?" I ask.

Her eyes light up. "A hidden safe."

"*Ellie.*" Annie Laurie gives her a scornful look.

"Oops, was I not supposed to tell?"

"No." She darts a sideways glance at Carl and Jasmine.

"*Sorry,*" Ellie says, then turns back to us. "Y'all don't say anything."

"Not to worry," Carl says with his hands up. "Your secret's safe with us."

About that time we hear a knock and a lady pokes her head inside their door. Ellie jumps up. "Mom!"

"May I come in?"

"Sure. What are you doing here?" I notice Carl stands up when she walks in.

By the sweet look on Ellie's mom's face when Ellie hugs her, I'm struck by how much she adores her daughter.

"How did you get in?" Ellie asks. "Everyone has to show their ID."

Her mom cups a hand next to her mouth, and whispers, "I slipped in behind another mom and her daughter."

"Is everything okay?" Ellie asks. Her eyes are troubled.

"Yes, everything's fine, honey. I probably should have called, but I didn't think you'd mind, and I have a surprise." She pauses. "Lilith has talked me into taking a Rush Advisor position with Alpha Delt. Isn't that cool?"

Ellie wrinkles her nose. "I guess. What does that mean?"

Annie Laurie shoots straight up. "It means she'll get to know who gets bids and who doesn't, like, way before we do. My mom was one last year."

Ellie rears back. "Really, Mom?"

Mrs. Woodcock nods.

"Cool." Ellie turns to us. "This is Cali and Jasmine, by the way. Our next-door neighbors."

Before I can say hello, Carl rears his head back, holds his palms up. "What am I? Chopped liver?"

Ellie laughs. "Sorry, Carl. And this is Carl, Jasmine's boyfriend. This is my mom, everybody. Wilda Woodcock."

Instead of shaking our hands, she hugs every one of us. I can tell by Mrs. Woodcock's smile that she is warm and kind, and I love the way she's dressed: white jeans and a long flowing top made of silk. She looks a lot like Ellie.

"How nice that y'all are already getting to know one another," Mrs. Woodcock says. "My roommate and I became instant friends with our Martin next-door neighbors."

"You lived here?" Jasmine asks.

"I sure did. Boy, did Lisa and I have a blast. I'd tell you some of the stories, but I wouldn't want to embarrass my daughter." She laughs and Ellie rolls her eyes. "Did you girls move in today?"

"Yes, ma'am," I say.

Jasmine stands up. "Wanna see our room?"

Mrs. Woodcock claps her hands together. "I'd love to."

"Then come on over." With a sweeping motion of her hand Jasmine moves to the door. As we all walk back toward our room, she apologizes. "I haven't unpacked everything yet, but Cali's side is perfect."

Carl says, "Jasmine here is in no hurry to do anything."

Mrs. Woodcock lags behind, pats Jasmine's arm. "There's plenty of time to unpack, Jasmine, don't you worry one bit." Seconds later, once inside our room, she glances around with a sweet smile. "Why girls, this is lovely."

"We're proud of it," Jasmine says. "Aren't we, Cali?"

I nod. But only slightly. I was proud. Five minutes ago.

Mrs. Woodcock taps me on the shoulder. "All of you girls like the same colors."

"Pink and gray," I say with a halfhearted shrug. Compared to theirs, our pink and gray looks like Pepto-Bismol and elephant skin.

We haven't been in our room five minutes when another lady pokes her head inside. She must notice us, though she doesn't say hello. Just looks right at Ellie and Annie Laurie. "Dinnertime. Let's go, girls."

A mystified expression transforms Mrs. Woodcock's face and I watch her turn around slowly toward the lady. "Lilith, meet Cali, Jasmine, and Carl."

When I see the lady's eyes roving around our room I have a strong feeling about whom she's related to. "Where are my manners? Hi, I'm Mrs. Whitmore, Annie Laurie's mom." As she limply shakes our hands, I can't help comparing her to Mrs. Woodcock. And I can't help noticing the pin on her breast, or that she keeps looking at Jasmine and Carl.

"I wish we could stay and chat, but we have reservations at City Grocery in fifteen minutes." She turns to Ellie. "Do you like my surprise? You weren't expecting to see your mother so soon, were you?"

"No, ma'am," Ellie responds with a coy grin.

"I guess she told you she's the new Alpha Delt Rush Advisor?" She slips an arm through Mrs. Woodcock's. "She's going to be fabulous." Then she looks at the girls. "Y'all ready?"

Annie Laurie and Ellie tell us good-bye and walk out behind Mrs. Whitmore. Mrs. Woodcock follows, but before leaving she turns back around. "I'm sorry I didn't get to meet your parents, girls. Maybe next time?"

Jasmine and I both nod and I force a smile. I'm not sure what Jasmine's thinking, but I'm dripping with gratitude that Mrs. Woodcock didn't ask any more questions. Neither one of us have fathers, at least not fathers we know. Relief over not having to explain this, or anything about my mother, floods through me like a roaring tidal wave.

FOURTEEN

MISS PEARL

Three weeks after move-in, I come into work before the crack of dawn, and find a Cisco eighteen-wheeler parked right behind the kitchen. *What's he doing here already?* I wonder, and make my way to the door. It's that pretty boy Fred Smithson, our favorite driver, but I'm in no mood to socialize. I didn't take time to put my face on before I left, and the first drop of coffee has yet to splash my tongue.

"What on earth are you doing here this early, Mr. Smithson?" I slide past his dolly with my head down, take my key out, and unlock the door.

"I'd be at this till ten o'clock tonight if I didn't get an early start. Between the University and the sorority and frat houses, I'm busy all day every day. Y'all happen to be my first stop."

I don't look right at him. The last thing I want is for him to see me looking like this. "Have you been waiting long?"

"Just pulled up five minutes before you did."

My weave is twisted up inside this cap. Can't cook unless it is. I catch him eyeing me. He's never seen me looking this plain. I didn't anticipate him being here when I agreed to come in extra early today. Usually Mama Carla meets him at the door, but before I left yesterday I told her to sleep in. Truth is I could do her job in my sleep.

I reach for my card to clock in, and see Aunt Fee's below it, already punched. Normally she doesn't come in until ten. "What are you doing here already?" I holler. I turn to see her standing in front of the stove stirring a big pot of red sauce. I can smell it from the door.

"Cooking up a surprise."

"Not a surprise. I can smell it from here."

"You know spaghetti and meatballs is one of the girls' favorites. Had to get here early to get this sauce on."

"It's smelling good already."

"Sure is, Miss Ophelia," Fred says, tipping his dolly forward to drop his first load.

"Thank you, baby," she hollers. "Why don't you stop by after work and get you a plate?"

"Wish I could. But I've got plans tonight. Thank you, though." Mr. Smithson heads back to his truck for another load.

"Five A.M. came mighty early for me," I say. "I wanted to throw that alarm clock across the room. What time did you get here?" I grab a white apron off the hook, tie it behind me.

"Been here almost an hour."

"Say what?"

"Got a doctor's appointment right after lunch. I needed to get a head start on dinner."

"Is something wrong?"

"Just a checkup. That's all."

Aunt Fee hasn't been to the doctor's for a checkup in as long as I can remember. None of us here have. Alpha Delt offers no health insurance benefits for anybody except Mama Carla. "You sure you're okay?"

"I'm sure."

When Mr. Smithson is ready to leave, I make sure to check each item with the order form—four towering stacks of dry goods. Mr. Marvelle will be busy unpacking all morning.

Fred passes me his pen. As I'm signing my name I notice his eyes on my arm. "What does your tattoo say?"

I hold up the inside of my right forearm, show him the small cursive letters a few inches from my wrist. *Absolvatus sum.* "It's Latin. Means I have been forgiven."

"Amen, sister."

We wish each other a good morning and I shut the door behind him. I sure wish I'd taken time to put my face on.

First thing I do when I get into work every morning is head out to the dining room to brew coffee. Our girls are mighty choosy when it comes to their joe. Last fall, they told Mama Carla they wanted a coffee tasting, so she ordered in four kinds of beans. They settled on a special brew from clear out in Portland, Oregon. Now I'm the one grinding those beans every morning.

Once I get that started, make sure there's plenty of sugar, Splenda, stevia, half and half, skim milk, *and* almond milk, I set out my breakfast bar. Bagels, three kinds of cream cheese, butter, an assortment of muffins, and fruit in case someone wants a grab-and-go. Then I head back to the kitchen and straight to the walk-in. Pull out a flat of eggs, milk, butter, and cheddar cheese—all the ingredients for my grits—then set it on the counter. Some of the girls like grits for breakfast. I like to make sure there's a plenty of oatmeal, too.

On top of that, we take special orders for eggs. Some order scrambled; some order fried. Others may want an egg-white omelet, especially if they're trying to reduce. There's a lot of pageant girls in Mississippi. Two or three of them right here in Alpha Delta Beta.

Auntie puts down the long wooden spoon she's been using, turns to me. "I've been thinkin' 'bout you, dahlin'."

"Is that right? What about?"

She's opening and closing her mouth, like she's struggling to find the right words. "I don't want you to think I'm steppin' up in your business, but . . . pretty as you are, you need a man."

I almost burst in two from laughing. I need a man. What else is new? I measure out my ingredients, pour them all in the pot. Then I turn on the eye. "Is this about our money talk the other night?"

"No, it is not. I just think you need a man." When I don't comment, she goes on with her own business, but a minute later says, "I haven't heard you talk about no one special since Les. What happened to him, anyway?"

I turn to see her staring at me. "Lester is married now. Don't you remember me telling you that?"

"Not really." She leans in toward me. "What about Gerald Sorrels? Last I hear, he single again."

I think about ignoring that comment, too, but that's not my way. "There's a reason for that."

She presses her lips together and stares me down. "Listen here. You're forty-four years old and you ain't gettin' no younger."

I'm not looking at her on purpose. I'm working on my oatmeal, stirring the ingredients around in the pot. Then I say, "Nobody knows that better than me."

She softens. Out of the corner of my eye I see her push up her glasses. "I know that, baby. I just hate to see my beautiful niece going to waste."

I look at her then. Press my hands into my hips. "I'm not going to waste."

She hangs her head. Her feelings get hurt over the least little thing. She can dish it, but she sure don't like to receive it. "Forgive me, sugah. I didn't mean it that way."

Seeing how ashamed she looks takes away all the irritation I'm feeling. "Don't worry about it. I'm all right."

Aunt Fee adjusts her apron, looks back up. "I'm only tryin' to tell you it's a shame a girl as pretty as you's not married."

"I tried that once. It didn't work." My ex-husband is the last person I want to be thinking about right now. And she knows it.

"That don't make a bit of difference. Plenty of women try it again. Queenie's daughter been married four times." She dips the long spoon back in her pot and slurps up a taste.

"That would be the difference between Queenie's daughter and me. No thank you."

We both laugh.

"One of the deacons at our church—you know Brother Carlson?"

I give her a slight nod.

"He ain't married. And he's a *nice*-looking man!"

"Aunt Fee." I shove my hands back on my hips. I'm dead serious this time. "He's an old man. What do you think I'm going to do with a man that age? Besides get him ready for his casket. *Shoot.*"

"He ain't that old. He's my age."

I sigh. This conversation is going nowhere fast. "I don't want just any man. I've got my sights set high."

"All right. That's good. Long as you're lookin'." She opens her mouth to say something else then pauses. Her words trickle out slowly. "You woulda made a wonderful mama."

Hearing that out of Aunt Fee's mouth gives me a jump. She hasn't brought that up in years. I feel my shoulders droop. "I've got all the children I can handle right here." I say it like I mean it. And I do.

Auntie goes quiet. I watch her disappear into the walk-in, then bring back a large jar of chopped garlic. She dumps a few tablespoons into all three stock-pots, stirs it in, then taps her spoon on the edge. "Sometimes I think about what your life would have been like today if you had been older when all that happened."

A wave of sorrow catches in my throat like a vise, nearly strangling me. Then that permanently etched image of the sterile hospital room flashes across my mind. I don't answer her right away. Instead I ruminate on things I shouldn't. The hiss from the gas burners is the only sound in the room.

After an extra-long minute I say, "You know I don't like to look backward. Mama always said, 'things happen for a reason.' If you think too much about that road you never took, it will make it impossible to enjoy the one you're on."

She closes her eyes. I can tell she's regretting her comment. "You're right, baby. Don't listen to me." Once a few seconds have passed she studies me again. "Every now and then I get that ... what you call it? Stinkin' thinkin'?"

"That's it. And it can rot you to the bone." I seize the chance to switch topics. Now it's my turn. "How much longer do you intend to do this, Aunt Fee? You're sixty-four years old." The girls are always telling her she can't ever quit. I heard one alum tell her she can't retire till she's a hundred. They can say it all they want, but this is a big job and the sorority is growing larger every year with more and more mouths to feed.

"You're changin' the subject."

"Yes, ma'am, I am. But I want you to answer me."

She stops what she's doing and turns to face me. Her big ol' eyes are see-ing red. "How do you think I'm ever gone retire? Makin' fourteen dollars an hour after thirty-two years. Shoot."

"Social Security," I say, watching my grits start to bubble.

"You know that ain't enough. I caint ever retire. And neither can you if you keep working here." Now I've got her all steamed up. But Aunt Fee's been a working woman since she was twelve years old. I want to make sure she enjoys some time for herself on the back end.

"I'll take care of you."

This seems to quiet the waters. "I know you will, baby. But I ain't gone be no burden to nobody. Especially you."

While Mama was over to Mrs. McKinney's working for her family of three kids, every waking hour of every day, not to mention every holiday, Fee was taking care of me. That's back when she worked as a seamstress and an ironer out of her home, before she came over here. Mama would drop me off at her house, a few streets from ours, before she drove our old raggedy Plymouth over to Mrs. McKinney's. Mama never meant for me to be raised by her sister, but she did what she had to do. My daddy wasn't around.

Auntie has three sons, all older than me. Marvin lives in Chicago. He set out after high school and discovered big city life. Tony followed in his big brother's footsteps. He said he wouldn't come back to Oxford, Mississippi, if his life depended on it. But Leroy, he only moved as far as Memphis. He comes down here every now and then. But not as often as he should.

All three of those boys love their mama, but they don't take care of her like a daughter would. Fee's got six grandchildren, some of them girls, but they live up in Chicago. She goes up to see them in the summertime when she can. But that costs money she doesn't have.

I sidle up next to her, put my arm around her thick waist. She's nearly twice as big as I am. "Listen here." I pull her chin around so she can see the seriousness in my eyes. "You would never be a burden. You understand me?"

"You are the sweetest child I know." Aunt Fee's eyes gloss over with tears. "I just want you to have a good life, baby. Find a man; get another job. Go back to college." She wipes a tear away with the hem of her apron. Her voice is shaky. "You are my special daughter, the closest I ever got to one of my own. And a mother never wants her girl to be alone. Sometimes I can't sleep for worryin' 'bout you all by yourself in that apartment way out on the County Road, nobody to look after you. I ask the Lawd every night to protect you."

"I'm fine, Aunt Fee. You should spend more time worrying about Tony. He's the one needing your prayers. That wife of his is the laziest woman I've ever seen—besides Kadeesha. She'd walk her dog while she was riding a scooter if she could get away with it."

Auntie's tears turn into tee-hees. "I know that's right. Land sakes. Tony caint get her to work for nothin'. She acts like it's her right to be a stay-at-home mama. I told her I worked the entire time I was raisin' my boys—and you. I told her every other woman in our family had, too, as far back as I can remember."

The swinging door squeaks and that cute little Brennen Davidson pokes her head inside. "Good morning, Miss Pearl. Oh hi, Miss Ophelia!"

"We'll pick this discussion back up later," I whisper. "Hello, Brennen. You're up mighty early."

"I'm going to work out." She dashes over to the stove and gathers us into a group hug. "How was your summer?" Her eyes dart back and forth between us.

"Fine, baby. Yours?" The words tumble out of both of our mouths at the same time. It makes us all laugh.

Brennen grins. "I know you're aunt and niece, but you sure act like mother and daughter."

Auntie takes me by the hand. "I was just tellin' her that this mornin'."

"Aww. I wish my aunt was as sweet to me as you are to Miss Pearl."

"What you mean? Come here dahlin'," Fee says. "As sweet as you are?" She reaches out and envelops Brennen in her arms again. And they stay that way for what seems like a full minute. It's hard to pull away when my auntie wraps you in one of her embraces. Her large cuddly body radiates warmth and it feels like you're a cub in the arms of a mother bear. Who would want to break away from that? "Tell us what you want for breakfast this mornin'."

Brennen pulls away. "Let's see." Her head bobs from side to side. "May I please have two egg whites with a side of fruit?"

"That all you want?" Aunt Fee asks. "No wonder your little arms look like toothpicks." She laughs and nudges Brennen playfully. Even though she means it, she would never want to hurt her feelings.

Fee clutches Brennen's shoulder and escorts her to the door.

When Fee turns back around I could swear I catch a grimace on her face, like she's in pain. My eyes follow every step she takes as she strolls back to the stove.

"What's the matter?"

Her sauce is simmering with a vapor of steam rising from the pot. She leans over, whiffs. "Nothin'." She avoids looking at me.

"Then why did you get that look on your face?"

"What look you talkin' about?"

"The way you knitted your brows and squeezed your eyes."

"I was thinkin' 'bout that tiny girl and wonderin' what she thinks is pretty about bein' string-bean skinny. I bet she don't weigh but a hundred pounds."

"Looks like you're hiding something to me."

"I ain't hidin' nothin'. Must be your imagination."

Imagination my foot. She forgets I know her better than anyone else in the world, including her three sons. I narrow dubious eyes her way as Carli Cone knocks on the door with another breakfast order.

FIFTEEN

MISS PEARL

It's close to ten o'clock by the time I make my way up to the second floor. Same as every morning, I head down the hall emptying trash cans the girls have left outside their doors. If I see a liquor bottle, a wine bottle, or even a beer can in the trash I'm supposed to report it. But I'd never do that. That's their business, not mine. Besides, I'm not the housemother. Not officially, anyway. If a sister were to get caught she would have to go up before the Standards Committee and risk getting kicked out of the sorority for good.

"Good morning, Miss Pearl," most every girl says, when seeing me in the hall—wearing towel wraps and in a big hurry to get in and out of the bathroom. Every now and then I pass a girl who keeps her head down. I try not to let that bother me. I know what kind of family she comes from and that's what she's been taught. What bothers me is when I get to the toilet and find it backed up, seeing that the contents are not from number two, but vomit instead. All these girls pressured to stay thin, *that* breaks my heart.

As I empty the last wastebasket into my trash bag, Allie Blakley from Laurel, Mississippi, eyes me in the hall. She's got her hair twisted up in a big towel, furry slippers on her feet, and a silk bathrobe wrapped tightly around her. We've not run into each other a single time since school started. I watch her eyes blink. "When did you do that to your hair?" she asks, like it's something strange.

"Over the summer. Do you like it?" I flip a long piece off my shoulder with two fingers.

"I love it. Can I touch it?"

"Go ahead." Allie cautiously runs her hand across my hair like it's a zoo animal. "It won't bite," I say, laughing.

"How do y'all do that?" she asks. "Do you go to a salon?"

"Mmm-hmm. I can't do this myself."

"Didn't you do your own box braids?"

"Yes I did. But that's fairly simple. This has to be done right or it looks fake."

She grabs me by the hand and pulls me inside her room. "I want Kerry to see you. Kerry," she calls in a high-pitched voice. "Look at Miss Pearl."

Kerry has the same reaction. Only she doesn't ask for permission to touch it, she jumps up from her makeup mirror and runs over to me, patting my head down. Sometimes these girls forget their manners something awful. "It feels so real," she says.

"It *is* real," I tell her.

"It's real hair? Like real extensions?"

"Of course it's real hair," I say with a chuckle. "What else would it be?" White girls are so funny when it comes to a chocolate sister's hair.

"You look so pretty," they both say at the same time, almost surprised. Like this was the first time they had seen me for who I really am. I know they don't mean any harm. Sometimes people say things and the words tumble out all wrong.

"Were they expensive?" Kerry asks.

"They weren't cheap. I'll tell you that much." I paid $150 plus tip to Shirley, and that didn't include the cost of the hair. That was another $160. When I wore box braids, they were significantly cheaper—about sixty dollars for a whole head of synthetic braids. I'll go back to that next time, but I wanted to try this weave. Just once I wanted to look glamorous, like Beyoncé, even if she is ten years younger.

"I'd be wearing them, too, if I were you," Allie says. "Money for hair comes first. If it were a choice between food or hair, I'd choose hair any day of the week."

"You and me both," I say. "This girl wants to look sharp." For fun, I swing the hair off my shoulder the way Beyoncé does on the TV set.

Both of the girls laugh.

Then a picture of my bald tires crosses my mind. All of a sudden I feel shame. I might look glamorous today, but what about my car? It's hard to pray for safety when I've spent all my money on beauty. Allie and Kerry may can do that, but who do I think I'm fooling?

Kerry takes her hair out of the towel, swings it free. "And speaking of, I better get this mop ready before I'm late for class."

I move on over to their door. Before leaving, a thought pops into my head. Something I've been wondering for a long time. "Can I ask y'all a question?"

They nod.

"Why do you girls get your face and hair looking all pretty, then put on those big T-shirts and exercise pants every day for class?"

They both look at each other, kind of bewildered like, and shrug. "Because everybody else does it?" Kerry says, glancing at Allie.

"Okay then. Thanks for solving the mystery. I'll see you babies later." They wave and I shut the door behind me, chuckling. Why doesn't this surprise me?

As soon as I step into the hall my phone goes off. I answer on the first ring.

"Pearl? It's Carla." I don't know why she insists on identifying herself. I know her voice and she knows her number is in my phone.

"Hi, Mama Carla. You need me for something?"

"It's not urgent, but when you're done up there will you please stop by my apartment?"

"Of course. It won't take me but another twenty minutes."

"That's fine. Just stop in when you can."

I'm almost finished with trash pickup, but after lunch Mr. Marvelle and I will be performing shower surgery. That's my term for cleaning the drains. We work as a team. He unscrews the drains, then uses his scalpel—a plumber's tool with teeth on both sides—to lift all that long nasty hair out. I stand by with gloves and a plastic trash bag as he empties the mess inside. Then we move on to the next shower stall, till we finish the whole operation. With all that hair, and as many showers as the girls take, we have to do this every month. Not something I look forward to, but it's necessary.

When I make it to Mama Carla's apartment, I find her on the phone. Her door is always open. Once she notices I'm standing there she holds up a finger. "Okay, stay calm," she says to whomever is on the other end of the line. "I'll see you tomorrow. I love you." Then she softly lays her phone down on the table next to the chair and hangs her head.

"What's the matter?" I ask, while sitting down in the chair next to hers. It troubles me to see her this way.

She looks up. I can tell she's been crying.

"Are you okay, Mama Carla?" I reach over and touch her on the knee.

"I'm okay." She stares down at her lap again, lightly shaking her head. "But my child is not." Finally she looks at me. "It's Patrice. Philip walked out on her and the kids two days ago." She wipes her nose with the back of her hand before disappearing into the bathroom. Trudy hops down, trots right behind her.

Moments later, Mama Carla returns with a box of Kleenex in one hand, Trudy in the other. They both settle back down into the chair. "I knew something was wrong. Mother's intuition," she says with a sniffle. "Patrice hasn't mentioned his name in months. Never talks about him unless I do. She used to sing his praises." Mama Carla's dabbing her eyes with a tissue. Her nose is red.

I'm not sure if I should pry or keep my mouth shut. I might not be raising children of my own, but I know what it's like to have a marriage fall apart. I reach over, touch her on the knee. "He's not cheating on her, is he?" Soon as I say it, I regret it. "I'm sorry, it's none of my business. I just know what that's like."

She sniffs, blows her nose before answering. "It sounds that way. They haven't slept together in six months. And they're only thirty-six."

"Men are so ignorant. They always let that other head do all the thinking."

That makes Mama Carla laugh and I'm glad to see it. "Why do you think I'm alone? I was done with that little head a *long* time ago."

Now I'm the one smiling. "Me, too."

She shakes her head. "No way, Pearl. You're too young to be done with men."

"Now you sound like Aunt Fee."

"Well, it's true. I've seen the way men look at you. You are a very attractive woman."

"Why, thank you. You are, too, Mama Carla."

"For a sixty-two year-old, I guess I'm all right." She puts her hands on either side of her face, pushes up her cheeks. "If only I'd had the money for a facelift. I might have had a chance."

"Now, Mama Carla. You still have a chance."

"Maybe one day. But right now I have to think of my daughter. I told her I'd be there this weekend. I know it's terrible timing with school just getting started, and our first home game, but she's my child. She needs me."

"Of course she does. Nobody can take the place of your mama." Hearing my own words makes me miss my mama. If it weren't for Aunt Fee, I'd be out of my mind.

"You never stop needing a mother, do you? No matter how old you are." She turns around in her chair to face me, tucks her Kleenex under her thigh, and puts both hands on my knees. "Do you have plans this weekend?"

I think about it for a second. "Let me check my date calendar." I laugh, pull out my phone for fun, and check. "I'll be right here working the game."

"I mean the whole weekend. I'm wondering if you might fill in for me while I'm gone."

As housemother? I'm so shocked I don't quite know what to say.

"Sure, why not?"

I just look at her. We both know why not.

"You're every bit as qualified as I am. And you know my job backward and forward."

"You've got a point there."

"Patrice lives down in Ocean Springs. It's a five-hour drive down to the coast so I won't be home till late Sunday evening. I can pay you fifty dollars a day."

That's one hundred and fifty dollars toward my tires. I blurt my answer before I have time to think it through and talk myself out of it. "Why sure I will, Mama Carla. I'm honored you asked."

"The girls will love it. You'll sleep right here in my bed."

Now that I've said yes, doubt creeps in. I'm quite sure there's a faraway look about me, but Mama Carla doesn't seem to notice.

"And don't hesitate to reprimand Kadeesha if she needs it. I'm not so sure about her anyway."

I'd been wondering when this would come up. "Better tell her that. Matter of fact, please tell that to everyone on staff. I don't want any of them saying I think I'm better than they are."

"The only one with more seniority than you is Ophelia, and you and I both know she'll be happy you're subbing for me."

"All right then," I say, feeling better about my decision. "I guess I have myself a job." I relax into the wingback chair, feeling the soft cushion against my head.

"You'll be fantastic, Pearl," Mama Carla says reassuringly. The last time I had a compliment like this is hard to remember, but I know one thing: Mama Carla trusts me more than I thought.

She lays her head back, too, and stares up at the ceiling. She's thinking hard on something, so we sit in silence until she says, "I miss my daughter and grandchildren. As much as I like this job, it's hard to be so far away. Especially when they need me like they do now." She sighs. "I'm not sure how much longer I can keep doing this."

Hearing her say the words out loud doesn't necessarily surprise me. She's alluded to it in the past. "I understand. Family comes first." With the exception of my cousins, all my family is right here in Oxford.

We talk a little longer, then I move over to the door, put my hand on the knob. After a pause I turn back around. "You sure about this?"

With a stiff spine and her chin held high, she looks at me confidently. "Of course I'm sure."

"You don't have to ask anyone's permission?"

"No, Pearl. I don't have to ask anyone for permission. I can ask anyone I want to substitute, as long as they're qualified. You know as much as I do about this job. You are qualified."

I draw in a deep breath then release it slowly. Every time we've had a substitute the lady has been white. There isn't a black housemother on the entire campus. In either sororities or fraternities. Never has been.

Projections of how the alums and parents may react are swirling in and out of my mind already. I can't help picturing their faces when they see me. Will I be welcomed into the fold or treated like a black sheep? It's one thing for a black lady to cook or clean in this milky-white House. It's another thing altogether for a woman of color to be the one in charge.

SIXTEEN

CALI

She would do that?" I ask Ellie when she offers to have her mother write me an Alpha Delt rec. I'd gotten into the habit of coming over to her room when Jasmine and Carl start their last phone call of the night, and I am sitting on the end of her bed. It's late, midnight, but no one in Martin goes to bed early.

Most of the girls on our floor get their homework done in the library during the day and reserve nighttime for socializing. And partying. And tons of laughing. Though we only met two weeks ago, it feels like Ellie and I have known each other two years. Friendships come fast and easy when you're living on the same floor of the dorm.

Ellie and I are sitting together on her bed with our backs up against her headboard. She reaches over and pats me on the arm. "Of course. My mom would be happy to do that for you."

"That would be sweet," I say.

"Email me your rec packet." She writes out her email on a notepad by her bed and hands it to me. "I'll call her in the morning."

After speaking with a girl in the Panhellenic office last fall about how to join a sorority, I started putting my rec packet together. She said I needed a résumé stressing community service, leadership, and academics. Fortunately, I am strong in all three areas.

Mamaw has a friend in Memphis who has a friend who was a Kappa Kappa Gamma and she was willing to write me a rec. After she saw my résumé, that same lady offered to find more friends who could write recs. She seemed to think I would be a great candidate for a sorority, and that I shouldn't have any problems. But I do.

After not having a pedigree, the next problem is: I don't have recs for all thirteen sororities on campus. And the third problem is: I don't think I have enough money. From what I learned in that same phone call to Panhellenic, I might need as much as five thousand dollars my first year and I've only managed to save three.

It wouldn't hurt, I learned, to have several additional letters of reference from other alumnae. The girl I spoke with in the Panhellenic office told me to ask my mother's friends for the letters. She said I'd be surprised to learn how many of them had been in sororities. I told her thank you very much for the information and hung up the phone. What I didn't tell her was that my mother has no friends.

Annie Laurie looks up from the Spanish textbook she's been reading with a cool smile. Her face always confuses me. Is she genuine or…is she fake? She doesn't offer to have her mother write a letter of reference: not that it matters all that much, but I still wonder why. I shrug it off and hop down from the bed. "I'll go do that now and let y'all get ready for bed."

"Is Jasmine asleep?" Annie Laurie asks, before I get to the door.

I glance over my shoulder. "Not yet. She and Carl are having their final lovey-dovey convo of the day. Those two are on the phone, like, constantly," I say, with a giggle.

"Black people are always on the phone."

What an odd remark. "Really? I haven't noticed."

"Next time you're walking to class, pay attention. You'll see what I mean." She's talking, but her eyes don't leave her Spanish book.

That's good because my eyes are on the pill bottle on her vanity, right next to her makeup mirror. Annie Laurie Whitmore. Adderall 10 mg. Take 2x day. Not that I care, but it does strike me as curious why she takes it. She doesn't seem like she has ADHD.

My hand is on the doorknob when she adds, "Cali? Why didn't your parents move you into your room?"

Everything inside of me tightens. My head feels light and my body grows warm. How long has she been dying to know the answer to this? "I live with my grandparents," I say, without turning around.

"How come?" I can feel her eyes burning into the back of my head.

Slowly, I turn around to face her. "Because my parents are dead." Annie Laurie's forehead shoots up and she flies a hand to her mouth. By the look on her face, I can practically hear the questions coursing through her mind. My heart is pounding loud enough for the whole dorm to hear.

"That sucks," she says. "I'm sorry."

I zip the cross hanging around my neck back and forth on the chain, something I do when I'm anxious. "It's okay."

"Cali. That's horrible," Ellie says crawling to the edge of her bed. "I'm so sorry."

"Thanks. But it's all good. My grandparents are better than parents."

"How—" Annie Laurie opens her mouth to ask, I'm certain, another of the nosy questions she stores in her arsenal—about how they died or when they died—but Ellie blurts, "I'm not trying to be rude, y'all, but I have to go to sleep. I have a test in the morning and I don't do well without sleep."

"I'm off," I say. "Have a good night's rest."

As I shut their door I hear Ellie's voice. "Night, Cali. See you tomorrow."

Before walking inside, I stop in front of my room to steady myself. All the blood has disappeared from my head. I feel like I might faint. Ellie saved me. Was it on purpose? Or on accident?

Now I feel like vomiting. Because I've lied. Majorly lied about my past. Having them discover that I've lied scares me to death, but I'm even more afraid of them learning the truth. Ever since I've been here I've been careful. Trying my best to be inconspicuous. I hadn't anticipated someone like Annie Laurie would be my next-door neighbor, incessantly pressing me for information.

I slip quickly inside our door. Jasmine is on her bed rubbing cocoa butter on her legs. Her cell phone is charging on the bedside table, but she's wearing the Bluetooth device that's usually attached to her ear when she talks to Carl. When I walk in she waves. We've only lived together two weeks and I already know her Carl voice. It's sultry. Dragged-out words. Lower tones.

First I grab my PJs from the chest under my bed, then move over to my closet for my robe and shower caddy. I'm not comfortable changing in our room. Jasmine, on the other hand, is the complete opposite. She strips down to nothing in front of me. The first time she did it I couldn't help noticing the heart shape of her pubic hair. I know you aren't supposed to stare, but the first time I saw it I was so caught off guard *all I could do* was stare.

With my shower caddy, robe, and PJs in hand, I head down the hall to the bathroom. As I'm brushing my teeth, I look in the mirror and imagine myself as a sorority girl. I've literally been dreaming about it since I was twelve years old. Miss Mississippi made a special stop in Blue Mountain to visit our school. I remember her saying that she was in a sorority at Ole Miss and that she wanted to be governor one day. I can recall sitting in the gym, listening to her talk, and wanting to be just like her.

With the addition of Mrs. Woodcock's I'll have recs to seven out of the thirteen sororities. If I make it, I vow right here and now to be the best pledge in the sorority. I'll become president. Then I'll become a lawyer. And after that, just like many of our former state leaders who became Greek, I'll be governor of the great state of Mississippi. The first lady governor, unless someone beats me to it, and then I'll be the second.

Once back in my room, I grab my laptop out of my backpack and climb up onto my bed. Ellie's email address is on my desk so I hop back down, grab the note, and do it all over again. Jasmine looks at me with confusion, and I point to the note in my hand. "Ellie's email."

After emailing her my rec packet, I type my mother's name and info, "Jennifer Suellen Watkins Mississippi California," into the search bar. Once I hit return, Google brings thousands of websites into view. I scroll down to the bottom of the first page, and do it again on the next ten pages before closing the window. There's everything from obituaries to homicides to missing persons and adoption records for Suellens and Jennifers, but nothing on Jennifer Suellen Watkins in Mississippi or in California.

Satisfied, I close my laptop and put it in the drawer on my nightstand. After tucking my prayer stone inside my palm, I scoot underneath my covers and face the wall, rubbing my worries into the stone. Its cold texture matches the temperature of my heart as I picture my mom: long brown dreadlocks. Glazed blue eyes. Dark circles. Gross clothes.

I hear Jasmine tell Carl she has to go. And that she loves him. It makes me long for a boyfriend. I'd love to be hearing sweet words from the man of my dreams. But thoughts of my elusive prince are replaced with my new life at Ole Miss, thousands of miles away from my biological mother.

SEVENTEEN

WILDA

Somewhere far off I think I hear my phone ringing. When I slowly open my eyes, there's a low light in the bedroom, and all I want to do is fall right back to sleep. But then a loud thunderclap jolts me out of grogginess. My cell phone *is* ringing. When I see seven on the clock I bolt up, lean over, and pick up my phone charging on the nightstand. *Ellie.*

"Heart," I say, with a scratchy voice. "Is everything okay?" She's never up this early. And her first class is not till nine.

"Of course it is. Why?"

"You don't have class till nine and you love your sleep. Why in the world are you up?"

"I've *been* up." She sighs deeply. "Annie Laurie wakes up at six. To do her hair and makeup." A small, sarcastic giggle follows. She's not pleased.

"Maybe she's got a cute boy in her first class."

"Whatever. I wake up to the sound of her annoying blow dryer every morning."

"How's it going otherwise? Did you get all your homework done last night?" As soon as I hear my words I want to take them back. I'm trying not to hover.

We had talked yesterday afternoon. And the day before that. I can't keep myself from dialing her number once a day.

"Yes, ma'am. It's easy here compared to high school."

Ellie's prep school education is actually paying off, I think. *As it should.* "That's a relief." From the angle of my bed, I can see the condensation on the panes through the crack in the curtains. Moist, opaque. The heat must be intolerable already.

"Hey, I need you to do something," Ellie says.

I sit up, prop the pillow behind me. "Anything." She's been gone two weeks now, and the emptiness feels like I've been starving myself. To be needed feels like savoring a five-course dinner at Antoine's.

"Remember Cali? Our next-door neighbor?"

"The one with the black roommate?"

"Mom."

"Sorry. I don't know why I said that. I meant it as a qualifier. Not a description. Yes, I remember Cali."

"You have to be more careful when you say stuff, Mom."

"I'm scared to say anything these days. Next thing I know you'll be telling me I can't say Oriental rug."

Ellie emits a loud irritated noise into the phone. "Whatever. So will you please write Cali an Alpha Delt rec?"

I pause before answering. Lilith's face has popped into my mind. Remembering what she said at the Rush meeting about the cutoff. I don't know Cali or anything about her family and the rec specifically asks that question. But the truth is Ellie's recommendation is good enough. "I'd be happy to do that." Thrusting my legs over the side of the bed, I jump up and head into the bathroom.

"Good, because she's incredible and doesn't have a rec from Alpha Delt yet. Plus no one in her family has ever been Greek."

"No problem, honey."

"I feel really sorry for her, Mom. Her parents are dead and she was raised by her grandparents in a little town close to Oxford called Blue Mountain."

"How awful. Bless her heart." Just hearing this news makes me excited to write her a rec. Alpha Delt could change her whole life.

"Ew. Are you peeing?"

"I just woke up. You pee and talk all the time."

"But I cover the phone. That's *gross,* Mom."

"Sorry. Gosh. I can't do anything right this morning."

"Do you think it's too late?" she asks, ignoring my comment.

"Is what too late?"

"To write Cali a rec?"

"I think September fifth is the deadline, so we're good."

Ellie sighs again, but this time from relief. "Thank God. Will you do it today? I want to make sure she has a chance. We're already good friends." No mention of Annie Laurie as a good friend. I'd like to press her about it, but I know better.

"Yes, I'll do it today." I move into the kitchen with Daisy at my heels, and rinse out my coffeepot from yesterday.

"Good. I've already emailed you her rec packet."

"That was fast."

"I knew you'd do it."

"You were right," I say. "Hey, who did you decide to invite to the game this weekend? Annie Laurie?"

"No, I invited Cali."

I pause. "Does that make things weird between you and Annie Laurie?" I'm trying my best to temper my voice. She'll bust me, big-time, if I don't.

"Not at all. She's already going with her parents."

"Well that worked out perfectly."

"Yep, sure did," she says. "Okay, better go. It's gonna take me a while to put my hair in a ponytail."

"You're a mess, Ellie Woodcock."

"Bye, Mom," she says with laughter in her voice.

Daisy needs to do her business so I let her out the patio door. She just stands there looking back at me with the rain drenching her body. "Go on, girl. Hurry up, Daisy. It's okay," I yell from the door. She's doesn't want to do it, but she prances over to the closest patch of grass and squats anyway. Then she races back inside like she's been caught in a hailstorm. After a shakeout, she lays her face sideways on the rug and scoots around in a desperate attempt to dry her mustache.

That Cali certainly is a sweet girl. It makes me feel good to be able to help her. And it's tragic about her parents. *What's her story?* I wonder. I'll find out soon enough when I get her résumé.

EIGHTEEN

WILDA

I'm supposed to meet Mama for lunch. Truth is, I'm making myself meet Mama for lunch. I love my mother, I do, but she's a thespian from the grandest of Shakespearian repertories, the ilk of which defies duplication. Yesterday she called to tell me my baby sister Mary, who lives with her family in Dallas, was dying, *"literally dying,"* she said, of heatstroke. Naturally it scared me to death when she said that and after almost dying from a stroke myself I finally recovered enough to ask what the heck had happened.

"The tempatuah in Dallas has hovered over the hundred-degree mark for twenty-foah days straight," she said, in her thick Mississippi drawl. "Their entiah family will be dead by the end of the week." That, in a nutshell, is Mama.

When I walk into The Cupboard, one of our better-than-average restaurants, Mama is seated at a table holding her cell phone. She's already ordered water and tea for both of us, and there's a basket of two rolls on her side of the table. I give her a hug, notice she's looking at Facebook, and take my place. When I sip my tea, I can tell it's unsweetened. I'm glancing around the restaurant, packed with diners, when Mama asks what I'm doing.

"The waitress made a mistake. This is *un*sweet tea."

Mama pats my hand, which is still wrapped around the glass. "She made no mistake, Wilda. You really need to stop ordering sweet tea. Your hips don't get any smallah the oldah you get."

That crawled all over me. "Mother. I am fifty-eight years old, five foot eight, and I weigh . . . well I weigh less than I did a year ago. I hardly think ordering sweet tea is the end of the world."

"Do you still wear the same size you wore last year?"

I give her a small shrug. "In some things."

"That"—she squints one eye, pops up her pointer finger, and adds a loud clucking noise inside her cheek—"is the end of Haynes's world."

Every single cell of my body winces. When we were young, Mary and I would kick each other under the table whenever she did it, all the while knowing what the other was thinking . . . *she makes me siiiick.* We call it the ick. "Mama did the ick today," one of us might say, or "She icked the lady in the checkout line." It's without question *the* most annoying thing in the world. Mama, by the way, is a four. Still. At eighty years old. Her arms are the size of my big toes.

"Did you invite me here to spend the afternoon insulting me?" I ask her. Haynes is forever preaching to not let her bother me. But she always has, always will.

"No, but you have to think of Haynes."

"What about Haynes? He loves me just the way I am."

She lightly strokes my forearm. "Honey, men keep their sex drives much longah than we do." She leans forward. "Is Haynes still having luck . . . down theyah?"

I lean in toward her, our foreheads nearly touching. "I refuse to talk with *my mother* about this subject. I'm going to pretend like she never asked me that question." Settling back in my chair, I take a sip of water. And stare at her.

She purses her lips, then tents her fingers together. "Your fathah died so young. I never knew if his would still work when he got ol—"

"That's it!" I slap my hand on the table. A piercing screech fills the room as I push back my chair. Standing up, I grab my purse.

The room chatter dies a sudden death and Mother glances around at the onlookers with indignant eyes. "Wilda, *please*," she mutters through clenched teeth. *"Sit down."*

Slowly I lower myself back in the seat, still clutching my purse. I lean in again. "What in the world makes you think I would ever have any interest in my daddy's penis? Either change the subject or I'm leaving."

"Okaaay." After scanning the restaurant to see who's still looking, she clutches my hand, which is still resting on top of my purse. With a much kinder expression she says, "How is Ellie? And how's it going with her roommate? It's Annie Laurie, right?" Mama picks up my napkin and hands it to me. I've been in the restaurant entirely too long not to have placed it in my lap.

I sigh, resigned to my fate, and wrap my purse strap around the back of the chair. "I think they're doing okay. It seems they're fairly different, but I'm sure they'll be fine."

"I can't tell you how glad I am they are rooming togethah. The girl is from such a fine family."

I ignore her comment. Her definition and my definition of fine family differ inexhaustibly. "She's made a new friend from next door whom she adores. A girl from Blue Mountain, Mississippi. I met her. She's a lot like Ellie."

"Where is Blue Mountain? I've never heard of that. Actually"—she points a finger in the air—"I have. It seems to me there's a character from one of Tennessee Williams's plays from Blue Mountain. But I can't seem to recall which one."

"I can't believe you remember that."

Mama lifts her readers from the chain around her neck and places them at the tip of her nose. Then she glances at her menu. "It's because of the great depth with which I studied Tennessee Williams at Sweetbriah."

She wants me to acknowledge this, but I don't. I've heard it a thousand times. "Anyway. Ellie wants me to write her an Alpha Delt rec. I guess the girl doesn't know many alums and needs all the help she can get."

"Are you going to do it?"

"Sure, why not?"

"Because you don't know a thing about her."

"That's a snobby attitude."

After pinching off and buttering a small corner of her roll, Mama lays her knife at the top edge of her plate, the proper way to place it. Then she peers at me over the top of her glasses. "It's not snobby. Why, it's responsible."

"You were never in a sorority, Mama. It's a big deal these days. Especially at Ole Miss. Everyone should have an equal opportunity whether they come from the *correct* family or not. It should be based on the person, not the parents."

"For your information, I was in the best Tap Club on the Sweetbriah campus. I've told you Sweetbriah didn't allow sororities. We were too busy horseback riding. It was Vahginia, after all." She looks away, shakes her head, and *tsks*. "I always wanted my granddaughtah to ride. It's a shame she wasn't allowed. She would have been a champion."

I glance at my watch. I still have forty-five more minutes of this. "Mama. You know English riding is a very expensive sport."

She purses her lips, cocks her head to the side. I know exactly what she means by this gesture. I've forbidden her to say it out loud, so she's taken to expressing her words through body language. What she means is: You should have married a man who makes more money. Haynes is an extremely gifted attorney. He heads up a small firm and provides pro bono representation for several of his underprivileged clients. Needless to say, however, he didn't go into it for the money.

The tempo inside my chest feels like a metronome that's been set to high speed. I close my eyes and try to figure out a way to escape the madness. No wonder I feel like I don't measure up.

Once we've ordered and the waitress has delivered our food, Mama seems to be preoccupied with inspecting her meal instead of meddling. My heart is just regaining its natural rhythm when she says, "Let's switch subjects. How is Ellie liking that elegant dorm room I paid foah?"

This is the one place in my life I've given my mother license to meddle. I should never have told her about my predicament with Lilith Whitmore. Then she never would have offered to loan me the money. Then I would have been forced to tell Lilith no. I have no one but myself to blame. If only I could have a redo.

"It's beautiful, Mama. She loves it. Thank you again." I take my first bite of green beans and am pleased to know they aren't overcooked.

"The pictures on Facebook are simply stunning. I particularly love the one of Ellie and Annie Laurie with their arms around one anothah." The day Mama got on Facebook was a dark day in the Woodcock household. "Now that girl's a beauty."

I nod. "She is pretty." The fried chicken is cooked to perfection—dark brown and extra crispy. I practically salivate when I pick up the first piece.

Unlike me, Mama eats to live. So far she hasn't taken a single bite. "Two pretty girls. Living in what must be the most magnificent room on the floah."

"Oh, it is. I think Ellie may be a little overwhelmed by it to tell you the truth. It's nicer than any room in our house." The absurdity of this makes me giggle out loud.

Mama nods. "I'm sure the Whitmoahs have extraordinary taste."

I'm in the middle of chewing, so I cover my mouth. "There's no question about that."

As I'm nibbling on the chicken leg I can see her staring at me out of the corner of my eye. She slices off a small corner of meatloaf, then changes her mind about eating it and puts down her fork. "Now. Let's discuss your loan."

When she offered the loan she insisted there was no hurry to pay it back. I swallow. Put my chicken leg down. "Okay."

"I'm assuming you're still keeping this from Haynes?"

My eyes close on cue. Hearing her say it out loud makes it worse.

"I think you should go on and tell him. He won't mind. He adores Ellie." Finally she takes her first bite of meatloaf, all the while staring me down as she chews.

"Read my lips. I'm not telling him. He wouldn't understand." I lean back in my chair. "I've decided to get a job and pay you back myself. The only reason I'm waiting is because Lilith has asked me to serve as an Alpha Delt Rush Advisor. Rush doesn't begin until October ninth, and I'll have to be in Oxford an entire week."

She taps her mouth daintily with her napkin. "I think it's a shame the University has pushed Rush back to the fall. What a terrible inconvenience for the girls. The very idea of having Rush while attending class is ludicrous."

"Apparently they were losing big money. Girls were dropping out of school when they didn't get the sorority they wanted—while they still had time to enroll somewhere else."

"Well, thank God for Lilith Whitmoah. Now that her daughter is Ellie's roommate I'm sure that will go miles toward ensuring Ellie's chances at a bid."

"Ellie doesn't need Annie Laurie to get a bid!" My pulse is pounding again.

"I didn't mean it that way." She presses a hand to her heart. "I simply meant having a girl with an outstanding pedigree for a roommate could only help Ellie."

There is no point in arguing with or challenging my mother. My prevailing thought—flashing in neon to plague me with regret—is something she taught me long ago, something I had forgotten about until right this minute. The borrower is *always* slave to the lender.

NINETEEN

WILDA

After lunch, I run to the cleaners for Haynes's shirts, and to the grocery to pick up fish for dinner. Once I'm back in my car a cursory glance in my rearview mirror confirms what I already know: My hairdo is shot. If I'd been smart, I would have taken my umbrella into the grocery when I saw the dark cloud in the distance, and my hair would still look okay. I try lifting the roots, but give up. It's no use. I'll have to fuss with it again before Haynes gets home.

Rifling through my purse, full of receipts and other superfluous junk, I find my cell phone resting at the bottom. As I call Ellie, Haynes's voice echoes in my mind. "Try not to call her every time you think about her. Let her be independent. No smothering."

I hang up, and call Cooper instead.

He's "temporarily" living in North Carolina, managing the Apple store in Raleigh. He knows that I know he'll never move back to Memphis, but he won't admit it. Even though I know he's at work, I call anyway. It goes straight to voice mail.

So I call Jackson.

He's in Nashville, where he at least admits he's never leaving, working as a medical supply rep, and picks up on the first ring. I'm in the middle of breathing a deep sigh of relief at having at least one child to talk to, when he says, "Mom, I'll have to call you back. I'm only halfway though a report I have to turn in tomorrow, and I'm stalled for words."

"Can I help you with it? I'm good with words. I made an—"

"A in all your English classes at Ole Miss. You've told me a thousand times."

"*Jackson.*"

"You wouldn't get this, Mom. I have to have to call you back." Then he's gone.

And I'm empty.

For the first time the thought strikes me in a profound way just how empty I really am. I am officially an empty nester and I don't know what to do with myself. Maybe Lilith asking me to be on the Advisory Board was no coincidence and rather a gift from God. Rush starts in five weeks and it can't come fast enough. I'll get to be in Oxford an entire week.

When I get home to my computer, Ellie's email is in my inbox. As curious as I am to read Cali's résumé, I check Facebook first. And I can't help but get distracted by the Nordstrom ad flashing at me from the right side of my home page for the exact pair of boots I had decided, over a week ago, were entirely too much money. As hard as I try to keep my eyes from floating over to them… I can't. It's killing me. How in the world am I not supposed to click on it?

Click.

And I'm drooling at that same pair of boots I shouldn't have looked at in the first place. And I love them. And dammit, I do want them.

Click.

I add the most adorable pair of booties to my cart in a size 8 and buy them before I have a chance to talk myself out of it. Now the thank-you-for-your-order page is staring me in the face. $215.27 after tax.

But I'm getting free shipping. I convince myself they probably won't look good anyway, and I can use the free return-shipping option and send them right back. But the only way to know for sure is to try them on. Right?

The phone rings and my face lights up when I see: Ellie. I push the talk button. "How's it going, El?"

"Hey, Mom. Did you send the rec?"

"I've got my computer open right now." I was so busy buying booties I had forgotten why I was on the computer in the first place.

"Okay, please do it now. We're counting on you."

"I'll call you when I hit send."

"A text is fine."

I roll my eyes. "Okay, I'll *just* text you."

Once I pull up Ellie's email, and Cali's rec packet is open, I'm happy to see there's a great close-up picture of the girl, standing in a cotton patch. She's adorable—not as pretty as Ellie, in my humble opinion, but just as cute as she can be. The second thing that practically leaps off the page is her GPA, and rightfully so. She has a 4.20. And a 32 on her ACT. My goodness, this girl is brilliant.

As I scroll down the page I learn she was valedictorian of her class at Blue Mountain High School and class president as well. She's in the National Honor Society, belongs to the Methodist church, has done loads of volunteer work—including several mission trips with her church—and works for the Daisy Chain Gift Shop in Blue Mountain. She's even an interpreter for the deaf and hard of hearing. On the second page I learn she ran cross-country for four years and plays the piano. What's not to like? What about this girl is not perfect Alpha Delt material?

She's listed no Greek affiliations; Ellie warned me about that. Instead of parents, she's listed her grandparents, Charles and Margaret Watkins, both professors at Blue Mountain College. Bless her heart. I can't imagine how Ellie or the boys would feel if they lost Haynes and me. My heart is breaking for her, and I don't even know her.

Filling out the Alpha Delt rec is easy. We used to do this longhand, but having it online is much more convenient. The rec form asks about everything from leadership skills, interests, and talents to academic and service achievements.

There is also a question asking how I know her. I'm tempted to say I've known Cali for a long time, to help the girl out, but the more I think about it Lilith's face pops into my mind's eye. She knows perfectly well I don't know Cali Watkins and, considering she will probably add in her two cents, I better not lie.

Finally it asks if the potential new member understands there are financial obligations in joining a sorority, with an option to check yes, no, or unknown.

I *text* Ellie to find out and within two minutes she texts right back: yes.

The real and more pertinent question is: can *we* meet the financial obligations? I now owe Mama ten thousand dollars we don't have. A sorority for Ellie will cost us another five hundred dollars a month—at least. What happens when Ellie wants another sundress or a nice pair of shoes? I just spent her sundress money on my own boots. *But,* I think, with momentary relief, *I have a college degree in journalism. I will get a good job within the month.*

Immediately a mental picture of the interview I'll have springs to mind: Man behind big messy desk at the *Commercial Appeal* with me sitting across from him, hands folded in my lap, legs crossed at my ankles. "So, Mrs. Woodcock," he'll say. "You're fifty-eight with no experience? No problem. Of course you can have a top job with our newspaper. How's seventy-five thousand to start? Go on down to Personnel now and sign your paperwork. Congratulations, Mrs. Woodcock! And welcome aboard."

TWENTY

CALI

While walking to class this morning all I could think about was: Ellie's mom is writing me a rec. Alpha Delt is one of the oldest, best sororities on campus! Once she sends that in, I'll have eight recs total. Kappa, KD, Pi Phi, Chi O, Tri Delt, AOPi, Alpha Phi, and now Alpha Delt.

Even though this helps my chances at membership, there's another important detail I must address. And that's money. I must save more money. First thing this morning, before my math class, I stopped at the Union. There's a giant bulletin board there with all kinds of job opportunities for students. I tore off stubs for three babysitting jobs and one helping out with the girls' volleyball team on weekends. Yesterday I went over to the employment office to see if I could get a signing job. That was something I got interested in when I was little. Sometimes I sign during church when the regular lady is away. But mostly I practice at home. I've never been paid for it, but I love it.

Our math teacher actually let us out of class early. Something about an appointment she couldn't avoid. Although she offered numerous apologies, no one could have cared less. We all dashed out of there to soak up the sunshine. Today is one of the prettiest days we've had so far. Not a cloud in the sky.

Nearly every tree in the Grove has students underneath its canopy with their noses buried in books.

Now, on the way to writing class, when I happen to look ahead, I see Annie Laurie walking toward me. She's texting and hasn't seen me yet. I think back to what she said about black people always being on their phones. She's on hers more than anyone I know.

She's wearing a big T-shirt and Lulu shorts. I'm wearing a regular-size T-shirt and blue jeans. When she's only ten feet in front of me I call out to her. "Annie Laurie."

She stops walking, and glances up from her phone. A smile is on her face, a rarity for sure. "Hey."

"Where you headed?" I ask.

"English, but I'm starving. Wanna go eat? I'm dying for something delicious. If I have to eat this campus food again I'll puke."

I shrug. "I wish I could. I've got writing class." As much as I want to be friends with her I know I have to keep a little distance between us. Because of that nosy streak of hers.

"So skip."

"I . . . I don't think I should." I shake my head lightly.

"So you miss a class. What's the big deal? You make good grades." The way I'm hemming and hawing gives her another opportunity to try and persuade me. "We won't go that far away. You'll be back by your next class."

I know I shouldn't go, but there's . . . something about her. Something alluring. Something enigmatic. Yet paradoxically repelling at the same time. I don't want to go, but I think I'm afraid to tell her no. Afraid of getting on her bad side. Hesitantly I say, "I guess I could."

"Good. Let's go to Southern Craft." She hooks her arm through mine and nudges me forward, picking up the pace as we walk.

My heart steps up, pounding louder and louder the farther away I get from my next class. I know why I'm doing this, but I'm still conflicted as hell. I know I shouldn't be missing class, but if I piss her off do I run the risk she'll keep probing into my past? Which is worse?

Out of nowhere my scholarship letter flashes across my mind. Maybe I willed it there. I stop abruptly, untwine my arm from hers. "On second thought. I better not."

"Why? Don't you like Southern Craft?"

"It's not that. It's—" Southern Craft is not cheap. In fact, it's pricey. I've never been, but I've heard other girls talking about it. Maybe lunch is more affordable, but that's not the real reason. "I just remembered I promised my teacher I would meet with her after class. It's about a job. There's someone she wants me to tutor." It's only a half-lie. There really is someone my teacher wants me to help. But we don't actually have plans to meet today.

"What? Are you lying?" She doesn't say it all that mean, but she still says it.

My nostrils flare. "No, I'm not lying. It's the truth." So it's a half-truth. No one will ever know that but me. Still, my pulse is racing and as much as I hate to admit it I'm sort of afraid of her.

"Why do you have to work anyway?"

Oh God. Here we go. This is exactly why I didn't want to go to lunch alone with her in the first place. I blurt my answer before I have time to shut myself up. "We're not wealthy people. My family has had to spend so much money on—" I catch myself mid-sentence. I almost told her they've spent all their money trying to get my mom sober.

"On what? Your family has spent all their money on what?"

Shit. "On . . . I don't know. Blue Mountain is not a booming metropolis."

Annie Laurie wrinkles her nose. "Working while you're in college must be tough. Poor you."

I breathe a silent sigh of relief—for dodging a big one. "It's not like I have a choice." After a pause I add, "Don't worry about me, though. I actually enjoy working." Then I glance at my phone for the time. "I better go. Hope you have a great day, Annie Laurie."

I turn around and haul ass to class.

TWENTY-ONE

MISS PEARL

Once work is over, after walking briskly around campus for an hour—all alone, I might add—I drive through Handy Andy's for a barbeque, a side of beans, and a nice slice of chess pie. Having that bag of sweet-smelling goodness next to me on this long drive home has nearly killed me, but I'm waiting to eat once I get in front of my television set. I've got my heart set on a dinner date with the man of my dreams—Usher.

At least once a day, I daydream he's single, makes it to Oxford for some reason, and fate brings us together. Maybe he's on his way to Clarksdale to play at Morgan Freeman's Ground Zero Blues Club. Maybe it's a fender bender. Or how about we see each other over the top of a gas pump? It's love at first sight. Then he takes me home with him—wherever home is. Lord Almighty, I'd be a willing, sinning fool if I could get just one face-to-face minute with that man.

My apartment is on the second floor, right out front and open to the parking lot. Every time I walk up these rickety metal steps, I'm reminded that I need to check to see if there's an opening on the ground floor.

When I turn the key and open the door, I glance at my watch. It's seven o'clock already. Where does the time go? Seems like I just picked up my pocketbook this morning, now I'm laying it back down in the same spot.

First thing I do is hunt for my remote, which I find stuck behind the couch cushion, then I flip on the box and scroll through my saved shows till I find *The Voice*. Once I hit play, Usher's fine face is the first thing on the screen. "Here I am, baby," I holler at the TV. "Come on to Oxford. You are looking sharp tonight." Then I set up my TV tray. Mrs. McKinney gave the set to Mama when it didn't sell in her carport sale. When Mama died, I took it home with me. Use one every night.

As soon as the first commercial comes on I head into the kitchen, pop my sandwich and beans in the microwave. But only for a few seconds, there is nothing worse than hot cold slaw. Then I take it out and put it on a plate. I grab a roll of paper towels—barbeque is messy business—and head on back out to the den to wait on my man to return to the screen.

Just as I'm raising the sandwich to my mouth—sauce oozing out the sides— here comes a rap on the door. Lord have mercy, it's that fool James Hardy down the way. He's the sole reason I can't let light into this room. I haven't opened my blinds since I met him, the day after I moved in. He can keep on knocking because I'm not answering.

I take my first bite, feel it melting on my tongue—the bread, meat, slaw, and sweet sauce mixed together lets me know what heaven tastes like—and here comes the knock again. Only this time it's louder. Seems like I hear a faint voice, too, and it's not from a male. I reach over for the remote, turn town the volume. "Pearl, baby, are you home?"

Fee? What's she doing here? She's usually wiped out and home by this hour. Once her feet slide into her bedroom slippers she never leaves the couch. I put Usher's pretty face on pause, scoot around the tray, and unlock the door. Still in her uniform, Aunt Fee's standing there with her pocketbook hanging from her shoulder.

"What are you doing all the way out here this late? I almost ignored your knock." Fee lives in town, on the east side, near a smattering of other low-income folks.

"I need to talk with you. Mind if I come in?"

"I was just sitting down to watch *The Voice*. Come on in."

Now she knows I love *The Voice* and she really knows I love Usher. But she pushes on past me. "These old knees," she says, straining to sit, "keep lettin' me down." Her behind is big like Mama's was, and I notice the sofa cushion curl up underneath her. "Fetch me a glass of water, baby, if you don't mind. My mouth is dry as toast."

"All right," I say, and head into the kitchen. "What's on your mind? The suspense is killing me."

"I'll wait till you get back. I'm in no hurry," she hollers.

"Maybe not, but I sure am," I mutter under my breath.

I bring her a Co-Cola with ice, because I know that's what she's after, and sit back down next to her. I pick up my sandwich, hold it out her way, but she shakes her head.

"All right then, tell me what's on your mind. You drove a long way. Must be important."

"It is important." She gulps half of her Coke down without a breath, then finishes with a loud, "Ahhhh."

Before I take a bite I ask, "Is this about me finding a husband again?" Then I dig my teeth in.

She never answers that question, just slides onto something else, and puts a serious tone in her voice. "I promised your mama on her death bed I would look after you. Like I've done since you were a baby."

I hurry up and swallow. "You've told me this before."

She raises a palm. "Let me finish, please." Lord knows what's coming. I may as well forget Usher. "I think she asked me that, not because anything is wrong with you, but because of your heart." Now the tone in her voice changes. The sweet Aunt Fee shows up. "She knew you'd be taking care of everybody else but you. She knew you wouldn't be thinking about yourself—" I try to object but she holds her hand up again. "And *she knew* somebody needed to point it out to you." Then she just looks at me.

"I think about myself a-plenty."

"No you don't. I know you love our girls, but you're selling yourself short. You are smart, Pearl May, and you know it." She raises her finger. "You've been working at Alpha Delt since you were nineteen years old. That's almost twenty-five years. And what do you have to show for it?"

"What do you have to show for thirty-two?"

"Not a damn thing. And that's my point. No retirement. No health in-surance. Granted, we get paid time off at Christmas, spring break, and Thanksgivin', too. But look what happens in the summer. Nobody can live on unemployment."

"Tell me about it."

"They're talkin' all about Obama's care. We can't even afford that. Then get penalized for not having it. *Shoot.* I can't give up one more penny of my check. And neither can you. Your check less than mine."

"At least I get a tip every now and then."

Fee's lips press into a straight line and she gawks at me with eagle eyes. My tongue has slipped into muddy waters. "You better hope Uncle Sam never find out about that." An arthritic finger wags my way. "And that's another thing. You get all kinds of tips and fine, pretty things. But they don't come for free." She picks up one of the throw pillows on my couch. Then gives me the hard stare. "You're workin' overtime for every one of these. Have you thought about that?"

I don't say anything. But I know she's right.

My lips part to ask what she thinks I'm supposed to do about it, when her tone softens. "You're workin' too many hours, baby. And you don't take time for yourself. I want more for you than all this. Your mama would, too."

After laying my sandwich back down on the plate and wiping my hands with a paper towel, I pat her on the knee. "Thank you for loving me like you do. I don't know what I'd do without you."

She smiles, puts her arm around me. "Your mama knew you were a rare treasure the day you were born." With her other hand she touches the pearl dangling from my neck. "I remember the day she had your pearl made into this necklace. She carried me along with her to the jeweler. It was your six-teenth birthday. Ain't that right?"

I nod. "Seems like yesterday."

"That jeweler said Mississippi pearls are extremely rare and very valuable. Just like you. You make sure you hold on to it, you hear?"

I give it a feel. "Don't you worry. I'll never let this go."

My great grandmama and her people liked to go "musseling." They'd wade out in the Mississippi River feeling for freshwater mussels with their toes. In all her years of exploring she only found one pearl. Now it's mine—baroque with a pink cast. Due to the mother-of-pearl button craze back in the thirties, Mississippi River pearls have all but vanished from the riverbeds. All the freshwater mussels and clam beds were depleted and never replenished. No wonder they're so valuable.

I figure now's as good a time as any to drop the bomb on her. "Mama Carla asked me to fill in for her this weekend."

With a gasp, she rears back. "Say what?"

"Said she'd give me a hundred fifty dollars extra."

I watch a cautious smile sneak onto her lips. "You may as well have told me I have the power to fly."

"You and me both." My mind's been battling ever since Mama Carla asked me. One minute I'm imagining myself at the front door of the Alpha Delt House as the full-time housemother, the next I'm in the middle of a swarm of angry bees with their stingers pointed straight at me, daring me to disturb their hive.

"That Mama Carla is a nice lady. She knows a good thing when she see it."

I smile back at her. Mama Carla drips with honey. She's not one of the bees I'm worried about.

"But what's that new House Corp President gone say? What's her name? Lilith Whit*less*?"

I laugh so hard I snort. "Mama Carla acted like it was her decision, not Miss Whit*less*'s."

"Maybe so." She raises her finger. "But you be careful. You know what I'm sayin'?"

"I know what you're saying."

She shudders, then recoils back into the sofa. "There ain't no tellin' how that snake might strike when she finds out. She slithers into my kitchen, poking her pointy head into our business like she's Queen of the House and we're her subjects."

"She thinks she is, anyway. But I'm not afraid of her."

"And neither am I." Her eyes turn into half-dollars. "You fill in for Mama Carla this time. Then you think about findin' something else. You hear?"

"It's not as easy as you think, Aunt Fee. Where would I go? Have you thought about that?"

"The University pays benefits—all kinds of jobs over there. They'll be tickled to have you."

"I'll think about it."

"That's all I can ask." She takes ahold of my hand, stares at it for a while, then massages my ring finger. "This hand would look a whole lot nicer with somethin' shiny on top." She squeezes one eye shut, tilts her head to the side. "I thought of someone else. What about James Pearson?"

After I let my mouth fall open in surprise, like she's just presented my shining prince on a silver platter, I hold up my left hand and stare at the empty space on my finger. "Fee, that's such a coincidence. I thought of someone else, too."

Her eyes sparkle and dance like two kaleidoscopes. "Who's that?"

I lift the remote from the couch and push play. "Usher."

TWENTY-TWO

CALI

Bump-bump-bump, the bass pounds through the wall, right next to my bed. My lungs feel like they might explode from the reverb.

"Make it stop," I say out loud, covering my head with my pillow.

"God, oh God, God, oh God." Even with the pillow smashed up against my ears I can still hear Big Sean, Annie Laurie's favorite rapper, like he's in the room with me. *It's too early for music*. Tossing and turning, I fling my pillow around, desperately trying to block the noise.

We pregamed in Ellie and Annie Laurie's room—it's become the official pregaming room due to its size—till three thirty in the morning. And now they're at it again. It's our first game-day morning in Oxford, and I may as well face it. Sleep is over.

My phone is next to me on the bed. I check the time. God, it's ten o'clock already. I turn over and Jasmine's not there. She had spent the previous Friday night with Carl, but when I drifted off to sleep a few hours ago she was in the bed next to mine. My phone rings while it's still in my hand. The music blasts even louder as I say, "Hello."

"Hey," Ellie says, all bright and cheery. "Where are you? We're pregaming over here."

"I can tell. *Uhhh,* I feel like I just fell asleep," I say with a frog in my throat. A flash of nausea rushes through my stomach. "And I don't feel all that great."

"Me, either. And we didn't even drink all that much."

"I think it's all the crap we ate. Too many Cheez-Its gets me every time." Maybe I'm fooling myself. It could have been the bourbon. Either way, I'm swearing off both for the next month. Well, the next week. "When are we meeting your parents?"

"In three hours. Still wanna borrow my dress?"

I sit straight up. "Yes, is that still okay?"

"Of course. Come get it."

"Sweet. Be there in five."

As soon as Ellie mentioned borrowing her dress, a burst of energy collided with the queasiness in my gut, and now I'm raring to go. Last July, before school started, I had driven to Tupelo, forty-five minutes away, and bought two cute dresses at Reed's. But I really want to save them for Rush.

I jump out of bed and head for the bathroom. Every single shower is running and each sink is occupied with girls brushing their teeth or washing their faces. As I wait for a toilet, I daydream about the day ahead. I knew I'd be excited about our first home football game, but never dreamed I'd actually get to go. Ellie's parents had two extra tickets and she invited me to come along. I asked her why she didn't invite Annie Laurie instead, and she said the Whitmores had tons of season tickets so Annie Laurie would be sitting with them.

When I push open the door to their room, Annie Laurie's in front of her makeup mirror. Her hair is already perfect, flat-ironed straight and hanging down her back, about six inches from her butt. She's wearing the cutest romper I've ever laid my eyes on—a pale blue V-neck, with eyelets and sleeves that brush the tops of her elbows. That pretty white-gold jewelry, that Yurman she always wears, matches perfectly with a blue gemstone dangling from her neck. Honestly, she looks stunning, with the exception of her dark eye shadow, thick black eyeliner, and heavy base. I don't get that, guess I never will.

Ellie's still in her pajamas with her hair in a messy bun on top of her head, texting. As soon as she sees me, she puts down her phone, leaps over to her closet, and pulls out the cutest red sundress ever, with a high halter neckline and a keyhole back. She holds it up to my front, still on the hanger. "Ole Miss red," she says, extra loud so I can hear her over the music. "It's gonna fit you perfect. But try it on real quick and see."

"Here?"

"Sure, why not?"

I strip off my T-shirt and boxer shorts and slip into Ellie's dress. By now, my modesty is waning. As soon as her dress touches my skin I already know it's perfect. I can feel myself smiling. And the excitement about today bubbling up inside.

"Turn around. I'll tie it for you," she yells over the music.

I do as she asks, holding up my hair. Catching my reflection in her vanity mirror verifies my feelings. I love this dress. It's short, but not too short—six inches above my knees.

"It looks adorable on you," Ellie says. "What do you think, Annie Laurie?"

"I love it," she says, awkwardly, while applying her mascara. With every sweep of the wand, her mouth opens wider. She never turns to look directly at me; she just glances briefly at my reflection in the mirror above her vanity.

"Turn around," Ellie says, scooting her back against mine. She slices one hand over both of our heads. "How tall are you?"

"Five two. What are you? Five three?"

She nods. "I'm the shrimp in my family. I take after my grandmother."

Annie Laurie screws the brush of her mascara back inside the tube, places it on the mirrored top of her vanity amid the other makeup strewn about, and picks up the remote from the clutter. She points toward their TV and the music softens. Then she looks directly at me. "It really does look great on you, Cali." A pause. "Do you have any sundresses?"

That punches my gut. I know I should say something snarky right back. But for some reason I can't. So I simply say, "Yes, but Ellie wanted me to wear hers today."

She smiles that smile again. The one I can't decipher. Her cryptic look, clear as dishwater. "That's really nice of you, Ellie." She gets up and walks over to their "entertaining station," as she calls it. There's a bucket with ice poking out of the top, and a pair of silver tongs to the side. A plastic Sprite liter is next to it, along with two big bottles of Tropicana orange juice.

I watch her pour a good amount of what I know is vodka, hidden inside the Sprite liter, into a large Ole Miss plastic cup, top it off with OJ, then stir it around with her finger. After licking her finger, she takes a sip and turns to us. "Y'all ready for a screw?" Then she bursts into laughter and jukes in place underneath the new addition to their room—a hanging disco ball.

"Too early for me," Ellie says with a forced giggle. "Do you want one, Cal?"

I shake my head. It's the last thing I want right now.

With an exaggerated eye roll, Annie Laurie reaches for the remote again and bumps up the rap volume five more notches. She throws the remote onto the couch and proceeds to dance around the room holding her drink high in one hand and flicking and circling her wrist with the other.

"Come on, y'all," she hollers and, after I exchange a green-light glance with Ellie, the two of us jump up and juke along with her. I know some pretty good moves from high school, but now, after living in Martin a few weeks, I'm, like, a pro. Ellie and I turn around and twerk our butts together, then laugh so hard we fall down onto their sofa. Dorm life is way more fun than I ever imagined.

"I still feel terrible about not asking Jasmine," Ellie says, a bit out of breath. "She's not upset, is she?" Ellie is literally yelling so I can hear her.

Shouting just as loud, I answer. "No, I swear. She and Carl have friends from Greenville who always tailgate in the Grove. Jasmine says they have this awesome flat-screen TV and no one ever wants to leave."

"I'd never want to hurt her feelings."

I shake my head emphatically. "Don't worry. It's all good." We sit a few more seconds listening to Drake before a thought occurs to me. It's hard to believe as a lifelong Mississippian, but it's true. "I've only been to one Ole Miss game. My grandfather took my friend Rachel and me as a sweet-sixteen birthday present."

Ellie is obviously surprised, but she reaches over and pats my cheek. "Then this game is long overdue." She looks over at Annie Laurie. "Will you please turn it down a few notches? I'm going deaf."

Annie Laurie obliges, then says, "I don't think I've ever missed a game in my whole life." She takes another big swig of her drink. "Daddy's pilot flies us to all the away games." Daddy's pilot? Now I know I'm not in Blue Mountain anymore.

Kickoff is at three o'clock against the Wofford Terriers but Ellie thought we should be ready by twelve thirty. She said her parents had been invited to several tailgate parties in the Grove, including the Whitmores', and we could tag along if we wanted. Ellie and I had discussed the warning about not going into the Grove before Rush, but we decided being with her parents was a safe way to go.

I glance at my phone. "Don't you think we should get our showers? It's ten thirty."

"Probably so," Ellie answers. "We're supposed to meet my parents in front of the Lyceum at one."

"Y'all are coming to our tailgate party, right?" Annie Laurie asks.

"Yes," Ellie and I both say at the same time.

"We should all walk over together. Let's say we leave here at noon."

"Sweet. I'll text my parents and tell them we'll meet them there." Ellie types the message out on her phone.

Standing up, I grab my PJs. "See y'all in a few." As I head out the door, four other girls from our floor step inside.

"Shut the door," Annie Laurie yells. "We don't need the RA barging in here."

TWENTY-THREE

MISS PEARL

The House is as quiet as falling snow when my alarm goes off at six, early on Saturday morning. Lord have mercy, it feels like I just slipped into this bed. The clock read three A.M. when my head finally hit the pillow last night. The last thing in the world I want to do right now is move out of this silky cocoon. So I lie in Mama Carla's bed a little longer, running my hand along the top of her comforter, feeling the slickness of the silk against my fingers.

Suppose I woke up every morning swaddled up this way? What if I really was the House Director? I'd make a good salary. Have a beautiful place to live. Get my insurance paid for. As crazy as that seems, I can't help but fantasize. Who wouldn't? Just for the fun of it, I let my mind drift, imagine myself as Pearl Johnson, House Director of Alpha Delta Beta sorority. Before I know it, I'm replaying every detail of the night before. But this time I'm the House Director for real.

I stayed outside the apartment door like Mama Carla does early on Friday nights, watching the girls come and go, each of them dressed up and ready for the town. After supper, around ten o'clock, I returned, ready for them to come on home. Now I see why she does it. If one of the girls gets over-served and needs a hand finding her room, someone needs to steer her in the right direction.

Poor little Cara Moore, that baby didn't know what day it was when she came stumbling through the door around midnight. Oliver, our security guard, told me she was all by herself when she walked up. When he passed her off to me her hair was hanging down in front of her face and she reeked of bourbon. I took her by the hand, led her straight upstairs, and tucked her safely in bed. I gave thought to her mama, living way down in Vicksburg, blissfully unaware of Cara's ways. I certainly would appreciate it if someone did that for my daughter.

Bless his heart. I can't believe Oliver ever came back for a second round. That poor man looks nothing like a security guard. He's chunky, especially around the middle, and his pale pudgy face has ruby red cheeks with very little facial hair. From what I hear, the girls teased him unmercifully last weekend. He told his supervisor that one of them actually spanked him on the behind. Said another girl squeezed his cheeks and called him her baby, only she liked to rip the skin off. I know they didn't mean anything by it. But all kinds of things can happen at that hour and I certainly didn't want another repeat on my watch.

Around one o'clock in the morning, I found several of my babies milling around the kitchen looking for treats. Mama Carla would have told them to take their hineys and skedaddle right on out of there. But I couldn't help myself. I did the opposite. Brought out all their favorites: chips, M&M's, popcorn. I know what it's like to get the late night munchies. I'm not dead yet.

When I roll over to get out of bed, my angry body is yelling at me to stay put. I have to force myself off the mattress and into the bathroom. After using the toilet, I wrap my head up in a shower cap to protect my weave. Looking around, I imagine for a moment this bathroom is mine. I run my hand across the pretty white tile, then feel the plush towels Mama Carla has hanging on the rack. What would it be like if I woke up here every morning?

After stepping inside the shower, feeling the water beat down on my back, I get to thinking about that ornery Kadeesha and how she's taking over housekeeping today. Lord, I hope I don't have to get on to her. I have a certain way of doing things, and I take pride in my work. Marinating on her nasty self only lasts another minute, though. Once I feel the hard pressure of this shower and enjoy how long the hot water lasts, I soon forget all about her and luxuriate in what I'm doing right now.

It's seven A.M. by the time I make it into the kitchen. We don't serve meals on the weekends, but Mama Carla always puts out a breakfast bar—bagels and cream cheese, sweet rolls, and fruit. Once that's done, and I get the coffee made, I take a bagel and a coffee cup and mosey around the house like Mama Carla does, feeling like I'm queen for the weekend.

By chance, I happen to glance out the front window at the Chi Theta House and notice a car pull up. There's a boy behind the wheel, and I watch him lean to the passenger side to kiss one of the girls. She steps out of the car barefoot, still in last night's sundress, with shoes in her hand. She shuts the car door, then scurries up to the House. Pushes in her code and she's gone.

Makes me think back to the last time I kissed a man. That was three years ago. I might be forty-four, but I am not deceased. I still want a man's arms wrapped around me, feeling my bare skin, working his way down my neck. I'm not sure why, but today I feel more ready and alive than I have been in a long time. Auntie's right. I do need a man.

Over the next few hours, pregame fever spreads all over the house. One of the alums brought over a cake—big enough to feed everybody—and put it in the dining room. It's in the shape of our mascot, the black bear, holding a little terrier in a headlock. A win over the Wofford Terriers today is just about guaranteed. For some reason a sobering thought strikes me. As long as I've been working on this campus I've never once seen the inside of Vaught-Hemingway Stadium.

As the girls prance down the stairs they look like they're stepping off the runway, wearing pretty sundresses, rompers, boots, and high heels. I try wearing heels but my feet get angry with me. So today I'm wearing a pair of flat gold sandals. Got my toes painted up Alpha Delt blue, like all the girls do theirs, and my fingernails, too.

I even dug out my favorite dress. Made sure it was clean and pressed up real nice. It's pale yellow, with buttons running clear down the back. Buttons are only for show, hiding a long zipper, but no one can tell. Donnie, my ex-husband, used to say this dress fits my curves in all the right places without being too tight. It's old, but nobody around here has ever seen it. Fee told me to be sure and wear my Mississippi pearl necklace. Pearl is the official jewel of Alpha Delta Beta.

I'm standing in the foyer, around noon, when I spot Miss Lilith hurrying through the front door. Her blond hair is pulled back in a high ponytail with a bump on top, like Barbie styles hers. The pale blue pantsuit she's wearing is some kind of pretty and her earlobes are so sparkly I can see them from here. She never looks in my direction, just makes a beeline to the powder room.

A few minutes later, when she flies out, my body tightens. That's not a smile on her face and the beeline she made into the powder room has changed course. Now she's buzzing straight toward me. "Hello, Pearl," she says, soon as she lights. "Don't you look nice?" I watch her eyes travel all the way from my weave down to my big toe, with a brief stop at my necklace. Then she stares at my arm. For a moment I wonder if I'm bleeding or if there's a spider on my arm, then I remember my tattoo.

"Thank you, Miss Lilith. You look nice yourself. I love your pantsuit and your earrings are gorgeous." Lord. Now I'm gushing over her, too. Same as Mama Carla.

"Perhaps you are unaware . . . but the ladies' room needs more toilet paper. *Two* of the three holders are empty and the trash cans are overflowing." Her eyes have left mine and shifted over to Mama Carla's apartment. "Pardon me," she says, as she pushes past and raps on the door. "Carla, yoo-hoo."

I turn to see the backside of her blue pantsuit as she disappears inside. Just walks right in Mama Carla's apartment, uninvited. I consider stopping her, but she's already gone.

Before I can blink, she's right back out. "Where is Carla?"

"She had to leave town."

"Oh?"

"Her daughter was in need and Mama Carla had to help her." It is none of my business, and certainly not Miss Lilith's, so I stop short of explaining the need.

Miss Lilith puts a hand over her heart, sucks in a pound of air. "Are you . . . who is her weekend replacement?"

I've been expecting this. "I am." I don't add an explanation. I simply let those two words soar out of my mouth, then float down and land softly, like a duck on a pond.

After a long pause she says, "Huh," and stares at me as if I should give her an explanation. I resist. So awkwardness comes between us. Similar to that feeling you get when you call someone by the wrong name. "Have her call me, please. The minute she gets back."

"I sure will." I smile after I say it, but she never smiles back. The urge to explain jumps up again, but I swallow it right back down.

As she's walking away she says something about being away from her Grove party too long. She gets all the way to the front door, and I think I'm in the clear, but she turns back around. At first it looks as if she'll head my way again, but instead she rushes through the kitchen door.

By now, I have worked myself into a state. Between Miss Lilith's reaction and being so ticked off at Kadeesha for skipping out on housekeeping duty, I want to kick a soccer ball, or hit a punching bag—anything that might relieve this angst.

Checking both the downstairs restrooms, ladies *and* gents, it gets worse. They look more like outside lavatories at an old nasty gas station, not powder rooms in a fine sorority house. Wastebaskets are overflowing with wadded up paper towels, holders are empty with no way to dry your hands. Soap dispensers are still okay, but there are black scuffmarks all over the tile floors. Miss Lilith was right. Two of the three stalls in the ladies' are clean out of paper. With the close proximity to the Grove most of the alums and their husbands come here to use the toilet.

I debate whether or not to let Kadeesha have it right then and there, or just do it myself. After taking a deep breath and praying for the strength to calm myself down, I choose the latter. I'm the one who has to work with her every day. It is not worth the headache.

I'm reaching for the door when it jerks open from the other side. Miss Lilith is standing there with both Kadeesha and Mr. Marvelle. He has a bucket in one hand and a mop in the other. Kadeesha's hands are empty. She's just standing there smacking on a piece of gum.

"Where are the supplies kept?" Miss Lilith asks with an angry tongue.

"In my maintenance closet," I say matter-of-factly.

She turns to my coworkers. "Please, one of you, go get the supplies. These powder rooms are atrocious."

"Pearl has the key," Kadeesha says as if that's the reason for the mess. Before God, I want to strangle that woman.

Stretching out her hand, palm up, Miss Lilith asks, "May I have the key, please?" Upon which I remove the plastic bracelet around my wrist and hand it over. "Thank you. Please come with me," she says to Kadeesha and Marvelle. Then that lady struts down the hall and enters my closet as if it's hers.

Before long she emerges with an armload and practically shoves toilet paper and hand towels at both of them before kicking the door closed. Then she strolls back to me, holding the key away from her like its something nasty, drops it inside my hand, and never says another word to any of us. We all watch her swish toward the foyer and out the front door.

"Why did you have to do that?" I ask Kadeesha as soon as Miss Lilith is gone.

"Do what?"

"Ignore these washrooms. Do you hate me or something?"

With that gum rolling around inside her mouth, it appears Kadeesha is in no hurry to answer. "Why do you say that?" she finally asks, followed by two more smacks and a loud pop.

"Don't you know my substituting for Mama Carla can only help us? This is about progress, Kadeesha. Not me having more seniority than you."

"Pearl's right." Mr. Marvelle shakes his head in disgust. "Land sakes. I would have done it myself if you didn't wanna do it. Now look what you've done. We'll be lucky if all three of us don't lose our jobs."

The rest of our staff is off today. Sororities don't serve meals on weekends.

"This ain't my fault," Kadeesha says, then sashays on past us, straight for the ladies' room. Before she opens the door she stops. "I'm not sure I even want this job."

Marvelle cuts his eyes my way without moving a muscle. Soon as the door closes behind her he shakes a finger toward the space where she last stood. "Well, take your junkie butt and get on outta here, then."

TWENTY-FOUR

WILDA

I can't get over how much Oxford has changed," I say, peering out my window as Haynes and I inch around the Square. "Thank goodness Square Books is still here. The way bookstores are dying, it's a small miracle." The traffic is backed up all the way from Highway 7. We left Memphis early to secure a good parking spot, and it seems the rest of the Rebel fans had the same idea. "Look at all the new restaurants and gift shops."

"Who would have ever thought," Haynes says, looking out his side, "the population of Oxford, Mississippi, would double. Actually, I think it's tripled since we were in school."

I reach over and mime holding a microphone under his chin. "So, Mr. Woodcock, to what do you attribute Oxford's population explosion? I'm told it's grown faster than any other city in Mississippi."

He leans into the imaginary mic. "Well, Ms. Couric, that's an easy one. Aside from the hundreds of baby boomers swarming here for retirement, Eli and Archie Manning are Oxford's real stars. Football has turned our community into a gold rush."

We look at each other and laugh. Then he leans over again like he wants to continue the interview. "There's one more thing I'd like to add."

Holding the "mic" back toward him I say, "Yes, Mr. Haynes Woodcock. Please do continue. You are very handsome, by the way."

"Thank you, Ms. Katie Couric, you are extremely beautiful yourself." Looking straight ahead at the car in front, he clears his throat, then leans in closer. "Oxford may have had its trials and controversies over the years, but I can assure you it's one of the best small towns in America."

Ironically, at that very moment, I spy the bronze statue of William Faulkner sitting on a bench near City Hall. "Why, you must be speaking of the silly hubbub over the Faulkner statue."

"I had forgotten about that one but, yes, you are correct: that was inane . . . in my opinion, anyway." Haynes grins and I melt all over again at the sight of his luscious dimples.

About twenty years ago, a local artist was commissioned to sculpt the statue. The $50,000 project was paid for with both private and public funds, but no one could agree on a place to put it. There was a bit of an outcry when the mayor ordered that an old magnolia tree be cut down to make room for the statue in front of City Hall. Twenty-five people held a memorial service for that magnolia tree. They even laid a black wreath at the stump.

"If not the statue, to which controversy were you referring?"

"Actually, I'd rather not comment. I prefer to let negativity die. I'll finish this interview by saying, it's always something in Mississippi."

I withdraw the mic and place my hand back in my lap. I know exactly what he's talking about. "I hate to rebirth negativity, but whatever happened to those kids?"

He sucks in a breath, exhales loudly. "Last I heard only one's going to jail. The second guy cooperated with the prosecution, pled guilty, and was given a year's probation. The third was never charged."

"What's fair about that?"

He simply shakes his head without commenting.

A few years ago, three college guys put a noose around the James Meredith statue. That despicable stunt almost killed Haynes. He was on the University committee that had worked to erect it in honor of the fortieth anniversary of the admission of the first black man to Ole Miss.

It's always something, all right. Now my thinking shifts to the money I owe Mama and the terrible predicament I've gotten myself into. It was the dumbest decision of my life. My desire for Ellie to have a transcendent college experience has caused me to lie to the person I love most. But I'm determined to pay it off before he finds out. "By the way, I've decided to get a job as soon as Rush is over," I say. "To help pay for Heart's sorority dues."

"That's great, babe. Proud of you."

"If I take it now, I'll have to give up the advisor position. What do you think?"

"Whatever makes you happy. Have you thought about where you want to work?"

"Well, considering I'm fifty-eight and haven't worked a real job since the kids were born, I'm thinking about that store where Vicki works—What's Hot. You know that pale green sweater you love on me?"

He nods.

"I got it there. She thinks she can hire me."

"That's great, honey. Why don't you work part-time? Even that would be a big help."

There's talk Haynes's law firm may be hired by the family of a former UPS employee who was killed on the job, but who knows when or if that will happen. And considering the new tunic I'm wearing cost another two hundred dollars, on top of the money for my new booties and the ten thousand I owe Mama, working part-time is not an option.

Driving onto campus always gives me a warm nostalgic feeling, no matter how many times I do it. First of all—and maybe I'm biased—I think it's the most beautiful campus in America. The old buildings with their rich histories, the monuments, the Grove, the grand sorority and fraternity houses, even the smell of the place—it all makes me happy. Haynes and I both love it so much. We're making Ole Miss one of the beneficiaries of our estate—if there's one left after I've finished paying Mama back.

"Haynes! I see a spot." I point frantically down a hill with a grassy area that's been turned into a parking lot on the outskirts of campus. "Hurry before someone gets it."

"Great eye." He whips to the right, rolls down his window. "How much?" He asks the guy taking the money.

The fellow leans in with a wad of cash in his hand. "Twenty bucks."

Haynes turns to me. "A casualty of growth," he says, then hands the man our money.

After pulling down the visor, I flip open the mirror and apply lipstick. "It's going to be a tight—" Suddenly, we bounce hard in our seats, "Fit." He's looking at me with a barely contained snicker. I turn from him back to the mirror and see an amber-colored line between the top of my lip and the bottom of my nose. We both explode with laughter.

Despite the pothole, Haynes expertly manages to maneuver our Expedition into the parking spot. With his hand on the gearshift he turns to me, squeezes his lips together. "Just so you know, I'll have one beer at the Whitmore tent. That's it."

My shoulders slump in disappointment. I'm just sure it's the hottest ticket in town. Why doesn't he see that? "You told me that already," I say. Then, gripping the door handle, I turn to him with a pleading face. "Lilith says it'll be really nice. Trust me, the food will be incredible."

"I have no doubts about that, but I'm not interested in spending my whole day off with the Whitmores." He glances at his watch. "It's eleven now. Let's stop by Frank and Judy's, then we'll meet Ellie and Cali at the Whitmores' at one. That's the time you told her, right?"

"Yes, but I thought we could get there earlier to have lunch."

He reaches out, clutches my wrist. "You know how I feel about them."

I do know how he feels about them, but I like Lilith. Sure, she's bossy and overbearing, I suppose, but she's Ellie's roommate's mother. And she's gone out of her way to be nice to all of us.

"Frank and Judy will have good food," he says. "They always do."

I nod in reluctant agreement, and we get out of the car.

As we're walking up the hill, perspiration building with each step, I stop suddenly. Hot and out of breath, I say, "Do I look snappy casual?"

Haynes curls his lip, then laughs out loud. "That's random. What the heck are you talking about?"

I stop, look down at my white jeans, new booties and new top, breathing heavily. "It's the dress code for the Whitmore party. According to Lilith, that's how the British say it."

Wearing one of his signature saucy expressions, he glances down, scanning his attire—blue jeans, tennis shoes, and a red golf shirt. "By George, I jolly well suppose I'll have to stay at Frank and Judy's then," he says in a British accent. "Do enjoy yourself, dahling."

I don't even have enough breath to comment. By the time we get to the top I'm soaked and nearly wheezing, but I push on. My hair is frizzed out to the max. Reluctantly, I tie it back with the ponytail holder I always keep wrapped around my wrist. Haynes notices, and with an amused smile says, "I love you, Wilda."

Twenty minutes later, we finally see the edge of the Grove. Haynes stops moving when we round the corner, pausing to take it all in. "Would you look at that."

A red, white, and blue tent city is laid out before us, ten acres of American patriotism under a canopy of live oaks, magnolias, and elms. Every inch of earth is crawling with football fans who love to party. Nothing is more fun or more Americana. You could tailgate in the Grove every fall for the rest of your life and never begin to see it all. Each tent is different, some decorated with themes, some fancy, some not, but it's pretty much guaranteed that the food inside any and all of them will be delicious.

We spend the first hour and a half with Frank and Judy. They've been hosting Grove parties for the last twenty years and always have plenty of good food and drink. But as sweet and hospitable as they are, the whole time we're here I keep imagining Lilith's face. And how she'll be wondering where we are. Knowing Haynes only wants to stay for one beer is giving me pre-diarrhea.

TWENTY-FIVE

CALI

When we walk into the Whitmores' tent, at about twelve fifteen, I can feel my eyes practically pop out of their sockets. Seriously, I'm not exaggerating. This place doesn't look a thing like the other tents we've passed. It's...well, besides Ellie and Annie Laurie's room, it's the most incredible thing I've ever seen. The space is *gi*normous and there's even a crystal chandelier. And the food. Oh my gosh, the food. Just the smell of it makes me salivate. Uniformed workers are walking around passing little bites to all of the guests. All of a sudden I'm so hungry I want to run off with one of the trays and eat every single morsel myself.

Mrs. Whitmore, who is wearing an outfit straight from a fashion magazine, is talking with a group of women who are dressed up almost as lovely as she is. She sees us and hurries over.

"Annie Laurie, you look gorgeous. Turn around and let me see your hair." Annie Laurie spins a small circle and I watch Mrs. Whitmore study her daughter's entire body, spending most of the time on her feet. Her tone shifts. "I told you there's a chance of rain today, Annie Laurie. I hope those pretty suede booties make it through."

Annie Laurie simply shrugs.

"Oh well. If you ruin them don't come crying to me." Ellie and I stand there in awkward silence. Just when I feel like it can't get any weirder, Mrs. Whitmore finally acknowledges us. "Hello, girls. Don't you both look nice?" She briefly eyes us up and down.

We smile and tell her thank you.

"You look so pretty, Mrs. Whitmore," I say. "Is that your Alpha Delt pin?"

Reaching up to finger it, she gives me a saucy smile. "Yes indeed. I don't go anywhere on this campus without it." She lowers her voice to a whisper. "I'm a former president."

"My mom told me you were," Ellie says. "That's cool."

"My blood runs true blue. I'm a third generation Alpha Delta Beta. And hopefully Annie Laurie will be the fourth."

Ignoring her mother's comment, Annie Laurie tugs on the front of my dress. "Cali's wearing Ellie's dress. Doesn't it look good on her?"

Now it's me Mrs. Whitmore is studying. Thoroughly. And it makes me feel super uneasy. "It sure does. I saw the rec Mrs. Woodcock wrote for you, Cali." She crosses her arms and a smile builds slowly. "That was very kind of her. I'm sure you've written her a nice thank-you note?"

"Yes, ma'am. I'm very grateful," I say.

"Ever since I read it I've been curious about something. Tell me, what is your given name?"

"Ma'am?"

"Your real name. Surely it's not Cali. It must be short for something?"

I freeze. She's caught me so off-guard. Ellie and Annie Laurie both turn to look at me. Unable to speak, I just shake my head.

"Cali's your *real* name?"

"Yes, ma'am."

Mrs. Whitmore tilts her head curiously like she knows better. "The spelling is sooo... unique. It looks like it was shortened from California." She chuckles. "But what do I know?"

Her smug expression makes me think she does know it's California, but how could she? Unless she knows someone from Blue Mountain who's known my family since I was little. And what are the odds of that?

I'm relieved when she drops the subject and snuggles her daughter. "You girls get some food. I'm sure it will be a big relief after eating all that abhorrent

University food." As we're walking off, she pulls on Annie Laurie's arm. "We'll be leaving here around two thirty. Your daddy does not want to miss kickoff. Okay?"

Annie Laurie yanks her arm free with a scowl. *"Okay."*

Mrs. Whitmore ignores the offense and turns to Ellie. "I've been looking for your parents. I thought they'd be here by now."

"Oh, they were—"

"Lilith. There you are!" A lady with the exact same hairdo as Mrs. Whitmore's—a high ponytail—pulls her away.

"Not too much alcohol, girls," she says while dashing off.

Ellie and I steal a stunned, sidelong glance before Annie Laurie steps between us, looping her arms through ours. "Let's head to the bar."

"Wha— Are you serious?" Ellie asks with shock written all over her face. "Maybe yours doesn't care, but my dad will kill me."

"How will he know?"

"My breath?"

"Hang on," she says, withdrawing her arms. "There's a fix for this." Anne Laurie digs inside the Louis Vuitton cross-body bag she's wearing, and hands Ellie a handful of Altoids. "Works every time."

Ellie slips them in her own bag but adds, "You have no idea how smart my dad is. He'll know."

"They aren't even here."

"Yet."

Thoughts of my scholarship swirl through my mind. And the warning Ellie heard about being extra careful about your behavior until Rush is over. But I keep my mouth shut.

"When my brother was in school," Ellie says, "before he turned twenty-one, my dad caught him drinking at a Grove party and he, like, almost pulled him out of school."

Annie Laurie's nose wrinkles. "Why does he care? The drinking age was eighteen when he was young."

Until now I've had nothing to add to this conversation. I'm not sure why I want to admit this, but I go ahead and say, "I've never even seen my grandparents drink."

Both Annie Laurie and Ellie turn their heads at the exact same time and look at me like I'm from outer space. As if this is the strangest thing anyone's ever said.

"Not once?" Annie Laurie asks.

After a shrug, I shake my head. "Nope."

"Not even a glass of wine?" Ellie adds in a gentle tone.

I shake my head a second time.

Furrowing her brow, Ellie tilts her head to the side. "Is it a church thing?"

"Pretty much."

"That's okay," Ellie says reassuringly.

"Yeah, but…it's still weird." Annie Laurie moves toward the bar, but glances back over her shoulder. "Even Jesus drank wine."

Once Annie Laurie has moved away from earshot, Ellie whispers, "Yeah, and Jesus would tell her she doesn't need any more today."

Ellie and I trail behind as Annie Laurie walks right up to the bar. There are two men serving drinks. "Well hello, Miss Annie Laurie," one of the bartenders says. "Don't you look lovely today?"

"Thank you, Robert," she says with a confident grin.

"What can I get you girls?" Robert's happy expression and the tone of his voice make me feel welcomed.

Annie Laurie glances around at the display of liquor bottles on top of the bar. "I'll have a…a…mimosa." Robert pulls a large cup from the stack, pours a generous amount of champagne, then tops it with orange juice.

He hands it to her, then turns to us. "How about you two ladies? What's your pleasure?"

"I'll have a glass of orange juice, please," I say.

"No champagne with it?" Robert chuckles.

"No, sir. I'm good."

"Oh come *on*," Annie Laurie says, then looks at Robert. "They'll both have a mimosa."

The next thing I know we all have mimosas. With little bar straws. And Colonel Reb stir-sticks. While following behind Annie Laurie to the food table, Ellie rolls her eyes and we share an irritated look. But we get over it quickly when we see the food. The smell of it makes me want to drool.

Working our way around the table the three of us fill our plates with roast beef, eggs, bacon, grits, and fruit.

Once I sit down in one of the cushioned chairs and dig into my meal, I relax. I didn't realize how hungry I was until I took my first bite of thick, crispy, maple-flavored bacon. When I carve into the roast beef and pop a bite in my mouth, it melts, literally melts, on my tongue. It's juicy and pink, and although I was hesitant to try meat this undercooked, the moment I taste it I have to restrain myself from shoveling the rest in my mouth immediately.

Annie Laurie only eats a small portion of hers before putting the tray on the ground underneath her seat. Ellie and I watch as she strolls up to a towering display of oysters, which, personally, I have zero desire to try. Annie Laurie sure does, and fills an entire plate, with cocktail sauce in the middle.

"I should be a horny toad by the time I finish all these," she says, laughing, and almost misses the edge of her chair when she sits back down.

Ellie and I steal looks at each other.

Three oyster shells fall onto her lap and slip between her legs onto the ground. Cocktail sauce has rubbed onto the hem of her romper, so she dabs at it with her napkin. Then her phone beeps. Balancing the plate on both knees, she pulls the phone from her bag, reads the text—hiccups—then types frantically with her thumbs. "Let's go, y'all," she says, jamming her phone back inside her bag.

Covering my mouth with one hand, I thrust my other her way. "Wait, I'm not through yet." My words are garbled from the bite of scrambled eggs I had just taken.

"There'll be plenty more when we get back," she says. "My friend Carter just texted me. He's with two of his pledge brothers. We're supposed to meet them in five minutes."

"Can't they come here?" Ellie asks.

"They've already eaten." Annie Laurie puts the plate of oysters on top of the other plate under her chair, wobbling a bit when she stands up.

I look at Ellie. She looks at me. We know we shouldn't go. What is the hold Annie Laurie has on both of us that we follow our tipsy friend right out the front of the tent anyway?

TWENTY-SIX

WILDA

At twelve thirty, Haynes finally agrees to mosey on over, but we can't move ten feet without running into someone we know. It takes us another thirty minutes just to plow through the crowd. When we see Bill and Becky Barkley, the sweetest couple in the world, I hardly speak to either of them, because by now my anxiety about being late is killing me.

Lilith said their tent was directly across from the Lyceum, next to the road, and impossible to miss. When we finally come upon it, impossible to miss is an understatement. HOTTY TODDY THE WHITMORE WAY is screen printed in large white letters on an oversize navy blue tent, taking up *three* Grove spots. I've heard college boys get paid well to secure spots when the University opens for setup, around midnight, but to get three in a row, in this prime location, has to be a costly challenge.

There is only one way in, at the center of the tent, and when Haynes and I step inside, the smell of bacon, eggs, and sausage makes me feel like we've left the Grove and entered New York's Plaza Hotel for Sunday brunch. A mammoth table with silver-domed chafing dishes is set up beneath a crystal chandelier hanging from the apex of the tent. The flowers on either side of the table look like something out of Versailles. Two gigantic arrangements of white lilies, red roses, and blue hydrangeas are masterfully and artistically displayed in elegant French urns.

In one corner, a black man wearing a white jacket and a chef's hat is behind a prime rib carving station: in the other corner a different chef is flipping made-to-order omelets. In elegant dinner party fashion, three servers—all African American—are strolling around with silver trays, each wearing black pants and white jackets, their first names embroidered in black.

After stopping dead center of the tent, and shifting his neck from side to side, Haynes scratches his jaw and mutters, "Holy God Almighty." He then slides his hands into his pockets and strolls over to the food table.

At the bottom of every domed dish sits a little card with the name of the food item contained within. Each is written in perfect calligraphy. Even though he knows it drives me crazy, Haynes opens and closes every single dish, one at a time, to peer inside. Eggs Benedict, eggs Sardou, and plain scrambled are in the first three. Benton's maple bacon and homemade pork sausage links are next, and Belgian waffles with Vermont maple syrup are in another. Gouda cheese grits and hash browns make up the final two. A tiered fruit display with a carved watermelon cornucopia, spilling over with every kind of fruit one can imagine, is on one end, and a large spread of fresh oysters on the half shell is on the other. Citronella candles are burning on both sides.

"Honey!" he says, moving toward the table. "You told Gage how much I love oysters."

"Will you please *stop it,*" I say in a hushed tone.

Knowing it works every time, he shoots me one of his disarming winks, then slurps an oyster right off the shell.

As luscious and wonderful as this food looks and smells, there is something else more jaw dropping than all the decadent cuisine put together. Hardly anyone is here. Perhaps the size of the tent dwarfs the crowd, but after a quick scan of the guests, I guesstimate only twenty-five people. Frank and Judy must have had sixty. And they only have one Grove spot. What is going on?

We both spot Lilith at the same time. She's on the far side of the tent in front of a massive big-screen TV, in all her glory, wearing a stunning pale blue ensemble, holding court with a small audience of women I don't know. From all the way over here I'm drooling at her outfit and her rail-thin body. Light-weight pants, slim cut, with a matching scooped neck T-shirt that has a thick banding around the bottom of the elbow-length sleeves. A wide taupe leather belt with a large silver buckle ties it all together.

She sees us, waves, and points at the bar. Haynes, waving back, wraps an arm around my waist, then guides me in that direction. A server stops in front of us with a tray of sausage balls, and we each take one, along with a cocktail napkin embossed with the same message as the tent: HOTTY TODDY THE WHITMORE WAY.

Another couple is at the bar, so we step in behind them. Lilith had told me I'd probably know several people, but oddly enough, I don't recognize a soul. And it makes me feel sorry for her. By the massive amount of food they've prepared—well, the food someone else has prepared—it's obvious the Whitmores had planned on a large crowd. What has gone wrong?

Two bartenders are mixing drinks, and it only takes a minute before one politely asks for our order. "Gage Whitmore does not hold back," Haynes says, while scanning the bottles on top of the bar. Ketel One vodka, Woodford bourbon, Glenlivet whisky, Bombay gin, and Schramsberg champagne are displayed off to one side, as well as a large crystal pitcher of Bloody Mary mix with a sign that reads, BIM BAM BEST BLOODIES. Another pitcher containing orange juice has a sign in front of it that reads, FLIM FLAM FRESH SQUEEZED.

"I'll have a Bim Bam Best Bloody, please," I say, my words sounding a bit tongue-tied. "That sounds delicious."

"Yes, ma'am. Comin' right up." He pours, then hands me a large red cup with the Whitmore party slogan imprinted in white.

Haynes orders a Heineken, which incidentally must be concealed in a cup as an ancient law prohibits beer in The Grove. The bartender pushes the beer toward Haynes. "Thank you, sir," my husband says, tapping the top of the bar, and we step aside to let the next person in line place their order.

"I cannot wait to dive my face in that food," I whisper after my first sip. "The smell is killing me."

"Knock yourself out, babe."

"You aren't eating?"

He shakes his head. "I'm full."

"How can you resist?" I deliberately starved myself at Frank and Judy's, knowing what was to come.

I'm beelining it to the table when Gage's voice booms over a loudspeaker. *"Welcome, friends!"*

I turn around and see that he's at the far side of the tent, holding a microphone. It's the way he's dressed that has me startled: a navy blue blazer, white dress shirt, and red tie. Under normal circumstances I wouldn't think twice, but it's ninety degrees outside and a hundred and ten inside this tent. Haynes moves over to me, and we, along with their other guests, give Gage our undivided attention.

"Lilith and I…where's Lilith?" He scans the pitiful crowd. "There you are, darling." He beckons her with a flutter of his fingers. Lilith smiles bashfully, and strolls over to join him. Placing his arm loosely around her waist, Gage holds the mic a few inches under his mouth. "Lilith and I want to welcome you to our first tailgate party. We're tickled you're here…aren't we, darling?"

Once he squeezes Lilith's side, she leans into the mic, her lips brushing the top of the ball. "Sure are. We—" One of those awful microphone squeals stops her mid-sentence, and after making a dreadful face, she backs away. Gage whispers in her ear and she tries again. "We've been excited about this party all summer. It's the first of many to come. So make sure you eat up. Drink up. And Hotty Toddy *the Whitmore Way*," she shouts, and Gage punches the air with his fist.

I start to nudge Haynes, but when I see a quarter-inch vein throbbing in his temple I reconsider.

"Listen up," Gage continues, stealing the mic back from Lilith. "Make sure you come back after the game. Lilith has a victory celebration surprise. We're going to stomp those Terriers into the ground!" Everyone around us whoops and hollers and claps loudly. "Are you *ready*?" Gage yells into the mic.

Every guest—myself included, my husband excluded—replies, "Hell Yes, Damn Right." Then everyone, including Haynes, who is reacting to the sneer I've just flashed him, finishes the fight song. "Hotty Toddy Gosh All Mighty, Who The Hell Are We? Hey, Flim Flam, Bim Bam, Ole Miss By Damn." A round of high fives and cheers follows before the Whitmore guests resume their conversations.

"Alrighty then," I say, turning to Haynes. He simply lifts his forehead, and offers a cool smile.

Someone tugging on my arm causes me to whip around. It's Lilith. "Hey, y'all," she says, all bright and cheery.

I give her a big hug. Haynes only offers a pat on the arm. "What a party," he manages to say. "Thank you for inviting us."

"Oh my gosh, Lilith. This is the most incredible thing I've ever seen. Thank you so much."

"You're welcome, glad you're here. The girls were here a little while ago, but they left to find a better party." She finger quotes "better party" and tightens her lips.

"I was wondering where they were." Haynes glances behind him and then at his watch. "We were supposed to meet them at one."

"You know young girls. Boys always win out over parents." She claps her hands together. "Have you tasted the stuffed figs?"

"Not yet," I say. "We haven't even made it around the food table."

"Rosetta is passing them around. Oh, where is she?" Lilith cranes her neck around the tent. "They are to die for. You've got to try one."

Haynes, who only minutes prior told me he knew absolutely no one, says, "Excuse me, ladies, I spot a buddy of mine," then moseys off.

The second he walks away Lilith jams her hands into her hips. "Have you been to the House?"

I shake my head.

"Be glad you haven't."

"Why?" I try to look her in the eyes, but am distracted by her beautiful jewelry. Floral medallions made of aquamarines and diamonds set in platinum circle her neck. I look up and see matching earrings hanging from her lobes. And she's wearing her Alpha Delt pin again. *My gosh, I haven't worn mine since I graduated. Give it a rest, Lilith.*

"Apparently Carla is away this weekend for some . . . *personal need*. At least that's what I've been told. You'll never guess who's filling in for her."

"Who?"

"The maid." She says it with such disgust I flinch.

Right then a server walks by and offers us a fig. As I stuff one in my mouth my taste buds explode. "Yum. What's in this? Goat cheese?"

Lilith nods. "Wrapped in prosciutto. But back to the House."

Now another server walks up and stands off to the side. I can't help noticing she's twisting her hands together and chewing her bottom lip. Lilith deliberately ignores the poor thing. Trying to help I look at the woman, then back at Lilith, hoping she will at least acknowledge her.

"What is it, Tilly?" Lilith finally asks, with a light stomp.

"Mrs. Whitmore," Tilly replies in a soft voice. "I'm sorry to interrupt, but there's a problem with the generator and the party manager asked me to find you or Mr. Whitmore."

"*Jesus.* I'll be right back, Wilda. In the meantime go indulge yourself. The food is fabulous."

On the way over to the food table I spot the desserts. Football-shaped sugar cookies inscribed with HOTTY TODDY THE WHITMORE WAY, and individually baked brownies and lemon tarts in the shape of Colonel Reb, the outlawed Ole Miss mascot. Before I can lift a plate from the stack of fine china, Haynes taps me on the shoulder. "Ready?"

I turn my head slowly with a murderous glare.

"Just kidding," he says with a playful grin. He relents—how could he not—and gets a plate of his own. Then we mosey around the table, loading up on what looks like the best brunch food we'll ever put in our mouths. There's another server at the end of the table handing out trays and red linen napkins with utensils rolled inside.

The perimeter of the tent is lined with wooden vineyard chairs. We grab two seats near the TV, which is broadcasting the Ole Miss pregame show. Only a few bites into our meal Gage spots us and makes his way over. Haynes stands up, lays his tray on his seat, and shakes Gage's hand. "Man, you sure know how to throw a party." I stand up, too—reluctantly. I so hate a cold egg.

"Thank, you. Thank you. So pleased you could make it."

"Gage," I say, "this food is delicious. I feel like I'm at the Plaza, not the Grove."

He laughs. "Well, it's been quite an undertaking, I must admit. Getting all these moving parts together has certainly been a challenge. But Lilith is the one to thank. She's made it happen." Raising his chin, he gives us a booming laugh. "That wife of mine can make *anything* happen. And God bless the poor soul who tries to stand in her way."

"I remember that well from our college days." I steal a glance at my eggs, which are growing colder by the second.

"Make sure you come back after the game. Lilith's got quite the surprise planned." Leaning toward us he whispers, "She's hired a Motown band."

Out of the corner of my eye I'm watching Haynes. His mouth has stopped moving. I think he has shock-jaw.

"We're taking the big table out to make room for a dance floor. A couple of my boys are bringing it in during halftime."

Haynes tightens the grip on his beer. "I didn't know you had any sons."

With a Bim Bam Best Bloody in one hand and the other shoved inside the pocket of his pants, Gage shoots Haynes an awkward smile. "You know what I mean."

Although Haynes returns a polite grin, I know he's uncomfortable. So am I. From the composed looks on our faces, though, Gage would never know it. As Southerners we hear "microaggressions" like these quite often and ignore them out of… politeness or fear, I don't know what. It doesn't make it right, but we do it. And… we're at their party.

"Have y'all ever heard the Motor City Band?" Gage asks.

Haynes and I shake our heads.

"Lilith and I heard them back in June at a wedding in Jackson, and we knew we had to hire them. You'll be impressed. Might even want them for Ellie's wedding."

"Good God. That better be a long ways off," Haynes says. "What do ya say we pay for college first before we start talking about weddings?"

Gage laughs. "You've got a point there, my friend."

Haynes reaches out for another handshake. "Great party, man. Thanks for having us."

"You're welcome," our host replies, then strolls off, disappearing into the paltry crowd.

Once he's out of sight, Haynes grips the back of my elbow and practically pushes me out of the tent. "Don't ever ask me to come anywhere near this place again." Much to my chagrin, his voice is way louder than it should be.

"But what about my lunch?" As we leave the party—the one I was just sure was the hottest ticket in town—I glance back at my barely touched, cold eggs Sardou.

TWENTY-SEVEN

CALI

When we walk up to the Lyceum, three boys who look like triplets in their navy blue blazers, red ties, and khaki pants—a game day requirement for new fraternity pledges—are huddled together. We introduce ourselves, and although I feel a little weird at first, it only takes a few minutes to feel comfortable around these guys.

Will is super cute, so is Carter, although Ben is a little on the chunky side. Not that I have anything against chunky boys; I'm just being honest. He's sweet, though, and funny. They're all genuinely nice and for the next hour we stroll through the Grove, people-watching. It's fun to be with three fraternity guys. In fact, it actually makes me feel quite popular. Carter and Annie Laurie went to high school together and from what Ellie tells me, Annie Laurie's always liked him.

I get a sense that Will likes me. Several times now he's touched my arm, and he keeps asking if he can get me anything. At one point he steers us all into a random tent, which he declares "beer friendly." "Friends of my parents," he says. All the guys, as well as Annie Laurie, fill their cups from the keg. Ellie and I simply grab cookies.

With one hand carelessly gripping her beer, and the other hooked to

Carter's belt, Annie Laurie narrows her eyes at Ellie and me. "You two are wimps," she says with a giggle. I suppose she thinks she's being funny, and saying it in jest, but actually it's rude. Her words are slurred. I'm wondering how she'll ever make it to the game.

"We aren't wimps," Ellie says. "We're just not jeopardizing the one chance we have at joining a sorority. And you shouldn't either."

"I'm just kidding," Annie Laurie says, with a drunken grin.

A few minutes later, we're in the middle of one of the walking lanes between the tents—headed in the direction of the stadium—when the heel on Annie Laurie's bootie turns under. She falls into a random lady, spilling beer all over her pretty white blouse.

The lady jumps out of the way, looks down at her shirt. *Pissed.* "Watch it," she says harshly, sneering at Annie Laurie. But by now Annie Laurie is too wasted to care. Carter and I reach out to steady her and the other two boys back away.

Ellie *leaps* out of the way, making a disgusted face. "I can't believe this is happening," she says, checking her phone for the time. "We're supposed to meet my parents in fifteen minutes."

"What should we do?" I ask, although the answer is bubbling underneath my tongue.

Ellie's nostrils flare. "*Dammit.*" She combs her fingers through her hair, pushing it back from her forehead. "I'm *so* pissed right now. I knew I shouldn't have come with her, but I did it anyway."

We both look at each other, then at Annie Laurie, whose coloring seems to have changed. It's paler, despite her dark makeup. She doesn't even seem coherent. Her hair is messy and the sleeve of her romper is hanging off her spray-tanned shoulder. Both of her arms are carelessly wrapped around Carter and if not for him, she wouldn't be able to stand. Makeup smears are all over the sleeve of his navy jacket.

"If we take her back to the dorm, we'll be ridiculously late to the game," Ellie says. "I can tell my mom, but I'll have to make up an excuse to my dad. I'm always on time and he knows that. *Shit.*"

"You go on to the game and I'll take her back. Just make up something about why I'll be late." *This is the right thing to do,* I keep telling myself. Even though it's the last thing I want to do.

"No. I'm not gonna do that."

"Why? It's okay," I say, pushing Annie Laurie's sleeve back onto her shoulder.

"No it's not. I don't want my dad thinking you've done something wrong when you haven't."

"We need to do something," Carter says. "She could throw up right here." He backs off slightly, but holds on to Annie Laurie's shoulders to steady her.

"Let me think, let me think." Ellie exhales loudly.

"Take her back to her parents," Ben says, with a goofy face.

Carter shakes his head. "No way."

"I'm only kidding," he says with a laugh.

Will just shrugs.

There's a battle going on in my head. I do not want to take her back. I want to leave her right here and go happily to the game with Ellie. So why am I even considering it? Yeah, I suppose it's the right thing to do, but Annie Laurie's been such a jerk. The battle must have something to do with my mother. All the times I saw her like this, out-of-control-wasted on God knows what, barely able to walk a straight line. Like it or not, I don't have a choice. "Okay. I've made a decision." I look straight at Carter. "Will you help me walk her back?"

He tips his head back, sighs.

"I can't do it myself."

After another long sigh, he glances at the guys, then back at me. "I guess."

"Okay, great. Ellie, you go meet your parents. Tell them Annie Laurie's not feeling well and I walked with her back to the dorm."

"That's not fair. She's my drunk roommate. We'll both go."

"There's no point in both of us missing the first part of the game. Plus, your parents are waiting right now. Carter and I will get her back to Martin, and then I'll text you when I'm at the gate."

"I hate this, Cali." There is genuine concern in Ellie's eyes. I can tell she's fighting her own battle between right and wrong.

"Me, too, but there's no other choice. It's the only way."

"Could y'all take her?" Ellie says to the guys. "Since you're not going to the game."

"Excuse us." Before any of them has a chance to answer I pull Ellie off to the side, just out of earshot. "As nice as these guys seem to be," I tell her, "the truth is we don't know them. I think it's better if I walk with Carter."

Ellie gives me a halfhearted shrug. "You're right. You're so nice, Cali, and she doesn't deserve it."

It always comes back to my mom. I'm too nice. Even when I shouldn't be. *Sweet little Cali. How'd you get to be so nice when your mother treated you like dirt?* "You're sweet to say that, but I think it has more to do with my general distrust of humanity. It's very unhealthy." I laugh nervously.

"You're still nice." She gives me a hug, and we walk back to the group.

"Sorry," I tell them. "We needed a short pow-wow."

Ben puts his hand on his mouth and starts an Indian war whoop, to which Ellie reacts with such an intense eye roll that it looks like her pupils have rolled back inside her head.

"I'll meet you guys back here in thirty minutes," Carter tells Will and Ben.

"See ya around, Cali," Will says.

"Yeah. See ya." I hate telling this cute guy good-bye before we've had a chance to get to know each other. After I give him a look that must indicate how I feel, Carter and I prop Annie Laurie's arms on our shoulders and begin the long walk back to Martin.

"Cali," Ellie shouts. I turn to see her waving her room card. She runs over and slips it into the pocket of my dress.

"You should probably stop by and tell the Whitmores Annie Laurie's sick," I whisper. "They'll be frantic with worry when she doesn't show up for the game."

Ellie squeezes her head in her hands. "This whole thing makes me madder by the second. I hate lying to people. Especially to my dad. He always figures it out."

"I know, but it'll probably save us a lot of grief in the long run."

What should have been a fifteen-minute walk actually takes thirty because of the number of times we've had to stop. I had to hold Annie Laurie's hair back when she threw up in the bushes. Not once but twice. Carter ended up having to carry her the last ten minutes, all the way down the long, awful flight of stairs back to Martin.

I swipe my room card to get us inside the building. Carter's still holding Annie Laurie—like a baby—and I'm holding the door open for them, when, unfortunately, Tara Giles and her mother walk out. My heart sinks down to my toes when I see them. Tara lives closer to the elevator on our floor and we've become pretty good friends. She'll not be all that surprised about Annie Laurie, but it's her mother I'm worried about. She's a Pi Phi advisor.

I do the only thing I can do. I smile and say hello. Tara is friendly—she's always friendly—and her mother gives me a warm grin. I pray she doesn't hold this against me. If only she could smell my breath she'd know. I haven't had a thing to drink all day, except three measly sips of a mimosa back at the Whitmores' Grove party. As we're walking through the lobby I realize I'm anything but inconspicuous. I may as well have a look-at-me sign pinned to my dress. The whole way up on the elevator I keep envisioning Tara's mother's face. I try interpreting her thoughts. But it's futile. And stupid. Besides, there's nothing I can do about it. What's done is done.

Once upstairs, Carter places Annie Laurie on top of her unmade bed and within moments she's fast asleep. Their room is a disaster—half-empty cups all over the place and clothes strewn over the floor. Such a contrast from the first time I saw it.

"I've seen her hammered before, back in high school, but never like this," Carter says.

I can't take my eyes off her. Is it anger? Is it pity? Or even sorrow I'm feeling? I honestly don't know, but whatever it is the emotion is super strong.

Carter's looking at her, too, probably feeling . . . I don't know what the heck he's feeling. "How much has she had? I mean, look at her," he says. "She's, like, passed out."

"I'm not really sure." I look at my phone. "Ellie said she started around nine and it's quarter after three." And kickoff was fifteen minutes ago.

"Has she taken anything else?"

"I have no idea." His question reminds me of her Adderall prescription. I look over my shoulder. "There's a pill bottle over there." I point toward her vanity.

Carter moves over and picks up the bottle, reading the label. I watch him unscrew the cap and empty a few pills into his palm before slipping them inside the pocket of his pants. He looks straight at me. "She'll never miss these."

Then he screws the top back on, places the bottle down where it was. "Thank you, Annie Laurie. You just made me a hundred bucks."

Something inside me stirs. I want to ask him how he'll sell the pills, but I don't.

"So, do you want to walk back with me?" he asks.

I look over at Annie Laurie. She's looks horrible. *Just like my mother.* "I do, but I feel like I need to stay with her."

Carter sighs, stretches his neck from side to side. "Look, Cali, I'd stay with her, but all the pledges have to be at the House before the game ends. We have a big party tonight and we're required to help the band set up. If I'm not there I'm screwed."

I've heard about what happens to fraternity pledges if they mess up. I don't want that for Carter. "It's all good. Really." I'm sure he feels bad that I'm not going to the game now, so we look down at our feet, then out the window, over our shoulders, anywhere but at each other.

Finally he moves toward the door. "I guess I'll see you later. Sorry about all this."

"It's not your fault. Thanks for helping. I'm sure she'll be calling you when she wakes up."

Chuckling, he opens the door. "I'm sure she will. See ya, Cali."

I wave, then watch the door shut behind him. Now everything is oddly quiet. It's never like this in the dorm. No music. No laughter. I can't even hear Annie Laurie breathing. It scares the crap out of me to think she might not be breathing. So I go over and put a finger under her nose. When airflow warms my skin I'm relieved.

Becoming more and more resigned to what I must do, I sit down in the desk chair, the gorgeous, linen-covered desk chair with Annie Laurie's fancy pink monogram on the back. Her pill bottle is right in front of me. I can't take my eyes off it. Or stop picturing Carter's hand shoving the pills inside his pocket. So I pick it up. Rolling it around inside my palm, I hear the tiny pills clinking against the side of the plastic. Something inside urges me to unscrew the top. I could make money, too. Money that I need. Desperately. Carter made it seem so easy. There are plenty left inside. Would she even miss them?

I slam the bottle back down. Am I crazy? Why would I want to risk everything I've worked for? Willing my idiocy away, I dig inside the pocket of my dress for my phone. My thumbs fly across the keys in a text to let Ellie know what's going on, and to tell her I'm afraid to leave Annie Laurie this way.

Right away she texts back: It's okay. I'll think of something to tell my parents. I feel so bad, Cal. I'm sorry you're the one who had to take her home.

Don't worry. Smiley face emoji. I'll be fine. Enjoy the game. See you soon. Three heart emojis. That's my final text.

Annie Laurie's phone is dinging like crazy, but I ignore it.

The TV remote is atop their upholstered coffee table. After searching through what seems like a thousand channels I finally find the game. Sinking into their fancy gray and white sofa, the colors of the gloomy sky out the window, I find comfort as I wrap their furry throw around me and watch my Ole Miss Rebels take down the Wofford Terriers.

TWENTY-EIGHT

WILDA

While Haynes and I were at the Whitmore party, Ellie had texted me to say she and Cali would meet us in front of our regular gate at two thirty, a half hour before kickoff. Ever since she was little, Ellie has loved watching the pregame activity down on the field: the cheerleaders, our superb band—the Pride of the South—and the Rebelettes.

On the way to the stadium, as Haynes and I dodge hundreds of other hurried fans desperate to be seated before kickoff, I can swear I hear someone calling my name. Between the sound of the band playing inside and all the cheering outside it's hard to know for sure. I stop briefly to look around, but don't see anyone, so I catch up with Haynes and we keep striding toward the gate.

"Mrs. Woodcock, Mrs. Woodcock!" I feel a tug on my arm and turn around to see Lizzie, the Recruitment Chair of Alpha Delt. I remember her well from the Rush Workshop. Even though she's a senior, she looks as though she's barely eighteen—her adorable dimples will always be her fountain of youth. The red sundress she's wearing is similar to one of Ellie's. "Hi, Mrs. Woodcock." She's panting like she ran a six-minute mile to catch up with me.

"Well, hi, Lizzie. I thought I heard my name."

"Thank goodness I caught you." She places her hand on her heart, as if she's trying to slow it down. She must be desperate to talk to me.

"I'm glad you did, too. What's going on?"

"Do you have a minute?"

Haynes is in a hurry to meet Ellie and Cali, but I look at him with anxious eyes. "Sure, we have a minute." I place my hand on his shoulder. "This is my husband, by the way. Haynes Woodcock. And this is Lizzie, our wonderful Recruitment Chairman."

Haynes shakes her hand. "Hello, Lizzie, pleasure to meet you."

"Thank you. You, too," she says, then turns right back to me. "I was gonna call you this week, but I'd much rather tell you this in person." A funny expression washes over her face and she winces, tucking her arms into her sides.

"This looks top secret to me," Haynes says. "How about I go on to the gate to meet the girls and let y'all finish this discussion?" He pulls a stack of tickets from his pocket and hands me one.

"Great, see you in a sec." When he walks away, I quickly turn back to Lizzie. The suspense is killing me. "What did you want to tell me?"

Her smile is wavering. "This is, like"—she starts to talk, then stops as if she's struggling to find the right words—"so awkward, to be honest."

I reach over to pat her arm. "It's okay, honey. You can tell me." My mind is already down the road to crazy. *What have I done? What has Ellie done? Did I have poop on my pants in the meeting? What the heck is it?*

"So, at the last Recruitment meeting, when Mrs. Whitmore introduced you, I was a little surprised because . . . well, like, she had never told me you were taking Anne Marie Norton's place. Technically, a Rush Advisor is not supposed to have a daughter in the sorority. Especially not one going out for Rush."

My hand involuntarily shoots up to my mouth, and I gasp loudly. "I had no idea."

"We figured you didn't." Lizzie nervously tucks her hair behind her ears and shifts her feet.

"We'll find someone else to take my place."

"Actually, I spoke about that with our president, Selma James, and the other alums on the board and we all decided to make an exception. It's too late, plus we all think you're awesome. You're so nice and—" She leans over and whispers, "Promise not to tell anyone this?"

With a rapid nod, I try to reassure her.

"We love Ellie. She's gonna get a bid to Alpha Delt."

At least I think that's what she says. A kid walks by and blows one of those ear-splitting noisemakers not five feet from us. Covering my ears, I lean in closer. "Did you just say Ellie would get a bid?"

"I'm ninety-nine point nine percent positive."

"I'm so relieved." I lightly clap my hands together, beyond happy to know the other girls like Ellie.

"I'm sure you are." She reaches out, touches me on the shoulder. "I'd never tell you that in normal circumstances. So please, please keep it on the down low?"

I give her the Alpha Delt secret-swear—four fingers across my heart.

Lizzie smiles, gives it back. "The whole thing has been awkward this year because, technically, Mrs. Whitmore is, like, not supposed to be in Rush meetings." Her voice speeds up as she's talking. "She's the House Corp President, and that's great, but Recruitment is not her job. We keep wondering if she knows all this, but keeps doing it anyway, or if she just doesn't understand the rules."

Holding my palms up, I say, "I'm not sure either, but we should probably give her the benefit of the doubt. Things have changed a lot since we were in school."

With heels lifting off the ground, she clasps her cheeks. "I know! And this is her first year as House Corp President. Maybe she thinks Recruitment is still part of her job?" She stares at me with pleading eyes, like she wants me to break all this to Lilith.

"Are you wanting *me* to explain that to her?"

"Would you?" Her eyes bug out and she puts her hands together, like she's praying.

"No! I mean, maybe. I'd have to think about it, Lizzie. Lilith is over the moon about her position. I don't know what I'd say."

"None of us know what to say, either. It's been, like, *so weird* and caused some intense issues in the House."

I'm not surprised by any of this. Lilith's performance in the Rush meeting I attended was certainly awkward. But what about the other Alpha Delt advisors—Sallie and Gwen—surely one of them can break the news? They've been on the board longer than I have.

Lizzie looks down at an empty cup on the ground. After squatting to pick it up, she peers at me with a pained expression. "Please think about breaking the news to Mrs. Whitmore. We all feel like you'd be the best one to do it. Since your daughters room together."

I groan, press my fingers to my temples. I can see her point—but if she only knew. "I guess I'll do it," I finally say, and a hot flash instantaneously creeps up my back. I may as well be inside a kiln. I'm that hot. Thousands of people are rushing past and I've just agreed to tell Lilith Whitmore she can no longer attend Rush meetings. Now my entire face is wet.

Lizzie doesn't seem to notice. *"Thank you."* She presses a palm to her heart, lets out a small moan. "Thank you *so* much. It's been, like, *so* weird."

Yeah. It may have been weird for you, I'm thinking, *but what about me?* To think I have to be the one to break this news to Lilith is nothing short of getting a diagnosis of Fish Odor Syndrome. How in the heck does someone ever handle that?

Ten full minutes later, when I finally make it to the gate, I spot Haynes standing with Ellie. Picking up my pace I race over to where they are, and nearly slip on someone's spilled beer. Haynes reaches out to steady me then guides us into the line. "Where's Cali?" I ask, looking around at the people near us.

"Annie Laurie's sick," Ellie says. "She volunteered to walk her back to the dorm. She'll be here soon."

"What a sweet girl," I say. For some reason Haynes doesn't comment.

Ellie moves ahead, and as we walk through the security check Haynes whispers in my ear. "I smell a rat."

"Honestly, honey," I say, in a soft voice, while the security person checks my bag, "Cali is a really nice girl. You have to trust me on this."

Haynes, ever the lawyer, turns his head, looks me straight in the eye. "She's not the one stinking up the lab."

TWENTY-NINE

MISS PEARL

Sunday evenings in the House are always mellow, as most of the girls are either studying or watching TV. I'm happy for the peace and quiet and it sure feels good to get off my feet. The only thing better would be to have them soaking in a hot tub with sweet-smelling bath salts. But Mama Carla should be walking in this door any minute now, and I have a suspicion she'll be dog-tired. Driving all that way after a stressful weekend would do anybody in. That's why I made sure to leave her apartment cleaner than I found it.

I'm trying to read *The Triumph*, the Alpha Delta Beta bi-annual magazine—its title based on the ADB motto: Triumph Over Adversity. But with every page I turn I can't stop thinking about what happened yesterday. It was bad enough that Miss Lilith wasn't happy about me taking Mama Carla's place, but add Kadeesha's stinky attitude into the mix, and, well, I'm still angry. There I was doing a fine job as housemother and Kadeesha tries ruining it for me.

If truth be told, it's made me wonder why I ever decided to work at a sorority house in the first place. I love our girls, don't get me wrong, but it's hard. Hard to be a surrogate mother instead of a real one. The Alpha Delt girls are a daily reminder of the decision I made all those years ago and every now and then it about chokes the life out of me. How was I to know I would never give birth again? Plenty of unwed mothers put their babies up for adoption hoping it won't be their only chance at motherhood.

Is my daughter's adoptive mother good to her? What about her father? How about college? Did she graduate? And what about the man in her life? Is she married now, with children of her own? Once again that voice inside my head gets going. It speaks loud and clear, the way it always does, reminding me of who it was that made the selfish choice in the first place to give up my own flesh and blood. I have nobody to blame but me.

At a quarter past ten, I look up from reading and here comes Mama Carla, dragging herself inside with Trudy trotting at her heels. I hop up, help her with her bag, and she and Trudy both plop down in the other chair. No "How are you," or even a simple, "Hello, Pearl." The first words out of her mouth are: "Philip left her."

"Tell me that's not true, Mama Carla."

"It's true." She lets her head collapse back into the chair and closes her eyes. "I was hoping that wouldn't be the case. You and I both know how hard it is to go through divorce."

"Sure do." I put the magazine down on the coffee table and give her my undivided attention.

"It's nasty and it keeps the children in a constant state of upheaval."

"That it does. Any chance of reconciliation?" I ask.

"It doesn't look like it."

"I am so sorry, Mama Carla."

"Somehow she'll get through it."

"Yes, she will. We both know how that works." I yawn, cover my mouth. "Excuse me."

Mama Carla yawns, too, laughs. "I bet you're as tired as I am. How did it go here?"

"It went well," I tell her.

"No hiccups?"

"Nothing I couldn't handle." A part of me wants to get her opinion on the big hiccup that happened here yesterday, but I don't want to worry her. Not tonight.

"You must be ready to get in your own bed."

"I might be spoiled by yours. It sure is comfortable. I felt like I was queen for the weekend."

She chuckles softly, gets a sparkle in her eye. "Would you be open to doing it again sometime?"

"Of course." Despite the brouhaha with Miss Lilith, the thought of this still makes me happy. Like I told Kadeesha, progress.

"Pardon me," she says, talking through another yawn. "I'm afraid I lost too much sleep this weekend."

I figure that's my cue to head on home, so I stand up. "Something struck me as funny while I was lying in your bed, Mama Carla. Before last night, I'd never spent one night in this House."

"Never?"

"No, ma'am. After all these years." I gather up my pocketbook and overnight case. "By the way, there are clean sheets on your bed."

"Oh, for goodness' sake, Pearl, you didn't need to do that."

"Yes, I did. I knew you'd be too tired to do it yourself."

"Well, thank you. You're a dear. On the way in I noticed the House looks spotless. Did Kadeesha behave herself?"

"That's another story. We can talk about it tomorrow." We both chuckle, too tired to say much more. "Oh, I almost forgot. Miss Lilith asked me to have you call her soon as you get back." I search her face, looking for her reaction. I'm not going to give her a blow by blow, but I feel as if I have to at least pass on the request. If not it could borrow trouble for Mama Carla.

She puts a finger to her chin. "Did she, now?"

"Yes, ma'am." I cut my eyes at her. She knows we're both thinking the same thing. "Soon as she saw it was me taking your place."

She leans her head back, shuts her eyes. "Well. Whatever *Miss Lilith* needs will have to wait until tomorrow. Good night, my dear."

"Good night, Mama Carla. Get some rest."

Our pudgy-faced security guard stops me as soon as I walk out of her apartment. "Finally going home, Miss Pearl?" he says, sweet as he can be.

"Yes, Oliver, I sure am."

"Want me to walk you to your car?"

"No, thank you, baby. I'll be just fine. But you're mighty sweet to ask." I've trekked to the parking lot a thousand times by myself. And I imagine I'll be doing it plenty more.

It's quiet in the kitchen when I walk through to the back door. The only sound is the soft hum from the icemaker. When I push the door to and lock it from the outside I feel a deep sense of pride in how I've spent the last sixty-two hours. A soft rain is falling; Lord knows we need it. I start toward the parking lot, but something makes me turn around. I look up at the second story. The upstairs study room is brightly lit and through the blinds I can see some of the girls' silhouettes bending over their books. A thought comes to mind. Something I can see as clearly as Paul saw Jesus on that road to Damascus. I haven't thought about it much in a few years. But now I believe the timing is just right.

THIRTY

WILDA

The second I woke up, Monday morning after the game, Lilith Whit-more's face popped into my mind's eye. Four months ago she was a tiny head on an old composite in my attic. Now she's occupying more space in my worry room than I ever knew I had. I've been practicing what I'll say to her over and over again and by now, ten A.M., I'm about to have a nervous break-down. I've been on the toilet all morning.

In my mind, I get as far as: Hi Lilith, this is Wilda, how are you today? Nice weather we're having, huh? Then I hear her say: Actually it's the hottest September on record. Did you really call to talk about the weather or is there something else on your mind? Spit it out, Wilda, I don't have all day. Or even: Wilda, I'm glad you called. There are a few things about Rush we need to discuss. Particularly that Cali Watkins. I saw the rec you sent in for her and heard you and Haynes invited her to the game. Do you honestly think she's Alpha Delt material?

Define Alpha Delt material for me, would you please, Lilith? Because a daughter who is falling down drunk in the Grove does not seem to be in line with your definition. Ellie made me swear not to tell Haynes but, apparently,

Annie Laurie had to be carried back to the dorm. And that sweet Cali Watkins sacrificed her seat at the game to take care of her. Ellie also told me that Lilith was not very friendly to Cali at the Grove party. The irony of that is astonishing.

On the way home from the game I told Haynes about my talk with Lizzie. He thought it was hilarious. I told him that there was nothing in the least bit funny about me telling Lilith Whitmore she can no longer attend Rush meetings and that he was no help at all. He reminded me how few people were at the party, and said I shouldn't be in the least bit afraid of her. After nearly thirty-five years of marriage, wouldn't you think he'd know me a little better than that?

Now I'm staring at her contact on the phone in my hand, her picture in the tiny round circle above her name—like the composite in my attic. Poor Daisy hasn't been fed yet and my house is in desperate need of a scrub-down. I'm walking around in circles wondering what to do first. Instead of punching in her number I put the phone down and clean our toilets. Then I vacuum our entire downstairs like I'm OCD.

When the phone rings, thirty minutes later, I'm as jumpy as a dang flea. I creep over and peek at the name. *Mama*. Reluctantly, I push talk. It's been awhile. "How's it going, Mama?"

"Not well. We have a problem." *We* is the key word here. With every passing day I'm more and more jealous of Mary living in Dallas.

"What's wrong now, Mama?"

"If Hugh Freeze thinks that defense will carry us through till the end of the season he's got anothah thing coming." My mother doesn't know the first thing about football.

"We won thirty-eight to thirteen," I say.

When she snickers and clicks her tongue my entire body cringes. I can feel my face contorting like I've just gotten a whiff of spoiled milk. A throwback to childhood.

"Against the Wofford Terriers. Freeze better do something if he hopes to have a sliver of a chance against the Tide. The talk is he's going to be let go."

"The talk from whom, Mama?"

She pauses long enough for me to realize she's made the whole thing up. "I don't know, Wilda, I've heard it in passing."

I switch the phone to speaker mode and set it down on the kitchen counter. When I come back from the laundry room she's still talking. "And then I called both Coopah and Jackson and they agree with me. Hugh Freeze is in big trouble." I know she has embellished this way out of proportion, but there is no point in challenging her. I just let her talk. "But enough of Ole Miss football. How is Ellie?"

"Fine. We took her to the game. She's Miss Ole Miss. Couldn't be happier."

"Well. That makes me happy to hear. How is her roommate?"

Mention of Annie Laurie gets me thinking about Lilith all over again, and I feel that familiar pit constricting my stomach. I'm just about to confide in Mama about Lilith when, thankfully, my better sense takes over. "She's fine, too."

"I am delighted the Whitmoahs are in your life. They are such a fine family. What luck their daughtah needed a roommate and chose Ellie."

Hearing her choice of words, "chose Ellie," does me in. "I better go, Mama, I've got a ton to do today."

"Well," she says, completely ignoring me. "How's the job search going?"

"I told you. I can't take a job until after Rush is over."

She never responds. Just rolls right onto something else. "It's a shame neither of my grandsons are married. I'd certainly like to see my first great-grandchild before I die."

Now my head is pounding. Between Mama and my impending phone call with Lilith, I might combust. This calls for drastic measures. "Mama? Mama? Are you there?"

"Yes. I'm heah."

"Shoot, I must have lost you. If you can hear me I'll call you later. My tub is overflowing. Have a great day."

I push the red end-call button and I'm free.

For now.

I'm convinced a good hot soak in the tub will calm my nerves. But when I get out twenty minutes later, panic returns and I find myself once again staring at the phone in my hand. It's getting impossible to come up with more stall tactics so I go ahead and take a deep, *deep* breath and punch in her number.

Lilith answers on the first ring, without a hello. "Hey, stranger, we were hoping y'all would come back for the band."

"I know. I really wanted to, but Haynes wasn't feeling well. I had to drive the whole way back." Little Southern white lies numbers one and two.

"I'm sorry to hear that," she says. "Please tell him Gage and I hope he feels better."

"I sure will."

"By the way, I never got to finish telling you about the maid."

"Rosetta?"

"No. The Alpha Delt maid," she says.

"Pearl?"

"Yes, Pearl. Anyway, *she* was filling in for Carla last weekend."

"Aw. She's so sweet. I met her when I was there for the Rush meeting."

"Sweet, yes, I'll give her that. But a House Director she is not. When she told me she was Carla's fill-in I nearly died. We're the finest sorority on campus. What is this world coming to?"

Oh my God. Did she honestly say that? "You know we have an African American active member now. Right?"

"Don't remind me."

I'm hideously uncomfortable. All I want to do is hang up the phone, but there's still so much to talk about. I'm beginning to wonder why in the world I took the advisor position and, more importantly, why I ever encouraged our daughter to be a part of this.

I pause. A little too long.

"Wilda?"

"I'm here."

"I thought I lost you."

"No, I'm still here." I breathe deeply. It's now or never. "Lilith. The funniest thing happened on the way to the stadium. Right after we left your tent."

"Oh?"

"Yeah. I ran into Lizzie Jennings. The Rush Chairman for Alpha Delt?"

"I know Lizzie. Very well, in fact. She's doing a great job."

"I think so, too. I was very impressed with her at that Rush meeting I attended, and how she kept it moving forward. Things sure seem to run more smoothly than when we were in school. Don't you think?"

"I'm not so sure about that. But I suppose they run a fairly tight ship. Now, as you were saying?"

"Well, funniest thing. It seems there's been a mistake." I'm balled up in the corner of the couch with my thumb in my mouth.

"What kind of mistake?" she asks in a cool tone.

"This is not coming from me—as you know I don't know all that much about Alpha Delt."

"*Wilda*. I can tell something's wrong. Please tell me what it is."

"Lizzie asked me to tell you . . ."

"Tell me what?"

"The House Corp President is not supposed to be handling anything that has to do with Rush."

My voice is practically shaking. And it only makes things worse when a deafening silence on her end follows—dead, dead air.

Now I'm terrified. "I told her I was sure you didn't know and you were only—"

"You're exactly right. I had no idea," she says in a surprisingly calm, kind voice. Relief is oozing from my adrenal glands when she adds, "I'm glad you told me. I'm going to hang up right now and call Lizzie. I need to thank her for telling you, reassure her all is well, and let her know she has nothing to worry about."

To think all the gray hairs I added to my worrywart head in the last thirty-six hours was all for naught. "You're not upset?"

"Upset? Heavens no. Why would I be upset?"

"I . . . I was afraid it might hurt your feelings."

"Wilda. You need counseling, girlfriend," she says in a somewhat jovial tone. "If that's all it would take to hurt your feelings, I suggest you find a good therapist."

THIRTY-ONE

MISS PEARL

It's here. Rush. The biggest week of the entire year. Most days I'll clock in at five forty-five and won't leave till one the next morning. By the time the week runs out, this forty-four-year-old girl will be completely outta gas. The *only* thing positive about working that many hours is the number I'll see on my check. It's one of two weeks out of the year I get overtime pay, and it can't come at a better time. My tires are still bald.

There are traces of October in the air when I park my car. My sweater is in the back seat so I reach behind me and slip it on. By the time I walk all the way to the House I'm five minutes late. Mama Carla is rambling around the kitchen when I clock in. She's got an order sheet in one hand and a pencil in the other. I'm surprised to see her.

After placing my card back in the slot, I mosey toward her. "Why in the world are you up working so early?"

She's still in her bathrobe, has last night's makeup on her face, and her hair is a big mess. "Lordy, Pearl. I've been up all night."

"Uh-oh. What's happened now?"

She sucks in a deep breath then expels it slowly. "Sometime in the wee hours of the morning, one of your *babies* took the liberty of propping the side door open. When her boyfriend snuck inside the stairwell, drunk as Cooter Brown, he fell all the way to the bottom, splitting his head wide open."

I gasp.

"She found him unconscious, so she had to call an ambulance, which, naturally, woke not only me, but the rest of the house."

"Mercy me. He is okay?"

"He's fine. A little embarrassed, but physically he's fine."

"Whose boyfriend?"

"Do you really want to know?" She leans on the wall for support. "She's one of your favorites."

"I don't guess. I'm the maid, not the housemother." We both chuckle.

"You should have seen our poor security guard, bless his heart."

"What did Oliver do now?"

"When he heard the commotion, he banged on my door first. Then, as we walked through the house, he had both hands on his gun." She stretches her arms out to demonstrate. "He ducked around every corner, like he was a cop on *CSI*."

I can't help but laugh. "Bless his heart. He's our own Barney Fife."

She chuckles, shakes her head. "Needless to say, I've been up ever since."

"I was up late myself."

"What called you to the witching hour? Something fun I hope."

"I wish. Nothing bewitching about last night for me. I was right here. Till eight."

"Don't tell me; let me guess. You were rescuing another pair of thong panties from the agitator in the washing machine?"

"That was last week."

"Hang on. Give me another try. You were teaching someone how to make instant oatmeal."

"Hush now, Mama Carla. That's my baby you're talking about."

She puts a hand on her hip. "I give up. What were you doing?"

"Cleaning upchuck." I lift my hand to stop her from getting the wrong idea. "But it wasn't from drinking."

She throws her hands up. "Thank God for small favors. What happened?"

"Well, I'll tell you."

After I left work, about five o'clock, I was headed out toward Handy

Andy's for a barbeque. Shirley and I were on the telephone, talking about her new boyfriend. I was only fifteen minutes from home when someone with an unknown Memphis number started blowing up my phone. I ignored the beeping the first time, and the second, but when I heard it a third time I told Shirley I had to go. When I switched over, I'm sure there was a plenty of annoyance in my hello.

"Miss Pearl?" I heard someone say.

There was a mama on the other end of the line. So I put a little more nice in my voice. "Yes, ma'am."

"This is Kathy Peabody calling you from Memphis. I hate to bother you at nighttime. Do you have a minute?"

"I'm driving home from work, Miss Kathy, how can I help you?"

"Sara Beth is sick. Really sick, I think. She's in her room at the House and doesn't have any of the right meds. She's been throwing up since two o'clock this afternoon."

"Oh no."

"None of her girlfriends want to go near her for fear they'll get it, so she's isolated. My husband called her in a prescription for nausea. It's ready at Walgreens. I'm happy to pay you extra if you could pick it up for her."

As enticing as the extra cash sounded, I sure didn't want to go backward. *Remember your tires, Pearl.* I turned into a driveway and was headed back to Oxford before I could talk myself out of it. "I can do that for you," I said. "Is there anything else she needs?"

"A Sprite would be good. And some ice in a bucket. And maybe a wet rag for her face. Oh and how about some trash bags? She says the bathroom is so far down the hall she's been throwing up in her room. She's afraid she'll throw up on the rug if she makes a run for it." I had a clear picture of that in my head. And I knew exactly who would be cleaning it up. "You can get everything at Walgreens," she said.

As tired as I was, I couldn't remember going through the last red light. "Okay, Miss Kathy, I've turned around and I'm headed to Walgreens."

"I'm writing you out a check now. If you'll give me your address I'll mail it to you in the morning." After I gave her my address, she thanked me a hundred times and we ended the call.

I lean into Mama Carla. "After cleaning up a nasty mess, and making sure Sara Beth was doing okay, it was eight o'clock when I left here."

"I hope you don't get it." She backs away with a smile.

"I've learned my lesson. I wore a mask and gloves."

"What would these mamas do without you, Pearl?"

"They'd find someone else, I suppose."

"I have my doubts. On that note, I think I need a nap if I expect to make it through the day." She sighs deeply then hands me her clipboard. "Would you mind finishing this order for me, please?"

"Of course. You go ahead and lie down."

"Thank you, dear. I'm not feeling too well. I've got a lot on my mind. Plus we have a big week ahead."

"Sure do. Try to get some rest. I'll see you when you wake up."

To make room for all the girls coming through Rush, Mr. Marvelle and I used to have to break down all thirty of our dining tables and tote them clear down to the basement. Had to take most of the chairs down there, too. This year, praise the Lord, Mama Carla has hired a moving company to pick them up, store them, and bring them back once Rush is over. My back has been thanking her ever since she told me.

Right before nine, Mr. Marvelle and I are toting all of the glasses we use for water parties up from the basement when Sarah Mason sprints down the front hall in front of us.

"Woo, where you headed in such a hurry?" I ask her. I can barely see over the top of my box, but I know it's her by her pretty legs.

"To the Union. Did I tell you I'm a Gamma Chi this year?" she says over her shoulder.

"That's right. Sure did."

"We're handing out Greek Day T-shirts to all the rushees. My shift starts in ten minutes."

"Have fun, baby."

"I will," she hollers back, before dashing out the front door. Gamma Chis, the term Ole Miss uses for Greek Counselors, play an important role during

Rush. Once the rushees get divided into groups, the Gamma Chis escort them to all the Rush parties and give advice, even comfort the girls if they happen to be cut.

Seeing Sarah gets me wondering about her parents' divorce. And what it feels like to be in her situation. Trying to hold it together when she's supposed to be enjoying the best years of her life. Sarah is kind and good, exactly the type of girl I would want my daughter to be like, and yet she's dealing with terrible heartache. Heartache she didn't bring upon herself and certainly never asked for. It makes me wonder about Autumn's parents. Are they still together? Do they love each other? I gave my baby that name close to ten years ago. She was born the first day of autumn, and I, well, I suppose I just needed to name her.

After putting the last box of glasses in the kitchen I head to my closet for window cleaner and a roll of paper towels. Then I head over to the composites on the ground floor. I always start on the one closest to the foyer. Two thousand fifteen. With each swipe I focus on one picture of one girl, think about what she meant to me, then move on to another. Twenty-five years of knowing and missing these girls often brings a tear to my eye. Some of them, well, many of them, come back to see me when they're in town. But there's plenty I've lost contact with completely. Occasionally, I wipe the face of one who never wanted to know me. But that's life. I don't let it get me down.

I'm so lost in thought I don't notice Mama Carla's head poking out of her apartment door. Before God, it looks like there is no body attached to that little blond head. *"Aaahhhh!"* I scream, like I've just seen a spirit in a graveyard, and throw my rag way up in the air. My heart jumps into overdrive and beats so fast I have to lean against the wall to get ahold of myself. "Mama Carla! You liked to scared me to death." Before long I get to laughing so hard I can hardly catch my breath.

"Pearl. When you're done, may I have a word with you, please?"

Her reaction takes me by surprise. Normally she would have laughed along with me. I have never heard her use such language. Or that tone. It's as sharp as one of Fee's kitchen knives. This morning, before her nap, she was joking with me. Seemed to be in a great mood. What in the world has changed?

"Of course. Let me finish this composite. Be there in a minute."

After I'm done, I lay my supplies down on the floor in front of the next

picture and rap on her door, even though it's standing wide open. She's rifling through papers lying on the table next to her and looks up when she
hears me.

"Come on in. I'm looking for an EOB I got in the mail the other day. I can't
seem to find it."

"EOB?"

"Explanation of Benefits. From the insurance company?" She looks confused, like I should know what she's talking about, then taps her forehead. "Of
course you don't know. It's a statement the insurance company sends out after
a doctor's appointment. It gives your portion of the bill."

I smile at her. Not her fault the rest of us don't have health insurance.

"Pearl, I want you to be the first to know something. Sit down, why don't
you." She points to the empty chair. Her tone has changed. And it fright-
ens me.

I take a seat, feel the hair on the back of my neck rise.

"It's terrible timing with Rush this week, but I suppose there's never a good
time for sad news."

My heart stops. The medical bill she had in her hand. Her tone of voice.
"Please don't tell me you have cancer."

"No, no no. It's not anything that bad, thank the Lord." She swallows and
chooses her words carefully. "I may as well just say it. I've decided to leave
the Alpha Delt House."

I'm not completely shocked by this news. She had mentioned she might
not be able to keep doing her job if things with Patrice got worse, but the reality of her leaving is flooding my heart with all kinds of emotions. Not only
will I miss her terribly, but the mere thought of the transition is horrid.

The House Director we had before Mama Carla was nothing to get excited
about. It's not that she was unlikable, just boring—no personality. Nothing
like Mama Carla. And the one before her—now, *she* was a living nightmare.
Some of my friends who work at other Houses have told me more heinous
House Director stories, and as much time as I spend engaging with the House
Director, this gives me reason to sink down further into the chair. "I bet
you're fixin' to tell me you're moving down to Ocean Springs."

Her bashful smile lets me know I'm right. "In the house with Patrice and
the kids. She's overwhelmed, Pearl. Sad all the time, and my grandchildren

are acting out. Looks like they've got a messy divorce and custody battle ahead. I don't want her losing them because she's a stressed-out wreck. I'm afraid she needs me there a lot more than y'all need me here."

I can feel my body shrinking. And my heart squeezing shut. "When are you leaving, Mama Carla?"

"As soon as the board can find a replacement. I wish I could stay till the end of the year, but I'm afraid that's not possible. I'm hoping to leave by Thanksgiving."

"That soon?"

She lets out a sigh. "I suppose I could stay a little longer if it takes awhile to find the right person, but as soon as possible."

I have no words.

"Do me a favor and keep this to yourself. I'll tell the rest of the staff after I've let Lilith Whitmore know."

"Of course," I force myself to say, but all I can think about is whom they might get to replace Mama Carla, and with Miss Lilith at the helm it will certainly not be me. The thought of that leaves me with only one option. "If you're leaving then I'm leaving, too."

She uncrosses her legs, sits up straight. "No. Pearl. That's the last thing I want to happen. Please don't quit."

"A few weeks ago, when I was leaving here, you know the night you got back from Ocean Springs?"

A nod lets me know I've got her attention.

"Something hit me clear as day when I was leaving out the back door."

"What was that?"

"I looked up at the study room, at all the girls doing their homework. Right then and there I knew it was time to get my butt back to school. And once and for all, finish the degree I started all those years ago."

Mama Carla leans toward me with her hands on her thighs. "Pearl. That's the best thing I've heard you say in a long time."

"I know it's what I'm supposed to do."

"Have you registered yet?"

"No. I'd never be able to afford Ole Miss tuition, so I've decided to apply to Rust College in Holly Springs." When I graduated from Oxford High School, I had a full scholarship to Ole Miss, but had to give it up after my first year. Mama Carla only knows I dropped out of school. What she doesn't know is why. She's never asked and I've never told her.

I had worked hard to earn my scholarship. Finally there would be a woman in our family to break the legacy of career housekeepers and graduate from college. Yet one fateful choice reversed my plan. Once I gave up my daughter, I could no longer concentrate on my studies. My grades suffered and my scholarship was lost.

"Rust is a fine school. Can you get financial aid?"

"I looked into it when I got home the other night. I can get a partial scholarship, so I've been thinking I might get a job in Holly Springs, long as I'm driving all that way. Who knows, I may even move there. Might be able to find a better deal on rent." Rust College is forty-five minutes away from Oxford.

Mama Carla doesn't say anything for the longest time, but I can tell her brain is spinning. She does that sometimes when she's searching for the best answer. After a long minute she says, "May I offer you my opinion?"

"Why, sure." I relish any advice Mama Carla has to offer.

"I think you should cut back your hours a little bit here while you're working on your degree. The girls would love to have you up in the study room with them. Or find your own nook somewhere else. This House is certainly big enough."

"But you won't be here. Maybe the new housemama won't feel the way you do."

"Once she gets to know you, and how you hold this ship together, she'll be eating out of your hand."

"What you're saying sounds good, but … I'm hardly making it as it is, Mama Carla. I'm not sure I'll be able to cut back. That's why I'm thinking of moving down to Holly Springs."

"It's a conundrum. I can see that. Let me think on it and get back with you."

I feel fatigue setting into my body and it's only eight thirty. "Let me get back to work, then," I say, slowly rising from the chair. "Why folks feel like they have to touch the composite every time they see someone they know is beyond me. But it happens every day."

"You do know everything there is to know about this place."

"I know more than you think I know."

"Like what?" she asks with a mischievous grin, rising from her chair.

"Some of the Alpha Delt secrets. I know the handshake and that secret swear. But don't tell it. I would never want to get anybody in trouble."

Touching her heart with four fingers she winks. "I wouldn't dare."

"You know the secret swear, too?" I say from the doorway.

Her eyes crinkle at the corners. "I have my own sources."

We both laugh. Then I walk out the door.

I'm already past the staircase when Mama Carla calls my name. I turn around to see her waving me back. "I had a thought," she hollers, so I move toward her. When there's not but a foot or two between us she glances behind her, then side to side. "What about you?"

"What about me?"

"Why don't you apply for my job?"

I glance around the foyer to make sure she's not talking to someone else. "Are you listening to yourself, Mama Carla? Me, a black woman, housemother of a lily-white sorority house? You have lost your mind." I don't want to tell her that I'd thought about it when I woke up in her bed a few weeks ago. After the way Miss Lilith acted, I put a heavy pipe in front of that dream.

"I most certainly have not. You did a great job when you filled in for me. Besides, you've been working here far longer than I have, and you're smart as a whip. You have a year of college under your belt and you're going back to get your degree. Of course you should apply for the job."

"Unh-uh. It would never happen."

"Just give it some thought. You'd have health insurance. A lovely, paid-for apartment. A nice salary, plus a paid vacation all summer. And you could study at night. In fact, you could take online courses. That's become common among working professionals."

The more she talks the better it sounds. Until Miss Lilith's hateful mug pops into my mind. "Even if I were to consider it, what do you think Mrs. Lilith Whitmore would have to say? After the powder room incident?" I had told her all about it the day after she got back from Ocean Springs.

"Pooh. I filled her in on Kadeesha's ways. She knows it wasn't your fault."

"Maybe, but that's not the only issue. I heard the talk when I filled in. You know she, and a few others for that matter, were not happy."

"I'll admit Lilith Whitmore has high standards for Alpha Delt. But, she'll have to agree you are every bit as qualified as I am. No one knows more about the inner workings of this House than you do; I'm a novice by comparison. I, for one, would love to see you get the job, and I'm sure the girls would, too."

"I do know every inch of this place. And I should after working here all these years."

"Give it some thought."

I let her words marinate a few extra moments. "I might just do that."

THIRTY-TWO

MISS PEARL

Even though I promised Mama Carla I wouldn't mention it to anybody, I run straight into the kitchen to tell Fee. I have to tell somebody before these nerves of mine jump out of every pore on my body. She'll keep it to herself. I know that. Whenever Aunt Fee gets top secret information she locks it up like she's storing it in a vault.

She's up to her elbows in flour. It's down the front of her bosom, on her white apron, and in her hair, too. I see chicken, eggs, butter, and milk right next to where she's working. Helen's pulling chicken off the bone and Latonya is a few feet away, chopping onion, parsley, and celery. I know what's on tonight's menu. Chicken and dumplings.

"Aunt Fee," I call from the side of the stove. "May I talk to you a minute?"

"Lemme get my hands out of this mess, and I'll be with you in a minute, baby."

"I'm in no big hurry," I tell her. "Take your time."

"Looks like you in a hurry to me," says Kadeesha, who is standing in front of the dishwashing station with her hands in a sink full of dishwater. The front part of her hair is poking out of her hairnet. "You came running in here like you had a big story to tell. Like you know something nobody else know."

That fool woman tries to pick a fight with anyone who will let her. I want to give her a piece of my mind, but instead I angrily—but calmly—say, "I run because I need the exercise, Kadeesha." Then I just stare at her.

"Kadeesha," Auntie hollers, "you finished washin' my utensils yet? I am two minutes away from needin' everything Helen and Latonya are choppin'. That means I need my utensils. You don't need to be concernin' yourself with whether Pearl run or she walk. You need to keep your own mind on your own business. You hear me?"

Kadeesha shuts up then. But I see her eyeing me, narrow slits following me around the room. Somebody needs to tell her there is nothing pretty about her face with that ol' ugly scowl spread clear across the front.

"And cover your whole head. I ain't gone tell you that again."

"I'll be in the pantry helping Mr. Marvelle when you're ready," I say to her, sliding over to where he's working. Then the two of us finish emptying the morning's delivery onto the pantry shelves.

Ten minutes later Aunt Fee walks by, and motions for me to follow her out the back door.

"Look at her," Mr. Marvelle says after she walks past. "You see where her hand is, don't you?"

Stepping out from the pantry, I catch a glimpse of her holding her stomach the instant before she opens the back door. I turn back to him with worry written all over my face.

After rubbing the nape of his neck, he looks me straight in the eye. "I see her doing it all the time."

"I asked her about it a few weeks ago and she told me it was nothing."

"It ain't nothin'."

I knew it. I knew something was bothering her. Why didn't she own up to it? "This time I'm not letting her get away with it." With a firm push on the screen door, I head on out to the backyard.

Fee's taken a seat in her favorite chair. She pulls her tobacco pouch out of the pocket on her apron and pops a big piece behind her bottom lip. With a deliberate shake of her head she lets me know something or *someone* has got her goat. "Woo-whee. That Kadeesha. She gets on my last nerve."

"You and me both." That might be true. But we have a more important matter to discuss. We sit there in silence awhile before I speak. "Okay, now.

Don't be telling me nothing's wrong with you. I saw you holding your stomach again."

"It ain't nothin' but a cramp." She won't even look at me when she says it.

"What kind of cramp? Your cramps been gone a long time. You're sixty-four years old."

"Shoot." She closes her eyes, plays like she's napping.

"Don't 'shoot' me. How did it go at the doctor's last month? You never told me."

"You never asked."

I swallow and press my lips together. She's exactly right. "Forgot all about it. So much going on around here." Here I've spent time thinking about my hair weave and a job I'll never get, and forgot all about asking my own auntie what happened at the doctor's. "I'm sorry. Please tell me how it went."

"Listen here," she says, in a rigid tone. Her eyes are big as saucers now. "Doctor say I'm okay. If it keeps on bothering me I might have a little surgery. That's all."

"What kind of surgery?"

"Exploratory surgery. But I ain't gone worry about that unless I have to."

"Then why are you still holding your stomach?"

Her voice softens. She turns to look at me dead-on. Our knees are rubbing together. "It's fine, baby, and I don't want to talk about it no more. I want you to talk. What is it you wanted to tell me?"

I squeeze one eye shut, let her know I'm on to her. I'm not ready to switch subjects but Aunt Fee is the most stubborn woman alive today. Finally I say, "Mama Carla's leaving."

Her eyebrows shoot to the sky with wrinkles lining her forehead.

I put a finger to my lips. "Shhh, now. Be quiet about it. She doesn't want anyone knowing. She said she'd be telling you soon. After she tells the board."

She leans her chair back against the brick, the way she always does. The front legs rise a little. "Here we go. Another new housemother. Lawd have mercy on us all. Just when we had something good."

"That's not all."

"Uh-oh. What else happenin', baby?"

"She thinks I should apply."

Fee whips her head around. "For housemama?"

I nod. "Yes, ma'am."

She doesn't respond and I could swear she's thinking it's a bad idea, but then, "That's wonderful, dahlin'." Her lips curve into a big smile.

"You mean it?"

"Anything has to do with you betterin' your life is good news to me." She picks up the Gatorade bottle and spits inside. Then I see her face transform, switch from glad to mad as fast as a rabbit can run. "The idea of you spendin' all these years in front of a toilet, disposin' of everybody else's number two. *Shoot.* It's about time you put down that ol' nasty plunger, and put it down for good." After crossing her arms in a huff on top of her large bosom, I see her jaw clench. "Doing all that nasty work all these years—for eleven dollars an hour. *Hmmph.*"

"Eleven fifty."

She just looks at me.

"Mama Carla gets that. I know she does," I say.

"Mama Carla ain't dumb."

"She thinks I'm well qualified."

Fee rears back. "You *are* well qualified—smart as a whip. But!" She whips that finger in the air, the way I've seen her do a thousand times. "You've got one major strike against you and we both know who that strike is. Lawd," she shakes her head. "I don't know if I need to be tellin' you to go for it or to get out of harm's way, 'fore you get hurt."

"I don't know either."

"I do know one thing. That Lilith Whitless got a cold black heart. And nobody can convince me otherwise."

The next day, Auntie seems okay. She's back to her old self and if there's something wrong with her, I don't see it. She's laughing and loving on everyone as usual. I know she's better because she's back to bossing poor ol' Marvelle around. Sometimes I think she's sweet on him. I know he is on her. I've seen him throwing his eyes her way when he thinks no one's looking.

When he watches her cook there's a tenderness about him, eagerly anticipating the first plate of the night, which always has his name on it. If there's something she needs and it's high up on the pantry shelf, he's scrambled up his ladder before she has a chance to ask him for it.

Mr. Marvelle, he can get grumpy sometimes, but never around Aunt Fee. One time, when he asked her how she knew everything he's doing, she said, "You see this big head I've got sittin' on my shoulders? I've got two more eyes in back and they're bigger than the ones in front. That's how I know."

THIRTY-THREE

CALI

"Look out, Sorority Row. Here comes Cali Watkins." Jasmine's got her arms crossed and she's inspecting my first-day-of-Rush outfit. Still in her PJs and silk headscarf—the one that hides every hair on her head—she's as cheeky as ever. "It didn't take you long to look like the rest of these Martin girls."

"Busted." I peer down at my workout shorts, Nike tennis shoes, and extra-large Greek Day T-shirt. It's seven fifteen on a mid-October Sunday morning and we have to be in the Grove by eight.

"What time does all this Rush hoopla finish, anyway?"

"Somewhere around or six or seven. I think." Rush parties start at four the rest of the week. My last class on Monday, Wednesday, and Friday—Honors Spanish—doesn't get out till three. I'll have to be dressed and ready before I leave for class.

I turn back to the mirror on our door to finish applying my makeup. Specially for Rush week, I treated myself to a brand-new tube of L'Oréal mascara. The first day has me so jittery I'm surprised I've got a steady hand.

"Perfect timing. Carl gets back from Greenville around then. Wanna go to dinner with us?"

I sigh. "Damn. I'm already going with Ellie and a bunch of other girls to Volta. Why don't y'all come, too?"

She puts her hands on her hips, pushes out her chest. "Are you kidding me?"

"Why would I kid about that?" I ask, looking at her through the reflection. Our entire conversation is taking place in the mirror. With her headscarf on—only her ears showing—the beauty of her face and skin is accentuated. It's as smooth as brown velvet.

"Don't get me wrong. It's not that I don't like all a y'all," she says, even more Jasmine-like. "I don't want my man in the middle of ten women. He might not make it out alive." Her delivery—the cadence in her voice—cracks me up. Jasmine's sense of humor has become one of my most favorite things about her.

"We won't hurt Carl. We love Carl."

"Yeah. And that's the problem. His heart might give out."

"That Carl loves one woman and one woman only," I say, punctuating my words with my mascara wand.

"That may be. But that one woman is no dummy."

We both laugh and I get back to my mascara. Ellie has taught me a new trick. "Sweep from the root," she's always saying. "It makes your lashes look super long." There's only problem with this execution—the dim light near the door.

As I'm sweeping—careful not to poke my eye out, a phrase Mamaw always uses—I notice Jasmine's expression change. I could almost swear she's a little blue. So I quickly finish and shove the mascara back in my drawer. Stepping toward her, I ask, "Are you sad you're not going out for Recruitment?"

Jasmine opens her eyes as wide as they will go. "Cali. Be serious. Do I look like the type of woman who would want to join a bleached-blond sorority?"

"I have red hair," I say with a wink.

"You know what I mean."

"*Well?* You live in a dorm full of sorority girls." We've spent considerable time on this subject. I know I'm well within the boundaries of our friendship to talk with her frankly. "And there are only a couple of other black girls living here as far as I can tell."

"First off—and you already know this—I'm only staying here because I plan to be an RA next year. It's helping me to understand the needs and de-sires of the residents firsthand."

That's incredible, I think to myself. *So unselfish.* "I can't imagine anyone else doing something like that. You'll be the best RA ever."

"Well, I hope so." Our rug has been curling up on the edge and she mashes the corner down with her foot. "Can I tell you something you don't know?"

"Sure." I back up and sit on the edge of my bed.

"You're playing a big part in all that. Living with you is helping me to un-derstand white girls and how y'all think."

"Aww, that's so sweet. I'm glad."

"As far as a sorority goes, I might join. But it'll be a black one." She takes off her headscarf. "You can be sure of that." When her braids fall around her shoul-ders, she reaches back and ties the scarf securely around them, making a big fat ponytail. "Look around today. You won't see many chocolate sisters going out for your Rush."

I shrug. "I'm sure you're right."

"And why the ones who *do,* do it in the first place—has me unzipped. You know what I'm sayin'?" The way she emphasizes "unzipped," and teeters back and forth—like she's a bobblehead—makes me laugh out loud.

But something else about what she said pulls me down. "There's something really sad and wrong about all that. Don't you think?"

"What do you mean?"

"I mean . . . we're still so divided around here."

"It's not just here, Cali; it's everywhere."

"I know. And I'm not sure of the answer, but I still hate it."

She bends toward me. "All we can do is our part. And I think we"—she flicks a finger back and forth between us—"are doing just that."

"We are. I know that. But . . . I wanna do more. That's why I want to be governor one day. I really want to make a difference in people's lives."

When Jasmine reaches out to hug me I stand up, pull her in tight. After she lets go she keeps her hands on my shoulders. "You are a sweet person, Cali Watkins. You're always concerned about me and everybody else. I love that about you."

"You're a sweet person yourself, Jasmine Crawford. And I'll always be concerned about you. Probably till I'm ninety and can't remember my own name."

"We might be old ladies together. Never can tell." She turns around to make her bed.

So I do the same. As I'm fluffing my pillow, I turn back around. "Does that mean we'll move to Florida and knit all day?"

She looks over her shoulder. "Either that or crochet. And when we're finished, we'll get in the car and drive twenty miles an hour down the beach highway."

"It would have to be in a convertible."

"Of course it'll be in a convertible." She tugs on her pajama shorts. "We'll wear granny bikinis. Take our tops off and swing them high in the air while we're driving."

The thought of that—the two of us topless with the top down—gets me laughing. "And then we'll park the car, run across the sand, and take a buck-naked dip in the ocean."

A hard pounding on the door interrupts our banter.

"Who is it?" Jasmine says, in a loud voice.

"The Resident Advisor's boyfriend." It's no guy. It's a girl, disguising her voice, and it's followed by laughter from a gaggle of ninth-floor rushees. "Open up. *Now.*"

Jasmine sashays over, snatches the door open. "Why if it's not the ninth-floor Martinian sextuplets. Come on in," she says, waving them inside.

Ellie, Annie Laurie, Bailey, Tara, Hannah, and Claudia—all wearing identical yellow Greek Day T-shirts—come rushing in. Ellie holds the hem of her shirt. "Whatever makes you say that?"

Everyone laughs.

Hannah and Bailey lift their legs and touch their matching Nike tennis shoes together. "Great minds," they both say at the same time.

"Jasmine and Carl may come to dinner with us tonight," I say.

Tara's hand flies to her chest. "I thought you knew we canceled Volta."

I shake my head. "Why?"

"My Gamma Chi said there's a good chance we might be at Weir Hall till nine or ten tonight."

"Depending on your schedule, you might wait in line three hours to rank," Bailey adds. "We'll have to eat at different times."

At the end of every Rush day we'll be ranking our bottom three sororities. I know that from Rush Orientation.

"I wasn't going with y'all anyway," Jasmine says.

"And why not?" Ellie asks, with a hand on one hip.

Jasmine mimics Ellie, puts a hand on her own hip. "Because Carl couldn't get enough of all y'all."

"Whatever," Hannah says. "Carl hasn't seen *nothin'* yet."

"We better go, y'all," Tara says, looking at her watch. "We have to be there in twenty minutes."

I start to grab my phone from the nightstand when Ellie puts her hand out to stop me. "Remember? No phones allowed."

"Oops. Almost forgot."

"Wait. *What?*" Jasmine asks. "Y'all can't take your phones?"

Annie Laurie pulls hers out of her bra. "No one is gonna tell me I can't bring my phone."

"You go, girl," Jasmine says, and they give each other a high five.

No one else comments.

THIRTY-FOUR

CALI

After taking the steps down from the ninth floor—the line for the elevator was ridiculous—we have to get in another line. It seems like a thousand of us are making the trek up the gargantuan flight of stairs from the Martin parking lot to Rebel Drive. It'll take a little longer to get to the Grove this morning with all of us walking over at the same time.

When we crest the hill, not far from the back of the Union, I can already hear the chatter, and when the Grove is finally in view I literally feel like pinching myself, because the moment I've been living for is here. The Grove looks like a giant sunflower field, with thousands of girls clustered together in yellow shirts—their cheery faces beaming in the sunlight.

I had heard there would be this many—the largest Ole Miss Rush ever—but seeing everyone congregated together is *insane*. I'm not exactly sure, but it seems like blondes have the majority—with a smaller percentage of brunettes and a tiny spattering of us redheads. Every now and then I spot a black girl sticking out like a raisin in a bowl of milk, but Jasmine was right. Not many.

Sarah's arm is high in the air, and she's waving at me when I walk up to our designated spot: the far right corner of the Union steps. She's wearing the cutest purple Gamma Chi T-shirt, khaki shorts, and leather flip-flops.

"Hey, girl. How are you?" she says with that sweet voice of hers. Instantly I feel my muscles relaxing. Her bubbly personality and sparkly eyes remind me of one of the reasons I wanted to join a sorority in the first place. When she wraps her arms around me, I'm reminded of her kindness. During Rush Orientation she made it a point to give every one of us in her group private time, to divulge any fears we had about the process. I never told her my biggest fear, but I still felt like the luckiest person on earth to have gotten her as my Gamma Chi.

"Honestly? I'm nervous," I tell her. "But I'm super excited at the same time."

She reaches out, takes both of my hands in hers. "Please don't be nervous. It's all gonna be fine. We have thirteen sororities on this campus and they're all looking for great girls like you."

"Aww, thanks, Sarah. I know there's a House for me. I'm just... I don't know... *nervous*." A part of me is dying to explain the reason for my fear—that I don't have a pedigree and I'm just a girl from a tiny town where people don't belong to sororities or fraternities—but I don't. She wouldn't understand.

"I don't want you to be. Today is gonna be a blast. Just enjoy it, okay?"

Even though I nod in agreement, I'm still worried.

Five more girls in our group walk up at the same time and Sarah embraces each of them, too. No one on my floor is in my Gamma Chi group, but I do know Bridgett, a girl in my Honors English class. I try looking around the massive crowd for Ellie, but quickly realize there's no point. She's just another blonde.

All of us spend the next fifteen minutes engaging in high-strung small talk while we eagerly await our first Water Party at nine. Turning a slow circle, I look around at thousands of happy girls, bouncing on their toes, full of excitement and hope, and I'm reminded that some of the girls I'm watching right this minute will have their hearts broken. And that one of them could be me.

At eight twenty, Sarah climbs up to one of the higher steps with a small box in her hand and corrals us for a brief meeting. She has to raise her voice a little so we can hear her. "The most important thing I want y'all to do today is have fun. I know a few of you have been telling me how stressed you are, but I want y'all to try and relax. And enjoy yourselves. Rush is meant to be one of the best experiences of your life. You'll be meeting tons of new people," she says, while handing each of us a Ziploc bag labeled with our names. Our official Rush name tags are tucked inside. "But don't let that worry you. You aren't required to remember all their names."

Everyone laughs.

"I'm sure y'all remember me mentioning these bags at Orientation. Feel free to use them for all your necessities: your student ID, money, *tampons*," she says, with a warm smile. "Lipstick. And, most importantly, keep your schedules in here."

A girl named Maddie Patton raises her hand. "What if we need to go to the bathroom?"

More laughter erupts from our group.

"Good question," Sarah says. "Hopefully, it'll be on your lunch break, which, by the way, is at noon today. Or you could go on your afternoon break. But if at any time you're dying, and can't possibly hold it another second, tell me. I'll escort you into whatever House we happen to be closest to."

"I have one," I say.

"Of course. Ask anything you want," Sarah replies.

"I've heard something about a variable quota this year? What exactly is that, and what does it mean for us?"

"That's another good question, Cali, thank you. So, this year Panhellenic is trying to help the newer sororities on campus get more members. In order to do that they've put a restriction on the quota for older, more established sororities, and given the newer ones a higher quota." The way she's tucking her hair behind her ears and the smile on her face make me think she considers a variable quota a good thing. "It does mean it'll be a little harder to get a bid from the older sororities, but we have so many great Houses on this campus. Please don't worry about that."

"I've heard the older Houses rushed way more girls than they should have last year because they only learned about variable quota a few months ago. What, then?" Bridgett asks.

Sarah shrugs. "That's anyone's guess. But the good news is newer sororities will have a chance to catch up. It makes the whole thing much more fair. Don't y'all think?"

I'm starting to wonder if Sarah might be in a newer sorority. She's required to keep her affiliation a secret, and my curiosity is driving me crazy. Old or new, I'd kill to be her sorority sister.

"Honestly, y'all. Please don't worry about this. On another note, we'll all be together today, but for the rest of the week you'll be in new groups, depending on which Houses invite you back. But there will always be Gamma Chis waiting outside every House to help you with whatever you need."

The chatter in the Grove is climbing, so Sarah makes a megaphone with her hands. "I'm always here for you if you need to call or text me. Okay?" Her eyes rove around at each of us. "I mean that."

Another girl in my group raises her hand. "Sarah, I have a question."

"Sure, Whitney, go ahead."

"Do we take our plastic bags into the Houses?"

"Actually, the Gamma Chis keep them for you. And I meant to tell y'all, I have Advil and plenty of breath mints, and granola bars if you're starving." She holds her arms up and looks at the sky. "Can y'all believe how lucky we are? As of right now it's not supposed to rain all week. But it could get chilly a little later in the day, so don't hesitate to wear a jacket. The Gamma Chis will hold those for you, too, when you go inside for the parties."

Sarah reaches into her back pocket and glances at her phone. "So it's eight thirty-five now. Oh, one more thing. Everyone left their phone at home, right?"

We all nod.

"Unfortunately," Bridgett says.

Sarah laughs. "I know it's a pain. Everyone hates it." Another Gamma Chi walks by and waves her over, away from our group. I watch them talk among themselves a minute before Sarah hurries back. "Everyone ready?"

We're all looking around at one another, nodding.

"Alrighty then. First up, Chi Omega."

THIRTY-FIVE

CALI

Sitting here in this classroom at Weir Hall, after the overload of noise and conversation we've had all day, is like stepping out of a rock concert into a prayer chapel. After standing for three hours in a line that ran all the way back to the Union, I'm relieved to finally be sitting down. I can't believe it's already dark outside.

Now I am trying to rank—well, I'm agonizing over—my bottom three choices. I loved every single sorority. Granted, some knew all about me, and others didn't, but that's because of my lack of recommendations to every House. I'm sure of it. And even more sure now—after meeting the members and seeing the kindness they showed me—that I have a real chance. I would be happy with a bid from any one of them.

All fifteen of us in this room seem to be more confused than sure. One girl has her head on her desk. Another has her arms crossed with her pencil on top of the sheet in front of her. Not only are we supposed to circle our top ten choices, and rank our bottom three, but there's a place to choose how we wish to be contacted should we not get invited back to *any* Houses: by phone or in person. I check phone. I'd rather get it over with in a single phone call.

Sitting right in front of me is a girl who seems more baffled than I am. A

Gamma Chi is kneeling next to her desk with her hand on the girl's arm. Sarah had told us that Gamma Chis would be here tonight to talk us through our ranking, should we need help choosing. "They won't try to sway you," she said. "They'll offer you an unbiased ear."

When the Gamma Chi gets up, I raise my hand and she walks over, kneels at my desk. "Hi," she whispers. "Having trouble?"

"A little," I whisper back. "I would love your advice on something."

"Sure." She shifts knees and smiles.

"Should I rank the sororities I didn't have recs for as my bottom three? Even if I loved them? Like a ton?"

She tilts her head, takes a minute to ponder, then slowly nods her head yes. "I think that's wise. Especially if you're having trouble choosing. Only because all the Houses here require recs. Make sense?"

"It does. Thank you," I whisper.

"Of course." She gives me a light hug and moves over to the side of the classroom.

I am dying to talk to Ellie. We haven't crossed paths one time today, not even at our lunch break in the Union. I can't wait to hear which Houses she's circled as her top ten. It would be awesome if our choices were the same. But even if they aren't I'm still thrilled over the thought of having a big family of sisters I can grow old with. Be in one another's weddings. Hold one another's babies. Support one another when life takes a crippling turn. Never having had a sister of my own, this is my chance.

My one negative out of the entire day is the money issue. Like I thought, I will probably need five thousand dollars my first year. Aside from the baby-sitting jobs I've had, I've not taken a steady job since school started. So far I've been concentrating on my grades. It's a dilemma. Somehow, though, I will come up with the extra money.

The line at Chick-fil-A in the Union was almost out the door, so I decided to go back to the dorm for dinner and grab chicken fingers at the C-store. Totally starving and dying from the smell, I dive into the bag while riding the elevator, and finish every single one by the time I get back to my room.

After fumbling for my room card, I unlock the door, hoping to find Jasmine, but instead our room is dark and empty. One glance at my phone tells me it's not too late to head next door, so I throw the empty chicken finger bag in the trash and head over. Of course their door is open, so I poke my head inside. Both of them wave when they see me, but Ellie slides right off her bed and pulls me down on the couch next to her. "I looked for you, but *forget it.*"

"I know. Right?"

"Crazy."

"I think I saw you leaving the KD House," Annie Laurie says. Still in her Greek Day clothes, she's on top of her unmade bed—amidst all of her gorgeous throw pillows—flipping through *Cosmo* magazine.

"Really? I never saw you."

"I was leaving Tri Delt; you were talking to your Gamma Chi."

"Oh my gosh," Ellie says, twisting her hair up. "I loved, loved the Tri Delts."

I'm feeling the same way, so I pull my knees up and lean in toward her. "I agree."

The temperature outside has dropped and the dorm feels a little chilly, so I wrap up in their furry throw. Ellie moves closer. I cover her up, too. "Do you have a preference?" she asks.

"Not really. Do you?"

She tilts her head. "The Phi Mus were great, so were the DGs, and the Chi Os." She marks each one off with her fingers. "The Alpha Phis. Of course I loved the Alpha Delts—honestly, I loved them all." She pulls the throw up under her chin.

"Me, too. It took me forever to rank."

"Same here. What's it gonna be like after Philanthropy parties? We can only choose five."

"I can't think about that right now. But truly, I'm not just saying this . . . I'd be happy with any sorority."

"Not me." Annie Laurie has finally found something to comment on. "There were a few you couldn't give me a million dollars to join."

Ellie and I look at each other slyly, out of the corners of our eyes. I don't even want to know which ones she's talking about. So I change the subject. "I guess I'll have to be ready for Philanthropy when I go to class tomorrow. I don't get out till three."

"That sucks," Ellie says.

"I know. I'm just happy it doesn't conflict. You know we'll be dropped from Rush if we miss a class?"

"That's ridiculous," Annie Laurie says, slapping the magazine down on her lap. "How would they even know?"

"I'm not sure, but I'm not taking any chances," I say.

"You're such a rule-follower, Cali. You need to chill." It seems by the tone of her voice that she's joking, but knowing her, she's not. "Are any of your friends from Blue Mountain rushing this year?"

I hesitate before answering. She's such a snoop. "I don't think so."

"That was random," Ellie says looking at her with a what-planet-did-you-come-from look on her face.

Annie Laurie either doesn't notice or doesn't care. "Huh. How come?"

My patience is running dry. "I'm not really sure, Annie Laurie."

"My mom said a lot of poor people live in Blue Mountain." The girl doesn't let up.

"Blue Mountain doesn't have many wealthy families, if that's what you mean."

Ellie pats my leg. She knows me well enough to know I'm wearing thin. "That's okay. Who cares?"

I've had about as much of Annie Laurie as I can stand for the day. "I'm about to drop," I say, standing up from the couch. "Guess I'll see y'all at the Grove tomorrow." I wave and Annie Laurie waves back.

"Let's try to find each other." Ellie's eyes are full of anguish. It's hard to be in her position. Roommates need to get along, and confrontation makes living together unbearable.

"Sounds good. Y'all have a good night's sleep."

Before I walk out the door Annie Laurie shuts her *Cosmo* and sits up straight. "I'm sure Blue Mountain is a sweet place."

The heat of anger rises up the back of my neck. I whip around, stare at her briefly. "It really is, Annie Laurie."

After stepping into the hall, I shut the door—harder than I should—behind me.

The next afternoon in the Grove, when Sarah hands me my schedule for Philanthropy parties, only five of the ten time slots are full. The others say: No Event Scheduled. I've been dropped by five of my top ten choices. I'm not going to lie. Seeing this in print stings. But I suppose it makes sense.

I followed the advice from the Gamma Chi in the ranking room, chose sororities I had recs for, but even still some of them dropped me. *It's okay, no big deal,* I tell myself, because, more importantly, I still have Alpha Delt and Tri Delt. And they are Ellie's top choices. But the scary thing about that is, they're both older sororities. Their pledge classes will be smaller. *Don't get too attached,* I tell myself. *Concentrate on the other three, the less-established sororities who have invited you back.*

The sound of someone trying to catch her breath startles me. When I look to my right, Rebecca, a sweet girl in my Gamma Chi group, is crying. She's holding her schedule in one hand, and her stomach with the other. Now she's shaking. I want to comfort her, but I'm not sure what to say. I turn a slow circle, my mouth opening wider with each step, and now I'm freaking out because lots of girls are blinking back tears. Yes, there are many more who are happy, but others are full-on crying.

I never expected to see tears today; it's early in the week. But it's going on all around me. All over the Grove, teary-eyed girls are walking around aimlessly looking for someone, anyone, to give them comfort. One girl with tears rolling down her cheeks passes right by me, and I overhear her tell the girl she's with that she's transferring to another school.

I feel terrible for Rebecca. I don't want to ask her about her schedule because I can tell she's devastated, but I feel like I need to say something. "Did you not get your first choice?" I finally ask. I can't stand seeing her cry.

She shakes her head and with tears pooling in her eyes, asks, "Do you know Elise Davis?"

"No. I'm sorry I don't," I say.

"Will you please, please go with me to find her?"

"Sure I will." I mean, it's the least I can do, so we set off on a journey to look for Elise Davis.

"I need to find her or at least one of my other best friends," Rebecca says. "I wish we could have our ph-phones." Her voice is shaking and tears are streaming down her cheeks. She's using her fingers to wipe them away, but they won't stop.

We see other girls running into the Union so we follow along behind them. There's a super-long line of crying girls waiting for the bathroom. Instead of taking a place in line, she wants to keep looking for Elise. But we only have twenty minutes before the first Philanthropy party starts and there are hundreds of people in the Grove. There's no way we'll find her in time.

"Why don't you talk to Sarah?" I say, in my most tender voice.

"Okay. I guess I can."

Taking Rebecca by the hand, I lead her back to Sarah, who takes one look at her and immediately wraps an arm around her shoulder. Then she moves her away from the group, off to a private spot near a magnolia tree.

Not wanting to appear as though I'm eavesdropping, I stand off to the side. While scanning the edges of the Grove, I notice other crying girls with their Gamma Chis. Should I be crying? I've been cut by several sororities, but for some reason I feel strong. I'm not sure what that's about, but I'll revel in my strength for as long as I have it.

Several minutes pass and I'm thinking of rejoining our group when Sarah and Rebecca walk back toward me. "Clean up your makeup," I hear Sarah say. "You still have five great Houses left. Let's go in and open your heart up to possibility. Okay?"

Rebecca nods in agreement, but it seems she'd rather just go home.

"Cali, will you please walk with Rebecca to the Union so she can splash her face? I need to get back to our group."

"Sure. I'd love to."

As Rebecca and I are walking toward the bathroom I can't help wishing I could join Sarah's sorority. She's exactly the kind of person I want for a life-long friend. But after witnessing all these tears today I'm reminded of how real the possibility is that I might not be joining a sorority at all.

THIRTY-SIX

WILDA

It's two o'clock in the morning when we park my car in front of Lilith's condo after the final round of Sisterhood parties. Lilith not only laid down the law about me staying here during Rush, but she insisted both of our other Rush Advisors, Sallie and Gwen, stay, too. Why in the world any of us agreed is the question.

Our initial thinking made sense. Since Lilith's invitation would save the sorority scads of dollars on hotel rooms, all three of us said yes. Albeit reluctantly, at least on my part, but what was I going to say? Rush Advisors are required to be in Oxford an entire week, so that's a considerable amount of money saved. I'd rather see Alpha Delt put it toward something more meaningful, like the impoverished people of Oxford. Or the Care Walk for Breast Cancer. Or how about a raise for the staff?

On the short drive home from the House, all we've been talking about is falling into bed. But when we stumble into the kitchen, Lilith, whom we all believed would be fast asleep by now, is sitting on a stool at the kitchen counter—fully dressed—flipping through the latest copy of *Garden & Gun*.

On the far side of the island, I spot a bottle of red wine and three Waterford wineglasses. Right next to that, elegantly displayed on a large McCarty tray, is a spread of cheeses, olive tapenades, grapes, three kinds of crackers, and turkey sliders. The first night we were here, Lilith catered in a tender-loin supper. Every night since she's had a unique spread of tapas waiting on us. But all this glorious food and wine doesn't change the fact that her daughter, Annie Laurie Whitmore—*a triple legacy*—was cut from Alpha Delta Beta two hours ago. And we have to pretend like all is well. Every time I think about it I dry heave.

"Hey. How did it go?" Lilith says, cheery and full of energy. She slides off her chair and moves over to her six-foot, Sub-Zero wine cooler. Sallie shoots me a glance from the corner of her eye while Gwen checks her phone, as if there's anything new to see at two A.M.

"Exhausting," Sallie says. "This is my last year on the Board."

"Sallie, you can't quit. Alpha Delt needs you." Lilith has removed a wine bottle that's already been corked. She pours a full glass, then slides it across the marble counter to Sallie. It's that nails-on-a-chalkboard sound. And so is her voice. "Sounds like you could use a large one."

"That's nice of you, Lilith, but we're all dead tired." Sallie looks at Gwen and me for backup. The two of us bounce our heads off in agreement. The awkwardness we're all feeling is worthy of an epic nervous breakdown. Just shoot me.

With a flick of her eyebrows, Lilith shows Sallie the label. "Not too tired for this, are you?" It's Newton Unfiltered Chardonnay. Sallie's been talking about it all week. But given that it's seventy dollars a bottle, she rarely drinks it. Imagine that. Here it is in Lilith's kitchen.

"What?" Sallie says. "You bought *Newton?*"

"I thought it was your favorite," Lilith replies.

"It is; but it's my celebration wine."

"It's time to celebrate, girlfriend. Rush is almost over."

Sallie takes a sip, closes her eyes. *"Mmmm."* Then she starts that contagious, coveted laugh of hers, and I don't know about Gwen, but it gives me momen-tary relief.

Now Lilith's reaching for the bottle of red. She holds it in front of Gwen and me. "It's your Prisoner."

Prisoner is new to me. At least since I've been here at Lilith's condo. She pours a glass and before she can pour another Gwen pushes her hand out.

"None for me, thanks. I can hardly hold my head up." After picking a grape off the cluster, she says, "Thank you for all this, Lilith, but honestly I'm too tired to breathe, much less drink. I'm hitting the sack."

I so admire the young generation. They know how to be direct.

Stepping toward the hallway, Gwen turns. "Good night, you guys. See you early in the morning." And there she goes down the hall, away from Sallie, and me, and what has turned into the most disturbing, cringeworthy night of our lives. Seriously, it's as bad as accidentally forwarding a nasty email about someone *to* that someone.

"What's different this year?" Lilith asks Sallie, refilling her own glass. "I don't remember you wanting to quit after last year's Rush."

"You know about the variable quota, right?" Sallie, very calmly, asks.

Lilith presses a hand to her heart. "There will be some tears this week-end."

By the stoic look on Sallie's face, one would never know how prescient Lilith's words actually are. Sallie is a master of disguise. I, on the other hand, must be a dead giveaway. I'm flipping nervously through the *Garden & Gun*. I'd rather be having knee replacement surgery—and for me that's saying something—than be sitting here in Lilith's kitchen.

She spreads a cracker with one of the tapenades. "So how did the final round of Sisterhood go?" Then she takes a delicate bite, holding her hand underneath to catch the crumbs.

"Fine," I say, in a breathy tone, even though it was anything but.

"We had to cut several legacies," Sallie says. Okay, she's preparing Lilith for the fall.

But Lilith doesn't react. All she says is, "Surely that tramp, Amber Maples, got cut."

"She got cut earlier in the week," Sallie tells her.

"Do they still have the Pref rule?" She's referring to Preference. If a girl makes it that far she's guaranteed a bid. No matter what.

Sallie reaches for a slider before answering. "It's not a guarantee that you'll get your first choice, but yes—if a girl gets invited back to Pref she'll get a bid."

I can tell Lilith's calculating all of this, because Annie Laurie was only invited back to three sororities for Sisterhood. This is a fact she has not shared with us, but as Rush Advisors we know all. With the exception of Alpha Delt, all the older Houses cut her. The other two who invited Annie Laurie back are newer sororities that Lilith would never want her joining in the first place. Apparently, and unbeknownst to Ellie or me, Annie Laurie was not well liked in high school. She had a zillion reference letters from Lilith's lionizers, but none of Annie Laurie's peers can stand her. How Lilith is keeping her cool right now is mind-blowing.

"What time does Panhellenic need the list in the morning?" she asks, casually. "Last year, if I remember right, it was seven A.M."

"It's the same this year," I say.

"Then I'll have coffee and chocolate croissants ready for y'all by six."

"Lilith," Sallie says. "Please sleep in. You've been too good to us already."

"Nonsense. This has been my treat, having y'all here."

I find it very interesting that Lilith has yet to ask me which sororities Ellie has been invited back to. No doubt, she must be getting all of her information straight from Annie Laurie.

After Sallie and I have said our good nights we drag ourselves upstairs to our en suites. When we're safely out of earshot, Sallie creeps into my room. "I swear," she says, locking the door behind her, "if I live through Sunday it will be a flipping miracle."

"Do me a favor?" I ask.

"Sure."

"Please find a gun and put me out of my misery."

Thank God for Sallie's laugh. It cackles and she puts a little yell behind it. Hard to do it justice, but it's about the only thing getting me through this Hell Week. "I took a week off work for this. Gwen did the same thing." She squeezes her cheeks. "I work *hard* for my vacations. I need to use that gun on myself... for being so stupid!"

"Five months ago, Lily Turner was a distant memory," I say. "Now Lilith Turner Whitmore is ruling—I take that back—*she's ruining my life*." I stagger over to the bed, sit down on the edge. "And to think Ellie could have gone to UT."

"Is it true?"

"Is what true?"

"About the dorm room costing each of you ten thousand dollars?"

I fall back, splaying my arms and legs out wide. "How do you know about that?"

"Uh, I think everybody knows about that. I guess Annie Laurie told Mary Crockett, who told her mother, and, well, you know how that goes."

I bolt back up. "Believe me. I walked into a booby trap on that one. My husband doesn't even know about it. *Yet.*"

"Uh-oh."

"'Uh-oh' is putting it mildly."

"I also heard Lilith sent Annie Laurie to a ten-thousand-dollar intensive Rush workshop in New York City." She puts an uppity aristocratic tone in her voice. "To learn the art of Rush conversation, and how to dress properly and accessorize for all the parties." She sits on the edge of my bed, leans in toward me. "Did Ellie go with her?"

"I know you think I'm crazy, but I can assure you I'm not that crazy." I sigh, loudly. "I'm living a nightmare. And there's no end in sight."

"Looks like it'll get worse before it gets better. For you, anyway." Sallie laughs again. And this time, I laugh along with her. What else can I do?

THIRTY-SEVEN

WILDA

I smell the coffee when my alarm goes off at six fifteen. Half of me is seriously considering opening the window, sliding down the gutter, and making a run for it. I think of calling Haynes for comfort, but I remember what he said when I left home: "I have officially removed the words Lilith and Gage Whitmore from my vocabulary."

So I move on past the window and head into the Jack and Jill bathroom I'm sharing with Sallie. Her door is open and she's already awake, her laptop resting on her thighs. I notice she's taken the liberty of wrapping herself in one of the luxurious spa robes that's been hanging on the back of our bathroom door all week. When she hears me she waves.

I walk over to the bed and slide in next to her, propping her other pillow behind me. "Coffee smells good. Want me to get you a cup?"

"Nah. I'll go down with you. I'm just looking over our list again." Most of the sororities on campus have hired an online company to compile a final tally of all the active members' votes. Sisterhood Select is ours.

"Ellie's on it, right?" I ask timidly.

Sallie points to the screen. "Right here. But no Annie Laurie Whitmore." Then she groans loudly, looks up at the ceiling. "If anyone had told me I'd be staying in the home of a woman, wait…*the House Corp President,* whose trashy daughter would be cut from Alpha Delt after Sisterhood, I'd have resigned a loooong time ago."

"I'm still wondering if Lilith has a revolver." I flop back on the pillow.

She laughs, keeps her eyes on her laptop.

"Clearly God's trying to punish me," I say. "It's His payback for when I froze Celia Opp's bra at Becky Goodwin's slumber party." *Or more recently— my big whopper to Haynes.*

Sallie lays her head back and chuckles. "That's nothing. I did waaay worse."

"Really? Lay it on me. You're making me feel better."

She sits up straight, propping herself with her hands. Then she peers at me over her readers. "I made fun of a boy in my Sunday School class with a lisp. *To. His. Face.* I can still see him. I leaned over two people and said, 'Hi Bwad, when did you get your bwaces off?' He almost cried." She flops back down, stares at the ceiling. "As we all know, karma can be a real bitch when she wants to."

"Speaking of karma, did you hang out with Lilith in college?"

"No. But, to be fair, she wouldn't have wanted to hang with me, either. We were different then and we are total opposites today." She blesses me with her laugh again.

"She hung out with the other officers, if I remember. Right?"

"Yep. Don't you remember her mother?"

With a slight nod, I wrinkle my nose. "Maybe."

"I'll never forget her. She was some sort of an advisor. Always at the Alpha Delt House. She'd drop an N-bomb like she was part of the Klan."

"Ew."

Sallie shudders and makes a scary face. "That was Mrs. Turner."

We lie there wallowing in our misery a little longer before the coffee aroma stirs me to action. "Let's go get coffee," I say, scooting off the bed. "It'll give us a lift." Then I look back at her. "It's the best coffee I've ever had."

"It oughta be." Sallie stands up, takes a big stretch. "They have it flown in from Brazil."

Lifting my arms overhead I say, "Of course they do!" then head into the bathroom.

I'm tying the sash on the other spa robe when I hear, "I saw Lilith set the timer on the coffeepot. Maybe she decided to sleep in."

"Don't get your hopes up," I say with a mouthful of toothpaste.

While creeping down the stairs, we hear the whooshing of the milk steamer on Lilith's cappuccino machine. I turn to Sallie and mouth, "Told you."

When we poke our heads in the kitchen, Lilith has her back to us, expertly bobbing a metal cup under the arm of the steamer. Due to the noise, she doesn't hear us walk in.

Gwen is seated at the island behind her, holding a frothy mug of cappuccino with both hands. Banana and kiwi slices, raspberries, and a chocolate croissant are on a plate in front of her. When she sees us, she rolls her eyes dramatically.

The sound of the steamer stops abruptly and Lilith turns around. She seems surprised to see Sallie and me. "Good morning, ladies, did y'all sleep well?"

I pull out a stool. "All three hours of it."

"If that," Sallie says, settling down herself.

"I have some surprises for y'all this morning." I watch Lilith pick up a mug and fill it with steamed milk, then garnish it with chocolate shavings and a rock candy stir-stick. "Who's first?"

Sallie shifts in her seat. "Give it to Wilda. She needs it the most."

When Lilith hands over the mug, she gives me an impenetrable grin. *Hmm,* I think, *what does that face mean?* "Thank you, Lilith. I feel like I'm at a restaurant," I say, mimicking her grin.

"You sound like Gage. He tells Rosetta that every night after supper." Once she's finished making a coffee for Sallie, she slides it to her, then glances up at the large watchmaker's clock on the wall. "Fifteen minutes till y'all upload the list. We're almost home free."

Home free until she finds out about Annie Laurie. Then all hell will break loose.

"Thank God," Sallie says, sniffing the aroma before taking a sip.

"All in the name of sisterhood." Lilith lays down the towel she's been using to wipe the steamer. "Enjoy your cappuccinos, ladies. I'll be back in a flash." She grips the doorframe. "I have one more surprise for y'all."

"Lilith, please," Gwen says. "You've given us everything we could ever need for the rest of our lives."

"Pooh." She swipes away Gwen's compliment and strolls off toward her bedroom.

When she's out of earshot, the three of us start whispering.

"This is getting weird," Gwen says with a sour expression. "I don't know about you guys, but I'm creeped out."

Sallie whispers, "It's almost like she knows something's up with Annie Laurie. And she's doing whatever she can to change the outcome."

I squeeze my temples with both hands. "Why didn't I encourage Ellie to go to UT? I could have saved my family misery." I look at Sallie. "And money."

Her nose flares. "I always wondered why I didn't have daughters. Now I don't have to wonder anymore." She slaps the counter and laughs.

"I don't think I want children," Gwen says. "After watching this whole thing go down. No thanks."

"I'm turning in my pin," Sallie whispers. "I swear. I am turning it in."

"Back at ya." Gwen takes another sip of her cappuccino. "Even I'm rattled. And I'm usually calm in the face of adversity."

"Triumph over adversity," Sallie says. Then looks toward Lilith's bedroom. "What's taking her so long?"

Gwen and I look at each other and shrug. "Who knows?" I say.

Sallie reaches across me for a chocolate croissant. "I can't even imagine how you feel, Wilda." She turns to Gwen. "At least we don't have a daughter rooming with Annie Laurie."

All of a sudden intense heat envelops my body and I'm cooking, like I'm inside a stockpot set at a roaring boil.

Gwen knits her brows together, touches my cheek. "Are you okay? Your face is bright red."

I take the *Garden & Gun,* the one from last night, and fan my face so hard I rip the cover. "I thought I had had my last hot flash, but that all changed when Lilith Whitmore reentered my life." I lift my hair, trying to get the back of my neck. But it doesn't help. So I dash over to the freezer and stick my head between two of the wire shelves.

I've been in there for what seems like two full minutes when Lilith finally decides to return. She opens the freezer door wider. "Wilda, what are you doing in my freezer?"

"Trying to kill myself," I mutter.

"Shut the door. It's getting cold in here, girlfriend."

Reluctantly, I drift back to my seat.

There are three gorgeous gift boxes in her arms, and she places one in front of each of us.

"What's this for?" I ask, picking up my box.

Lilith gives a light shrug then smiles impishly. "Just a little happy."

"Lilith. You didn't need to do this," Gwen says indignantly.

"Of course I did. It was the least I could do for all the hard work you girls are doing for Alpha Delt. My gosh. You've spent a hundred hours this week alone."

I might not know what's on the inside, but I certainly know from where it came. Gwen unties the white satin ribbon, then slowly lifts the lid of the finely crafted turquoise box.

Lilith puts her hand out to stop her. "Hang on, Gwen. I want y'all to open them together," she says, excitedly. "You're all getting the same thing."

After Sallie and I untie our ribbons, we all lift our box lids at the same time to find sterling silver key rings with a signature Tiffany heart. *Please Return to Tiffany & Co. New York* is on one side and each of our initials is engraved on the back, with our phone numbers underneath. I can hear the tape playing in all three of our heads: Oh. My. God. Oh. My. God.

"Lilith," Gwen says, firmly. "You did way too much."

"Oh my gosh, Lilith." Sallie holds hers up by a finger. "I don't know what to say."

"You don't need to say anything. You girls deserve it."

I have to say, I am no longer fooled by Lilith Whitmore. The woman is calculated in every single thing she does. So I force a smile and add a cryptic response. "You are something else, Lilith. Wow."

"Uh-oh, look at the time," she says. "It's three minutes till seven. Don't y'all need to upload the list?" There's a bit of haughtiness in her tone.

"Well, crap." Sallie hurries off her barstool. Then scampers out of the kitchen. "Thank you for reminding me," we hear her say as she's pounding up the stairs. "Do y'all trust me to hit send or do you want to look at it one more time?"

"Go for it. I'm tired of looking at it," Gwen hollers, with a hand beside her mouth. Then she looks at me. "Upward and onward to Pref. It'll be a loooong night."

It will be a long night, all right. In fact, we should probably all move to Canada. Once Lilith finds out that Annie Laurie has been cut from Alpha Delt, her scream will cause a magnitude-ten earthquake and split the foundation of the Alpha Delta Beta House. We'll all be enveloped into the bowels of the earth together.

THIRTY-EIGHT

WILDA

Why is Annie Laurie Whitmore coming to Pref?" Lizzie asks the minute we step inside the chapter room at eleven o'clock. She and Selma James are seated next to each other staring at a laptop, which is on the table we've set up as a workstation.

"What are you talking about?" Sallie asks, setting her bag down on a chair.

"She's on today's schedule!" I can tell Lizzie is beside herself. Not only is she gnawing on her fingernails, there is sheer panic in her voice.

"Let me see that." Sallie sits down next to her, turns the laptop her way. "Well, I'll be darned. If her name isn't right here I don't know whose is." Sallie looks up at me. "You saw the list we got from Sisterhood Select this morning. She wasn't on it, right?"

I'm shaking my head. "No."

My mind drifts to our protocol. Last night after Sisterhood parties, around nine o'clock, all the active members voted from the Sisterhood Select app on their phones. Then Sisterhood Select compiled a list of the results and sent it back to us sometime before six o'clock this morning. Sallie submitted that list—all the girls we were inviting to Pref—to Panhellenic this morning at seven. Annie Laurie was not on it.

"I don't get it," Lizzie says, scratching the back of her head.

Selma leans back, runs her fingers through her hair. "We're in trouble."

"Hang on, girls. Whatever the mistake is, we can fix it," Gwen says calmly. "Let's call Panhellenic. They'll get it all sorted out." Gwen, I've learned from this turbulent week, is the eye of the hurricane.

"Let's all go over it one more time before we do," Lizzie says. Gwen and I step behind the others and we all lean into her laptop as she slowly scrolls down each name on the screen. Sure enough, Annie Laurie Whitmore's is right there in black and white, scheduled to be at Alpha Delt for our second round of Pref.

"Let's call Panhellenic. It's the only way we'll know for sure," Gwen says.

Lizzie takes out her cell phone, places it down on the table, and presses the speaker button. When a lady picks up, she leans in. "Hi, this is Lizzie Jennings, Recruitment Chairman for Alpha Delta Beta. We have a discrepancy and we're hoping you can help us."

"Sure thing," the lady says. "What's the discrepancy?"

"So we submitted our list of the PNMs we're inviting back to Preference to y'all this morning at seven. And a certain girl was *not* on it. Yet now, she's on our schedule for today. We're confused, to say the least."

"I guess so. I'm Terry, by the way."

"Hi, Terry," Lizzie says.

"We'll get to the bottom of it. But in the meantime I can assure you our system is accurate. What is the Potential New Member's name?"

"Annie Laurie Whitmore."

"Okay. Let me look at something." We hear her typing in the background. "May I put you on a brief hold?"

"Sure." Lizzie glances at us and we all agree.

Nervously I take a sip of my coffee and a bite of the doughnut I brought from upstairs. Bits of sugar glaze fall onto my blouse and I brush them off in haste. Then I replay every detail of the morning in my mind: Sitting on Sallie's bed. Looking at the list. Making sure Ellie's name was on it. Going down for coffee, getting a monster hot flash, Lilith going to her room to get our Tiffany key rings—

Now Terry is back on the line. "Lizzie, are you there?"

"Yes. I'm here. And so are our Rush Advisors, Sallie, Wilda, and Gwen, and our chapter president, Selma James."

"Hi, ladies."

"Hi, Terry," we all say at the same time.

"Okay, so, I've got the list you submitted pulled up on my computer. It's in alphabetical order, as you know, and I'm scrolling down to the bottom." A pause. "Annie Laurie Whitmore is the second to last name on the list. Ellie Woodcock is last."

We all look at each other. "That's impossible," Gwen says, calmly. "She was never on our list to begin with. In fact, she didn't get a single vote."

"Huh. I'm looking at the list you uploaded this morning right here on my computer, and—"

"There has to have been a mistake. Y'all must have pulled from the wrong list," Lizzie says, desperately.

"With all due respect," Terry's tone is kind, but authoritative. "I'm not doubting there's been a mistake, but we've never made one like this before. I'm the Greek Life Advisor and I've been here four years. Are there any other discrepancies?"

Each of us looks at the other and shrugs. "We haven't looked that closely," Lizzie says. "It was only when we saw Annie Laurie's name that we knew something was wrong."

"Would you mind going over your original list again—to make sure all the other names on today's schedule jive with yours?"

I get a sinking feeling—a knot in my stomach. Someone has deliberately messed with our list.

"Sure," Lizzie says, desperately. "We'll do that and call you right back."

Sallie gets up and pulls out her own computer from her bag, then sets it up on the table. "I know I'm crazy, but not this crazy." She opens her laptop. Then laughs her incredibly fun, infectious laugh, the one she could bottle and sell for a million dollars if that were possible. I love how she never takes life too seriously. "Okay, here's the list I submitted this morning. I'll read the names on mine," Sallie says to Lizzie, "and you check them against the Panhellenic schedule." Since they're in alphabetical order, Sallie begins with Becca Billings. We have no As this year. Then she proceeds down to the Ws. "The last two names are Cali Watkins and Ellie Woodcock."

"That's it! Cali Watkins is not on the schedule." Lizzie turns around to face Gwen and me.

"Let's call Terry back," I say, desperation settling into my own voice. "It's human error. Whitmore and Watkins are right next to each other. Surely they'll correct it for us." Bless Cali's heart. Ellie told me she'd only been invited back to five sororities for Philanthropy. There's no doubt in my mind it was her lack of recommendations. I didn't even have to work hard to convince everyone here of her sweetness. All of our girls loved her right away. Goodness me, her résumé alone touts her bright future. She is perfect Alpha Delt material.

"We can call, but . . . I don't know." There's sheer exasperation in Lizzie's voice as she redials Panhellenic. When Terry answers she dives right in. "Okay, so, we've found the mistake, but it wasn't on our end."

"Huh. Be specific, please," Terry says.

"Cali Watkins is our second to last name on the list. Not Annie Laurie Whitmore."

There's a pause, then with slow, deliberate words Terry responds. "I understand there's been a mistake, but . . . it didn't come from our end. Honestly, I'm looking at the list you submitted this morning and Cali Watkins is not on it. Annie Laurie Whitmore is."

Selma leans in toward Lizzie's cell phone. "Terry, hi, this is Selma James, President of Alpha Delt. There must be something we can do to correct this."

"Hi, Selma. I'm afraid there's not. All the schedules have been printed and delivered to the Gamma Chis. They've made their phone calls already—it's . . . eleven fifteen. The PNMs will be at the Union in forty-five minutes dressed and ready for Preference."

Lizzie sighs loudly. "Okay. Thanks for your help. We'll just deal with it. Have a good day."

"You, too." Before Terry hangs up she says, "Wait, Lizzie, are you still there?"

"Yes, we're still here."

"Out of curiosity, are you ladies the only ones with passwords to your Panhellenic account?"

"I think so," Lizzie says, looking around at all of us.

A rush of adrenaline floods through me at two hundred miles per hour. My breath catches. Selma and Lizzie whip around, eyeing me curiously.

"We'll look into that, Terry," Selma says, keeping her gaze on me. "Thanks for your help."

When Terry ends the call, Sallie, Gwen, and I shoot disgusted looks at one another.

"Why are y'all looking at each other like that?" Selma asks.

Gwen shakes her head, chews on her bottom lip. Sallie forces a smile. I make sure my face is expressionless, but my heart is running faster than a cheetah. Finally, Sallie peers at us. "I smell a rat. Just sayin'."

Selma breathes deeply, then presses her lips together. "We never thought to revoke Lilith Whitmore's password—after she rolled off the Advisory Board. Is she the rat you're smelling?"

"OMG," Sallie says. "That's what took her so long this morning."

The Tiffany key rings, the wine, the beautiful meals, asking me to be on the Advisory Board—it's all making sense.

Lizzie crosses her arms in front of her. "What do we do now?"

"What can we do?" Sallie says. "Unless we want to create a stink that'll bring the House down."

And to think I was ever happy about reacquainting with Lilith Whitmore. Or our girls living together. What's wrong with my judgment? "We could never prove it," I say, staring into space.

"And she knows that," Gwen adds, moving over to a chair. She sits down and drums her fingers together. None of us can speak.

After a long moment of silence another inescapable truth occurs to me. "May I make a suggestion?"

"Go ahead. We need all the suggestions we can get right now," Selma says, in an angry voice.

"We'll never be able to prove Lilith Whitmore changed the Rush ballot, do y'all agree?"

Everyone nods.

"Then I seriously think it's in our best interest to keep this among the five of us. If it gets out . . . well, we can all imagine what that will look like. Like it or not, Annie Laurie will be an Alpha Delt. And—like it or not—we need to be kind to her."

Lizzie puts her head down on the table. Then raises it slowly. She blows a long puff of air, then turns to me. "I guess you're right. We don't have a choice. We have to embrace her. Love her like a—"

"Sister," we all say.

"But everyone will know something's up. No one voted for her," Lizzie says.

"If anyone asks, just say there was a computer error," Sallie says. "But affirm there's nothing that can be done and," she sighs, "everyone must accept her."

"If anyone has a problem with it, send them to me." Selma taps her hand on the table. "I hate to say it, but this is what sisterhood is all about. We have a chance to become role models."

"But what about Cali Watkins?" I ask. "It's not fair to her."

"I know. It's sad; we all loved her," Lizzie says. "But it's not like she was one of our tip-top rushees. No one even knew Cali before this week."

I start to plead her case but Gwen speaks first. "It's too late anyway." She glances at her watch. "She's already gotten the news. I just hope she hasn't been cut from Rush completely."

THIRTY-NINE

CALI

My covers are pulled up under my nose when I hear the knock. There is no one I want to talk to. Not my grandparents. Not Jasmine. Not even Ellie. All the girls on my floor have been so caring and consoling upon learning I'd been cut from Rush. Even Annie Laurie has been sort of nice. But I still don't want to talk to any of them.

I can hear them outside my door. They're all running around getting ready for Bid Day. Their music and their laughter are unwelcome reminders of what life at Ole Miss is supposed to look like. I can barely breathe from the pain piercing my heart. Every time I think of what happened yesterday I get sick all over again.

Another knock.

It couldn't be Jasmine. She would use her room card. And besides, not wanting to be around all the "Rush hoopla" as she calls it, she went home to Greenville for the weekend with Carl. If I don't answer, whoever it is will eventually go away.

Now there's a third knock, this time with a voice. "Cali, are you in there? It's Sarah."

Sweet Sarah. She's been totally amazing. Even though I put my phone number down as a way to contact me should I not be invited back to any Houses, she came over here anyway to tell me in person. When I saw her, yesterday morning, she took me by surprise. I had no idea I'd been dropped. I mean up until Friday I'd only been cut from nine sororities. My Sisterhood schedule still included three Houses.

After the final round was over, completely torn by the choice I had to make, I walked over to Weir Hall, stood silently in line another hour and ranked my bottom choice. I put Alpha Delt and Pi Phi down as my top two choices. Everyone knows if you get asked back to Pref, you're guaranteed a bid. All of the girls, at all three Houses, were so, so sweet. Genuinely sweet. I never considered every one of them, including my bottom choice, would cut me completely. I thought that I had a real chance.

It was ten o'clock yesterday—the morning of Pref—and I had the door to my room open. Everybody's doors were open. Music emanated from most every room on the hall and girls were running in and out of the bathrooms getting ready. My new dress, the pale blue one I bought at Reed's that matches my eyes, with the long red zipper down the back and a square neckline with spaghetti straps, was laid out neatly on my bed. My brand-new heels were underneath. I had already washed my hair and put on my makeup.

When Sarah stuck her head in my door I was surprised to see her. Like I said, I felt good about getting invited back for Preference. As soon as I saw the bitter look on her face I knew something was wrong. "Cali, can I come in?"

"Of course. What are you doing here?"

She shut the door softly behind her. The way she lowered her head confirmed my worst fears.

All the blood drained from my face. "Have I been cut?"

She looked up, nodded slowly. "I'm so sorry."

Tears flooded my eyes, as if they had been there all along, waiting for someone to turn on the faucet. They poured down my cheeks; there was no stopping them. I don't think I could have cut them off if I wanted to. In fact, they surprised me. I hadn't cried that hard in two years. Not since I lost Annabelle, my beloved black and white kitty.

Slowly I sat down in my desk chair. Sarah moved Jasmine's chair right next to mine and pulled me in close. I cried and I cried. Then I sobbed. Geez, looking back on it, I'm super embarrassed. Mascara smudges were all over the shoulder of her white Gamma Chi shirt. I kept wiping my eyes with my fingers, but it still got soiled. She even stroked my hair while I cried, like a mother would do. "It's okay," she kept saying. "So many girls have been cut this year. With the variable quota and all. Several of them even suicided the one they wanted and were cut. You're not alone. It's messed up this year, Cali."

Moving off her shoulder I met her eyes. "I didn't care which sorority I got. I just wanted to belong." My nose had been dripping nonstop so I wiped it with the back of my hand. When I finally got up to look for a Kleenex, I couldn't find one so I grabbed a bath towel from the rack behind the door.

"I know there were Houses that would have loved to have had you as a new member, but perhaps you cut them early on. Sometimes it just works that way. It's hard to know what to do."

"It's hard when you don't have a pedigree." Without a Kleenex I had no choice but to blow my nose into the towel.

"A what?"

"A pedigree. Last fall when I was at work one day I heard these ladies from Memphis talking about Rush here at Ole Miss. They said you have to have a pedigree to belong to a sorority. I knew I didn't have one, but I still wanted to try."

"That's ridiculous. They didn't know what they were talking about. Maybe that's a holdover from the past, but we look for girls who are sweet and kind and well rounded. Like you."

"I wasn't able to get recs for all the Houses, either."

"Now that's a problem. You have to have recs."

"I know. But when I called the Panhellenic office last fall, they told me to ask my mother's friends for recs. My family is crazy, Sarah. You don't even want to know how crazy."

"My parents are going through a messy divorce. I know all about crazy. Trust me."

I felt so close to Sarah in that moment—so close I almost told her about Mom. Because the reason I was crying uncontrollably was because of her. I was sure that somehow, someone found out my mom got addicted to meth— or God knows what kind of drug—moved to California with some guy, and abandoned me when I was five years old. Just ran off and left me like I was a doll she grew tired of playing with. Didn't she consider what that would do to a little girl's self-confidence? To grow up thinking her own mother couldn't care less about her? Sure, she left me with her parents and not in an orphanage. But she didn't even have the decency to consider how it would break my grandfather's heart to have his only child leave her family behind. And cause my grandmother to drink from the same bitter cup day after day. But, as usual, I decided to continue the lie.

Now—Bid Day morning—Sarah's back at my door again. I love her, I really do, but I still don't want to talk to her. Even though I know she's come to console me again. I can't take much more consoling. My thumb is sore from rubbing my prayer stone. My eyelids look like I've been stung by two bumblebees. My head is pounding, I'm sick to my stomach, and I want to die. The death of a dream is worse than I ever imagined.

I feel like a baby bird on the edge of her nest trying to get up the courage to take her first flight, but when she finally, finally takes the leap and tries to soar, her wings fail and she falls twenty feet down on her fragile little head. And she's dead. Before she ever gets started. Before she ever gets the chance to prove herself.

I am leaving. I am getting as far away from here as I possibly can. If only I could do it all over again. Choose another school where sororities don't exist. In Maine or Washington State, maybe—as far away as possible. On second thought, Washington is too close to California. And the entire West Coast is not big enough when it comes to staying away from my mother. I'll transfer to Blue Mountain College next semester. My grandparents will be happy to have me back; I know that. And while I'm home I'll apply to a college in the Northeast for my sophomore year. Surely I can get another scholarship.

So I choose to stay silent and let Sarah leave. I can hear her footsteps as she's walking off. There's a conversation going on outside my door, but I can't hear what's being said.

Five minutes after Sarah leaves, my phone rings. I pick it up to read the name, and, *surprise,* it's Sarah. But I silence the ringer and let it go to voice mail. I'm still staring at my phone when a text pops up: Cali, it's Sarah. Can you please please please call me. I've got good news! Three heart emojis. Three smiley faces. And a slice of cake.

What could be good news? I've been cut from Rush. What news can Sarah possibly tell me that will make me feel better? I don't want to call her back. *I really wish she would leave me alone,* I think, as I press redial.

She answers on the first ring. "Cali! Where are you? I've been looking everywhere."

I sigh. Loudly. Right into the phone.

"No one on your floor knows where you are."

"I'm going home," I say softly. "Why would I want to stay here? It's Bid Day. I'm not getting a bid." I'll take a cab, if I have to, back home to Blue Mountain. I've certainly saved enough money to afford one.

"Yes, you are!"

I sit straight up.

"I can't tell you who it is, but you've been given a bid! I know it sounds weird, and it is, but sometimes sororities are given another chance to hand out more bids."

My head is splitting from pain and she's talking so fast I have to squeeze my face to keep up with her. "Wait. I don't get it."

"It's totally weird. And I never told any of you in my group about this because it doesn't happen that often. It's called a snap bid."

"I've never heard of that."

"I know. Like I said, it doesn't happen that often. And you're going to want to think you were second choice, but I promise you this sorority is over the moon about you. I can assure you they would never offer a bid to a girl if they didn't love her. I mean really *love* her."

"Sounds sort of weird."

"This whole Rush season has been weird," she says. "With the variable quota and all. So many things got turned around. Tons of legacies were cut. And, like I told you yesterday, several girls decided to suicide and they ended up not pledging anything at all."

I finally let go of the breath I've been holding the whole time she's been talking. "Okay, so—"

"So get up, girl. Put your Bid Day clothes on and meet me in the Grove in an hour. *You are a new member!*"

Hearing those last five words finally convince me this is truly happening. But I still can't speak. I'm ... I'm starting to cry, again, and I don't know why. If what she's saying is true I should be dancing. But I'm not. I'm crying.

When I whimper into the phone I feel the pangs of embarrassment all over again.

"Cali, do not worry about this. Everything that has happened will become a faded memory. When you walk inside your new sorority House today and meet your pledge class and all the actives, you'll be so happy. Please get excited and enjoy this. It will be one of the best, most fun days of your entire life."

"Thank you," I manage to say, in a soft voice.

"Are you okay, Cali?"

"Yes. I'm just a little shocked. And . . . embarrassed."

"Don't be. Please don't be. It's all gonna be great. You'll be there today, promise?"

I suck in a deep breath. And swallow my pride. "Yes, yes. I promise." My pain is subsiding and I feel a little energy moving through my body. "Sarah?"

"Yes?"

"Is this really happening?"

"It's happening, baby. I'll see you in an hour. Don't be late."

"Okay." The tone in my voice is finally starting to lift. "See you soon." Once we hang up I climb down off my bed, steady myself against the mattress, and let the last two minutes sink in.

My hands are trembling. I can hardly punch in the numbers to Ellie's phone. "Answer, please answer," I say out loud.

Background music is blasting when she picks up. "Hey. Are you okay? Your Gamma Chi's been here looking for you."

"I know. Can you come to my room?"

"I didn't know you were in there. I'll be right over."

By the time I make it to my door, Ellie's already here. When I open it, I see her studying my face. "Oh, Cali. I'm so sorry." But then I smile and she smiles with me. Her eyes light up along with mine. "What's going on?"

I pull her inside, shut the door. "Sarah came here to tell me . . . *I'm getting a bid!*"

"*What?* I'm so happy!" She hugs me and we spin around, holding each other's arms.

"Can you believe it?"

"Yes, I believe it. What happened?"

I tell her everything that Sarah told me five minutes ago. Almost word for word.

"This is freaking awesome! Get dressed, Cal. Right now. We need to leave here in thirty minutes."

I glance at myself in the mirror, and my shoulders fall. "What about my eyes? I'm so embarrassed."

"Oh forget it. There have been so many girls around here with swollen eyes this week. Who cares?"

"I feel like I'm dreaming, El." Purely for fun, I pinch myself on the arm. "Am I?"

She laughs. "No, you're not dreaming. And don't worry about washing your hair. Just wash your face and I'll come by here in thirty minutes to get you. Okay?"

I can feel my cheek muscles lifting as I shoot her my best smile. Then I shut the door behind her.

"Yes! Yes!" I say out loud, wanting to scream at the top of my lungs, but instead I fall to my knees, tip my head back, and lift my arms high in the air. "Thank You, Thank You, thank You, God," I say, before crawling back up. Then I jump around the room. As fast as I can get my hands on it, I open the iTunes app on my phone and turn it up as loud as it will go. It's J. Cole, my favorite rapper.

As soon as I hear his voice I jerk and slide around the room. Instead of his lyrics, I make up my own and sing out over his. "I'm getting a biiid," I sing. "It's official, I ain't lyin', and I sure ain't dreamin'. *Yeah.* A bid's coming my way. Did you hear that, Martin, I told you, I ain't being left out in no cold. *Yeah.* That Cali Watkins…she the bomb. *Yeah.* 'This slang that I speak, don't change that I'm deep.' *Yeah.*"

J. Cole fades and I scroll though my phone till I find Alicia Keys. When I hear the first chords, I dance over to the door and study my reflection in the mirror. Jerking the rubber band out of my hair, I watch it cascade onto my shoulders. Then I sing with her.

"She's just a girl, and she's on fire." I bend down and flip my hair over.

"Hotter than a fantasy, longer like a highway." Then jerking back up, I watch myself juke my hips from side to side, like I am *the* coolest dancer on earth. I'm not—I'm terrible—but I imagine that I am, until Alicia finishes her last note.

Thirty minutes later, dressed in my official Ole Miss uniform, I'm headed to the Grove with Ellie.

FORTY

MISS PEARL

I t's the calm before the storm," Mama Carla says when we meet each other in the foyer. I'm just getting into work and exactly two hours from now this House will be exploding with 140 new Alpha Delta Betas. "You've got to see this." She takes me by the hand and leads me toward the downstairs study lounge.

Trudy is jogging right behind us wearing her ADB doggie jersey. One of the girls gave it to Mama Carla last year.

"See what?" I ask.

"This year's present crop." She swings open the door and before God every inch of the floor, the tabletops—even the cushions on the sofas—are loaded down with gift baskets full of every Alpha Delt novelty one can imagine—cups, headbands, pencils, beach towels, clipboards, and picture frames, just to name a few. Clusters of blue and white balloons are covering the ceiling and the scent from what must be three hundred bouquets of roses makes me imagine I'm stepping inside a perfumery. All the parents and grandparents—even the boyfriends and other girlfriends—send congratulatory gifts to the new pledges.

There's a stuffed orca, the Alpha Delt mascot—taller than I am—on a stand with his fins up, like he's dancing at Sea World. Sometime early this morning, all of the florists and gift boutiques in town got their own secret copy of the final bid list from Panhellenic. They're all sworn to secrecy, not even the parents or gift givers know who is pledging which sorority. By the looks of this place I'm quite sure they worked their arms and legs off putting these baskets together.

"Lord, Mama Carla, I'm not sure I've ever seen this much loot. In all the years I've been here."

"And the crazy thing is, because of that variable quota deal, we have fewer pledges than last year. Take a gander, Pearl." Mama Carla sweeps her hand from one end of the room to the other. "Try to guess which pledge got the most."

I scan the presents one more time, but I don't need to. "Are her initials ALW?" I say with a chuckle.

"You got it. When I saw that six-foot orca come in with her name on it, I said, 'Well now'"—she crosses her arms under her chest—"'isn't that a productive way to spend money.' Wonder how many starving children that thing could have fed?"

That Mama Carla. She's always got a wisecrack up her sleeve.

"Uh-oh, look at Trudy." I point toward the door. One of the baskets on the floor has been tipped over and that tiny thing is running off with a chocolate orca in its mouth.

"Trudy!" Mama Carla yells, and all I can see is her backside as she's running down the hall.

When I catch up with her I decide to tell her what's been on my mind all weekend. I've hardly slept from all the mental scenarios I've created. "I've been thinking about what you said on Monday and I've decided you're right."

She snatches the candy out of Trudy's mouth. "Bad girl, Trudy. Don't you know chocolate can kill you?" The orca is full of tiny teeth marks, but it seems Mama Carla has intervened just in time. "So much for this." She stuffs the candy into her pants pocket. "Now, what were you saying?"

"I'm ready to put in my application for House Director."

The elation on her face lets me know she's happy to hear it. "Pearl Johnson. That's fantastic."

"Well, I think so, too, Mama Carla. What's my first step?"

"I imagine you'll need to say something to Lilith Whitmore."

I shake my head, let out a moan. "That's what I was afraid of."

"Oh for heaven's sakes. What can that woman say? You're qualified and she knows it. Don't be afraid of her."

"Oh, I'm not afraid of anybody, and I'm sure not afraid of her. My only hesitation is, well, you know what it is. Something tells me she won't take me serious."

Mama Carla looks me dead in the eye. "She'll have to take you serious. This is 2016. She'll be here in a little while, so why don't you go up and tell her you'll be turning in an application."

"You think today is best?"

"Actually," she says, flicking a finger in the air, "today is perfect." She gives me a thumbs-up. "She'll be over the moon about Annie Laurie. You'll be catching her at just the right time."

"I hope you're right."

"You and I both know she's been living for this moment. You have no idea how many times I've wanted to tell her she needs to get a life and . . . never mind. I better shut up before I get myself in trouble. Let me go put Trudy up before she kills herself."

Mama Carla scoops Trudy in the crook of her arm and heads back to her apartment. I head on into the kitchen. Sleeping until eight this morning has made a big difference. I actually feel refreshed. Maybe Mama Carla is right. Today is the perfect day. Aunt Fee will be in soon, and I can't wait to tell her about my talk with Mama Carla. She'll have her own opinions on how I should approach Miss Lilith.

Once the kitchen door closes behind me, I go on about my business, making sure things are in order. This year the girls have decided to change Bid Day up a bit. Instead of taking the celebration off campus, we're having a big supper on the back patio to welcome all the new members.

When I drove in this morning I noticed both of the giant Bid Day banners hanging from the second-floor balcony and boulder-size balloons scattered all over the front yard. Streamers that had been placed on the porch railings, were fluttering with the wind. A blue-and-white balloon arch stretched over the front walkway, and a photo booth was on one side of the yard—oversize Greek letters on the other. No telling how late the girls were up last night getting it all done.

Around eleven, I look up at the clock and it's past time for Aunt Ophelia to make it in. Next time I look, a whole hour later, she still hasn't made it in. At first I figured she was in church, so I didn't worry. But now I'm ready to peel off a layer of my skin. Late-to-work is not her way. When I dial her number, there's no answer. Something is dead wrong.

Not two minutes later, here comes Mama Carla prancing into the kitchen, looking like she's got news. Mr. Marvelle, Kadeesha, Helen, Latonya—we're all here today and it seems everyone, besides me, is in a happy mood. Even though the staff is exhausted from Rush Week, right along with the members, Bid Day has everybody feeling good.

Mama Carla claps her hands together to get our attention. "Listen up, y'all." Everyone stops what it is they're doing to look at her. "The bad news is Miss Ophelia is sick today. But the good news is you've got me. I'm hoping we can all pitch in and get Bid Day dinner ready. Y'all okay with that?"

She looks around and everybody nods. Then she looks at Latonya, Aunt Fee's sous chef. "You might want to put me on chopping duty, Latonya. I've been known to burn up an oven before." She chuckles, turns back to the rest of us. "Don't start thinking that's the reason my husband left. That had more to do with a hot young nurse."

Everyone in the kitchen laughs, besides me. I can't laugh. Not today. I'm too worried about my auntie.

Mama Carla rubs her palms together. "Okay, y'all, put me to work. What can I do first?" She's not acting like she's worried about Aunt Fee. Could I be overreacting?

Mr. Marvelle doesn't seem worried either. He gives her a hearty chuckle. "You can march yourself right out that door, that's what you can do."

"What? I thought y'all might like to boss me around for a change."

"If you're still planning on hot chicken and waffles with maple syrup and a nice big salad, then we all know what to do," Mr. Marvelle says. "Latonya's chicken is almost as good as Miss O's."

"Hey now," Latonya says. "I know how to fry. Learned it from the best."

"So you're saying you can handle this without me?" Mama Carla asks, feigning disappointment with a hand on her brow.

Latonya flashes her a confident smile. "Go on, Mama Carla. We got this."

"It's not that hard," Kadeesha says. "I don't know what all the fuss is about."

I whoosh around and get up in that fool's face. I've had about as much of her as I can stand for one lifetime. "Nobody's putting up a fuss, Kadeesha. Nobody but you."

She backs away, holding her palms up. "Whoa. What's wrong with you?"

"I'm worried about my auntie. Can't you understand that?"

She narrows her eyes, shuts her mouth. But I can tell the venom is spewing backward, coating her tongue—all the way back to her throat—with spite.

As soon as Mama Carla leaves, I buy myself a Co-Cola from the machine in the buffet line. It's about the only thing I know of can calm my nerves—besides an extra-long menthol cigarette—and I put those nasty things down ten years ago last month. Then I walk straight out the back door. All the chairs are folded against the wall, so I pull one out and sit myself down.

I've had only one sip of my cold drink when I hear the door creak. Mr. Marvelle walks outside, pulls out his own chair. Then he sits down slowly, right next to me. "I'm telling you, Pearl. Miss O is not well." Hearing those words—especially from him—puts a twenty-five-below-zero chill through my body.

I take another sip, swallow slowly, then clear my throat. I look that man straight in the eye. "Tell me what makes you say that. Besides holding her stomach, what else have you noticed?"

"For one thing, she looks like she's dead on her feet. A few days ago, she toted one of these chairs back to the stove." He grips the seat. "Had to sit down back there. You know Miss O ain't like that. She runs circles around everybody in this kitchen."

"I know that's right." Why haven't I been paying more attention? My head feels heavy. I can hardly move. "Notice anything else?"

"Let's see, now." He's rocking nervously in the chair, dragging his teeth back and forth across his lip. "She told me one day that her legs was bigger than normal and that she felt full all the time."

"Wonder what that could mean?"

"I don't know." He's rubbing the insides of his palms, something I've seen him do when he's agitated. "I have noticed she uses the bathroom quite a bit."

That's all I need to hear. I reach into my pocket and yank out my phone. Once I punch in the numbers, it rings five times. "Come on Fee, pick up the phone."

After two more rings I think it's going to voice mail, but then I hear her answer. "Hello, dahlin'." Her voice is low and weak. "I was expecting your call."

"Why didn't you tell me you were sick?"

"Just a cramp; that's all," she says calmly. "Don't worry about it."

"This has been going on too long for me not to worry." She can always tell when I'm upset and today my voice has distress signals blinking at top speed.

Somehow she musters more strength. "I'm fine, baby. I'll see you tomorrow. Tell everybody I appreciate them fillin' in for me."

"What do you need, Aunt Fee? Tylenol? Food? Co-Cola? I'm coming straight there when I leave here, and don't you tell me I'm not. May as well let me bring you something you want." I dart my eyes toward Mr. Marvelle. He's sitting on the edge of his chair. Listening to my every word.

"How about a dinner plate?" she asks. "That would be right nice."

"What else?"

"I've got everything else I need right here."

"I'll see you after I leave," I say. "Around seven thirty."

"Don't rush. I'm not going nowhere."

I lay my phone down on my knee. Look over at my friend. "Something's bad wrong. I can hear it in her voice. I know it, Marvelle, I know it in here." I point to my heart.

He doesn't respond. All he does is close his eyes and let his chin dip down to his chest. We sit in silence a long while, until it's time for me to check the downstairs powder rooms for paper. The new pledges will be here in under an hour.

FORTY-ONE

WILDA

*O*nly *ten more minutes of this,* I think, as I zip up my suitcase. *Then I'm free!*
Sallie and Gwen are in their rooms getting dressed; then we're all
dashing out of here together. We've decided to drive our own cars to campus,
despite the crowded parking lots. None of us wants a reason to return to
Lilith's condo, plus I have a feeling we'll be mowing down anything in our way
to get the hell out of Dodge as soon as Bid Day is over.

I've decided to resign from the Advisory Board—effective immediately.
Aside from the obvious reasons, I need to get to the business of finding a job.
And putting this dorm room debt behind us, before Haynes finds out. All I've
been able to think about these last few days is the big-ass lie I told my husband. Yes, so Ellie could have a beautiful dorm room, but also, if I'm honest,
to get in good with Lilith Whitmore. Oh dear God. I must have temporarily
lost my mind.

Ellie told me this morning she wants to room with Cali next year. Once
that happens Lilith Whitmore will once again become a distant memory. I
may run into her every now and then at a game or at the Alpha Delt House,
but it will require no more than a wave or, at most, a brief chat. I can practically
taste my emancipation already.

Lilith left for the House early this morning, something about checking on Annie Laurie's gift baskets. Technically, she's not supposed to know Annie Laurie is getting a bid to Alpha Delt, but since we were the only House Annie Laurie visited on Pref, it's no secret.

Sallie is good friends with the owner of The Perfect Pick, a gift shop on the Square, and the lady told her confidentially they "could retire" on the profit from Annie Laurie's Bid Day presents. Sallie said the lady was kidding, of course, but she did say everyone would be shocked at the amount of loot Annie Laurie would be raking in this afternoon.

Haynes and I ordered Ellie a bouquet of roses from Oxford Floral, which I can't help hoping will be white, the Alpha Delt flower. We also picked out a gift basket full of Greek-lettered trinkets. Mama has also ordered her roses. It's funny when I think about it. The folks at Oxford Floral already know if our daughter will be a Tri Delt or an Alpha Delt. Yet I have no idea. The suspense is killing me.

The sound of a text message dings from the bottom of my purse. After rifling through the clutter I finally get my hands on my phone, but when I do I'm filled with an overwhelming sense of dread. Suppose it's a last-minute Rush catastrophe? Squeezing one eye shut I peek at the screen, then exhale when I see: Haynes. I sit back down on the bed and touch the message icon.

> Red Alert. Your mother is "surprising" you today. She wants to meet "the Whitmore girl" and her parents. Knew you'd rather know.

Just when I was starting to feel better. I groan and type back: Thanks for the warning. I thought you abolished "Whitmore" from your vocabulary?
Right away he texts back: I have. But I made an exception. Saving you from sudden-death-by-surprise was more important.

> Me: Thanks for the save.
> Haynes: My pleasure. It was the least I could do.
> Me: Why don't you come with her?
> Haynes: We have a toilet that needs fixing.
> Me: Lucky you.
> Haynes: I love you.

Me: I love you more.
Haynes: Impossible.

Closing my eyes, I bathe—actually, I saturate myself—in the warmth of Haynes Woodcock.

I'll never forget the first time I laid eyes on him. It was our freshman year—the Alpha Delt, Sigma Nu pledge swap. Back then, the membership chairmen—one from the sorority and one from the fraternity—got together and paired up the pledges ahead of time. We could put in requests if we had seen a cute boy we wanted for a date, but most of the time everyone went potluck.

We'd all be crammed in the foyer of the Alpha Delt House. The membership chairmen would call out two names and the pledges would meet in the middle. Then all the actives and remaining pledges whooped and hollered when the two, mortified and flustered, paraded out the front door.

Haynes was standing dead center of the Sigma Nu pledges. His thick, collar length, sandy blond hair flipped up on the ends, and even from where I stood I noticed his double row of dark eyelashes underneath thick sandy eyebrows.

The light from his eyes—so blue they looked like aquamarines—and the way he smiled, bobbing his head in response to whatever it was his fraternity brothers were saying, caught my eye. I watched him, and him only, praying we would be matched together, until he and Emily Kay floated out the front door arm in arm.

Later at the Sigma Nu House, after looking all over, I finally spotted them at the keg refilling their cups. There seemed to be an electrical current, a force beyond my control, pulling me toward him like a magnet, so I left my date and glided over.

After watching me standing there like an idiot with a pleading look in my eyes, Emily finally introduced us. "Wilda, meet Haynes Woodcock."

"Haynes who?" I had obviously missed that ever-so-important detail back at the House.

"Woodcock," he said, with a playful grin. Then he whispered in my ear. "Whatever you do, no rooster wisecracks. Only penis jokes allowed."

I laughed at his joke, probably harder than I should have. Standing next to him made me giddy and nervous. Then the reality of his last name hit me with a crushing blow. "Have you ever thought about changing it?" I heard my-self saying. Because at that point I was already down the road—down the aisle, rather—and the voice inside my head was screaming: *No! You can't be Wilda Woodcock!*

"When I was young. Then I got over it."

Once I realized what I had done, my face turned fifty shades of red. Who says something like that? And to a cute guy? No matter how bad his name is.

"Mind if I call you Wildebeest?"

Every guy I'd ever known from junior high to high school had called me Wildebeest. Disappointed, but grateful to still be chatting with him, I said, "Sure. But I should warn you, my horns are sharp and they can really hurt if you're not careful."

Then *he* laughed out loud. "I'm not afraid of a stinking Wildebeest," he said, with his chin in the air.

"Good. Then we should get along famously."

"Woodcock and Wildebeest. Now there's a duo for you."

I wanted to say, right then and there: I know. I've already thought of that, but if I marry you, I become Wilda Woodcock. And I have spent my entire life mad at my mother for naming me Wilda in the first place. But instead I said, "Actually, it should be Wildebeest and Woodcock. 'I' comes before 'O'."

"Fair enough. Wildebeest and Woodcock." We looked up and Emily was gone. From then on we really were Wildebeest and Woodcock. He must have seen something way more wonderful and attractive than a real wildebeest, which is one of the most unsightly animals God has ever created, with a hunch-back and a long-faced head with ears sticking out at right angles. And I ask myself why my self-confidence was in the toilet?

A few years later, when our partnership became official, Emily, who be-came one of my best friends and bridesmaids, told that story at our rehearsal dinner.

Six months earlier, I had been sitting at our breakfast room table when I told Mama I wanted to marry Haynes Woodcock. She took a dainty sip from her Herend china teacup and placed it slowly back down on the saucer with a light *clink,* her pinky high in the air. Sitting straight as a pencil, all the while staring out our bay window, she drummed her fingers against the teacup. "Wil-da Wood-cock," she said slowly, overenunciating each syllable. *"In-ter-es-ting."*

I jumped out of my chair, threw my arms overhead. "Why are you making this worse? You gave Mary your mother's name and I was your first girl. You could have given me a normal name, too. But *nooo,* you had to name me after a college roommate whom you've hardly seen since!"

"Why, Wilda is a lovely, old-fashioned name. But Woodcock." She pressed the back of her hand to her forehead. "How un*foh*tunate."

I stormed off to my room and we've never brought it up since. Despite that, and a host of other dramatic to-dos along the way, I still named Ellie after Mama. Even though Haynes wanted to name her Wilda. Love for our parents is deeper and more primal than any of us realizes, I suppose, despite the measure of childhood trauma. Haynes has spent the last thirty-four years telling me how beautiful I am, and how beautiful my name is.

Some days I actually believe him.

Years later Haynes told me that no one had ever asked him before if he wanted to change his name. But I'm convinced that question, no matter how cringeworthy, is the reason I'm Mrs. Haynes Woodcock today. And right now, after the week I've had, getting home to my husband is all I can think about.

FORTY-TWO

MISS PEARL

Miss Lilith is the only one in the present room when I walk past. She doesn't notice me, so I stand off to the side and watch her maneuver around the baskets, fingering each and reading the gift tags. Every now and then she'll take a second to smell one of the rose bouquets, but it seems she's more interested in checking out the sender.

She reminds me of my ex-mother-in-law. Always sticking her nose where it doesn't belong. When she happens to look up we lock eyes. She stiffens, stands up straight as a nutcracker, like she's been caught with her hand in that ol' cookie jar. The chain on that Alpha Delt pin she always wears on the end of her breast is still jiggling.

"Good morning, Miss Lilith," I say from the door. "Looks like Santa's workshop in here."

"That it does." She bends right back down, checks another gift tag. "I'm looking for the gifts Gage and I sent Annie Laurie. Making sure they're all here. I'm not supposed to know she's a new member. But I have my sources. How are you, Pearl?" she asks, stepping carefully between baskets.

I move on into the room, find a clear spot on the floor to stand. "Doing fine. Doing real fine. And what about yourself?"

"Couldn't be better. I've been waiting eighteen years on this day."

Mama Carla is exactly right. This lady is as happy as a rabbit in a two-acre garden.

"Annie Laurie will love it here," I tell her. "I remember you asking me to look after her back in August. Do you remember that?"

From a squatting position, she finally takes a moment to look at me. "If I recall we were standing right outside of this room. I had just bonked your poor nose."

Whacked is more like it. "Sure were. And I remember you telling me you would like me to be her third mother."

"Yes, and I'm hoping you're still up for the challenge." She stands up straight, puts a hand to the small of her back. "As her daddy likes to say, 'our girl can be high-maintenance.'"

"That's exactly what I want to talk with you about, Miss Lilith. I'd like to use this opportunity to tell you I'd like to take Mama Carla's place as housemother. That way I can really look after her."

She plays like she didn't hear me, going back to searching through the gifts. But I know she did.

"Miss Lilith? Did you hear what I said?"

She looks up. "I heard you say something about Carla. In the future, however, I would prefer to be called Mrs. Whitmore."

Here we go. I best buckle up. "I said I'd like to apply for the House Director's job—Mrs. Whitmore."

She doesn't respond. As I'm about to repeat myself a third time she does. "Pearl. You are such a dear to want to take that on. But you haven't been to college." Her tone is pleasant, but there's a distinct air to it.

"Yes, ma'am. I've been to college."

That woman's head turns around so fast she may have to be treated for whiplash. "You've been to college?"

"Sure have."

"Here? At the University?"

"Yes, ma'am. I attended for a year."

She puts a hand to her heart. "You *attended*?"

"Yes, ma'am."

"So you didn't graduate?"

"Not yet. But I've decided to go back and earn my degree." I smile when I say it. I'm proud of myself.

She *tsks,* loudly. "I'm sorry, but the House Director is required to have a college degree."

"It won't take me long. I'm a good student, Miss Lil—Mrs. Whitmore. My plan is to take online classes at night. And work school around my schedule here."

"I'm afraid that's not possible. Our Alpha Delt bylaws clearly state that the House Director *must* have a college degree." It doesn't take a dummy to read what's written all over this lady's face. Relief.

But that's not going to stop me. "I can promise you I would be an excellent House Director. I love these girls like they're my own daughters. I already know the job backward and forward. Mama Carla said it herself." As soon as those words leave my lips I know I've said the wrong thing.

One hand flies to her hip, another taps her thigh. She lowers her chin. "Carla has been talking with you about this?"

"We briefly discussed it when I told her I wanted to apply."

"I see." Her big eyes blink rapidly. "It's not her place to discuss her position with anyone. I'm the House Corp President." She taps her chest. "I do the hiring."

Aunt Fee's warning to be careful of Lilith Whitmore is echoing inside my mind. It's like she had a pair of binoculars into the future with a setting labeled: *Pearl, Beware.* "Mama Carla didn't mean any harm."

"I'm sure she didn't, but I'll have to remind her to let me handle this in the future. I best go tell her that right now."

"But—"

That lady moves right past me, pushes the door open with the palm of her hand, then blasts out of the study lounge, straight through the dining room toward Mama Carla's apartment.

I let about thirty seconds pass, then head on out myself. What I need is some time to think things through. This did not go anywhere close to the way I planned. If I can just make it to my closet without anyone stopping me, I can get some time to myself. Between Aunt Fee's illness, and now Miss Lilith's reaction to my application, I am second-guessing everything.

On my way there, I notice an older couple walking in through the front door. The lady's arm is hooked through the gentleman's. They stop in front of Miss Lilith. I can't hear what they're saying, but something tells me to change course and head that way, see if I can be of help.

Just as I'm within earshot I hear Miss Lilith say, "I'm afraid you're in the wrong place. Cali Watkins is not on *our* bid list. You should check across the street at the Chi Theta House. Why, they are a perfect fit."

FORTY-THREE

WILDA

Her fresh-out-of-the-beauty parlor Jackie O. hairdo is sticking out in the crowd like a penguin in a desert. She's got a high tease on top and the bottom flips up, three inches off her shoulders. I keep telling her to just go gray, but she insists on a dark dye job despite her age. Somebody, somewhere, once told her she favored Jackie Kennedy, so she's worn her hair like that ever since.

"Mama!" I let my mouth fall open and fly a hand to my chest.

"Surprise."

"What are you doing here?" We hug, but as always I'm careful not to muss up her hair. I've been warned since I was a little girl.

"Surely you didn't think I would let this special day in my granddaughter's life go by without me." She's standing amidst a zillion people in the Alpha Delt front yard, all waiting the arrival of our new pledge class.

"How silly of me," I say with feigned regret. "It is a bit of a drive, though."

"For pity's sake, Wilda, it's not but an hour and a half. I wouldn't have missed this for the world." Instead of looking at me she's craning her neck around the yard, inspecting the crowd like she's searching for a puzzle piece. "Where is Lilith Whitmoah? I haven't seen her yet."

"You don't even know what she looks like, Mama."

"Of course I know what she looks like. We're Facebook friends."

"Of course you are," I say, forcing a smile. "I'm sure she's around here somewhere." It's not the right time, but I plan to tell Mama every detail of Lilith's indiscretion.

When I turn to search for her myself I happen to spot my real surprise, standing next to a photo booth, waving like an imp. I gasp. Then I practically mow Mama down to get to him.

"You stinker!" I throw my arms around his neck and squeeze him harder than I have in years. Haynes and I haven't been apart this long since he went to a legal conference in Indianapolis after we were first married. "I thought you had to fix our toilet."

"Come on. Our little girl is joining an Ole Miss sorority today." He looks so dang luscious to me dressed in his khakis, a blue button-up, and a navy fleece vest. I've missed him so.

When I let go, Mama is right next to us, eavesdropping. "My darling son-in-law drove me heah. He is such a fine gentleman." She scans Haynes head to toe. "And looking so handsome today." I've not heard her speak his praises this much—ever.

"When will we know about Ellie?" Haynes asks me, stepping aside to let three active members with painted faces, dressed in frilly costumes and wigs, pass by.

"Not until she opens her bid card. Maybe you should go to the Grove and video her when she opens it. Then call me and let me know which one she gets."

"Then you can video her here or at Tri Delt. Got it." He nods, slides his hands in his pockets.

"What about me?" Mama asks.

"You stay here with your daughter. I'll be running back from the Grove."

"I suppose that's best." She turns to me. "I told Haynes on the way down, I can't leave here today without seeing that gorgeous dorm room."

I give her the evil eye behind Haynes's back. She shoots me one in return.

"That's one of your mother's missions for the day," Haynes says, chuckling. "I wouldn't tell her how much it cost. I didn't want her passing out in my truck."

I swallow, and calmly change the subject—not daring to meet Mama's eye.

"Honey, maybe you should go on over to the Grove. I got a text from Ellie right before I got here. She's on the way there." I push him on the shoulder, in an attempt to get him away from Mama.

"Trying to get rid of me?"

"No. I just know it will take you a minute to find her. Thousands of people are over there already."

"I can't wait to surprise her." He leans in for a kiss. "I'll call you as soon as I know something. Keep your phone handy."

"It will never leave my hand," I say, waving it in the air.

As soon as he's out of earshot I glare at Mama. "Why did you have to bring up the dorm room? You know I'll take you over there. Please leave Haynes out of it."

"Ohhh," she moans like a hospital patient. "You are wearing me out with this deception. Let's go ahead and tell him. He won't mind. Especially in light of who Ellie has for a roommate."

"Don't you know Haynes by now? He couldn't care less about that. I am not telling him."

"Spare me the details." She sighs. "Can you show me to the powdah room, please? I'd like to check my lipstick before I meet Mrs. Whitmoah."

Once she passes in front of me, I roll my eyes.

To get into the House we have to pass under a blue-and-white balloon arch over the walkway. Someone has turned up the volume on the rap music and it's honestly enough to make me turn back around. But I have to say, despite the razor-thin odds, if Ellie happens to pledge Alpha Delt instead of Tri Delt, the rap and this nightmare of a week will be well worth it.

Mama has to back away to let more members through. I see her jerk her palms up as if she's afraid of getting knocked down. After they pass she lifts her chin and adjusts her posture. "They're packing them in like sahdines these days."

"It's not like it used to be." The last thing I need is for her to fall, so I stretch an arm around her back and lead her through the front door.

While we're making our way toward the powder room I see her eyeing my hair. "Have I told you about my new hairdress'ah?"

"You've switched? I'm shocked. You've been going to Robert as long as I can remember."

"I was exhausted from hearing about his sexual escapades. At first I thought it was humorous, I even egged him on, but after thirty years I'm starting to wond'ah if he's actually a porn star in disguise."

I stop. "Mama. *Ew.*" This is not a subject I fancy speaking about with her.

She lifts her chin. "Tell me about it. That's why I switched to Brandon. He's young and cutting edge." She sighs. "He's gay, too, but aren't they all?"

Another mom is leaving the powder room. She holds the door for us as we step through. When Mama is in front of the mirror she stops. "Wouldn't you agree my hair is the best it's ever looked?" She lifts one side with her palm. "Brandon. Gould's in the mall. You should give him a call."

"Thanks, but no thanks," I say while looking at her in the mirror. "I have no desire to get my color done in front of a big mall window with everybody in Memphis walking past. A woman wearing a black plastic poncho with purple cream on her scalp is not an attractive look."

"Well. Don't say I didn't try." She inspects my hair once more before stepping inside the stall. I hear the latch click. "You're due for a new 'do."

FORTY-FOUR

CALI

If anyone could feel the pirouettes the butterflies are making inside my stomach right now, I think they might feel like they were about to see Jesus in person or at the very least take a walk on the moon. Am I really sitting here in the most beautiful grove in the country, with veins of yellow and red just beginning to spread onto the leaves?

Am I truly in the middle of two thousand pedigreed girls, listening to the president of Panhellenic welcome us all from the stage? There is breath moving in and out of my lungs and a pulse on my wrist, so this must be real. Maybe this is my first step toward becoming Mississippi's first lady governor.

I hate that I can't see Ellie. Her Gamma Chi Group is on the total opposite side of the stage. But this time we have a plan. As soon as we open our bid cards we are going to meet at the back of the last row of seats before we make the grand dash to our new Houses.

Even though I haven't the slightest idea which sorority has invited me to become a new member, Ellie knows for certain she will either be an Alpha Delt or a Tri Delt. She said it was the hardest decision of her life. After sitting in the ranking room for two hours after Pref last night she finally put Tri Delt first, although she really doesn't care which one she joins. Technically, I'm not supposed to know. Keeping our choices a secret is one of the Panhellenic rules. As much as I want to be in the same sorority with her, I have resigned myself that it's not going to happen.

I feel a tap on my shoulder, then someone whispering in my ear. "Cali, hey."

After whipping around in my chair, I see a girl I met at freshman orientation last summer. And she's sitting right behind me. "Mary Gaston!"

"I can't believe I'm just now seeing you," she whispers. "After all these months." She starts to say something else, but the Gamma Chis are dancing onto the stage for their big Reveal. Finally, we get to learn to which sorority each of them belongs.

I pat her on the hand and whisper back, "We'll talk in a sec."

Someone onstage yells, "Kappa Alpha Theta." Then all the one hundred Gamma Chis—it looks like there are at least that many—sing the entire Theta song, clapping and dancing like they're all Theta sisters. Most of the rushees around me aren't all that interested in the Reveal, but I'm super interested and I'm inspecting every girl up there, dying to spot Sarah.

When the song is over, about ten Gamma Chis break from the group, run to the front of the stage, and rip off their T-shirts to reveal their Theta jerseys underneath. Sarah is not one of them.

Next up is the AOPi song and like before, once the song ends, the real AOPi's run to the front, remove their Gamma Chi T-shirts, and strip down to their AOPi jerseys. ADPi follows. My eyes are hurting from focusing this hard. I've been insanely curious for over a week now, imagining which sorority Sarah actually belongs to. The same routine goes on for another three sororities, and still no Sarah.

When the Alpha Delts begin their song, I remember it right away. Having made it all the way through Sisterhood there, I'd heard them sing it for their door stacks. It's super catchy and I find myself singing along. When it ends and their Gamma Chis are bopping up to the front of the pack, I think I see Sarah. Wait… it *is* Sarah! She's an Alpha Delt? Oh my goodness, Sarah, you're an Alpha Delt? I'm so happy for Ellie right now I can't breathe. They could be sorority sisters.

When the Reveal is over, while the Gamma Chis are walking off the stage and heading back toward their groups, the Panhellenic president strolls onto the stage again. By the way everyone is screaming you'd think Ole Miss had won the National Championship. And she's taking her sweet time. Come on, girl, we're all dying here.

"Now for the moment you've all been waiting for," she finally says into the mic. All the girls scream louder—if that's possible.

"Listen up," she yells, over all of our voices. "Once all the Gamma Chis get back to their groups they'll be handing out your bid cards. *Do not open them.* Wait till your Gamma Chi tells you to do so."

Parents and grandparents, sisters and brothers—and college boys galore—are all over the Grove, sneaking in closer to get a better view. After learning I'd been cut from Rush, I told my grandparents I wouldn't be joining a sorority. I'm not sure which was worse, Papaw's tears or mine. I never thought of calling them back this morning to tell them otherwise. Dammit, I wish they could be here.

Now I see Sarah rushing back to our group, waving our bid cards over her head. She's wide-eyed and she can't contain her smile. I'm dying to tell her that Ellie is my best friend and to watch out for her at Alpha Delt, in case she joins, but there's too much excitement going on.

"Keep these in your hands," she says, while handing us our small white envelopes. By the way she's bouncing it seems she's as pumped as we are. "I want y'all to open them at the same time." Then she spreads out her arms and motions us to huddle in closer.

I'm staring at my envelope. The paper is thin and, if I really wanted to, I could press down hard enough to read the lettering. But I've come this far, waited this long, and I am not about to ruin my own surprise. Besides, I couldn't care less which sorority's name is inside. All I know is this might be the happiest moment of my life. I sure can't think of another one any better. Truly, I feel as though I might burst at any second.

Sarah seems the same way—buoyant and electric—and now she has to yell because other groups have opened their bid cards and girls are already screaming. "Here we go: five, four, three, two, one. *Open!*"

Everyone in my group is ripping into their envelopes, but my hands are shaking so hard I can't. Now they're all screaming and jumping. Some are already running. And I'm still trying to slip my damn finger underneath the flap of my envelope. My heart is literally pounding like it's trapped and begging to get out of my chest. Finally, I tear off a corner and rip the envelope in half. Once I'm able to pull out the card and see what's written, my jaw hits the ground. I suck in a pound of air and gasp. Then I blink about five times, certain there's been a mistake.

ALPHA DELTA BETA
CORDIALLY INVITES
CALI WATKINS
TO BECOME A NEW MEMBER OF
SIGMA MU CHAPTER
UNIVERSITY OF MISSISSIPPI

I'm staring at my bid card in shock. Everyone in the Grove is screaming. But my mouth won't move. I can't make a sound. Tears spring to my eyes. When Sarah said I was a new member I never considered it would be Alpha Delt. Never-in-my-wildest-dreams never.

"Hold up your bid card, Cali." I look up and Sarah's directly in front of me, holding her phone at eye level. How long she's been videoing is anyone's guess. "Had you fooled, didn't I?" She keeps going until I practically knock her down for a hug. "You deserve every bit of this," she says in my ear, then pulls away. "When I told you everyone was excited about you, I knew what I was talking about. Every single girl at Alpha Delt loves you. If it hadn't been for variable quota none of that craziness would have happened. *Now, run!*"

When I look around, I'm one of only a few girls still left in the Grove. I rush out to the end of the row, pushing over one, then two chairs trying to get to Ellie. But when I make it to the place where we both agreed to meet, she's not there. I'm too late.

So I run. Run like a track star, out of the Grove, past the Union, and down Sorority Row toward the Alpha Delt House. My adrenaline is roaring— I've never felt anything like it. Hundreds of boys are lined up on both sides of the street watching, and when I pass I look several of them in the eye with pride. Like I'm this new person, an adult peacock, well, actually a peahen, who has suddenly broken out of a shame shell that had bound and crippled her fan feathers far too long. When I pass the Tri Delt House I look for Ellie, but it's no use. Their crowd is enormous, spilling into the street.

I can see the Alpha Delt House in the distance so I race faster, remembering my cross-country days when I could see the finish line. When I finally make it to the curb, completely out of breath, the members are dressed in adorable costumes, lined up and holding hands across the front walkway—underneath a balloon arch—to form a human tunnel. *More than likely, I'm the last one here,* I think, so I take my place in line behind other new members. When it's my turn, I duck and run. Girls are cheering as I move through, patting me on the shoulder. I am free. I am alive. I am home!

At the end of the tunnel Sarah is waiting for me. She must have run as fast as I did to get here. She pulls me aside and slips a white Alpha Delta Beta jersey over my head, then hands me a much-needed bottle of water. After wrapping a ribbon name tag necklace around my neck, she squeezes the life out of me, then the two of us drain our water bottles.

After swallowing the last sip, I look around the yard. "This day seems surreal, Sarah. When will it all sink in?"

"Maybe by the time you graduate," she says, flicking her eyebrows.

There's fun music blasting and a giant crowd in the yard so it's hard to move around. Girls I don't even know are hugging me. When one of them grabs me, I happen to look out over her shoulder and lock eyes with a familiar face. It's Annie Laurie. Her mother and father are on either side of her, and she's holding an enormous arm bouquet of white roses. It's bigger than she is. Seriously, it seems like there are one hundred roses nestled in the crook of her arm. She acts surprised to see me, but still rushes over and offers a ceremonious hug.

"We're sisters," I say, careful not to squish her flowers.

"I'm so excited." I think she says that, but between the music and the screams it's hard to know for sure.

"Have you seen Ellie?"

"She went Tri Delt." Someone pulls her away and then another girl grabs me. I can tell she's one of my new pledge sisters by her name tag. I'd seen her at Martin, but we'd never met.

"I'm Becca Billings," she says.

"I'm Cali Watkins. Nice to meet you."

"Are you as happy as I am right now?" Her dimples and her big brown eyes are welcoming. I like her right away.

"Maybe happier. I was…I didn't think this would ever happen."

"Where are you from?" she asks.

"Blue Mountain, how about you?"

"Jackson. Well, actually Madison County. And I know what you mean. After hearing about variable quota I never thought I'd be here right now. But thank God I am!" She balls her hands into fists and raises them over her head.

Sarah, whom I thought I had lost in the crowd, hands both of us blue-and-white Popsicles. After introducing herself to Becca she huddles us in closer so we can hear her better. "Y'all are gonna meet so many people today, you'll think your heads are exploding."

"I can't wait to meet all the girls in our pledge cla—" I spot Mrs. Wood-cock a few feet away with her arm around a girl who looks just like...oh my God. *Ellie.*

FORTY-FIVE

CALI

I dash over and tap Ellie on the shoulder. When she turns around her look of sheer shock, mixed with over-the-top glee, is worth every second of the pain I've been through to get here. "Wha—*what?*" She bounces from one foot to the other, then grabs the sides of her head. "No freaking way!" She flings her arms around my neck and we dance in circles.

"I thought you went Tri Delt."

"I didn't get it. And now I know why." We pull apart from each other, but keep holding hands. She turns to her mother. "Mom? Why didn't you tell me?"

"And spoil the surprise?" Mrs. Woodcock reaches out and scoops me in her arms. "Cali. You have no idea how happy I am to see you on this lawn. Welcome home, sweetheart."

"Thank you, thank you so much. It truly does feel like I'm home." I'm hoarse. And hot. So I hold up my hair, fan the back of my neck. If only I had a ponytail holder.

"This is my dad and my grandmother," Ellie says, motioning to the two of them. "Cali's my next-door neighbor at Martin, my best friend on campus, and now my sorority sister."

We hug again, and nearly trip over the person behind us. "Sorry," I say, turning around, to a man who doesn't seem to mind.

Mr. Woodcock draws me in for a hug, too. "Well, Cali, I've heard a lot of great things about you, young lady."

"Thank you, likewise. Ellie talks about y'all all the time. And I'm sorry about not getting to the game a few weeks ago." I'm still embarrassed by this. Leaving them with an empty seat.

He swipes away my apology. "It's perfectly fine. No need to apologize."

"I'm Mrs. Dyson, Ellie's grandmothah. It's lovely to meet you, Cali." She extends her hand and I'm not all that sure of the carat weight, but there's a whopper of a sapphire on one of her fingers, and it's surrounded with diamonds.

"Thank you, Mrs. Dyson," I say. "It's lovely to meet you, too."

Mr. Woodcock runs his fingers through his thick hair. "Ellie tells me you're from Blue Mountain."

"Yes, sir. I've lived there all my life."

"Childhood home of Amanda Wingfield," Mrs. Dyson says.

My mouth falls open at the mention of Amanda. "Yes, ma'am. She's one of my favorite literary characters."

Mrs. Dyson looks surprised. "So you're familiah with Tennessee Williams?"

"Oh yes, ma'am. I've read *The Glass Menagerie* so many times I can practically recite it by heart." What a coincidence. Ellie's grandmother loves Tennessee Williams, too.

Mrs. Woodcock cuts her eyes at her mother, places a hand on my shoulder. "Cali, by the way, is a genius."

I hold my hands up. "Oh no, ma'am, far from it. But that's a nice compliment. Thank you."

"I hope you don't mind me bragging on you." Ellie's mom turns to the others. "Cali made a thirty-two on her ACT."

I cringe. It's not something I want made public.

"Wow," her dad says, leaning forward. "Ever thought of going into law?"

"Actually," I say with a winsome smile, "I have. Then I want to be governor."

Mrs. Woodcock reaches out to stop a member weaving through the crowd.

ADB Greek letters are painted in blue on her cheeks. "Selma, have you met Cali Watkins?"

The girl smiles when she sees me, claps her hands together. "Not yet. Hey, Cali, I'm Selma James. This year's president." Then she stretches out her arms and pulls me in tightly.

"Thank you so much for the bid," I tell her, once she lets go. "I'm really happy."

"Are you kidding? We're the happy ones. Cali, let me take this opportunity to tell you how much we all love you here."

"I can feel that. I intend to do great things for our sorority. I promise you'll never regret your decision."

"Phhh." Air escapes her lips. "None of us have a doubt about that."

Someone sneaks up from behind and puts a cheek next to mine. "Tired of meeting people yet?" It's Sarah. I love how she's keeping a watchful eye out for me.

I whip around, look at her like she's crazy. "Hardly."

"Speaking of meeting people," Mrs. Dyson says, "has anyone seen Lilith Whitmoah?"

I notice Ellie's mom and Selma exchange looks.

"No, ma'am," Selma says matter-of-factly. "I haven't seen her." Then she asks Mrs. Woodcock if she can speak with her privately. The two of them hurry inside the House.

Sarah puts a hand on Ellie's shoulder and one on mine. "Y'all have gifts inside."

"Gifts?" Ellie and I look at each other and grin. *Who would send me gifts?* I wonder. This day is getting better by the minute.

Sarah's arms reach around both of our shoulders. "Let's go take a peek. Then we'll get your faces painted."

As the three of us turn to leave, Mrs. Dyson takes Ellie by the hand. "I want to see your elegant dorm room, dahlin'. Before I head back."

"I'd love for you to see it, Mimi, but can Mom take you? I don't want to leave right now."

"I'll take you, Eleanor," Mr. Woodcock says before turning to Ellie. "Your mom won't want to miss a minute of this, either."

Ellie gets pulled away before we make it to the front door. Sarah and I keep moving, though, and when we step inside the House I am awestruck. Although I was here for Rush, all the members were crammed inside and I couldn't appreciate the decor. Now, standing here with my mouth open, I'm sure it's the most beautiful house I've ever been in.

I don't remember it from before, but the crystal chandelier hanging in the foyer is enormous, and it seems like it's beckoning all who come to call. A round table sits underneath with a massive display of white roses. A grand staircase twists and turns to another floor. The ceilings must be twelve feet tall, and the furniture looks like it's been staged for a photograph. My eyes travel all over the walls then stop at the composites in the foyer. Will my picture actually be on the one for this year? I feel like pinching myself.

Sarah can tell I'm speechless because my eyes are the size of baseballs and I'm turning a slow circle. "Pretty awesome, huh?" she says.

"It's . . . it's magnificent."

There's a dining room off to the side with enough formal tables to seat hundreds of girls at the same time. Sarah takes me by the hand. "Let me show you around."

First, we walk through the dining room, straight back to what's known as the study lounge. Today it looks like anything but. Hundreds of baskets and floral arrangements are taking up every centimeter of space. Sarah tiptoes through a sea of blue and clear cellophane until she finds a medium-size basket tied at the top with a bow. "Looks like this one's for you." She steps back carefully and hands it to me.

"This is crazy. I never expected this." After untying the bow, I dig in right away, finding all kinds of Alpha Delt novelties: a beach towel, a coffee mug, a sweatband, a picture frame, even an adorable stuffed orca. "Who would send this to me?"

"Read the card," Sarah says.

I place the basket down and open the small envelope.

To Darling Cali
With Love, Wilda & Haynes Woodcock

With a hand over my heart, I try to take this all in. "It's from Ellie's parents. I can't believe how nice they are." While I'm rifling through the basket she hands me two more. One from a few Alpha Delts I don't even know and the other from her. Both are jammed with more Alpha Delt trinkets, T-shirts, and game-day buttons. I can see them inside the cellophane.

"Tell you what. Save these for later," Sarah says. "Everyone just takes their baskets home when they leave. Besides, you have one more surprise."

She guides me down the hall, back to the foyer, and leads me to what she calls the Receiving Room. The first thing I notice is a black baby grand piano, which I can't wait to get my hands on. Then I notice a tall grandfather clock behind it. The room has elegant furniture with floral draperies, fine artwork on the walls, and a lovely oriental rug. In the corner are two formal chairs…I gasp. Mamaw and Papaw are seated in those chairs and Mamaw is holding a vase of long-stemmed white roses. Just the sight of them brings mist to my eyes and I stretch my arms their way. "Who told y'all?"

They both stand and we hold on to one another. I do not want to let them go.

"This lady right here," Papaw says, moving over to Sarah. He nudges her playfully into his side.

When I look at her, she's grinning. I give her a playful push. "You keep a good secret, Sarah Mason."

Mamaw hands me the roses. "We're very proud of you, Cali."

"How long have y'all been here?"

"Let's see now." Papaw props his chin on two fingers. "We got to town around nine this morning. Had breakfast, then took our time walking over. We've been here a couple-three hours, I believe."

"And we spent a good deal of the time talking with the nicest lady." Mamaw glances over her shoulder. "She was here a few minutes ago. Pearl. Pearl Johnson. She's the housekeeper here."

"Oh my gosh. Miss Pearl's our everything," Sarah says. "Don't you love her?"

"We certainly do," Mamaw says. "She's worried about her aunt, though. Apparently she's sick today."

"Miss Ophelia's sick?" Sarah looks genuinely concerned.

Papaw nods. "Pearl told us she had some kind of stomach issue. She seemed mighty upset about it. But I could tell she was happy for the distraction." He pats me on the back. "She's looking forward to meeting you, Cali baby."

Annie Laurie's mom peeks inside the room. I wave at her and smile. There's no doubt she sees me, but she plays like she doesn't and never waves back. She's still within earshot when Papaw calls to her. "Excuse me, ma'am. *Ma'am.*"

Mrs. Whitmore stops, turns around slowly.

He stretches an arm across my back, squeezes my shoulder. "See? We were right. Our Cali is an Alpha Delta Beta."

At first it seems Mrs. Whitmore doesn't want to acknowledge my grandfather. A long, awkward second stretches into five until at last, she puts a hand over her mouth. "I must have made a mistake." She squints one eye, then shoots me a hard smile. "Welcome to Alpha Delt, California. You are a very lucky girl."

FORTY-SIX

MISS PEARL

Around one o'clock I heard the screams. I looked out the front window and there they were—the new crop of Alpha Delts—running down Sorority Row like bears after honey, crying and laughing at the same time. In a matter of minutes every inch of the lawn was covered with hundreds of people and all things Alpha Delt. Between the costumes and the balloons, the painted faces and snowcones, it looked like a carnival.

Normally I like to go outside, join in on the festivities, but today my mind is stuck on Aunt Fee. One minute I'm worried sick, the next I'm so mad at her I can't see straight. It's one thing to be stubborn, but it's something altogether different to be dumb. And that's what I'm calling her this morning. Plain dumb.

All I keep thinking about is why she hasn't told me what's going on with her. I would have made sure she had seen a good doctor a long time ago—health insurance or not. Lots of our girls have doctors for parents. Surely one of them would have been happy to see her. I'd have carried her anywhere in the state she wanted to go.

My other concern—my conversation with Miss Lilith—well, that has had to take a back seat.

On my way up from the basement, I see Trudy sneaking down the hall toward the present room, so I go on and scoop her up before she gets herself in trouble again. On Bid Day, Mama Carla always stands at the front door, welcoming our new members. I have a feeling she must have left her apartment door cracked open by mistake.

When I walk up with Trudy in my arm I give Mama Carla a wink, put her back in the apartment, then close the door. It's only when I turn around that I notice whom it is Mama Carla's talking with. I had only met him once, on move-in day, and I don't like him.

"Have you ever met Sarah's dad, John Mason?" Miss Carla asks.

What I'd like to do is bite his head off, but instead I smile politely. "Yes, I have. How are you, Mr. Mason?"

"Very well, thank you."

"I sure am proud of Sarah. Gamma Chi is not an easy job."

"You're right about that," he responds with a chuckle. "I talked with her yesterday. One girl in her group was cut from Rush completely."

"I don't find many reasons to be glad I've got some years on me, but that's one of them," Mama Carla says. "I don't miss those days. Girls getting cut from Rush. That just bothers me. If I could change the whole darn system I would."

"Good luck with that," he says. "Where were you in school?"

"Millsaps. I was a KD, but sorority life was nothing like it is here. Trust me."

John Mason leans closer to the two of us. "In my day, guys didn't get cut from Rush. We'd just send the nerds over to the Farmhouse frat at State."

I suppose he thinks he's funny. He's chuckling with a hand covering his belly. But neither Mama Carla nor I laugh back. It was a rude thing to say. I turn to leave, but that man reaches out to stop me. "Did you go to college, Pearl?"

I turn back around. There's nothing upbeat about my tone when I answer. "I attended Ole Miss for a short while. I'm planning on finishing at Rust soon as I can."

"Rust College in Holly Springs. I pass right by there on my way from Memphis to Birmingham." He shifts his weight from one foot to the other, slides his hands in his pockets. "My company has locations in both. I've been making that drive twice a month now for years."

Exactly what does he think interests me about that?

"The only good thing about it is I get to see Sarah more often." As coincidence would have it, here comes that baby now, walking up from behind with a new member. "Speak of the devil," Mr. John says to her.

"Hi, Dad." She sounds annoyed. "When did you get here?"

"About fifteen minutes ago."

"Are you alone?" Uh-oh. Sarah's wondering if his young girlfriend has tagged along. She's talked with me about her so many times I feel like I know the girl.

"I am." After an awkward pause he ogles a new pledge standing next to Sarah. "Who's this pretty girl with you?"

Sarah rolls her eyes. "Cali Watkins. One of our new members."

Cali Watkins? So this is the young lady Miss Lilith lied about. Told her sweet grandparents she wasn't getting an Alpha Delt bid. That woman has stooped to an all-time low. I shudder to think what she'll do next.

"Hi, Mr. Mason," Cali says. "Your daughter is an angel."

"Well, I think so." Mr. John's eyes travel all the way down to Cali's toes. "Alpha Delt needs a pretty redhead around here."

With a bashful smile Cali mutters, "Thank you."

Sarah makes a quarter turn. "And this is Mama Carla. Our fabulous housemother."

"Hello, Cali. It's great to meet you."

"You, too. Should *I* call you Mama Carla?" Cali asks, hesitantly.

"You better."

Sarah scoots over and throws her arms around me. "Last but not least, this is Miss Pearl. She's our everything."

"Welcome to the family, Cali. We'll take good care of you." I reach out and snuggle her into my other side. She's a little-bitty thing. Redheaded with freckles and pretty blue eyes. I already want to protect her. From Miss Lilith, I mean.

Cali starts to say something, but Sarah interrupts. "Miss Pearl is, like, our in-house therapist. She always has great advice. You can tell her anything."

"No appointment necessary," I say.

Cali's eyes sparkle with an inner glow.

"You two will get along famously. I just know it." Sarah's smile fades as she turns to her father. "I've got a bunch to do today, Dad." She steps toward the door. "You coming, Cali?" Sarah's anger is not something she intends to hide. I've counseled her through many an hour of her pain. And I must say I can't blame her. She'll have to forgive him sooner or later. But it can't come until she's ready.

"I know when I'm not wanted." He smiles bitterly at the rest of us, then moves on out the front door without a good-bye.

"Well. I think I'll check to see how dinner's going," Mama Carla says, flashing a horrified look in my direction. "I'm looking forward to knowing you, Cali. See y'all a little later."

Sarah bristles. "Sorry. He makes me furious."

"No worries," Cali says. "I totally get it."

"Maybe I better tell him good-bye. I'll be right back." She looks at Cali. "You're in great hands."

After Sarah leaves, when it's just the two of us, Cali reaches for my shoulder. "How's your aunt? I heard she was sick."

"Tell you the truth, I'm not sure. But I'm praying she gets better soon. Thank you for asking, baby."

"My grandparents told me. They met you earlier today?" She says it like she's not sure I'll remember. When I give her a reassuring smile she adds, "They loved meeting you."

"Likewise. They're sweet as they can be."

"They said the same thing about you." Now Cali's fingering her necklace and her little eyes are darting around the foyer. Her smile has faded. Seems like she's worrying over something.

"What's wrong, baby? This is supposed to be a happy day."

"Oh, this is the best day of my life, but…" Seems like she's trying to get up the nerve to tell me something, but she's afraid.

"If there's something on your mind, go ahead on and tell it. Didn't you hear Sarah say I'm the in-house therapist? You can trust me."

She looks down, shuffles her feet, then finally locks eyes with mine. "You know Mrs. Whitmore, right?"

I nod, trying not to laugh. But a giggle is in my voice. "Oh, I know Mrs. Whitmore."

"Is she—" Now she's zipping her cross along its chain. "Does she…ever stick her nose where it doesn't belong?"

I can't keep from busting out now. "I'm afraid so. Don't quote me—if you do I'll swear on my mother's grave I never said it—but my advice to you is to have as little to do with her as possible."

"That's not so easy. Her daughter's my next-door neighbor. And now my pledge sister."

"Uh-oh." I nudge her with my elbow. Let her know I'm playing with her. Now I've made her laugh. I won't tell her about witnessing Mrs. Whitless lie to her grandparents, but I am curious about her story. "What's making you ask that, Cali?"

"I have reason to believe she's been snooping around Blue Mountain, my hometown, trying to dig up my past."

Lord have mercy. That woman knows no boundaries. There's nothing she won't do to have her way. "Well, she can't hurt you. I know that. You're an Alpha Delt sister now." I reach over, pull her into my side. "Don't you be afraid of her."

"I'm not really afraid of her . . . it's a long story."

"Look here. We'll talk about Mrs. Whitmore another time. You go ahead on and enjoy this day. Just remember who you are and whose you are." I let her go, pat her on the back. "Let me get back to the kitchen. We're shorthanded as it is. And with Aunt Fee gone . . . shoot."

"Okay. See you soon, Miss Pearl." Cali takes a step toward the door. Then whips back around. "I guess we've already had our first counseling session." Her smile tells me it won't be our last.

"You remember what I told you now."

"I'll remember."

"I got your back."

I've been taking care of these white girls a long time, but there's something special about Cali. When she smiles, it seems like she's opening a window, giving me a glimpse inside her heart. I don't know what's special yet, but I'm sure I'll find out. I always do.

After Bid Day dinner, once the kitchen is clean, and I've got Fee's meal all wrapped up in a to-go container, I hurry to my closet for my pocketbook. As the evening has worn on, my anger toward her has subsided, but anxiety has taken its place. Thinking about how weak her voice sounded on the phone has me on the verge of panic. Tears have flooded my eyes and I can't make them stop.

I see five gifts propped up on my closet door as soon as I round the corner, two wrapped and the other three in gift bags. It's not unusual, especially with the mamas around. I pull out my key, open the door, and flick on the light. Then I scoop up the gifts, pulling the door shut behind me. Since Aunt Fee's expecting me, I'll open them Tuesday. Tomorrow is my first day off in two weeks.

Tap, tap, tap. I think someone's knocking on the door, but with the loud music it's hard to tell. Easing it open a crack, I peek one eye out and see it's that sweet little Cali. She waves, and gives me a timid smile. I don't want her to see me upset, so I pull a tissue out of the box on the shelf, wipe away my tears before opening the door. "Hello, Cali. I see you found my office."

"Sarah told me where it was. I just wanted to say good night and thank you again for the pep talk."

"You're welcome, baby. You let me know what else I can do for you. You hear?" I don't mean to be rude, but I'm supposed to be at Aunt Fee's in twenty minutes. It'll take me twelve to get over there and my car's in the satellite parking lot, a quarter mile away.

"I will." She smiles at me with those pretty blue eyes, then hugs me goodbye.

After watching her take a few steps, I start to shut the door, but she turns around. "Miss Pearl?"

"Yes, baby?"

"Is there something wrong?"

Hearing her words makes me want to cry again, but I bite down on the inside of my cheek to keep from it. "I'm worried about my auntie. She's like a mother to me."

"I understand. That's how I feel about my grandparents."

"I'm headed to her house now to bring her supper."

An abrupt look of surprise springs across Cali's face. "Hang on one second, would you? I'll be right back."

Before I can stop her, Cali runs off down the hall. Two minutes later she's back holding a stuffed orca in her hand, breathing heavily.

"Please give this to Miss Ophelia. And tell her—" She pauses to catch her breath. "The new Alpha Delt pledge class can't wait to meet her." When she hands it to me, she beams.

Hesitantly, I take it from her. "Didn't you receive this today?"

She chews her lip, tilts her head. "Yes, ma'am, but I can get another one."

"That's yours. You keep it." I try handing it back, but she pushes her hand out.

"Honestly. I want her to have it."

I learned a long time ago, when someone aims to do something nice, it's important to be gracious. Telling her no might rob her of a blessing. "Thank you, baby. I'll give it to her. I'm going there now."

She grins. "And tell her I hope she feels better."

"That's mighty sweet of you, Cali. You run on now. You need to be enjoying yourself."

She hugs me once more, then waves as she's walking back to the party.

I knew there was something special about that sweet little redheaded girl.

FORTY-SEVEN

WILDA

Where are Haynes and Mama? My preoccupation with watching Ellie interact with her new pledge sisters, and getting to know their mothers, has made me lose track of their whereabouts. A hideous thought crosses my mind. *Did Mama ask him to take her to Martin to see Ellie's room?* I dismiss that notion as soon as I consider it. She's been sufficiently warned. They've most likely found a couple of chairs in an out-of-the-way corner. Neither of them can stand large crowds. But I am surprised Haynes hasn't left for home. He has court in the morning.

Watching my daughter, completely in her element amidst the Alpha Delt Bid Day splendor, has been like eating a giant piece of caramel cake. I've been savoring every single second of it. Well, the stolen seconds she's allowed me. Lilith, who I knew would be acting like Queen of the House, has been flitting around welcoming the newest members of her court. But she's avoided me like the plague. She's done the same thing to Gwen and Sallie. The irony, which has totally escaped her, is that we're all glad. We want nothing to do with her.

Mama, on the other hand, won't stop singing Lilith's praises. I wasn't able to witness their introduction, but apparently a new friendship has blossomed.

From what Mama told me they played the do-you-know game for nearly an hour. Gag me with a spoon, please. I can only pray Mama wises up soon. On the way home, I intend to recount every single detail of Lilith's impropriety.

For the third time I call Haynes's number, but it goes straight to voice mail. My goodness; I hope everything's okay. I glance at my watch. It's six thirty already. I'm one of only a few mothers left, hovering around the House like a helicopter parent, the very thing I swore I'd never become. Sallie and Gwen left a long time ago. Lilith, of course, is still here, the one and only alum on the back porch. She's been in the middle of the Bid Day party—the entire time—acting like she's one of the girls, casting her bewitchery on every one of them. That's the paradox. She's utterly charming when you first meet her.

I walk out onto the front porch considering calling Haynes again, when I spot him and Mama walking briskly up Sorority Row. I can't quite make out what he's holding, but there's something hanging from his hands and the closer they get it looks like . . . *Oh God*. It's one of the furry throws from the girls' dorm room.

Hurrying down the steps away from the House, I meet them in the street. "There y'all are. I've been calling you." I reach out to take the throw, but Haynes tightens his grip. "What are you doing with that?" I ask, my heart blasting out of my chest. My eyes dart over to Mama, but she won't meet my gaze.

"Sending it to the dry cleaners," he says, with a tone that slices through the night air—and me—like a razor blade. When he slings the throw around his neck he gets a stern look in his eye. I'd seen that look once before when he found out about a failed business venture that his little brother had coerced their mother into investing in. She tried protecting his brother and lied about it to Haynes for months. He felt terribly betrayed and—*oh my God*. "Did you like the room?" I ask Mama, hesitantly.

"Utterly spectaculah!" she says. "I told Haynes our Ellie has hit the jackpot with Miss Annie Laurie Whitmoah. Both she and her parents are so elegant. Why just look at the outfit Lilith is wearing today. Simply stunning. And that Gage Whitmoah. If he isn't the man of the hour I don't know who is. Lilith told me he flew in this morning on their Lear."

That same engorged forehead vein, the one that was throbbing at the Whitmores' Grove party, is pulsing again, even harder.

But Mama doesn't notice. She keeps on singing the Whitmores' praises.

"And their historic home. Why the pictures on Facebook have me convinced it's the grandest in Natchez. I feel sure it must have been home to one of our Confederate generals. It's so—"

"Will you *stop it*!" Haynes bellows with both hands covering his ears. "I can't hear another word of this."

Mama whips her head around to see who may be listening. By the grace of God no one is near.

"Is there anything else about that family, besides their money, that you deem utterly spectacular?" His eyes dart from Mama to me, then back to her. "Excluding that dorm room?" Now he's staring at me, but pointing at Mama. "That *she* paid for."

I look at Mama in utter devastation. She gives me an earnest look of her own.

His fists are clenched and I can see the whites of his eyes. "G—*dammit*, Wilda. You lied to me."

"Haynes. Watch your language!" Mama says. "You are in the presence of ladies."

He completely ignores her comment and glares at me. "After thirty-four years I thought I knew you. Obviously, I was mistaken."

"You do know me!" I reach out to touch him, but pull my hand back, unsure. Tears are bubbling behind my eyes. So I squeeze my face with all my might.

"Really? Then what made you feel the need to spend that kind of money on a dorm room? Then turn around and *lie about it* to your husband? Can you answer me that?"

"I—I don't know." His last question has opened my floodgate. Tears are streaming down my cheeks. I feel like the lowest form of life on earth.

"Was it to impress the Whitmores? To make them think we're rich like they are?"

"No. Hell no. There's a lot you don't know, Haynes. We've been apart so long I haven't had a chance to tell you what I've learned this week. I was waiting till I got home." I can't believe my mother is listening to this.

Even in the dark I can tell his face is red. "Learned what? How to live even higher on the hog?"

When he takes a step away I reach out and clutch his arm. "Of course not.

I've . . . Can we please talk about this at home?" I'm pleading with him, but he won't turn my way. "Haynes, *please,* look at me."

For a long moment he does look. Actually he stares, but doesn't speak, just shakes his head ever so slightly.

"Lilith and Gage Whitmore are—"

"Profligate, racist nutjobs." Now he's pointing toward Martin. "This is 2016. Who brings *the help* with them from home, four and a half hours north, to carve prime rib and shuck oysters at a Grove party? Do you suppose they provided them with hotel rooms? Or did they make them drive all the way back to Natchez at midnight?"

"Who said anything bad about colored people?" Mama asks, straightening the front of her jacket. "Certainly not I."

After giving Mama the evil eye, he shoves both sleeves up his arms. "I never said you did, Eleanor. I'm talking about *them.*" He points at Martin again. "Do you know anything about what kind of people they are?" He pauses, waiting for Mama to answer. She merely looks down and tips her head to the side. "How about the way they treat others?"

I can tell by the way she's hanging her head that she feels terrible. Even still, she never answers him.

"And now Ellie is living with their daughter. Really, Wilda, are they the kind of people you want as her role models?" The sorrow in his eyes shakes me to the core. Of course I don't want Ellie bearing any resemblance to them. I made a mistake—lots of mistakes. Somehow I have to convince him I regret all of it—the lie, the need to fit in, letting her use me. Somehow I have to make it up to him.

I start to respond, but he closes his eyes and drops his chin. "I am going inside to find my daughter, kiss her good-bye, then drive back to Memphis." He glances at Mama. *"Alone."* Then he turns back to me. "You two need to ride together. So you can lie about your means, and talk ad nauseam about Ellie's *utterly spectacular* dorm room." He shoves his hands in his pockets and strolls off. I watch him disappear inside the Alpha Delt House, leaving me alone in the street with Mama.

I grab her by the arm. And I mean *grab* her. "Why did you tell him, Mama? You knew how he would feel about it. I asked you not to."

"I never meant to, Wilda, honey. It just slipped out." She flinches and looks at my hand on her arm, so I let go.

"How? How did it slip?" My voice cracks because now I'm bawling.

"That elegant room was a *disastah*!" she says at the point of tears herself. "Clothes strewn about the floah. Makeup covering the vanities . . . cups every-wheah." She grips her temples and shakes her head. "Haynes picked up a full one and smelled bourbon right away. On the way to pour it out he tripped over something and it went all ovah that gorgeous couch, the wool rug, and that furry blanket. I couldn't help myself, Wilda. All I could think about was the money I had spent and it just spilled out."

"What spilled out?" I'm practically shouting at her.

"I told him we had to clean it up before Lilith Whitmoah sees it, and that I was sure she wouldn't take kindly to Coca-Cola and bourbon stains all over their twenty-thousand-dollah dorm room." At this point, Mama is weeping along with me.

I gasp. And feel my fingernails scraping the sides of my cheeks. Then I grip my stomach and release a loud groan. I'm about to vomit. I want to go over to Martin right now and throw up all over that damn couch. "Oh my God," I say, rocking my head in between my hands. "What did he say when he heard that?"

"He asked me to repeat myself. I tried to covah it up. But I've never been a good liar, you know that, so I finally said, 'Yes, Haynes, yes. It was very expensive, but look what Ellie got for that money.' Then I told him he couldn't put a price tag on Ellie's good fohtune. Why, landing the Whitmoah girl as a roommate is a rare coup. And I told him so."

I hold my face in my hands—unable to speak—tears covering my palms.

"We had to clean it up. That's what took us so long. Haynes scrubbed that couch, and the rug, too, with such fervah, I'm surprised the fabric isn't thread-bah." Mama reaches her arms out for me. "I told him I'd have the blanket cleaned, but he wouldn't hear of it."

Instead of folding myself into her arms I pace around her. "I need to go home. If I still have a home."

I'm walking off when she pulls my arm. Tears have flooded her eyes. "Don't you want to say good-bye to Ellie?"

I stop, look at her like she's crazy as a loon. "And have her and all her new friends see us like this? Crying our eyes out?"

Pausing to look up at the starlit sky, I notice the full moon. Mama looks up, too, and then gives me a small shrug. She always said a full moon causes all kinds of madness. Oh, the paradox of it all—like mother, like daughter. I hook an arm through hers and the two of us start the long walk back to my car.

FORTY-EIGHT

MISS PEARL

I've got Fee's dinner plate in one hand, a liter of Coke in the other, and Cali's stuffed orca under my arm. "Aunt Fee," I holler. "It's me."

I hear her stirring, but it's taking her awhile to get to the door.

Her house is in the last low-income part of Oxford on the east side. It was once Mama's. She had been renting it for years until William McKinney bought it for her after his mother passed. He gave twenty-two thousand dollars for it back in 2001. Standing out here, I can't stop my mind from flashing back to the good times and the bad. Of Mama, Mrs. McKinney, and of William.

I hear the sound of the chain jangling loose, then Fee's face peeks out. It's drawn, but she manages a weak smile. "Come in here. 'Fore you catch your death." Her voice is low and hard to hear.

"It's not that cold," I say.

"Cold to me."

I walk past her and she locks the door behind me. As she's sliding back to the couch, I notice she's hardly lifting her feet. The backs of her slippers are worn and so is the pink bathrobe she's probably been in all day. From the way her robe fits, I can tell she's lost some weight. Why haven't I noticed it before?

Grimacing, she lowers herself onto the couch. I set the food and the Co-Cola down on the end table. Then I hand her the orca.

"What's this?" She takes it from me and plays with its fin.

"Sweet new pledge sent it to you. Cali Watkins is her name. From Blue Mountain."

"Blue Mountain? Never had anybody pledge from there before."

"Now that you mention it, I believe you're right. How you feeling this evening?"

"I'll be better in the morning." She props the orca on her lap. "That food smelling mighty good."

"It's better than good." I pick up the plate, move into the kitchen, and pop it into the microwave. Once it's hot, I transfer everything onto a plate from her cupboard, grab a paper napkin, utensils, and a glass. Then I take an ice tray out of the freezer, crack out a few cubes, and fill her glass to the top. Her lap tray is sitting on the counter next to the sink, so I arrange everything, make it look real nice. The tray is in the grip of my hands when I spy a big fat pill bottle next to the faucet—preening like a peacock—daring me to look at it. I put the tray down and grab it by the throat. Oxycodone 20 mg.

Seething, I pick up the tray and march out to the den. Every part of me wants to demand that she tell me how long she's been taking Oxycodone, but once I see her petting on that orca I decide to keep my mouth shut. At least for now. So I go ahead and set the tray on her lap, then fill her glass with Coke. By the time I sit down next to her on the sofa, I'm all worked up.

"Sure smell good," she says. "Thank you for bringing it to me, baby." She puts the orca on the coffee table in front of her, dips a piece of chicken into the maple syrup, then takes a bite. "Latonya fry this chicken?"

I nod. "You taught her well." I'm biting my tongue to keep from mentioning the pills.

Aunt Fee grins. "She's a good student."

I go ahead and fill her in on the day; tell her about the new pledge class. I'm just fixing to tell her about my conversation with Mrs. Whitmore when she stops eating. Seconds later, she puts her napkin back on the tray.

"Can't you eat more than that? You've hardly touched a thing." Now she's really got me going.

"Not right now, baby, I'll save it for later."

I can't remember a single time when she hasn't finished her dinner. And I've eaten a thousand meals with this lady. That's it. I'm putting my foot down. "I saw that pill bottle," I say angrily. "I'm taking you to the doctor."

She hesitates and I'm convinced I'll have to fight with her to go, but instead she says, "Maybe in the morning. No, tomorrow your day off. I'll go the next day."

"That's exactly why we're going tomorrow," I say, my heart pounding. "Lord must have planned it that way."

"His plan always perfect," she says. "Don't have no appointment, though."

"Then we'll sit ourselves down in the lobby and wait till he can see us." I pause to collect my thoughts. "I can tell something's wrong with you."

In Aunt Fee fashion, she ignores my comment and slides onto something else. "Did you talk to that Whitless she-devil about taking Mama Carla's place?"

Despite my frustration with her, she's made me laugh. "Where in the world did you come up with that?"

"It's in the Bible somewhere. Lilith means she-devil."

"Say what?" That gets me going again. Then, despite how she's feeling, Fee chuckles, too. Pretty soon we're bending over, belly laughing. Can't stop. It's good to see her having fun.

But after a while she stops abruptly, holds her stomach, and squeezes her eyes. I reach over and touch her on the arm. "Please—"

"I'm okay, baby." She pats my hand. "Now tell me about that she-devil."

There's no use fighting with her; I'll let it go—for now. "I talked to her. She's insisting I call her Mrs. Whitmore."

Aunt Fee rolls her eyes.

"She says the job requires a college degree. Doesn't matter that I attended for a year."

A scowl reshapes her face. Her arms are crossed. Tight. "Forget her. Forget Alpha Delt, too. Go on back to college. You would have been finished a long time ago if things had turned out different."

A vision of my daughter springs into my mind. I picture her in a long hallway filled with doors. She's opening and closing each one, desperately seeking answers. About me, about her father, and why she was given away. As if she knows exactly what I'll say next she takes my chin in her hand and turns it toward her. "I know what you're thinking. And I'm gonna say it again. You did the right thing."

"I'm not so sure."

"Listen here. You gave your baby a chance at a better life. It was exactly the right thing to do. You hear me?"

I shrug, reflect back twenty-six years. In this very house. "It was selfish."

"Selfish? You had a choice and you kept that baby in your womb. You tell me what's selfish about that?"

I sigh, squeeze my eyes shut.

"You weren't but eighteen years old. Had just started your first year at Ole Miss—on a full scholarship. You weren't ready to be a mama."

If only I could reverse that decision. I'd be a mother. "Adopted children grow up with all kinds of abandonment issues, Aunt Fee. I've been reading about it."

"When that baby came out looking like she did, you done the merciful thing. I know you don't like to talk about it, but you stuff somethin' down long enough, it's bound to come out, one way or another. You know what I'm sayin'?"

Every cell in my body feels like it's on fire. There's no way around it. I gave up my own flesh and blood. The one and only chance to have a baby of my own is gone because I was too young and too selfish to raise her. "Have you ever thought about why I've worked at Alpha Delt long as I have?"

"You say it's because you love the girls."

"I do, but that's not the only reason. Suppose my baby had decided to come to Ole Miss?"

"Is that what kept you in this job? Thinking she could have been an Alpha Delt?"

"You never know. Things are changing. Lots of folks from Memphis come to Ole Miss. If she had decided to come here, I could have given her the money I've been saving for her college tuition."

"Pearl." She takes hold of my hand. "You go on and use that money on yourself." Then she looks me square in the eye. "You gave your baby a good life. And she loves you for it."

"What makes you so sure?"

"Just something I know. The Lord is looking after her, baby. He's looking after you, too, but He wants you to think of yourself for a change. Your daughter would want you to do that, too."

I start to tell her how much I long to see Autumn's face, hold her in my arms, but she puts a finger to my lips. "Shhhh, now. Stay still. Let His peace wash over you." Then she wraps her arm around my shoulders, pulls me into her side. I feel her hand on my head, stroking my hair. Sitting here next to her—warm arms snuggled around me—is the safest place I know. I don't want to move. Not now, not ever.

Before I know it she's humming. No words, just melody. With my chin nestled into her neck, I breathe in her familiar scent. The smell I've known and loved since I was a baby. Her harmony lulls me with calm as if she's an angel strumming a heavenly harp. *Don't leave me, Aunt Fee, please don't leave me,* echoes inside my head over and over again till I will it away, the way I always do when something breaks my heart.

FORTY-NINE

WILDA

Walking inside our house is like coming home and finding your pet dead. Because it feels like we're dead. The grandiose way in which I have disappointed my husband gives me an unfamiliar heaviness, like two bowling balls are tied to a rope around my neck. I can scarcely imagine looking Haynes in the eye. For the first time in our thirty-four-year marriage, I can't stand the sound of my own feet on the floor. It would be easier to lift a car off my foot than it would be to discard the cloak of shame I'm wearing. I am miserable.

My whole life, all the insecurity—and the ways I had coped—came to a head on the drive home. Every time Mama tried to say something, I had to stop her. I couldn't stand the sound of her voice. Or mine. For a solid hour all I did was think about the person I had become, why I had become that person, and what I was going to do to bury her. The *thought* of living one more minute as an insecure woman is more exhausting than actually living as one.

As much as I'd like to, there is no point in putting any blame on Mama for the deception. I did this. She kept insisting that I tell Haynes, but I wouldn't hear of it. Even though I knew I shouldn't, I still agreed to let Lilith Whitmore hire a dorm-room decorator. What kind of message did that send Ellie? Tomorrow can't come soon enough. If I have to deliver pizzas, I am finding a job and paying Mama back every red cent. Then I'll spend the rest of my life if I have to, begging Haynes to forgive me.

Daisy is waiting at the back door. As soon as she sees me, she hurls herself at my knees. I scoop her up and let her lick my face clean. Then I put her down and watch as she runs a victory lap at breakneck speed around the kitchen and our adjoining den, purely to celebrate my homecoming.

While watching her run, and the happiness she feels to have me home, I'm struck with a profound thought. Dogs are the purest, most authentic portraits of God's unconditional love we'll ever have on this earth. We humans eventually impose restrictions and let each other down, no matter the depth of our love. But God, like our beloved canines, loves and forgives us no matter what we've done wrong.

I head straight to the bedroom with Daisy at my heels. She runs right over to her little bed in the corner and curls herself into a ball. Haynes is not in bed yet, but I see a light under the bathroom door. So I stand outside and listen to the sound of water running. When it stops I hear him tap his toothbrush on the sink. Now I hear his footsteps padding toward the door. I step aside as he walks past. It's dark in the room so he can't see me. I watch him pull back the covers of our bed and slip inside.

Not wanting to startle him I tap on the wall. "Haynes," I say softy.

He lifts his head, looks my way, then falls back down on the pillow without uttering a word.

I creep over to his side of the bed. "Can we talk? *Please.*"

"What is there to talk about?" His voice is monotone. Not a hint of mercy. I knew he'd be mad, but I hadn't considered he wouldn't want to talk about it.

Taking a big chance, I lower myself down on the edge of our bed. Then, "Do you mind if I turn on the lamp?"

"Go ahead."

I turn the switch and a soft light washes over his face. With his head on the pillow, gravity pulling at his cheeks and forehead, his lines are softened, and I could swear he's thirty again. He's one of those Robert Redford types, with sandy blond hair that never bothers to gray.

We stare into each other's eyes. There's a lifetime there. We've been together since we were eighteen, long enough to teach each other how to laugh at life, how to breathe through pain. We've certainly been together long enough to know the importance of truth in marriage. *Dear God in heaven, what have I done?*

"I can't imagine how you must feel right now," I say softly.

"Pretty rotten." When he touches the side of his face I catch a glimpse of his gold wedding ring, scratched and dulled with age.

"I don't know how to begin to tell you how sorry I am."

"And I can't begin to tell you what this feels like. You lied to me, Wilda."

I hang my head. "And I can't pretend to know. You've never done it to me. At least not that I know of."

He rolls his eyes. "To have your mother, of all people, be the one to let the cat out of the bag, was…" He looks off, searching for the right word. "Emasculating. I don't know which was worse. The lie or the messenger."

I exhale a long stream of air at the mere thought of what that must have felt like. "I wouldn't blame you if you decided to leave me. For what it's worth, I'm deeply, deeply sorry."

His focus is on my face. But he has no words.

"I swear to you on our children's lives I will work every day for the next ten years if I have to and pay back Mama every red cent."

"Wilda. It's not about the money. It's the lie. I want Ellie to have a dorm room she's proud of as much as you do. Of course, I'd never have spent that much, but to think you'd go behind my back and lie about it is gut punching. Besides, I've never owed your mother a *dime*," he says angrily.

"I'd give anything for a redo. I knew it was wrong the moment I did it, Haynes, but for some reason I couldn't stop myself. I got wrapped up in the whole stupid dorm-room craze."

He shakes his head, closes his eyes. Then opens them slowly. "Why?"

"I've asked myself that question a thousand times. When Lilith's dorm-room designer called me last June, I was caught completely off guard. You remember her…Rhonda Taylor?"

"That chick was a *dorm-room designer*? Seriously?"

I nod.

"I thought Lilith hired— I don't know what I thought." His nose flares. "Go on."

"I had no idea Lilith had hired her till she called and asked me for a down payment. I know I should have stopped the whole thing right then, but it was like a force from Pluto swooped in and took over the real me. I mean, I heard myself agreeing to it, but I knew I shouldn't. Then when Mama offered to pay for it and sounded so convincing, like it was good for Ellie to be rooming with Annie Laurie, I don't know. I thought maybe she was right."

"You took your mother's advice over mine?"

"No . . . I guess." With my head hung again I feel tears stinging the backs of my eyes. But I don't want to cry because this is my fault. I don't want Haynes to think I'm looking for sympathy. I'm not. "Of all people to have hurt. You're the person I love most in the world. I am so ashamed."

"It's certainly not Rhonda Taylor's fault," he says. "If she can earn a living that way, God bless her. It just shouldn't have been from us."

"I know that now."

"Can you please tell me what it is about Lilith Whitmore you find even remotely attractive?"

"Nothing. Absolutely nothing." I'm desperate to squeeze back the tears so I tighten my face and swallow hard.

"What's changed? Because you certainly thought she was the bomb a few weeks ago."

"I don't know where to begin, but staying at her condo this week was not only an eye-opener, it changed how I feel about a lot of things."

He folds his arms outside the covers. "Like what?"

"For starters, Lilith used me. She never wanted to be my friend. It was her master plan all along to not only have our girls room together, but to get me on the Advisory Board so she could ensure that Annie Laurie would get an Alpha Delt bid."

"I'm not following you."

"Evidently, Annie Laurie had no friends in high school. All the top sororities cut her a few days into Rush. The only reason the Alpha Delts kept her is because she's a triple legacy and Lilith is the House Corp President. But after not one active member voted for her, we had no choice but to cut her after Sisterhood."

"Wow."

I take a chance and place my hand on top of his. He doesn't flinch so I go on. "It gets better. Lilith used her old password to sneak into the Alpha Delt Panhellenic account and put Annie Laurie back on the schedule for Pref.

That way she was guaranteed a bid. Anyone who goes to Pref gets a bid no matter what."

"So you're saying she deliberately manipulated the Rush ballot?"

"Yes. Right before Sallie submitted it. She distracted us with cappuccinos and gifts from Tiffany's while she crept back to her bedroom. Then she must have signed in with her old password, and added Annie Laurie back on the Pref list. The worst part is, she removed Cali Watkins in the process."

He narrows his eyes. "But Cali was there today."

"She and everyone else thinks she got a snap bid. But Selma James and I went to Panhellenic. After hearing what Lilith did, the president made an exception."

My husband's slow-moving head, back and forth, is his signature way of expressing sheer disgust. I can tell he's deep in thought.

"What are you thinking right now?"

"How to have her prosecuted."

I laugh because, I don't know, it's funny and I'm desperate for comedic relief. "There's no way to prove it, but we all know she did it."

"So what else has changed?" He turns onto his side and raises up on his elbow. "You said you feel differently about a lot of things."

"I've done a ton of soul-searching this week. Asking myself why I ever felt the need to keep up with her in the first place. And why I ever cared what she, or anyone else for that matter, thinks of me." A hot flash sinks in, so I yank off my jacket. "Another thing I've been thinking about is why I'm always comparing myself to other people. Why do you think I do that, honey? I mean, I have my theories, but I'd love to hear what you think . . . as my husband."

"I've said this before. I think it probably goes back to when you were a child. Not having a dad. Being raised by a whack job—sorry, a single mother who is, let's just be kind and say obsessed with her highbrow roots."

My eyelids fall. He's exactly right.

"Sadly, she values proper etiquette and pedigree more than her own family. I'm surprised you're as normal as you are."

"The sadder thing is, I've never thought I was like that. Before Lilith Whitmore reentered my life, I thought I was a reasonable, down-to-earth person. And look what I did to you. To gain her favor. Ugh, I feel like a giant louse."

He scratches his head, grimaces. "You're not a louse."

"I feel like one. I'd give anything if I could turn back the clock and never answer her phone call. Will you ever be able to forgive me?"

"I already have."

I stare at him in awe, and he stares back.

"What did I ever do to deserve you, Haynes Woodcock?"

"Uh, if I remember correctly, you locked those Wildebeest horns tightly around my heart, and I was a willing mate." He smiles devilishly, the way he does when he's in a goofy mood.

"I love you, Woodcock. I love you from the top of my horns to the tip of my tail." That was something I used to tell him when we first fell in love. It had been years since I'd thought of it.

He reaches up and strokes my cheek. "And I love you from the top of my rooster comb to the tip of my woody."

"You—" I dive at him and he flips me over on top of our bed, wrapping his arms around me. Then he peers down at me like I am Miss dang Marilyn Monroe. "I really missed you this week." Our lips are only centimeters apart.

"When you hear the rest of what Lilith pulled, you'll know how much more I missed you." I watch his lips brush mine, feeling the warmth of his minty breath.

"Right now, I'm much more interested in you showing me how much you missed me." The stubble of his whiskers tickles as he kisses his way down my neck, slowly unbuttoning my blouse.

FIFTY

MISS PEARL

At seven thirty in the morning, when I arrive to pick her up, Aunt Fee won't answer the door. I've been out here knocking and hollering ten minutes already. I'm trying to stay calm, but with each rap my stomach's churning with fear. Why I didn't get a key from her years ago is sitting heavy on my heart, but when I go around and find the back door open, relief settles in.

I push it open slowly, scared of what I'll find, because the house is as quiet as a graveyard. The kitchen looks exactly the way I left it last night. With one exception: the Oxycodone bottle is gone. I head into her bedroom, right off the kitchen, and spy it on her bedside table. Fee's underneath the covers. As still as the cold air in the room.

The floor creaks under my foot. Then I hear a frail voice. "That you, baby?"

Rushing over to her bedside, I say, "Of course it's me. I've been outside knocking. Can't you get up?"

She moves her head, but only slightly. "Having a hard time this morning." The strong scent of urine fills the room.

"What's your doctor's name?"

She bites down on her lip, whispers, "Nelson."

After rifling through my pocketbook, I yank out my phone. "You got his number around here?"

"I think you better take me on to the hospital."

Fear streaks through me like a runaway train. She would never go to the hospital unless it was an emergency. I punch 91—

"Who you calling?"

"The ambulance."

"No, ma'am. We ain't gone pay for no ambulance." She presses into the mattress with both hands, trying to rise. With lips mashed together, she grunts and strains. But after a few tries, she gives up.

"Aunt Fee, *please* let me call the ambulance. You're too weak."

She shakes her head. "Cost too much." Then she tries to push up again. "Give me a hand, baby. I can make it."

I take her by both arms and pull her to a sitting position, put two pillows behind her back, then let her rest. When she's got her strength, I help her swing both legs off the side of the bed, and put her slippers on her feet. She tries to stand, but falls right back down.

"Come on, Auntie, please. Let me call the ambulance."

"No," she says harshly. So I cup her elbow on one side, and she uses the bedside table to finally push herself up. It's then that I notice blood on the sheets.

"Can you walk?"

She nods. "Let's go."

It's taking us a long time to get to the car because the poor thing can't lift her feet. She just slides. The two steps down to the driveway are the worst part. I see her grit her teeth from having to bend her knees. When I finally get her in my car she lays her head back on the headrest, and never utters another sound. I have no idea if she is awake or asleep, but the fifteen-minute trip from her house to the hospital is the longest ride of my life.

The emergency entrance is the first I see, so I pull right up to the front door. Leave my car running and head straight to the desk. It doesn't take long for someone to meet me at the car with a stretcher, and take Aunt Fee back to a room.

Once I've parked and asked for her room number, I make my way down a long hall, stopping at number twelve. The bottom portion of a nurse's legs are visible underneath the curtain. When I pull it back and peek my head in, she motions for me to step inside. Fee's just lying there. Even though I try to talk to her, she won't utter a word.

After I fill the nurse in on all the details of what had happened before we got here, she takes Fee's pressure, checks her pulse, and draws two vials of blood. She slips out quietly. Less than five minutes later the doctor walks in. Fee can hardly open her poor little eyes to tell him hello. And now she's moaning. He takes one look at her then turns to me. "Good morning. Looks like we've got a sick patient."

"Yes, sir."

"We'll see what we can do to get her some relief."

"Thank you, doctor," I say.

He walks over to the sink and washes his hands. After drying them with a paper towel he turns back around. "Hello, Mrs. Smith. I'm Dr. Jensen. Mind if I do a little poking around?" Aunt Fee manages a slight nod, so he pulls a flashlight out of his pocket and points it into her eyes, then listens to her chest with his stethoscope. Once he's checked her pulse, he pulls back the sheet. "I'm going to press on your abdomen now, and I'd like for you to tell me when it hurts."

She never answers him, but she doesn't need to. She moans most everywhere he touches.

I watch him intently, every move he makes. After unwrapping the stethoscope from around his neck and replacing it in his pocket, he turns to me. "I'm going to send Mrs. Smith downstairs for tests. Are you her next of kin?"

"No, sir. She's my auntie. I may as well be her daughter, but she does have three sons."

"Do they live here?"

I shake my head. "Two are in Chicago. One's in Memphis."

"You may want to give them a call. I'll need someone to make decisions if need be."

I'm frightened by his words. "What do you think is wrong?"

"It's too early to tell. I'll have to get CT scans to know for sure."

"But do you have an idea?"

"It could be any number of things. But she's in quite a bit of pain. How long has she been like this?"

"I was at her house last night. She wasn't nearly this bad off. She was weak, but she was talking, and could get a few bites of her supper down."

"I'll get her started on an intravenous pain medication right away."

"She's been taking oxycodone. Twenty milligrams."

"Do you know when she had the last dose?"

"No, sir. Just found out about it last night. She's so stubborn. Never even told me she was sick."

He smiles. "I promise to let you know something as soon as I get the tests back." He steps toward the curtain, then turns back around. "By the way, does your aunt have a living will?"

My brows knit together. I'm not exactly sure what he means.

"A DNR. Her wishes on whether or not to resuscitate."

Now my eyes bulge. "Of course she wants to be resuscitated."

"Okay, just making sure." He smiles again, opens the curtain.

"Doctor?"

He turns.

"Is it cancer?"

He squeezes his lips together. "Like I said, I'm ordering several tests. We'll know then."

"But, is it possible?"

He gives a slight nod. "There's a possibility."

Auntie was moved to a private room on the third floor at Northwest Regional Baptist Hospital. It was the last thing we expected for someone with no health insurance, but that's what we got. The doctor ordered she be hooked up to a morphine drip. She's hardly woken since, but when she does, the moaning begins. It comes up from her gut and sounds more like an animal than a human.

Now, for the first time in eleven hours, she seems to be at peace. I'm anything but peaceful. Another doctor, Dr. Thomas, brought me the news thirty minutes ago. Aunt Fee has stage four, terminal uterine cancer. The CT scan showed it was not only smothering her uterus, but it had grown over her entire abdomen—in her ovaries, stomach, intestines, and, more important, her liver. "That's why she's in excruciating pain," he said. "The cancer has invaded her liver."

When I asked him how long she had, he said it was up to God. There's a chair in the room that folds out into a nice bed. I've put my name on it. Someone needs to be here, and that someone is me.

Her hand is in mine when I hear a creak in the door. I look over to see it opening real slow. There stands Mr. Marvelle. Seems like he's afraid to come any closer. He simply stays in the doorway, peering over at Aunt Fee in the bed.

"Come on in, Marvelle," I say.

It must take that man an entire minute to walk the five feet up to Fee's bedside. I go around and take him by his wrinkled hand, cold to the touch. His other grips a handkerchief.

"She'd be happy to know you're here," I tell him.

"She went down fast. Too fast." He lets go of my hand to put his on top of Fee's. "I tried getting her to see a doctor. She never would listen."

"That's her," I say. "You know that. Nothing any of us could have done to persuade her."

"Just hate it had to end this way." Marvelle wipes his nose, then stuffs his hanky back down in his pocket.

"Why didn't she tell me she was this sick?" Tears creep back into my eyes.

That sweet man reaches into his pocket, takes out a clean handkerchief, and does his best to wipe them away. "I imagine when she found out there was nothing she could do. If I know Miss O she didn't wanna worry you."

"She's the most stubborn woman alive." I look down at her. Bright red lipstick on her lips. Lying there as sweet as a sleeping baby. "I could just strangle her. I mean it, too."

Marvelle laughs. "She looks peaceful, Pearl. Pretty, too. You've got her all made up. She'd be happy about that."

An hour later, around nine o'clock, the door opens again and Mama Carla and Selma James peek their sweet heads inside. I don't have but a teaspoon of energy left, but I still find the strength to get up and take them in my arms. Once I'm able to let go they tiptoe over to the bed, look at Aunt Fee lying there, unresponsive.

Selma bursts into tears. "Half of our sorority is downstairs." I'm not sure if she's talking to Aunt Fee or to me. I pass her the box of tissues. She takes one, wipes her eyes. "We've taken over the entire lobby, Miss Ophelia. I'm not sure how happy the hospital is about it, but we're all here for you."

"Helen and Latonya are, too," Mama Carla says from the other side of Fee's bed. "So is Kadeesha." Then she smiles because she knows Kadeesha and I are not the best of friends.

"Doesn't that make you feel good, Aunt Fee?" I say, winking at Mama Carla. But Fee never opens her eyes. The morphine has her out cold.

Selma takes her by the hand. "We love you, Miss Ophelia."

Watching the three of them at Aunt Fee's bedside strikes a familial chord. These folks are my family. Fee would feel the same way if she were coherent. It would thrill her to know the Alpha Delts had taken over the lobby. Selma looks over at me. "We won't stay. We just wanted you to know we're downstairs in case you need us."

"I guess I'll go on, too," Mr. Marvelle says, standing up from the chair. "You need sleep, Pearl. You've had a long, *long* day."

As much as I'd like to have them in the room with me, I know he's right. "Thank you. I don't know what I'd do without all a y'all. I'm already out of my mind as it is."

"Pearl," Mama Carla says. "You listen to me. I want you to take all the time off you need. Kadeesha is covering your housekeeping shift, and everyone else is taking up the slack in the kitchen. I canceled dinner tonight and I'll do it again if need be."

"Thank you, Mama Carla. You're mighty good to me."

She reaches over and runs the back of her hand across Fee's cheek. "You sure look pretty, Miss Ophelia. Your Pearl has you made up nice. Your makeup looks beautiful."

"Doesn't she look good?" I ask.

"She looks gorgeous," Mama Carla manages to say, but now she can hardly talk.

I had run out to Walmart earlier and bought Fee two new pretty nightgowns—one blue, one yellow. The nurse helped me dress her in the blue one, in honor of Alpha Delt. Then I combed her hair back off her forehead, the way she likes it styled, and painted her nails. I made sure to color her lips with her favorite red lipstick. Unless you knew she was in her mid-sixties you'd think she was my age. Not a single line on her face.

When Mama was dying, Aunt Fee told me something I've never forgotten. "When peoples are getting ready to meet their Maker, they need to look their utmost best."

FIFTY-ONE

CALI

When Selma James told us in our first Monday night Chapter that Miss Ophelia had stage-four uterine cancer and wasn't expected to live much longer, many of the active members in the room cried. Some even wailed. There were even a few girls in our pledge class who got teary. It feels like a dark cloud decided to settle over the Alpha Delt house the day we pledged, and in a strange and somber way I feel bonded to my Alpha Delt sisters because of it.

Selma adjourned the meeting early and lots of us drove over to the hospital. Since the meeting was open, we were all casually dressed in Alpha Delt jerseys and T-shirts, so it looked like a blue and white river had flooded the lobby. Selma wouldn't let anyone go up to the room. I get that. It would have been too hard on Miss Ophelia and Miss Pearl both. Besides, the hospital wouldn't have allowed it. Lots of the girls were pissed though, as they felt strongly about wanting to see her one last time.

Now, another week has passed and Miss Ophelia's still hanging on. I feel terrible for Miss Pearl. Sarah told me she's not only unmarried and without kids of her own, but that Miss Ophelia is more like a mother to her than an aunt. I remember her making that exact statement on Bid Day. For some reason I have a feeling Miss Pearl's not only super sad about the thought of losing her, but she feels lonely. Most of the girls know her so much better than I do, but I felt a connection with her on Bid Day. She was kind and gracious to both my grandparents and me, and, well, I just want to give her a squeeze.

I know she's in her closet right now because I saw her go in there when I was on my way to the study lounge, not two minutes ago. After gathering my courage, I steal down the hall, and up to the door. Knocking softly I call, "Miss Pearl? Are you in there?"

It takes her a second, but she opens the door, though only a hair. We're eye to eye and I'm afraid I've bothered her when she says, "Hello, Cali." Then she smiles and opens the door wider.

"I hope I'm not disturbing you."

"No, baby, you aren't disturbing me."

"I thought you'd be at the hospital with Miss Ophelia."

"My cousin is with her. He ran me out of there. Said I needed a break." She laughs even though I'm sure she's sad.

"I won't keep you; I just wanted you to know everyone in our pledge class is thinking about you and we're all saying prayers."

She tilts her head back with a chuckle. "We could use every one of them, too."

As rotten as she must feel, she still has a good sense of humor. "I have something for you." I dig inside my pocket and remove the small cool rock. "It's nothing big. I just thought it might help you." I open my palm. "My grandfather gave this to me when I was little."

With inquisitive eyes, she takes the stone from my hand. "Why, thank you, baby." She peers at the lettering on top, then stretches out her arm. "I can hardly read anything these days."

"It's says: *The Lord Is My Rock.*"

Running her thumb across the top, she says, "He certainly is."

"I rub on it when I'm stressed or feeling down. I thought it might be a comfort to you."

"I know it will." She slips it inside her pocket.

"Are you doing okay?" I ask cautiously. I don't want to make her cry, but I do want her to know I'm concerned.

"Not really, but this is life." There's a faraway look in her eyes. She's fatigued. I know I would be.

"Life can suck sometimes," I say with a slight chuckle.

"We were never promised an easy ride. That I know."

"You sound like my grandfather."

"My mama told me that a long time ago." Her smile fades, then she shuts her eyes. "I sure wish she was here with us now."

"When did she die?"

"Let me see now." She uses her fingers to calculate the time. "She passed fifteen years ago the seventeenth of August." Biting down on her lip she adds, "Aunt Fee took her place. It's hard to lose a mother all over again."

Melancholy tugs at me now, for some surprising reason. I look down at the floor.

"Cali? Did I say something wrong?" She gently lifts my chin with two fingers.

I shake my head. "I'm sorry. It's just—" I stop short of spilling the details.

"What is it, baby?"

"Nothing. I didn't come here to talk about me. I only wanted to give you my prayer stone, and tell you we're all praying." I take a step back. "I'm sure you've got lots to do."

She steps forward, then stretches her arm across my back. "Why don't you step inside my office?"

"Oh no, I'm . . . with all you have going on, I'm . . ."

Guiding me inside, she motions for me to sit. There's not much room, but there are two stools. "Have a seat, baby." After taking the other chair, she pulls the door shut. Then she turns to face me with her hands on her knees. "Girls come in here to talk about all kinds of things. If there's something bothering you, go on and say it." Her face lights with compassion and she chuckles softly.

Miss Pearl is even nicer than I thought. I get the feeling she's a safe harbor, so I decide to test the waters. "When you said it's hard to lose a mother it hit home, that's all." Out of habit I reach up for my cross, zip it nervously on the chain.

"Did you lose your mother?"

"Yes, ma'am, but not by death." Okay, so I've admitted it to someone on campus. Now what?

"How did you lose her, baby?" Miss Pearl's voice overflows with tenderness.

I close my eyes, take a deep breath, then dive straight in. "She left me. When I was five. I haven't told any of my friends here about it. I'm not sure they could relate. They don't seem to have problems."

When she laughs out loud I'm a little confused. But then she says, "Might not seem like it, but there are all kinds of problems in this House. I don't mean to laugh. I just know what I'm talking about."

I smile, zip my cross again. "Maybe you're right."

"I'm right. You can trust me on that. Do you remember your mama?"

"Oh yeah. She still comes in and out of my life. She lives in *'Sunny California'* now." I sit up straight and mimic the way she says it. "The last time I saw her was about"—I look off, trying to calculate the timeline—"two years ago when she showed up at our house with her drug-dealer boyfriend. They wanted money. But my grandmother told her no. It was hard on my grandfather because he misses her so much. He wanted her to stay, but my grandmother is strong. She wouldn't let her." My honesty surprises me. But it's easy to be truthful with Miss Pearl.

"That's hard on you, I know."

"Yes, ma'am," I say with a sigh. "It was bad. I could tell she was using when I saw her grinding her teeth. Well, what teeth she has left. She got addicted to drugs about twelve years ago. Meth is a problem near my hometown." When Miss Pearl grimaces I'm afraid I've overshared. "Oh, sorry, I didn't mean to give you all the gory details. Especially with all you're going through." I bury my face in my hands.

"Cali," she says, gently removing my hands. "Didn't Sarah tell you I'm the in-house therapist? Nothing shocks me, baby."

"Yes, but I'm so embarrassed by her." The mere thought of my mother is revolting. "I just wish I could be a normal girl in a normal family."

"What's normal? You think these girls here are all normal?"

I shrug.

"Shoot."

Now she's made me laugh.

"Tell me about your daddy. Is he in the picture?"

As tight as it is in here I can lean back against the shelves, so I do. "I have no idea who the man is." It actually feels good to let that one out. And to support my back.

"That's okay. I only met mine a few times."

"Really?"

Miss Pearl nods her head tenderly.

It comforts me enough to tell her more. "To be perfectly honest with you, I wish my mother had given me up for adoption. Then I wouldn't have to know the bitter truth about her or my father."

A harsh look, erupting out of nowhere, replaces the tender face that only moments earlier had been kind and consoling. It's not mean, necessarily, just strong. And it takes me by surprise, because until now Miss Pearl has been so gentle. "Don't say that, baby," she says, in a commanding voice.

I drop my head. She can tell I'm hurt because she says, in a gentler tone, "Think about it from the other side. Suppose you had grown up never knowing who your mama is? Wouldn't you feel worse? Wouldn't there be a sinkhole in your heart you couldn't close no matter how hard you tried?"

"I haven't thought about it that way," I say, my heart still stinging. "I see your point. But…" My voice rises. "At least I wouldn't have to know the truth. My own mother doesn't give two shits about me." I touch her on the leg. "Sorry for the swear."

"Come here, baby." Miss Pearl pulls me into her chest. "That's not true. Even though your mama's on the wrong track right now, it doesn't mean she don't love you. Trust me. I know what I'm talking about. You're always in her heart."

"I seriously doubt that," I say, my chin on her shoulder. "Mothers don't abandon their children if they really love them." The way she's hugging me makes tears well up in my eyes. It feels good to be held by her. So much so, I imagine for a moment she's my mother.

Although I'm not ready for her to do so, Miss Pearl lets go and looks me in the eye. "Cali. I'ma tell you something I don't tell very often. There are only a few people living who know this about me." After a really long pause, she says, "I gave my baby girl up for adoption."

My mouth falls open.

Now Miss Pearl's eyes are pooling with tears. "When I was exactly your age."

"Eighteen?"

She reaches for a Kleenex behind her, dabs her eyes. "I was in my second month here at Ole Miss—on a full scholarship—when she was born. I had big plans. Wasn't sure what I wanted to be yet, but I was determined to make a name for myself. I would have been the first woman in my family to graduate from college."

I'm trying to take this all in. It's the last thing I expected out of Miss Pearl when I knocked on her closet fifteen minutes ago. The pain written all over her face matches the pain on mine. The most burning question on my mind shoots out before I can stop it. "Why did you give her up?"

She opens and closes her mouth, like she's not sure what to say. "It's complicated, baby. There were issues with her daddy's family. But the bottom-line truth is: I wasn't ready for a baby. I had spent all four years of high school working hard for my good grades. I had earned my scholarship and no one was going to take it away from me. Not even my own child. Motherhood was the last thing on my mind." She looks off. "I didn't know it at the time, but I'd live to deeply regret that decision. See there. You never know what's going on in your mama's head."

She's making a good point, but I'm still not convinced. Miss Pearl and my mother couldn't be more opposite.

"I long for my daughter almost every day. She turned twenty-five this past September the twenty-second."

From the way she's lamenting, it's obvious Miss Pearl did not abandon her daughter. "I think I see what you're trying to tell me."

"Hardest decision of my life. Took me fifteen years to believe she forgives me." She lifts her arm to show me a tattoo.

"What does it say?"

"I have been forgiven . . . in Latin. I paid that tattoo artist fifty dollars so I could remind myself of it every day. Aunt Fee liked to killed me." When she laughs, I'm comforted all over again.

We sit in silence a few moments, then I ask, "Did you ever go back to school?"

"Two days after I gave birth. But I only lasted through the spring semester. I started thinking about what I did, how I had given up my own flesh and blood. I fell down into a deep, dark pit. Started running around with the wrong crowd, acting out. Then my grades suffered. And that was hard because I had always made A's."

"I understand that. My grades are important to me, too."

"That's good. You keep it that way."

I can't help but smile. I love this connection between the two of us. "Then what happened? After you left Ole Miss?"

"I rebelled a little longer, made some more bad choices. Then Aunt Fee got me a job here. I started out as a kitchen aide. Nearly twenty-five years ago."

The stool is getting a little hard underneath my butt, so I adjust my posture. "That's a really long time."

"Yes it is." She looks me dead in the eye. "Now you keep that information to yourself. I only told you because I thought it would help you."

My eyes are wide. "I wouldn't dare tell anyone. Please don't mention what I told you."

"This is our secret," Miss Pearl says with loving eyes. "You and I can learn a lot from each other."

After giving her another quick hug, I pull back. There's something else I really want to know. "Miss Pearl?"

"Yes, baby?"

"Do you know who adopted your daughter?"

"All I know is it was a nice Catholic family in Memphis that could give her a better life. They'd been trying to start a family for a long time, but never could."

"Do you want to find her?"

"Sure I do. But that wouldn't be fair to her. If she wants to find me, she can. I put that in God's hands a long time ago. The way I see it is: If I were to look for her, it would be more selfishness on my part."

"You're not selfish. Look how much the Alpha Delts love you. You're their second mother."

"That's nice of you to say, baby, but I'm a plenty selfish. Guess we all are."

"I've learned if we don't take care of ourselves, no one else will."

"That's right. And I've recently decided to finish my degree so I can make more money. It's time I start looking toward the future. *Taking care of myself*," she says with a chuckle.

"No one else will."

"My auntie keeps telling me that. Matter of fact, she's been bugging me to get a new job."

I cover my heart with both hands, lean toward her. "You can't do that. What would everyone do without you?"

"Everyone would be just fine," she says, while patting me on the thigh. "Unfortunately, this job doesn't pay much. Eleven dollars and fifty cents an hour. And that's after twenty-five years."

I am not shocked by this news. Things are slow to change in Mississippi. All over the South, really. But I make that much babysitting.

"Aunt Fee does a little better, but the rest of the staff make less than I do."

"It must be hard for y'all to live on that."

"Yes it is," she says, before a deep line forms between her brows. "But I shouldn't have told you. It's not your problem."

"Maybe not, but I'm glad you did. I'm the kind of person that... dreams of changing things."

"There's no changing anything around here. Aunt Fee's been trying to tell me that very thing. She wants me to go to work for the University. So I can get benefits."

"I guess that means y'all don't have benefits here?"

She shakes her head. "Now it's all making sense why she's been harping on me to get a job with health insurance." With a hand pressed over her heart she leans toward me. "Here she is laid up with terminal cancer. Never went to see a doctor. That woman is as stubborn as a grape-juice stain. I want to strangle her sometimes. But it's too late now," she says, and bursts into laughter.

FIFTY-TWO

MISS PEARL

It came to an end on a Sunday, the thirtieth of October, right before Halloween. I'll always remember it as the day I became the oldest generation in my family.

Aunt Fee woke up the day before she passed like she was here to stay. I mean it. Everybody thought she would walk out the front door of the hospital and live another thirty years. She was feeling that good. All three of her boys, and all their wives and children, had made it to Oxford, and she was sitting up in her hospital bed, laughing and hugging on all of them. Telling everybody how much she loved them. Even talked to me about next week's dinner menu.

But it was only temporary. Within twenty-four hours her spirit left and she began her journey. I was in the room when she took her last breath. Right before she passed, she held her arms up in the air, even though she was as weak as a little ol' straggly weed. My cousins and I figured she was reaching for Him to carry her on Home.

When the news spread that Aunt Ophelia had passed, a hush fell over the House. The spirit of Alpha Delta Beta was put on pause. Mama Carla hung a wreath on the door made of white roses, the Alpha Delt flower, interspersed with lily of the valley, Ophelia's favorite. Since our church is relatively small, Mama Carla suggested we move the funeral somewhere bigger so everyone could fit inside. Pastor made all the arrangements to secure the Tallahatchie-Oxford Missionary Baptist Church. It's a good thing he did. Besides our family and friends, most of the Alpha Delts are planning on attending the service. Mama Carla said she'd heard several of the alumnae would be driving in, one from as far away as Atlanta.

As happy as Aunt Fee would be to know this many people wanted to honor and celebrate her life, there's one thing I know for certain. She would not be happy about the money going out the door. Marvin insisted on two stretch limos to carry us all to the church, then out to the cemetery.

About four years ago, one night after supper, when we were all sitting around talking in the kitchen, she was adamant. "I'm not leaving nobody with a fat funeral bill once I'm gone. Put me in a box in the ground and it don't have to be fancy, neither. Hurry up and do it, too, so the undertaker don't charge for no embalming fluid. But whatever you do, do *not* put me inside no oven. I want to be buried right next to Ruby. When the Archangel's voice comes and the Lord sounds His trumpet, I want to make sure there's bones left to rise."

FIFTY-THREE

WILDA

There was standing-room only by the time I slid into the back of the church. After thirty-two years as head cook, and with hundreds of Alpha Delts in attendance, there wasn't a seat to be had. From where I was standing, I could see an indisputable blond high ponytail, belonging to the one and only. Carla was seated on her left and Annie Laurie on her right. Lilith was sitting much closer to the front than I would have imagined. Even as House Corp President, it seemed a contrived show of support, especially in light of how incensed she was over Miss Pearl subbing for Carla.

It took a minute, but I finally spotted Ellie and Cali sitting with the others in their pledge class. Ellie was supposed to have saved me a seat, but since I was caught behind an eighteen-wheeler most of the way down Highway 7 and fifteen minutes late to the service, she must have given it to someone else.

By the time everyone in Miss Ophelia's family spoke and all the beautiful hymns were sung, the service lasted nearly two hours. Those of us who were late had to lean against the wall for back support. Carla and Selma gave moving eulogies. I couldn't have kept from crying if I'd wanted to. When I looked around the church I noticed there were only a few people without tears. And, I suspect, one board president.

Now, walking back to my car, I'm trying to decide whether or not I should go to the burial. Before I left Memphis this morning I'd heard the weatherman report that a thunderstorm, followed by a cold front, would be moving across the South later today. Although the sky has yet to fall, I can feel the drop in temperature.

The wind makes me think a tornado is about to blow through here at any moment. Dead leaves whirl around me, as high as my waist. My hair is standing sideways. When I finally make it to my car, in the farthest parking spot from the church, I tug at the door handle. After a hefty amount of resistance, the wind catches the door and it blasts away from my grasp. I jump inside; reach out as far as I humanly can, then tug the door shut with a thunderous *wumpth*. Once I start the engine and turn the heat on full blast, I point all four vents my way.

With my gearshift in reverse, I look over my shoulder and happen to notice a white Mercedes SUV pulling into the spot next to mine.

It's her.

What the heck am I supposed to do now? Ignore her? Oh how I wish I could be one of those nervy people who waves and blows right past. Instead, I slam the gearshift into park just before hearing three taps.

With her face pressed against my passenger window, I fumble for the locks then click them open in a hurry, because every time I'm in her presence I revert back to a spineless, yellow-bellied wuss. Before I can give any thought to what excuse I'll use to leave, she jumps inside my car and settles down into the passenger seat.

"Brrrr." She rubs the sides of her arms. "It's cold."

Reluctantly, I turn one—but only one—of the vents her way.

"That was different," she says. "I've never been to a black funeral before."

I probably shouldn't be shocked by this, but for some reason I am. "Really? I like them better than ours."

"Why do you say that?"

"Because African Americans seem much happier for the person who dies. Like heaven is much better than earth."

Lilith looks at me like I'm crazy. "Of course it's better than earth. The streets are made of gold." She forces a laugh. "Just kidding. I saved you a seat. But Ellie said you were running late."

"Thanks. I just slipped in the back. I was behind a very slow eighteen-wheeler most of the way down Highway 7."

"I've never seen so many people."

"Miss Ophelia was a beloved woman." Out of habit I reach for the radio, but retract my hand.

"Apparently so." She purses her lips, then changes the subject. "I saw Ellie sitting with Cali. Those two are spending a lot of time together these days."

"They have a lot in common."

"Hardly. I did some snooping. The girl's real name is California. Her mother is a drug addict and—"

I hold out my hand to cut her off mid-sentence. Hearing Lilith talk bad about Cali, after what she did to her, makes my skin crawl. "Honestly, Lilith, there's nothing you can tell me about that sweet girl that will change my opinion of her. Please just keep it to yourself."

"Well," she says indignantly. "She's hardly an Alpha Delt. But what can you do? I suppose we'll all need to be nice to her. She's one of us now."

"And she lives next door to our daughters." It's all I can do to keep my calm.

"With a Negr—" Now she stops herself. But not before igniting fire inside of me. The fire that should have been lit a long time ago. Perhaps my face gives me away because she quickly changes the subject. "By the way, your mother is an absolute doll. We know so many of the same people. You never told me she's from Eastover."

"Eastover is the neighborhood she grew up in," I say flatly. "She's from Jackson."

She looks at me like I'm off my rocker. "Several people I know live in Eastover. Trust me, I know the difference."

All I can think about is getting her out of my car, so I make up an excuse. "Are you going to the burial?"

"I was planning on it. Why don't we ride together?" She asks the question as if it's an invitation to go to lunch.

"I can't. I told Haynes I'd meet him for an early dinner. We have some business to discuss." I look at my watch. "In fact, I should probably get going."

"Speaking of business, you'll want to hear this."

Now I'm kicking myself for not running out of the church as soon as the service was over. But since I couldn't make the visitation I wanted to at least wave at Miss Pearl before she got in the hearse.

"Hear what?" I ask.

"Pearl wants to apply for the House Director job." Lilith moans like she thinks the idea is preposterous. "Can you imagine?"

I lean back in my seat. Put my hand on the gearshift, then take it off again. Pearl has just lost her aunt—her other mother—and Lilith has just left her service. I was right. Her appearance was purely for show. "Miss Pearl is the sweetest thing in the world," I say. "All the girls love her. She treats them like they're her own daugh—"

"I get that. But she's *the maid,* not a House Director. And besides, she has a tattoo—written in a foreign language." She holds her hands like claws, and makes a scary face. "That alone is enough to disqualify her."

Despite the indignant tone in her voice, I will myself, actually it's more of a command, to stay calm. In hopes of setting an example. "How did she do when she filled in that weekend?"

"I can tell you this: I went over to the House to use the ladies' room that weekend and it was a wreck. No hand towels and worse, *no toilet paper.* Thank God I had a tissue in my purse."

"Maybe she got busy with something important. I'll bet one of the other ladies on the staff had to fill in as housekeeper. Maybe Miss Pearl didn't know the bathroom was a wreck. I don't know much of the goings-on in that House, but I bet that's what happened."

"You should make it a point to know what goes on, *Wilda.* Not only are you an alum, but you're a Rush Advisor now. Not to mention your daughter is a new member."

I'm not a Rush Advisor for long, I think. I would have resigned by now if it weren't for the turmoil in the House—Carla leaving, Miss Ophelia dying. But I'll be sending my resignation email within the week. "I simply meant I don't know about the daily coming and going of the staff. Of course, I care about anything that has to do with Ellie, *Lilith.*"

"Having someone from a poor black neighborhood, with no college degree, as House Director of Alpha Delta Beta has *everything* to do with Ellie. She belongs to the finest sorority on campus."

I want to take her damn head off. But instead I close my eyes and count to ten, backward. After a deep breath I say, "Think about it. Many of us South-erners over the age of, what, forty-five had black ladies as second mothers. What's the difference?"

If an eye roll has a sound, she just made it. First a *tsk,* then a gurgle from the back of her throat makes me feel like I've said the dumbest thing on record.

"The House Director job"—her voice sounds ultra condescending—"is much more than a second mother. It's about responsibility. She has to liaison with the University and assist in setting up inspections, work with local ven-dors, recommend repairs and maintenance, manage the staff, plan the meals, order the food. All within a complicated budget. She runs the entire House."

"How do you know Miss Pearl can't do all that? From what I understand she's been there twenty-five years."

"She's *the maid.* And she doesn't have a college degree. Think about it. There are no other black House Directors at Ole Miss in sororities *or* fraternities. As a matter of fact, I've never heard about a black House Director at any other university. Why do you think that is?"

"I think that's ridiculous. If the person is qualified she should get the job. Regardless of the color of her skin."

"I never said anything about the color of her skin being the reason. I said she doesn't have a college degree."

"Yes you did. You just said there are no other black House Directors at Ole Miss."

She's playing with her hair, looking out the window. From where I'm sit-ting, I can see her breathing accelerate. After a few moments she turns and looks me at me with ireful eyes. "She is *un*qualified, Wilda. Our bylaws re-quire that she have a college degree. End of story."

"But we could amend the bylaws if we found a candidate with all the other necessary qualifications. Surely."

"Are you honestly telling me you're okay with this?"

With my eyes locked on hers I say, "I'm not only okay with it. I'm one hundred percent behind it. Miss Pearl is smart, dedicated, organized, *polite,* witty, and a great influence—not only on the Alpha Delts as a whole, but, more impor-tant, on our own daughters. I haven't noticed one thing that would tell me she's not qualified."

She *tsks* again. "I guess we'll have to agree to disagree. Obviously we place different values on a college education."

My pulse is throbbing in my temples and my poor heart is trying desperately to leap out of my chest. I vowed to stay calm, but now it's impossible. I had a feeling that's where she was headed, but actually hearing her say these things has made me sick, and sad, and frankly this is where the rubber meets the road, as my grandmother liked to say. You either stand up for what's right, or you don't. My wuss has morphed into a warrior. "I have to be honest with you, Lilith. I don't care about the color of her skin. I am not a prejudiced person."

Lilith gasps.

The dead air stretches on for an excruciating thirty seconds while the hair on my arms stands straight up.

"I am not a prejudiced person, either," she finally says. "For your information, I have given plenty of our hard-earned money to blacks. Have you forgotten I employ a black woman in my own home?"

"No, I have not. I—"

"And—for your *further* information—after Katrina hit, our church took up a special donation for the poor black people of the Lower Ninth Ward. I"—she taps on her chest several times—"was the very first person to stand up in front of the congregation and lead the way to the collection box."

Lilith's stab of pathos hits me harder than it should. I've heard of people snapping over the small stuff, but this comment sends me sailing over the edge. "I'm sure you did. As long as you knew people were watching."

By the look on her face, our friendship, or what she perceived as friendship, has just ended. "I should have never nominated you for the Advisory Board."

"You're right. It was your fatal flaw. I know exactly what you did."

"What are you talking about now, Wilda Woodcock?"

"Your little switcheroo," I say, holding up my hands and fluttering my fingers.

"I have no idea what you mean."

"Of course you do. I know what you did, Lilith, and so does everyone else on the Rush Committee. We can't prove it, but we all know."

For a brief second, and I mean brief, it appears as though Lilith regrets her indiscretion. Her shoulders slump and her eyes close. But a moment later, she stiffens. "I'm not even going to dignify that with a response. This conversation is over!" The force of the wind whirling outside is no match for Lilith's will. She lifts the door handle, uses her Prada heel to shove the car door open. Then she steps out onto the pavement, slamming the door shut behind her.

FIFTY-FOUR

CALI

Right after Miss Ophelia's burial, Ellie and I head back to the dorm, straight up to my room. I remember Jasmine telling me she had a big English project today, and would be in the library most of the afternoon and into the evening. The room is dimly lit from the thunderstorm outside, but I don't bother to turn on the light when we walk in the door. Somehow it feels appropriate to embrace the weather today. The darkness makes me ponder the funeral and how sad Miss Pearl looked in her black clothes walking down the center aisle of the church. Afterward, everyone was saying it was like Miss Ophelia was here one day and gone the next. No one even knew she had cancer. And now our pledge class will never get to know her.

Between the wind and the rain and the sudden drop in temperature, both Ellie and I are freezing. It's hard to get warm. So we pile up in my bed, and pull the comforter on top of us. "I feel terrible for Miss Pearl," I say once we're settled in. "Miss Ophelia was like her mother."

Ellie's lying on her back, sharing my pillow. "I don't even want to know how I would feel if my mother died." Suddenly she turns her head toward me. "I'm sorry, Cali. I shouldn't have said that. You know exactly what it feels like."

I'm still staring straight up at the ceiling, dying to tell her the truth. What's holding me back? Am I afraid she won't be my friend? "It sucks," I simply say.

"But your grandparents were just as good. Isn't that what you told me?"

"They were better, actually. Way better."

She turns to her side, facing me, propping herself up on her elbow. "What was your mother like?" She asks me this question with hesitancy, like she's not sure if she should.

I breathe in and breathe out. "I hated her."

From the corner of my eye I see her flinch. "Why?"

Turning my head toward her I say, "Do you really wanna know?"

"Only if you wanna tell me."

"She's a meth head." Surprisingly, I don't freak out when I say it. I stay calm. "*Was* a meth head."

I shake my head. "I lied. She's alive. At least I think she is."

Her eyes are as big as pumpkins now. I've no doubt shocked the shit out of her.

"She lives in California, where she ran off with some guy when I was five years old. We really don't know if she's dead or alive. I lied because I'm so, *so* embarrassed and ashamed of her." Shame is rolling around inside my gut, the way it has a zillion times before, but I'm still unruffled.

When she reaches out to touch my shoulder, Ellie's face is painted with compassion. "Don't be embarrassed. I don't care. I mean, I do care about you." By the sound of her voice, and the way she's trying to assure me, I can tell she's sincere.

"Yeah, but what about the rest of the girls in our sorority?"

"We don't know them yet, but I can't imagine any of them would care either."

"When I got dropped from Rush I was sure it was because someone found out about her. And held it against me." An image of my mother, the last time I saw her, floats across my mind. She's in our living room looking pretty, the way I remember her, until she opens her mouth and I catch a glimpse of her teeth, chipped and black.

"Like who?"

"I don't know," I say. "But I have a theory."

Ellie leans in curiously. I've got her attention. "What's your theory? Tell me."

"Remember when Mrs. Whitmore asked me if my name was California, back at the first football game?"

"Yeah."

"She was right. My real name is California. My mother named me that because she always wanted to live there. On Bid Day, Mrs. Whitmore lied to my grandparents. She told them I wasn't pledging Alpha Delt and called me California to my face. I'm convinced she went poking around Blue Mountain to find out about my past. I'm almost positive."

"Oh my God. I can't imagine she would do something that mean."

I shrug. "Like I said, it's just a theory. Maybe I'm wrong." Looking straight at her, I say, "Please don't mention it to Annie Laurie."

Her mouth gapes open. "Are you kidding me? Of course I won't."

A loud *bang* followed by a chorus of giggles out in the hall—a perfectly normal occurrence for Martin—momentarily stops our talk. Any minute now someone will barge into my room, but I want to continue our conversation. It feels like I've lost fifteen pounds admitting the truth to Ellie. "I'm sorry I lied to you, El. It's just been so damn hard. For me . . . and my grandparents."

With an understanding nod, she clasps my wrist. "What about your dad? You never mention him."

"Never met him."

Her eyebrows bounce on her forehead. Now I've really shocked her.

"Nope. My mom got pregnant with me her senior year of high school. She never told me or my grandparents who my dad is."

"Oh, Cali. I'm sorry."

"I overheard my grandparents talking one time. They think they know who he is. There was this older, redheaded guy who taught at Blue Mountain College named Will Smith. I remember his name because of the movie star. They suspect it was him, but no one knows for sure. Somewhere along the line my mom became rebellious because of her strict religious upbringing. At least that's what Papaw thinks."

"Do you want to find out who he is for sure?"

"Sometimes, but I'm not burning to know. Maybe one day. I wish my mom had put me up for adoption. But then again, I have the greatest grandparents in the world. If I'd been adopted, well, you know. I wouldn't know them."

"You're lucky there. I love my grandmother, but she's a piece of work. And I never knew my grandfather. What little my mom remembers of him is great, though." She slips out of the covers and moves off the bed. "I've got to get out of this dress. I'll be right back."

"Okay. Shut the door behind you, please."

The click of the door brings silence back into my room and as I lie here waiting for Ellie to return, the day my mother left me is as vivid as it was thirteen years ago.

"Just stay right here on the porch till I get back, okay?" Mama said, handing me the worn, dirty stuffed pony I'd had since I was born. "Neigh will keep you company. Don't move off this porch, California. Do you hear me?"

While my chin quivered, I poked my bottom lip out. I had no other response.

"Do you hear me?"

A man she called "Babe" had his head in the trunk of a beat-up Mustang, rearranging all kinds of stuff to squeeze in my mama's suitcases, her boom box, and a picture of the California coastline she had painted in high school. Our only pet, Frisco, the eleven-year-old beagle I loved with all my heart, hopped into the backseat and settled against the rear window. He had been my mother's thirteenth birthday present from my grandparents.

"Mamaw and Papaw will be home from work in fifteen minutes, okay?"

"Where are you going?" Clutching Neigh in my arms, I stepped toward her.

"It doesn't matter." She hurried back inside the house. Seconds later she was running down the front steps with Frisco's dog food. And his bowls.

"At this rate it'll take us a month to get there," Babe said impatiently, never once bothering to look my way.

"Who's he?" I asked, pointing my finger right at him. My left thumb was in my mouth, fingers gripping tightly around Neigh's tail.

"Just a friend."

I saw him cut arrogant eyes at her. But I didn't know why.

Mama knelt down in front of me at eye level. Put her hands on both my arms. "All you have to do is climb up in this chair." She patted the seat of the rocker. "Sing your songs till Mamaw and Papaw get here, okay? The time will go by like this." She snapped her fingers. Her eyes were watery and red. I didn't think she looked pretty.

Babe folded his arms, tapped his foot. "Any day now, Jennifer." I didn't like him. Or the way he was dressed. Dirty. Ugly. Mean man.

She glanced over her shoulder. "Quit your whining." When she coughed, it lasted longer than normal.

"Are you okay, Mama?"

Pulling me into her chest, she wrapped her arms around me. With my face buried inside her hair, the smell of smoke filling my nostrils, I could hear Babe start the car engine behind us. When she let me go my eyes filled with tears.

"Listen here. There's nothing to cry about, okay? You'll only be by yourself fifteen minutes." She backed her way down the steps and out to the car.

"No, Mommy. Please don't go."

After sitting down in the front seat and closing the door, she rolled down her window. At first I thought it was so she could stick her head out and wave. But I was wrong. She put one of those smoky sticks to her lips and propped her elbow on the windowsill.

The engine roared as Babe screeched down the road and made a left on Mill Street toward the highway.

Suddenly the door flies open and Ellie hops on one foot back into the room wearing sweats and a long sleeve T-shirt. "Uhhh," she moans, holding her toes.

"What happened?"

"I stubbed my big toe on Annie Laurie's stupid orca. There's no room for that giant thing and it's totally in the way. She just uses it as a catchall for her dirty laundry." She closes the door then crawls into her spot on my bed, against the wall.

I wrinkle my nose. "Poor you."

She sighs, wraps herself underneath my comforter. "Oh well. What can you do?"

After a few seconds I look straight at her. "I've been thinking about how Miss Ophelia had cancer and didn't know it. That's, like, insane scary, Ellie."

"I know."

"Miss Pearl said something about her not having health insurance so she never went to the doctor. But she also said Miss Ophelia was stubborn. 'Stubborn as an old grape-juice stain.'"

"Not even Obamacare?"

"Evidently not." I reach over for the cooler cup resting on my nightstand and take a big swig.

"I wonder why she didn't have health insurance. Does Miss Pearl have it?"

Swallowing in a hurry, I say, "I asked her that and she said no. Nobody on the staff has health insurance. Except Mama Carla."

"Do you know why?" Ellie's brows are knitted together.

"I asked her that, too. She said it's not offered."

Ellie scrambles up, leans her back against the wall. "That's, like, so wrong. I wonder why that is?"

"I don't know. But I haven't been able to stop thinking about it." We sit in silence another minute without talking. "Ellie?" I finally say.

"Yeah."

"Maybe we could, like, do something about it." I sit up to face her.

"Like what?" She leans in toward me as if she can't wait to hear what I'm thinking.

"What if everyone agreed to make benefits for our staff our pledge-class philanthropy project? I mean, think about it. They work so hard. They make sure everyone has amazing food—three meals a day—and that the House looks like a showplace. I know this is, like, an intangible, but look at Miss Pearl. She's like a mom and she's probably the nicest lady I've ever met. Honestly, and I'm not just saying this, I wish she was my mom."

Ellie reaches over and touches my knee. "I'm glad you have her."

"Wait till you get to know her. You're gonna love her."

"I know I will. My mom *adores* her. I can't wait to know everyone who works at the House. Staff benefits is such a great idea."

I take another sip of water. "I was thinking we could raise the money ourselves. At least for their health insurance."

"How would we do that?"

"I don't know, a big car wash, maybe? We did those for our high school cross country team."

"Nah. That wouldn't make enough. How about yummy Krispy Kreme doughnuts?" She laughs, pulling her knees to her chest. "I don't know. There has to be something we could sell."

"We need something big. I have no idea how much we need to raise, but it's more than likely going to be several thousand dollars."

"I have an idea," she says, sitting up straight. "Maybe we could pick out the prettiest tree in the Grove and sell the chance to name it. How about we make an appointment with Jeff Vitter—the Ole Miss chancellor—and ask him for permission? We won't know unless we try."

"That's a great idea! Who knows, maybe he would donate his time and let us add a dinner out with him and his wife? I bet all the parents would be willing to buy a ticket." All this talk is igniting a spark I'm not sure I'll ever be able to quench. It's, like, the very thing I've been searching for.

"My parents would buy ten," Ellie says.

"How much do you think we could sell them for?"

Ellie shrugs. "I don't know. Twenty dollars apiece?"

"Surely, that would be an easy sell. I mean, if there are, say, four hundred fifty girls in the sorority and every parent bought one ticket, that's nine thousand dollars. That would go a long way."

All of a sudden Ellie gasps. I mean, I've never heard her make a sound like this. Her face lights up like she's just won the lottery. "Cali! I just thought of something big." She drums her feet on the mattress as fast as a hummingbird flaps her wings.

"What?"

She squeals. And throws her arms up in a vee.

"You're killing me. *What?*"

With elation on every inch of her face, she beams at me. "Eli Manning. We could sell tickets for an evening out with *Eli Manning!*"

I rear back. Look at her like she's gone mad. "I mean, come on, Ellie, Eli Manning? How in the world are we gonna get him?"

"*My dad.* He's met him before. They were both Sigma Nus. Not at the same time, but they're still brothers."

"Okay, so what makes you think he can swing something like that?"

"If you knew my dad, you wouldn't even have to ask that question."

FIFTY-FIVE

CALI

We head straight to the House to find Selma James. The whole way over from Martin, Ellie and I had our fingers crossed hoping and praying she hadn't left for dinner. There's no meal tonight. In honor of Miss Ophelia, Mama Carla gave the staff the day off.

After skipping every other step up to the second floor, we actually find Selma in her room with the door open. She's sitting quietly on her bed reading. After knocking softly, we poke our heads in and wave. I think she's surprised to see us. She motions us in, then slides off her bed. "What's up, you two?" she asks while walking toward us. The first thing she does is give us hugs. "It's been a hard day, huh?"

"You did such a great job today," I say. "Your eulogy was beautiful."

"I was just gonna say the same thing," Ellie adds.

"Thanks. I wasn't sure I could get through it. Y'all would have loved her. She was sweet, funny . . . so loving." Selma looks off, shakes her head slowly. "I can't believe she's gone."

"I felt so bad for Miss Pearl today," I say. "I hated seeing her cry."

Selma presses her lips together. "They were really close. So were the rest of the staff. They all loved Miss Ophelia."

"That's why we're here," I say.

Selma looks at me curiously, then sits back down on the edge of her bed. "What do you mean?"

I sit down next to her. "Ellie and I were thinking it would be a great idea to do something life-changing for the staff."

As soon as the last words leave my lips Ellie's up on her toes and her voice speeds up. "We want to make staff benefits our pledge-class philanthropy project."

Selma looks at us, wide-eyed. "Okay. How so?"

"Since Miss Ophelia died from uterine cancer, and never went to the doctor because she had no health insurance, we want to honor her memory by making sure it never happens again." When Ellie gets excited about something you know it. Her hands swing all over the place.

Selma's gazing at us in disbelief, with her fingers splayed across her breastbone. "How do you know the staff doesn't have health insurance?"

"Miss Pearl told me," I say, feeling proud of the bond we had already made.

"I've never thought about that before." Selma props her chin on her fist. "It's not something the members get involved in. That falls under the auspices of the House Corp Board."

"Lilith Whitmore?" Ellie asks.

Selma nods. "Lilith Whitmore is the president, yes."

"So we'd have to ask her?" I ask.

She nods again. Without a smile or a frown, just a neutral face. "I'm sure you're planning on bringing it up at the new member meeting tonight, right? To see what the rest of your pledge class thinks?"

"Totally." We both say at the same time. We look at each other and grin— simpatico in so many ways.

"Wait till you hear how we're planning on raising the money," Ellie says.

Then we tell her our idea about Eli Manning and selling the tickets for twenty dollars apiece. Ellie tells her all about getting her dad to arrange it and about how he knows Eli personally.

"So you really think y'all can pull this off?" Selma asks. By the lift in her voice I can tell she's all in.

"I mean, we've gotta try. Right?" Ellie says.

"Absolutely." Selma presses her lips together, looks off to the side. "If every girl in our sorority bought one ticket, that would surely pay their health insurance for the first year. I don't know anything about it, but it seems like that would cover it."

"My dad would help with that, too. He knows about stuff like that."

"If Lilith Whitmore doesn't know how much it will cost, she can surely find out," Selma says.

"Don't you think the members will get behind it?" Ellie asks.

"I'm pretty sure no one has ever thought about our staff not having health insurance. But once they become aware, I have no doubt everyone will want to change things."

That night at our new member meeting, when Ellie and I presented our plan, there wasn't one person who opposed it. In fact, every single girl stood up and cheered. No one seemed to think selling five hundred tickets would be a problem at all, and there were a few who thought we might sell more. After all, Eli Manning is a sainted celebrity around here.

When someone asked who would make the final decision, Ellie got all excited. "We're actually very lucky," she told everyone, then glanced at Annie Laurie. "Annie Laurie's mom is the House Corp President. She's the one that can make it happen."

Although everyone in our pledge class seemed relieved, that it was surely a no-brainer with Annie Laurie as a new member, I'm not so sure. Call it a sixth sense, but after the way Mrs. Whitmore treated my grandparents and me on Bid Day, something tells me there may be trouble looming. I, for one, do not trust the woman.

FIFTY-SIX

CALI

Right after our new member meeting, Ellie texted Mrs. Whitmore to set up our own face-to-face with her. She responded right back by saying she would be in Oxford the next afternoon and we could meet her at the House at four o'clock, an hour before dinner. All Ellie told her in the text was that we had an amazing idea and we couldn't wait to share it with her.

Although Annie Laurie seemed to love our plan in last night's pledge meeting, for some reason she didn't want to be included in the one with her mother today. Who knows what that's about? Personally, I think she's making up an excuse. Something about a study date with an SAE. Yeah, right. No one has ever seen her study.

Mrs. Whitmore is waiting for us in the chapter room when we arrive. As usual, she looks like she's stepped out of *Vogue*. She's wearing a beautiful pants outfit with the same jewelry—the *Yurman*—that Annie Laurie always wears. And also her Alpha Delt pin. Every time I see her she's wearing it.

She must have gotten here early because Ellie and I are right on time. When she hears our footsteps she looks up from her Mac laptop and waves. "I'll be right with y'all."

"Right with y'all" turns into fifteen minutes, so Ellie and I stroll around the chapter room looking at old composites, marveling over how small the pledge classes once were. It's still hard to imagine my picture will be on next year's composite in the foyer. Besides the thought of that, something else has lifted my spirits. Admitting the truth about my mother, *and* my father, to Ellie has made me feel as though I've been set free.

"Okay, girls," Mrs. Whitmore finally says, closing her laptop. "I'm sorry to make you wait. I guess you've heard Carla Stratton is leaving Alpha Delt."

"No, I hadn't heard," Ellie says, glancing at me. "Have you heard that?"

I shake my head. "Who's taking her place?"

"I haven't gotten that far. Greek House Resource, a wonderful company who pairs prospective House Directors with sororities, is helping me. I've just uploaded our job description." She pats her Mac, leans forward. "So. What can I help you with? Your text said you had an amazing idea." She shows her enthusiasm by rubbing her palms together.

Ellie and I give each other confident smiles. "We really do," I say.

"Well, let's hear it. I can hardly stand the suspense."

"Miss Ophelia's funeral had a big impact on us," Ellie begins, scooting to the front of her chair.

Mrs. Whitmore's posture stiffens. "How so? You girls didn't even know her."

"No, we didn't," I say. "But her funeral was so lovely, and with the hundreds of people there it made us realize how loved she was. She must have done a lot for Alpha Delt."

"She worked here thirty-two years," Mrs. Whitmore says.

Ellie and I turn to look at each other. "Wow," Ellie says. "That's insane."

Mrs. Whitmore smiles. "We were lucky to have her. She was quite a cook."

"I wish we'd been able to have at least one of her dinners," I say.

Ellie doesn't comment. She's all business now. "After her funeral, Cali and I had this long conversation about the way she died. And how she didn't know she had uterine cancer."

Mrs. Whitmore rolls her eyes. "She should have gone to the doctor at the first sign. You don't get to stage-four cancer without symptoms."

"That's why we're here," I say.

She looks at me curiously.

I sit up tall in my chair. "She couldn't go to the doctor because she had no health insurance."

"We think health insurance should be one of the staff benefits," Ellie says with her chin held high.

Mrs. Whitmore uncrosses then re-crosses her legs, clasps her hands on her lap. "I'm afraid that's not possible."

"Why?" Ellie asks.

"That's a costly proposition. We are a small business here. If a staff member desires health insurance, he or she should find a job elsewhere."

"But we don't want them leaving us, do we?" Ellie's eyes are blinking rapidly.

Lilith Whitmore gives us a half-shrug. "If they must have health insurance, I suppose we don't have a choice."

"But they work so hard," I say, "and they don't get paid all that well."

"They do so much for us," Ellie adds. "It's the least we could do for them."

Now Mrs. Whitmore's arms are folded across her chest. She's tapping her foot ever so slightly. "You girls don't need to be concerning yourselves with House matters. That's what I'm for. You need to be enjoying your college days."

"But we are concerned, Mrs. Whitmore," Ellie says.

"What makes you think they aren't paid well? How would you even know that?"

"Miss Pe—" As soon as the words leave my lips I know I have goofed.

"Miss Pearl told you?" Mrs. Whitmore asks with a clenched jaw. "She was out of line. She should have never shared her salary information with you."

"She didn't. I asked her."

I can tell this has made her mad by the way her lips are mashed together, but she moves on and I'm grateful. "Here at Alpha Delt," she says, like we're children, "the staff gets perks you don't know about. Aside from *free* meals, they get paid vacations at both Christmas and Thanksgiving. Spring break as well. And you should see the Christmas gifts they haul in. They are darn lucky to have this job."

"And we're lucky to have them," I say.

Ellie leans forward. "It's not like they don't deserve it, Mrs. Whitmore. They are all hard workers."

"It costs a fortune to operate this House every month. You girls are too young to understand."

"That's where our pledge class comes in," Ellie remarks with an uncontainable smile.

"What do you mean, Ellie?"

Ellie looks at me and I smile along with her. "We are going to make staff benefits our philanthropy project this year."

Mrs. Whitmore looks down her nose. "How on earth do you plan to do that?"

Ellie pushes her hair behind her ears, sits up straight. "Well, we are going to sell tickets for a chance at an evening out with Eli Manning."

Mrs. Whitmore spreads her fingers into a fan against her breastbone. "An evening out with *Eli Manning*?"

"Yes, ma'am!" Ellie says. "We're inviting him and his wife, Abby, to Oxford. To go to dinner at the City Grocery with the lucky couple who wins."

Just when we think we're getting somewhere, the lady laughs in this crazy, condescending way, like she thinks we're ridiculous young juveniles who have no idea what we're doing. "Eli Manning is a busy quarterback in the National Football League. What makes you think he has the time or the desire to come down here and help you raise money for *our* staff?" She *tsks*, looking off to the side like she's talking to someone else. "Of all things."

"You don't understand, Mrs. Whitmore. My dad's gonna ask him. He knows him," Ellie says. Okay, she's pushing the truth a little, but she truly is confident her dad will make the ask.

"Your dad knows Eli Manning? Personally?"

"Well, he's met him before. They were both Sigma Nus."

"Meeting Eli Manning once and asking him for a favor of this magnitude are two totally different things." She presses a finger to her chin. "Ellie Woodcock. I'm surprised at you. And your dad, too, for that matter. Surely you know it's bad manners to ask a favor of someone you don't know. Especially a celebrity." She lifts a shoulder and flips her hair back. "Annie Laurie is not in on this, is she?"

"We asked her," Ellie says, the wind gushing from her sails. Her shoulders have drooped and her voice has lost its *oomph*. "But she said she doesn't have much spare time this semester."

"Well, thank God for that. My daughter knows she has to make good grades to be initiated in December."

"Please, Mrs. Whitmore," I say. "If Eli Manning happens to say yes, will you give us your blessing?"

"Even if he said yes, which will never happen, what happens next year? And the year after that?"

"Every pledge class can have their own fund-raiser," Ellie explains.

She points at Ellie. "Would you want the former pledge class deciding on your philanthropy project? I can't give you my blessing. It won't work."

"But—"

"Ah, ah ah," she pushes a palm toward Ellie. "My decision is made. I don't want to hear another word about it." Leaning in toward us, she adds, "Enjoy your college years, girls. These are not issues for you to be concerning your pretty little heads with. Find something more direful. Like cancer or heart disease. I'm sure there are millions of people who would appreciate your help." She stands with her chin held high. "Now, if you'll excuse me, I need to get back to the business of finding our next House Director."

Ellie and I both stand up slowly. Defeat is stabbing me in the chest. I'm sure she feels it, too. We get all the way to the chapter room door when we hear Mrs. Whitmore call my name. "Oh, Cali?"

I turn back around.

"What does your mother think of you joining Alpha Delt? A girl from Blue Mountain in the finest sorority on campus. Now that's something to be proud of. Don't you think?" There's a distant smile about her, as she slowly squints one eye.

"My grandparents are overjoyed for me, Mrs. Whitmore."

She sucks in a breath, covers her mouth. "Does your mother not know yet? California is a long way away."

Ellie looks at me, then back at her. Digs her hands into her hips. "You know what, Mrs. Whitmore? No one cares about the stuff you care about. Everyone here is just happy to have Cali as a new member."

"Cali is a very lucky girl. Snap bids are extremely rare. Especially for Alpha Delta Beta."

After grabbing the handle, Ellie yanks the door open. "Come on, Cal. Let's get out of here."

I put one foot forward, then whip my head back around. I can feel the flood of adrenaline rushing through me like a roaring wind. Deep inside my gut a match has been struck and the flame has reached my tongue. "You're absolutely right, Mrs. Whitmore. I am a very lucky girl. Lucky that I don't have you for a mother."

Ellie and I share a victory smirk as I shut the door behind us.

FIFTY-SEVEN

WILDA

The luscious smell of chargrilled filet fills the room when my husband opens the back patio door. He's spent the last fifteen minutes standing over our outdoor grill with a beer in one hand and a pair of long tongs in the other. The baked potatoes are done, the asparagus is roasted, and the table is set. We're celebrating our freedom. We have officially excommunicated Lilith and Gage Whitmore from our lives. Hallelujah!

"Potatoes ready?" he asks, swinging the small platter of meat over his head like he's playing airplane with one of the kids. Then he places it down carefully on the kitchen island. Haynes has a new pep in his step.

And so do I. "Yes indeedy. I'm about to take them out now." *Things may actually be getting back to normal,* I think, as I bounce over to the oven, sliding an oven mitt over my hand. I take that back. We are living a *new* normal. I am a new person.

Haynes reaches into the fridge, pulls out another beer. After popping the top he extends it my way. I reach back for my wineglass.

"Cheers," we both say in unison, clinking our glasses. We lean in for a kiss. Haynes strolls over to our docking station, slips his phone into the dock. After pushing play, Mick and the boys fill the room. "Under My Thumb."

I reach into the oven for the baked potatoes and plop one on each of our plates. After slitting them open and watching steam fill the air, I position several asparagus spears right next to the potatoes, singing along loudly with every word. "It's down to me . . . she's under my thumb." Haynes plops the smoldering filets in the middle and pours the juice from the platter on top. We're dancing over to the table when the door leading in from the garage flies open and bangs the wall. Ellie rushes inside with Cali right behind her.

"Heart! What in the world?"

Haynes whips around so fast he almost drops his dinner plate. "What's up, El?"

"Y'all have to do something about Lilith Whitmore!"

I look at Haynes. He looks at me. "To be free or not to be free. That is the question," he says theatrically.

Ellie sneers. "What are you talking about, Dad?"

Haynes puts his plate down on the table, moves over to her. "A little inside joke between your mother and me. Come here." He hugs her to his chest, then does the same to Cali.

I put my plate down and stretch my arms around them both. "Something big must have happened for you two to drive all the way home on a Wednesday. How on earth did you get here?"

"Jasmine loaned us her car," Ellie says. "Wait till you hear what Lilith Whitmore has done."

I can't believe I'm hearing that woman's name so soon after our emancipation. "First, let me get y'all a plate." I'm headed back to the cabinet when Cali stops me. "Thank you, Mrs. Woodcock, but we stopped for dinner along the way."

"Oh Lord, I hope it was good for you," I say with a sigh. "There's nothing but pickled pig's feet and fried pork rinds between here and Oxford."

Haynes adjusts his glasses and peers at me from across the room. "Wilda, stop worrying. I'm sure the girls went through the Whole Foods drive-in in Holly Springs."

"No, sir. We didn't see that," Cali says with a concerned face.

Ellie rolls her eyes, then looks at Cali. "He's just kidding you."

"No, I'm having a little fun at your mother's expense." Haynes pulls a chair out and motions for me to sit. He does the same for Cali and Ellie. "Would you girls like something to drink?"

"I'll have a beer, please," Ellie says. "Make it a tallboy."

Haynes points a playful finger her way. "How about two Cokes?"

Daisy, who had been on her hind legs pawing at Ellie's shins from the minute she walked in, jumps in Ellie's lap and kisses her face.

"Aw, she's so cute," Cali says, reaching over to pet Daisy.

"She should be," Haynes says from the fridge. "My wife feeds her homemade organic dog food."

Ellie, who is scratching up and down Daisy's back, kisses the top of her head. "You deserve homemade organic dog food. Don't you, girl?" After a few more scratches Ellie puts her down. Daisy sits back on her haunches, then innocently cocks her head at Haynes when he returns to the table with the Cokes. She's preparing her next move.

"Daisy, here," he says, peering down at her, "landed in a bucket of cream when she flashed those big browns at my wife."

Cali laughs. "I love dogs. My grandmother . . . not so much. I'm getting one as soon as I move into an apartment, though. I've already decided."

Haynes shoots her an exaggerated wink, points at Daisy. "You can have this one."

"She'll have to kill me first." I reach down to stroke my baby's head.

After handing the girls their drinks, Haynes shakes out his napkin and places it in his lap. "Okay. Lay it on us. What has that shameless silver spoon done now?"

Ellie giggles. "I don't even know where to begin." I notice her eyes shift over to Cali, who is shaking her head lightly. "Aside from insulting Cali in a way she'd rather I not get into, Lilith Whitmore shot us down on something before we ever got started."

Haynes lifts his hands over his head, the way he always does when he wants to make a point. "Never underestimate the evil power grab of a sorority alum with no other life." Then he cuts a small slit into his steak. "Hang on, El." He looks at me. "Is your steak okay?"

I slice into mine. "Perfect."

"Okay, keep going."

"After Miss Ophelia's funeral, Cali and I came up with this great idea for our pledge-class philanthropy project." She glances at Cali. "We wanted to raise enough money to give the Alpha Delt staff benefits, and Lilith Whitmore wouldn't hear of it."

Haynes leans in toward her with his fork in one hand and a knife in the other. "The staff doesn't have benefits?" He shifts his gaze to me.

I have no idea. So I simply shrug.

"No, Dad. They don't. None of them do. Miss Ophelia died from stage-four uterine cancer because she didn't have health insurance and never went to the doctor."

"I understand she had no health insurance, and I do think that's … absurd," Haynes says, slicing into his steak. "But she could have gone to a doctor, honey. There are free health clinics around Oxford."

"Maybe so, but it's still wrong," Ellie says, somewhat defeated. "And so sad."

"It sure is." This is news to me. I'd never thought about whether or not the staff had benefits.

Cali hasn't said much, but she finally opens her mouth. "Miss Pearl said Miss Ophelia was, like, super stubborn about going to the doctor."

"And she never wanted to spend any money," Ellie adds.

"Let's get back to the reason you drove all the way home," Haynes says, after swallowing his first bite of baked potato. "You two went to Lilith Whitmore with an idea and then what happened?" He slices off another bite of steak, then puts his knife down.

"She told us Alpha Delt is a small business and we can't afford to give the staff health insurance," Ellie says.

Haynes turns to me. "How many people on staff?"

I hurry to swallow before answering. "Six besides the housemother."

"Alpha Delt gives Mama Carla health insurance," Cali adds.

With one hand twirling her hair and the other holding her Coke can, Ellie's focus is on her father. "Dad, don't you know Eli Manning?"

"I wouldn't say I know him, but I've met him. At an Ole Miss athletic banquet. Why?"

"Do you think you could talk him into letting us sell tickets for a chance at an evening out with him and his wife, Abby?" Ellie has raised up in her seat. I can hear the excitement in her voice.

"Whoa!" Haynes puts down his fork, leans back in his chair. "I said I've met him *once*. I'm not sure I could pull off something like that."

Ellie's body deflates. She looks down, slumps her shoulders, like she used to do when she was little.

"That's a big ask, honey." I reach out to stroke her arm. "Your dad doesn't even know Eli Manning."

"But surely you know someone who does." There is pleading in her eyes when she looks at her daddy.

"I love that you girls are thinking like this," I say. "You're right to want to change things. Why don't we throw out some other ideas?"

"Hang on," Haynes says. "You girls might be onto something. Eli Manning was just nominated for the Walter Payton humanitarian award, the best award in the NFL, in my opinion."

Ellie and Cali look at each other with their mouths hanging open. Then Cali's cute little face lights up. "We were thinking if we could sell a ticket to each girl in the sorority, at twenty dollars apiece, that's right at nine thousand dollars. Surely that would pay for the staff's health insurance."

"It would pay for a lot more than that," Haynes says. "I'll have to run some numbers, but if each girl was assessed, I don't know, say, two hundred dollars a year, it would not only give the staff health insurance . . . I'd be willing to bet it could start a retirement fund, too."

"But *we* want to raise the money. We don't want to ask our parents for it," Ellie says.

Haynes and I look at each other. We're both thinking the same thing. Our daughter's head is screwed on the right way. "That's awesome, Heart. I'm so proud right now." These are the moments we parents live for.

Haynes puts his knife and fork down on his plate. "I'm proud of you both. The amount of money it would take to give everyone on the staff yearly benefits would be the equivalent of a discarded pair of Jimmy Choos at a frat house." Glancing at me, he winks, proud of his quip.

Ellie gives a mocking glance at Cali, then back to her father. "Dad. Since when did you become an authority on Jimmy Choos?"

"Another inside joke," he says, then sips his beer.

Turning toward him, I place my hand on his arm. "Actually, it would be more like a discarded pair of Nine Wests. Jimmys go for at least eight hundred dollars a pair."

Haynes chokes. For a minute I'm not sure he'll be able to catch his breath. His face turns beet red. "I did not need to know that," he says, coughing out his words.

"Okay, *whatever.*" Ellie waves a hand in front of her. "So. Dad. Can you call Eli's manager or his agent?"

"I can do better than that. A buddy of mine knows Eli well. I'll get in touch with him and we'll see where it goes. You never know. Maybe Eli and Abby will feel the same way we do."

"Daddy. This is freaking awesome!" Ellie gets up, throws her arms around her father.

Haynes pats her on the back. "Don't get too excited yet. We're a long way from a 'yes.' Besides, anything could happen."

Cali winces. "Like Lilith Whitmore? Can she stop us?"

"Not unless she wants mutiny in the House," I say. "By the way, what does Annie Laurie have to say about all—?"

"Not interested," Ellie blurts before I can finish my sentence. Then she sits back down and twirls her hair again.

Haynes and I glance at each other.

"Why is that?" he asks.

"Because she's a clone of her mother," Ellie says. "She does everything her mom tells her to do."

"What about all the other Alpha Delts? Were they in favor of it?" he asks.

"Yes. Every single person," Cali says. "The rest of our pledge class is all over it. And so are the active members."

"Then I'd like to see Lilith Whitmore try." A puckish smile crosses Haynes's lips.

"Everyone agrees the staff works so hard taking care of all of us, the least we can do is reciprocate by taking care of them," Ellie says.

"Absolutely." I secretly slip Daisy a bite of steak. "It's a beautiful thing to think that you young girls will be the ones to bring about change."

"We need to be doing this for the Sigma Nu staff," Haynes says. "All the sororities and fraternities do if they haven't done so already. Not only at Ole Miss, but Tennessee, Alabama, Georgia, LSU. Every university, really."

Cali picks up her glass and lifts it high in the air. "Here's to making a difference." All four of us touch our glasses together with a loud *clink*, then we each take sips—slow, delicious, hopeful sips—of making a difference in the name of Sisterhood.

Once the girls have left to drive back to Oxford—I mean as soon as the door shuts behind them—Haynes turns to me with a look I've seen him give jurors in the courtroom. "This all boils down to one thing. *Greed*. But you mark my word. Lilith Whitmore's rapacious thirst for wealth and power will be the very thing that brings her to her knees."

FIFTY-EIGHT

MISS PEARL

The cards and letters have been pouring in since Fee died. I must have gotten two hundred already. Selma James called to tell me she was ordering custom sympathy acknowledgments from Crane and that she and some of the other sisters would help me address every one of them. I have the sweetest, most loving girls in the world. The Lord has truly blessed me. And then some.

As a condolence, my dear friend Shirley volunteered to freshen up my weave. Then she treated me to dinner. But the whole way home from the restaurant, all I could think about was returning to work tomorrow. Everything in that House reminds me of Aunt Fee.

With her gone I feel as lost as a stray puppy. For the first time in a long time I am low. And, if I'm honest with myself, I'm angry, too. Angry at that stubborn woman for neglecting to see a doctor and for leaving me sooner than she should have. Didn't she think about what it would do to me? To lose a mother all over again?

When I get home, after hurling my pocketbook onto the couch, I don't take time to remove my coat or turn up the temperature. I walk right over to my silver service and carry the whole heavy thing to the kitchen. The tray must weigh twenty pounds on its own. I open the cabinet underneath the sink, pull out my rubber gloves, polish, three clean rags, and the old toothbrush I keep handy to work inside the nooks and crevices. I need a way to release this anger.

First, I pick up the coffeepot—the biggest piece—and get to work. Starting on the inside, I then move around to the front, lathering it up good with the pink paste. *Smells like rotten eggs,* I think while rubbing the handle, then the feet. *Rotten like the way you never told me you were sick, Aunt Fee.* After placing it back on the tray, I pick up the tea pitcher. Do the same thing all over again, then start on the creamer. There's a waste bowl and a sugar jar with a lid. And also a small kettle on a stand with a burner underneath.

Once I spread cream on all six pieces in the service, I pick up the toothbrush and go at the roses on that sugar jar like I'm scrubbing away blood. I maneuver the brush around each bud, working hard to get inside the petals and leaves.

While I'm brushing I'm seventeen again. And so is William McKinney.

I usually took the bus home every day from school. On this particular day, in mid-December, the temperature had dropped. All I had on was a light jacket. When William saw me shivering, standing at the end of the line waiting to board the bus, he rolled down the window of his shiny red Jeep. "Want a ride?"

I looked over, saw him smiling, and took a run for his car. We left the school parking lot a little too fast, as I recall.

"Up for helping me on the trig exam?" he asked first thing. We were both seniors in the same trigonometry class.

"I can do that."

"My dad will kill me if I get less than a B."

"Why's he so hard on you? He knows math's not your thing." I already knew the answer to this. William's father was harsh, "a mean good ol' boy," as William often called him.

"He doesn't care. All he cares about is A's. Even though he never made them. Bastard."

William had a gift for the creative arts. He could turn a blank canvas into a field of French lilacs in no time, and if there was a song you wanted to hear— any song—he could pick it out on his guitar and sing like he was getting paid to do it.

"Why don't you talk to him about it?" I said. "Let him know you're doing your best."

"There's no use. He doesn't care." Even from his profile, I could see all the varied emotions on William's face: Pain, disgust, anger.

Since I was Mama's only child, there had been times when Mrs. McKinney would allow the bus to drop me off at their house after school. I'd sit at the kitchen counter finishing my homework while Mama stood in front of the stove cooking their supper. Once Mrs. McKinney learned of my aptitude for math, she often invited me to their house to help William.

I remember the proud look on Mama's face whenever William and I would sit at the kitchen table working our math problems together. It was rare for me to bring home a report card without A's. But William, bless his heart, was a C student at best.

On the way home that day, William carried me by the Cream Cup. He knew I loved their chocolate shakes. Only about a mile from Oxford High, it was a popular after-school hangout, known for burgers, banana splits, and shakes. But on that cold December day, we were the only ones there. Once upon a time the Cream Cup had two walk-up windows. Blacks and whites couldn't order from the same one.

When we got our shakes we dashed back to his Jeep to stay warm. We were sitting with the engine running, sucking on our straws, when he said, "You're lucky, Pearl."

I thought to myself, *Me, lucky? You're the one who's lucky. Let's start with this car you're driving, why don't we?* Besides the Jeep, he was nice looking, wore nice clothes, lived in a big fancy house—his mama even drove a Cadillac car. I looked right at him and laughed. "Why am I lucky?"

"Because Ruby's your mom." Mama had been working for his family ever since William was born. He was the oldest of four.

"Why do you say that?" I asked him.

"For one thing," he said with a shrug, "she's the best cook in Oxford."

He was sure right about that. Mama was at their house fixing their supper at that very moment... like she did five nights a week, including every holiday. I wanted to say, "And you're the one eating it." But I didn't say it. I might think something, but generally I try to keep my thoughts to myself.

"And she's ... nice," he said, slurping the last bit of shake through his straw. "Much nicer than my mom."

"That's not true." I disagreed with him, but I knew darn well he was right.

"Yes it is. Ruby's much nicer to me than my own mother." A tear welled up in his pretty blue eye. He rested his head back so I wouldn't see it. Once a few seconds had passed he said, "I love your mother more than I do mine."

I sat straight up, turned to face him. "*William*. That's not true."

"Yes, it is."

"Don't say that."

He turned his head slightly, cut his eyes my way. "She cares about me, Pearl. She actually takes the time to ask me questions—about stuff I'm interested in. Girls ... my music. She even loves it when I sing for her."

"My mama is kind like that."

"So are you," he said.

I smiled.

"You're both kind. The other day, when I told Ruby I failed my math quiz, she didn't get mad. She just said, 'You'll do better next time, baby.' My dad grounded me for a week. Fucking asshole."

I flinched at his language, but I felt bad for him at the same time. He was always worried about what he had to do to please his parents. He only played football because his dad made him. Truth is, he hated it. Hated every minute he had to be on that field, which was hardly ever. There was a permanent spot on the bench with his name on it. Yet every day he still had to show up for practice.

I reached out and touched him on the arm. "I'm sorry."

"See, you are lucky."

"I suppose I am."

He put his empty cup into the holder between our seats. "Your mother feels like my real mother. I can't remember a day when she wasn't around. I've spent more time with her than my own mom."

Hearing him say those words out loud caused a stinging in my chest, like a bee was trapped inside. My chin dipped. I couldn't help it.

"What did I say?" I heard him ask with genuine concern.

I shook my head.

He reached over and gripped my hand, because William was the sensitive type. "Tell me. What did I say?"

I looked over at him. "You didn't mean anything by it."

"I . . . I know I didn't. Please tell me what I said."

I clutched the hem of my shirt, balled it up in the palm of my hand. "It's just . . . I can remember lots of days when Mama wasn't around."

He threw his head back, banged it on the headrest several times. "I'm such an asshole. I never thought about it that way."

"I know you didn't. Don't worry about it."

Neither of us said anything for a long while. Then he started his car and we left the Cream Cup heading down University Avenue for his house. When we reached the intersection he stopped for the light. "Can we study at your house today?"

We had never studied at my house. William had never even been inside. "Why my house?"

"If we study there my dad won't know you helped me. I want him to think I did it on my own."

"Fine by me, but don't expect much." My house wasn't much to look at compared to his and there certainly was no big TV.

When the light turned, he headed straight instead of taking a left toward home. Once we pulled in our drive, he took his keys out and set them on the gearshift. "You sure about this?"

I nudged his shoulder. "You scared or something?"

"Heck no."

"Then get out of your car and come inside."

He grabbed his backpack from the back seat and closed the door behind him.

When I opened our front door, I watched his eyes roam around the living room: at our family photos on the walls, our living room suite, our small dining room table. I showed him around, then one minute later we ended up in the kitchen. A tour of our home did not take long. Right away, his eyes darted to the front of our fridge, to a picture that had been hanging there for years. I'd looked at it so long I'd forgotten where it came from.

He lifted it off the fridge and studied it thoroughly. A drawing of what was most definitely his house with a lady, her skin crayon colored in brown, standing in the doorway. *To Ruby, I Love You, William.* "I can't believe your mom kept this. I don't remember drawing it." He looked over at me.

"She keeps everything. Don't open our closets. You'll be taking your life in your own hands."

He smiled, put the picture back where it was—underneath the teakettle magnet—and straightened it. "Do y'all have anything to eat?"

I laughed. "You just had a shake." That boy could put down a mountain of food, and still stay skinny as a reed.

"I'm always hungry." He pulled out a chair at our small kitchen table and took a seat.

I fixed him a Co-Cola and a slice of chess pie Mama had made the day before. Then I sat down next to him and watched him wolf down that pie like he hadn't eaten all day.

Once he swallowed his last bite I said, "Okay, you ready to study?"

"I'm never ready to study," he said with a chuckle. "Let's watch TV for thirty minutes. Then we'll study."

I shook my head playfully. "Whatever you say."

We moseyed out to the living room and settled down onto our couch. Once we finished watching a *Family Ties* rerun, and the five o'clock news had started, I asked him again. "Don't you think we better start studying?"

"I guess. But I'd rather play you a song I wrote yesterday." He got up and sprinted toward the door. "My guitar's in the Jeep."

"You better get back here, boy," I stood up and said before he could put his hand on the knob. "You're asking for it."

Reluctantly, he turned around. Then plopped back down on the couch. "Five more minutes?"

I shook my head and grinned. I already knew how hard it was for him to get started, but once he got going he usually did okay. "Five more minutes. That's all you get."

He leaned his head back and patted the seat next to him.

I sat down and leaned back, too. Out of the corner of my eye I could see his eyes were closed. He was thinking hard on something. Then he glanced around the room.

"I could live in this house. I used to feel bad for black people who had to live in small houses like this, but now that I'm here I realize I could live here, too."

"You're crazy," I told him. "You could not."

"Yes, I could." He shrugged, started to say something else, but stopped.

"What? Go on and say it."

"I was gonna say ... I could live here because I'd be loved." He turned to look me in the eye. "My parents don't love me, Pearl."

"William. You better stop thinking those things. They do love you."

"I can count on one hand the times I've actually had meaningful conversations with either one of them. They're much more concerned about Ole Miss football, and the furniture I can't sit on, than spending time with their kids. My mom is at the Alpha Delt house way more than our house. Still. After all these years. And my dad ... he still has posters of Archie Manning in his office."

I gave him an understanding nod.

"See, you are lucky." His once-smiling face had become expressionless. He looked at me with a longing gaze. "Wouldn't you hate it if your mom was like that?"

He was right. I would hate it. Listening to William talk, watching him mourn the divide between him and his parents, made me realize I was more than lucky. I was rich. But that didn't keep me from wishing I could take away his pain.

I can still see his tan corduroy trousers. And the way he nervously jiggled his leg. I reached over and softly patted his thigh. "Your mother does love you. She has a different way of showing it; that's all."

"Is it okay if your mom loves me, too?" Another tear seeped into his eye.

"Of course it is." I patted him again.

"That ... doesn't make you mad? Or sad?"

I shook my head no. And I meant it.

Then he let his tears flow. I don't know why he chose that day to vent; I guess he just needed to get it all off his chest. And I was a listening ear, someone he felt comfortable confiding in. William McKinney sat there on our sofa and cried like a little boy. I reached over, put my arm around him, and pulled him into my side. I needed to help him feel better, make him stop crying. He laid his head on my shoulder; his long hair covering my fingers. I stroked his head, because that's what I do. I'm affectionate and I touch people who need comfort. I sat up to look at him and wiped his tears away with my fingers. He reached up and put his hand behind my neck. The next thing I knew, we were kissing.

I've blocked it out for ages, but now, as I clean the silver service he insisted my mama keep, it's all coming back. The way he looked at me when our lips touched. How he stroked my cheeks, first one then the other, with the back of his hand. The way he held on to me like he never wanted to let go. How he stood up, took me by the hand, and led me into my bedroom. How we both sat down on my bed and fell back into the mattress. How he unbuttoned my shirt and told me I was beautiful. And how I knew by the sweet person he was, and probably still is, he was telling me the truth.

I had been at Ole Miss one month when I gave birth to our baby.

Bless Mama's heart. It almost destroyed her when she had to give up her only grandchild. She wanted to raise Autumn herself. But Mr. and Mrs. Mc-Kinney wouldn't hear of it. They learned of a family in Memphis who had been waiting five years on a baby, and she was gone two days after she was born. I didn't hold her but one time. The McKinneys never laid eyes on her.

She had dark hair and William's blue eyes. Mama said they might turn brown when she got older, but we never knew for sure. Her skin was light. Not perfectly white, just light, but she could pass for Caucasian. Looking like she did, everyone agreed it would be hard for us to raise her, especially in light of who her grandparents were and their place in the Oxford community.

William never once got to see her. When they learned I was pregnant, his parents quickly shipped him off to college—all the way up to Rhode Island. At least it got him out of going to Ole Miss; he never wanted to go there in the first place. He said his daddy finally gave up on him playing football and let him concentrate on his art. I think he gave up on William, period, once he learned he had a half-black grandchild.

Make no mistake about it. No one twisted my arm; I agreed to the adoption. The entire time I was carrying her I told myself I couldn't be bothered with a baby; my chief concern was me. I wanted to be the first college graduate in our family. I wasn't ready to be a mother. Not yet.

I gave birth on a Sunday morning, missed school on Monday, and was back in class on Tuesday. I stayed in college the rest of that semester, and the one after that. But as the days went on, I became depressed. As much as I wanted to make a name for myself, I couldn't find the strength to do it. I found myself falling deeper and deeper into despair. I regretted my decision. But it was too late. And I have spent almost every day since wondering where she is and how she's getting along. Who is treating her right, and who is breaking her heart. All the normal feelings a mother has for her child.

I hear William is doing well now. While he was in college, he met and married a nice girl and they still live outside New York City with a big family of kids. I read about him every once in a while in the *Oxford Eagle*. He's a landscape artist. Fairly famous, I believe. If it weren't for him, I wouldn't have a thing to show for our time with the McKinney family. Except for Aunt Fee's house, this silver service, and Autumn. But she's not mine to show.

Now all six pieces look shiny and brand new. Especially the sugar jar. It catches my reflection. I pick it up and stare into it for a long while. Looking at myself, I can't help but wonder if our baby girl holds any resemblance to me at all.

FIFTY-NINE

CALI

"Are y'all awake?" Jasmine and I are already in our beds when we hear Ellie knocking. "Open up. It's me."

I stumble off my mattress and head to the door. Although it's only ten o'clock on a Thursday night we're both exhausted from pulling study all-nighters twice this week.

Once I let her in, Ellie balls her hands into fists, swings them over her head, and glides inside. *At least someone's perky around this place,* I think, watching her squat with her legs shoulder-length apart, feet angled outward. She puckers her lips and sways her body from side to side, jutting her chin with each move. Obviously not as tired as she thought, Jasmine jumps off her bed and mimics Ellie, only she puts her facial magic with it. I can't sit still watching my two best friends dance so I squat, too, throw my arm in the air and whip with them.

"Cali?" Jasmine asks, rocking her body from side to side.

"Yeah?" Ellie whips a slightly bent arm above her head, then rocks to the same rhythm as Jasmine.

"Why are we whipping?" Jasmine asks. "With no jive?"

"Because I have something to tell y'all. And you might not hear me over the music." By now, Ellie's a little out of breath.

"Tell us already," I say, swaying to the imaginary beat.

"Eli Manning's people called my dad," she says as casually as she might talk about the weather. Then a sly smile creeps onto her lips. "And Eli said *yesssss!*" She screams and stands straight up, then throws her arms overhead, prancing in place.

Jasmine and I fall down on our butts.

"You're lying," I yell. "No freaking way."

"Your dad is the man," Jasmine says. "Wait till I tell Carl. He'll buy a ticket. So will the rest of his friends."

After we hear footsteps scrambling down the hall, Tara and Bailey pop their heads in our door. "What's up?" Tara says from the doorframe.

Bailey pushes her inside and they both plop down on our futon. "What are y'all yelling about?" Bailey asks.

Hannah and Claudia, our next-door neighbors on the elevator side, tumble in also. Hannah jumps up on my bed and Claudia scoots in next to Tara and Bailey.

"Remember how we were telling y'all we thought it was awful that the Alpha Delt staff doesn't have benefits?" Ellie asks.

The three on the couch nod, but Hannah says, "I don't know what you're talking about."

"That's right," I say. "You weren't here that day. Our pledge class wants to make staff benefits our philanthropy project." I scoot back a little so everyone can see my face while I'm talking. "Ellie's dad got freaking *Eli Manning* to agree to let us sell tickets for an evening out at City Grocery with him and his wife, Abby."

"That's crazy," Claudia says. "How much are y'all selling them for?"

"At first we thought, like, twenty dollars, but my dad has done tons of research and now he thinks we need to sell them for twenty-five." Ellie's about to lose it. Her hands are swinging all over the place. "So we'll have money for several years to come."

"How'd your dad do that?" Hannah asks. "Does he know Eli Manning or something?"

"He's met him before, but they're both Sigma Nus. And they have a good mutual friend."

Tara and Bailey, who are both Pi Phis, look at each other. "We should do something like that for our staff," Bailey says.

"We all should," Claudia, who is a KD, says. "Abby Manning was a KD here. Maybe she could help us."

I happen to look up and notice Annie Laurie in the doorway. There's no telling how long she's been standing there. She's not happy like the rest of us; she's frowning. When everyone sees me looking at her they look, too. "What are y'all talking about?" she snaps. Her voice is icy and accusatory.

Hannah, who is totally oblivious to the backstory, says innocently, "Oh ma God. I'm getting my parents to buy at least ten tickets for a chance at an evening out with Eli and Abby Manning. And if they win, I'm going." She pulls her legs up underneath her and leans back against the wall.

Claudia leans forward, puts her hands on her knees. "You're taking me with you, right?"

"Hell, yeah," Hannah says.

Annie Laurie's expression morphs from a frown to stone-cold furious. I mean, everyone knows she has bitchy resting face, but now she looks possessed. She's glaring at Ellie and me. It's scary. "My mom flat-out told y'all you couldn't do that. Why did you go against her wishes? She's the House Corp President. What she says goes."

A hush descends on our room. Everyone's eyes are darting around, looking at one another—looking anywhere—but at her. The tension feels as thick as mud.

Leave it to Jasmine to cut through it. She moves in toward her. "Annie Laurie. Let me ask you a question." Her arms are crossed in her usual audacious way, but her tone is surprisingly nice. "Why would your mother want to block something that could be a big help to people? I don't know the staff at the Alpha Delt House, but from what I hear they work their asses off." None of the rest of us says anything. But now, because of Jasmine, we're all looking right at Annie Laurie.

She crosses her arms in front of her like she's daring any of us to cross her. "Y'all don't know what you're talking about." Her tone makes her sound just like her mother. Like she's the smartest person in the room and we're all imbeciles. "Alpha Delt can't afford staff benefits. We're not Walmart."

"Really?" Jasmine tilts her head to the side. Her tone has sharpened. "You mean to tell me that everyone in Alpha Delt can't afford to pitch in a little extra?" She glances over her shoulder at the rest of us. "What does it cost y'all to belong to a sorority, anyway? Four or five thousand a year?"

Ellie tucks her hair behind her ears, then twists it across her shoulder. "At first my dad thought it would cost a lot more, but after researching he says it would only cost each girl *fifteen more dollars a month* to give our entire staff health, dental, *and* life insurance, *plus* a retirement fund."

"Shut up!" Hannah's bulging eyes make her look like a cartoon character. *"That's it?"*

"That's it," Ellie says. "Crazy, huh?"

"That's less than a T-shirt." Claudia's leaning forward with her elbows on her knees. "How many of those will we buy in a year?"

"It's the same as, like, three Starbucks venti lattes a month," Hannah says with a shrug.

Jasmine bobs her head. "Or two *cheap* glasses of wine."

"What if everybody gave . . . *ten* more on top of the fifteen?" Tara asks. "It would give the staff a better paycheck."

Ellie erupts from the corner of my bed. "Yes! That would be sweet."

"Y'all need to check with a real professional on that," Annie Laurie says in a condescending tone. "Someone besides Ellie's dad. If my mom thought it was a smart business decision for Alpha Delt, she would have done it already. She only has our best interests at heart, y'all."

"Best interests? Seems like taking care of your people is in your best interests," Jasmine says under her breath. "But what do I know?"

As awkward and weird and uncomfortable as this is, I pretty much can't take Annie Laurie anymore. All the mean comments she's made since school started, and the snobby way she's treated me—not to mention her mother snooping into my past and lying to my grandparents—all of it has pushed me to my tipping point. She's just like her mother. I step toward her. "What is it with you and your mother, Annie Laurie? I mean, seriously."

Her shoulders rear back, but I step closer. Now I'm only a few feet from her.

"Y'all's main concern is how Alpha Delt looks on the outside, not the inside. It's obvious you don't care that our staff barely makes enough to survive, as long as the house looks pretty and has a Southern aristocratic image—with only black people working there."

When a look of shock passes over Annie Laurie's face I have to admit I'm surprised at myself, too. But I keep going. "Have y'all ever stopped to think about *how* the House looks as nice as it does? Or about that delicious home-cooked meal you eat every day now? Maybe y'all think a genie lives in the kitchen and . . . abracadabra, *poof!* Four hundred fifty dinners appear on the tables by magic!"

I hear nervous laughter behind me, but I don't care. "Our staff work their butts off." When I say this my voice cracks because I can't help thinking about Miss Ophelia dead in the ground, and Miss Pearl missing her so much. And all the other things she told me about working there. "Don't you and your mother think they deserve to be compensated for the hard work they do?"

"They get paid holidays and perks you don't even know about," Annie Laurie says. "They rack in a ton of Christmas presents." Straight from her mother's lips to hers. But the way she said it seems like she was just quoting her mother. Her arms are no longer crossed. And she's rubbing the insides of her palms anxiously.

"Surely you don't believe that makes much of a difference for them, do you?"

Instead of her signature smirk, she gives a slight shrug with an uncertain gaze.

"You should *want* to help the Alpha Delts make a difference. You're a part of the sisterhood."

Now she's staring at the floor.

"Do you know why everyone in our sorority wants this change?"

She doesn't answer, but I sense she's paying attention.

"Because it's flat-out wrong. You say your mom has Alpha Delt's best interests at heart? If that's true, then you tell me what's good about paying our staff less than we get for babysitting jobs. Especially when they're the ones doing work most of us wouldn't be caught dead doing. Like cleaning all those toilets."

Her breath catches.

"It seems to all of us in this room"—I turn around to look at my friends—"and I'm betting most every sorority girl and fraternity boy on this campus would agree . . . providing benefits for the staff is well worth the fifteen-dollar-a-month sacrifice."

"Amen," Hannah says behind me.

"I wholeheartedly agree," Tara adds.

"Look. I know it's hard to go against your mother, but you don't have to be like her. Trust me. I know that firsthand." I shift a quick glance toward Ellie. "Wouldn't it be the right thing to make sure that when the people on our staff retire they have a few extra dollars to live on?" My voice softens. Now I'm pleading with her. "We should be the kind of sorority that goes the extra mile for people. We should be the kind of sorority that makes sure the people who work for us don't have to sit up all night worrying about how they'll feed their children or how to keep their lights on. We should be the kind of sorority that places a high value on those sweet people. *That*, Annie Laurie, is what it means to have Alpha Delt's best interests at heart."

My heart is beating super fast. Saying all this to her has taken every bit of courage I can muster. I'm trying to psych myself up for whatever nasty comment she's about to regurgitate, but the truth is I don't care what she says to me anymore. I know I'm right.

Instead of slinging another of her normal mud-coated remarks, Annie Laurie bursts into tears. Hands fly up, covering her face. It's not at all what I expected. I glance at the others to see what they're thinking, and their mouths are pretty much hanging open, too.

"Y'all don't understand," Annie Laurie says through genuine tears. "You have no idea what it's like to . . . She's not . . . My mom might not think the way y'all do, but I have Alpha Delt's best interests at heart. I love my sorority." Her eyes plead with us, like she's sorry, but instead of saying so she turns and runs off toward her room, leaving us all with our eyes popping out of our skulls. For a long, stretched-out moment everyone stays perfectly still. Then we hear a door slamming shut.

"That was so random," Tara whispers. "I never saw that coming."

We all look at Ellie, who holds her palms up. "Don't look at me! I don't know what's in that head of hers."

"Maybe you got to her, Cali," Jasmine says.

I stumble back in shock as my friends look at me in admiration.

"You were awesome," Bailey says.

"No joke. I'm so proud of you right now," Ellie says, hugging me from behind.

Bailey grips her forehead. "Seriously, though. What's wrong with her?"

Tara moves off the futon and peeks out the door. We watch her check both ways, then shut the door softly and turn back around. "Maybe there's something bad wrong with Annie Laurie's family? There's got to be a reason she's like that."

It crosses my mind that she's like that because of the way she's been raised—her mother's influence. My grandparents raised me. What if my mother had stuck around? Would I be different? Would I be on drugs? "It's because she lives in a house with a mean mother. It's her mother's influence; that's why she's like that."

"I've never met the woman, but"—Hannah exhales loudly—"she sounds like the bitch from hell."

"I met her the day we moved in," Jasmine says. "She's wound up tight. Very into herself and the way things look."

"That's an understatement," Ellie says. "Considering all that woman has done, Cali was nice. Y'all wouldn't believe the half of it."

"Like what?" Bailey is wide-eyed, eager for some good scoop.

Ellie shakes her head. "I don't want to stoop to her level, but she's, like, scary mean."

"So what started all this?" Hannah asks. "What's this about y'all going against her mother's wishes?"

Ellie rolls her eyes. "Her mom forbade us to take this project on. She said we'd never be able to get Eli Manning here. But my dad made it happen. He says she can't do anything to stop us if all the members are behind it. And we are."

"All but one," Jasmine says. "But you may have changed that, Cali. She wouldn't have been crying like that if something you said hadn't put a crack in her armor."

"How did she get into Alpha Delt, anyway?" Claudia asks. "I'm not trying to be mean, but, what the—"

"*Duh.*" Ellie blurts, flashing a tight-lipped smile. She throws her hands in the air. "How do you think?"

I see what they mean, but after tonight I see another side of Annie Laurie. Our situations may be different, but we're both wounded. Wounded by the person who is supposed to love us the most.

SIXTY

MISS PEARL

The kitchen is as quiet as a whisper when I walk in the back door some-time around eleven o'clock in the morning. There's no music, and there's sure no singing. Mr. Marvelle is in the pantry on top of the ladder, Helen is chopping onions—I can smell them from the time clock—and Kadeesha has her hands in the sink. I have to wonder if it will ever be the same around here.

"Good morning," I say, trying my best to be upbeat. Latonya is at the helm now and there's a new kitchen aide working next to her. Once I punch my card I head her way. "We haven't met yet. I'm Pearl."

"No we haven't. I'm Bernice, Latonya's sister. Happy to meet you, Pearl."

"Nice to meet you, too. Mind if I call you Bernie?"

"Go ahead on. Most my friends do."

Latonya waves like she's happy to see me, but that Kadeesha stares me up and down like I've done her wrong. *I don't have the time or energy for your lip,* I'd love to say, but I keep my mouth shut. She's not an early bird, and she's been taking up the slack ever since I've been gone.

I go on about my business, tidying up around the coffeepot, making sure the snacks in the buffet area are stocked. Once I get back into the kitchen I ask Kadeesha if she wants me to take over for her, but she tells me no. So I head on out, past the dining room, down the hall to Mama Carla's apartment. Her door is wide open. I poke my head in and see her on the phone. Trudy jumps off the chair and runs right up to me for a pet. Squatting down, I rub her on the head, then down her back.

Mama Carla holds up a finger and mouths, "One minute."

I nod and wait outside the door, in case she needs privacy.

Exactly one minute later she pokes her head out. "You could have come in. I don't have anything to hide from you, my friend."

"Same here." I take my usual spot in the chair next to hers. "You know almost everything about me."

"*Almost* everything?"

"A girl has to keep a few things to herself. I'm sure you've got some secrets, too, Mama Carla. And don't you say you're too old for secrets."

"Well, I am old, but yes, I do have my share of private fantasies."

We both laugh. I settle back into the familiar chair, thinking back to when I'd filled in for her. When I was queen for the weekend. "It's good to be back."

"We've missed you around here. How are things going?"

"As well as can be expected, I suppose. I knew I'd miss her, but it's harder than I thought. That ol' stubborn woman. I could wring her neck."

A smile sneaks up on Mama Carla's lips.

"But it's too late now," I say. Then we have us a good laugh. At the stubborn woman's expense. My anger has waned in the last few days. Now I'm just dealing with the unbearable pain of missing her sweet face.

Once we've calmed down, Mama Carla says, "You probably haven't had a chance to enroll in school yet, have you?"

"Not yet. But after what Mrs. Whitmore said, I'm more convinced than ever I need to do it."

Mama Carla leans in toward me. "*Mrs.* Whitmore?"

"I thought I told you. She said I can't call her Miss Lilith anymore."

"What?"

"Didn't I fill you in on that conversation we had? When I told her I wanted to apply for your job?"

"Bid Day was so hectic with Miss Ophelia out sick; we didn't get a chance to talk." She pulls her legs up underneath her. "But *she* told me. Asked me to keep my opinions about my successor to myself. I'm so sorry, Pearl. I feel responsible for putting you in this position. I thought it was a no-brainer. I still do."

"Don't worry about it. I've been giving it a lot of thought." I go ahead and tell her what's been on my mind. "When I looked out and saw her seated next to you at Fee's service, a thought crossed my mind. Maybe she's had a change of heart?"

Mama Carla snickers. "I think the roof would have to cave in on this House for that to happen. But I suppose anything's possible."

"Even so, I've decided to bring it up to her one more time." I've been mulling this over every day now since Fee died. I won't be able to live with myself if I don't give it one more shot. If Mrs. Whitmore still tells me no I'll move on, but I'll go down trying.

"I think you should," Mama Carla says, patting her thighs. "Just prepare yourself. I'd hate for you to be disappointed again."

"Mama Carla. I'm a strong woman. Don't you know that by now?" I laugh and think about how strong I am in all kinds of ways. Except my emotions over Aunt Fee dying. In that I've been anything but strong.

"You know I do."

"If that lady can't see I'm the right person for the job, that's her problem, but I owe it to myself to have one more conversation with her."

"Absolutely you do. And I'm behind you one thousand percent."

"For no other reason than progress. If I'm not qualified that's one thing, but it's not supposed to be about my skin color. That I know."

Mama Carla agrees by vigorously nodding her head. "I know that, and I'm betting the girls do also. I don't care if there's not another African American House Director in the entire South; it's high time that changed. Not only are you qualified; you're a good fit. It's as much about that as anything. Everyone already knows and loves you."

"Thank you, Mama Carla. Do you know when she'll be here in Oxford again?"

"Sometime today. She's got *an interview,*" Mama Carla says with finger quotes.

"I guess today's my day, then. When exactly are you leaving? Still thinking December?"

"If it weren't for my grandchildren you know I'd finish out the school year." She squeezes her eyes shut. "It's terrible timing with Ophelia's passing. I'm so sorry."

"No need to be sorry. You're doing the right thing."

"I'm doing what's right for me. Now you do the same. Lilith Whitmore has no idea who she's up against." She tilts her head back, chuckles.

"You know what Fee called her, don't you?"

"No. Tell me."

"The Whit*less* she-devil."

Mama Carla's eyes bug out of her head, then she splits, and I mean *splits,* in two. She gets to laughing so hard I think she may have a stroke. Her face turns as red and hot as a chili pepper. Watching her gets me going, then the two of us cackle like a couple of farm hens. She bends over, holding her stomach, then drops off the chair. I drop off mine, too, and we roll around on her carpet, so tickled we can't breathe. I mean it. We laugh and laugh like it's the last time we'll ever do it. Until a certain sound takes away our fun. All we hear is someone clearing her throat, but we both know from whom it came.

Mama Carla and I look up from the floor and there that she-devil is, dressed fancier than I've ever seen her: An ivory-lace dress—showing off all her curves—and a light blue silk scarf tied loosely around her neck, little short booties on her feet. And there's that pin again, dangling from her left bosom.

I resist the urge to scramble up off the floor, especially when I see Mama Carla taking her own sweet time.

"I hate to break up the party," Mrs. Whitmore says. There's a clipboard in one hand and the other is on her hip.

I put both hands on the chair and slowly pull myself up.

Mama Carla climbs back onto hers and Trudy, who usually welcomes everyone who stops by, jumps up next to Mama Carla, turns around on the edge of the chair with her curly tail pointed out straight, and growls.

"No party," Mama Carla says with a hand squeezing Trudy's mouth shut. "Miss Pearl just said a funny."

"Oh? Do share." Completely ignoring the growl, Miss Lilith tucks the clipboard in her armpit and claps her hands together. "I so love a funny."

And the tension over Trudy, who is still growling even with her mouth shut, makes things even funnier. Before I have a stroke from thinking how we're going to lie our way out of this mess, Mama Carla saves us. She sucks in her cheeks, then says, "Miss Ophelia's hearse got lost on the way to the cemetery." Then she tee-hees all over again, like it's the gospel truth.

Now I've known folks who take life too seriously, but I've never met anyone who can't grin when something even a little funny is said. This woman takes the cake. She gazes at us with a blank stare. Then says, "What's so funny about that?"

I better not look at Mama Carla. Between Trudy's growl, Miss Whitless's face and the undeniable truth that she was born without a funny bone, that strikes me funnier than the reason we were laughing in the first place. Out of the corner of my eye, I happen to catch sight of Mama Carla's shoulders shaking. I know I'm in trouble, so I excuse myself and run off to the ladies' room.

When I get back Mrs. Whitmore is in my seat. I wait for a lull in the conversation then I look at her and with my nicest voice say, "While you're here today, I'd like to sit down and talk with you when you get a chance."

She glances at a poker-faced Mama Carla to gauge her reaction, then turns back to me. "Can you tell me what this is regarding?"

"No, ma'am. I'd rather wait." I'm still smiling, but she's not.

After another glance at Mama Carla, she says, "All right. How about two o'clock?"

"That would be fine. Where would you like to meet?" I ask.

"Downstairs in the chapter room."

"Sounds good. I'll see you then."

I'm polishing the piano when I hear the grandfather clock in the receiving room strike one. Kadeesha's on her way to Mama Carla's apartment for her paycheck.

"Pssst. Can I talk to you a minute?" I call from the piano.

She stops, looks at me, then sashays over, smacking on Juicy Fruit. I can smell it as soon as she walks up. She studies the piano keys first, like she'd like to sit down and play, then looks at me.

"I'm sorry if my not being here these past two weeks has caused you trouble."

Smack, smack, pop, pop. "Forget it. I'm all right."

"I hate that you had to come in so early. I know you're not an early bird."

"Don't worry about it. It's not your fault." I hadn't anticipated this response. For the first time since she's been working here, I don't hear that haughty tone.

"Thank you for helping me out," I say.

"You're welcome." Now she's smiling.

All of a sudden I feel connected to her. Maybe it's the smile or the honey in her tone, but whatever it is, I lean closer. "Can I trust you, Kadeesha?"

She straightens. "Trust me? With what?" That ugly tone sneaks back in.

It's enough to make me want to shut my mouth, but instead I forge on. "I'm just asking: Can I trust you?"

She shrugs, juts out her bottom lip. "Sure."

"You know about Mama Carla leaving, right?"

She nods.

"I'm fixing to talk to Mrs. Whitmore about taking her job."

Her eyes bug like she's a little ol' tree frog or something. She doesn't open her mouth, just rolls that gum around. I honestly feel like she's about to say: *then I quit.* But instead she says, "That's good."

"You mean it?"

"I got your back," she says, then grins like she's real happy for me.

"Girl. Thank you for that."

Kadeesha turns, glances over her shoulder. "You're welcome." Then I watch her strut off toward Mama Carla's apartment. But she reverses her stride and strolls right back to me with a much faster gait. "You mean you're talking to Mrs. Shitmore, don't you?" Kadeesha wiggles her thick eyebrows, then sucks in her cheeks, holds her head high, playing like she's her.

Oh Lord, here I go again. Now it's Kadeesha and me cackling. "You and Fee. You know what she called her, don't you?"

Kadeesha nods. "Mmm-hmm. She used to say it all the time."

I lay my rag down on the piano so as not to get oil on her shirt and hug her around the neck. It's the first time the two of us have ever touched.

SIXTY-ONE

MISS PEARL

The chapter room door is closed when I arrive promptly at two o'clock. I'm not sure if there's someone in there with her, but I go ahead on and knock. No one opens. So I stand outside the door twiddling my thumbs. The thought crosses my mind she may be standing me up, but then I hear a pair of high-heeled booties clicking down the hall in my direction.

"Sorry I'm late," she says when she sees me. "I was meeting with a party planner about Annie Laurie's birthday party in February. Gage and I are throwing her a Mardi Gras ball here in Oxford."

Her hair is down today. Only half of it is in a ponytail, but it's still got a bump on top, like Barbie's, and her makeup is perfect. She takes out her key and opens the chapter room door. To my knowledge, it's never been locked before. "Have a seat, Pearl." She motions to a row of chairs. All the chairs are set up from Monday night's chapter meeting, so I pull one out from the back row and sit down. She pulls out another, making sure to keep a noticeable distance between us, then sits down herself. A pleasant smile spreads across her face, but I can't say it's genuine. "How can I help you, today?"

Looks like there'll be no small talk so I dive right in. "I'd like you to reconsider my application for House Director."

That smile fades away as fast as butter can burn. "As I told you before, we have mandatory qualifications for the position. Last time we spoke you didn't have a college degree. Has that changed?"

I refuse to be rattled by that snarky comment. "You know it hasn't." Folding my hands in my lap, I just look at her.

Now we're in a standoff.

"I do have a question for you," I say after a long fifteen seconds. "Does knowing everything about this House and caring about every girl here account for anything?"

Not one speck of emotion crosses her face. "Carla didn't know any of the girls when she was hired, but she did have a bachelor's degree, which prepares the mind for all the business decisions that come with this job." She holds up both pointer fingers to emphasize her words. "We have it recorded in the Alpha Delt bylaws that the House Director *must* have a college degree. If you like, I'd be happy to share that document with you."

"That won't be necessary."

She stands up, as if our conversation is over, wearing a smile as phony as a cheap silk flower. "Maybe next time we're searching for a House Director—if you have graduated by then—you can reapply."

But I keep my seat. I am not done. "Not everyone has had the opportunities you've had, Mrs. Whitmore. Have you ever considered that perhaps I had every intention of graduating from college?"

Now she just looks at me.

"Sometimes life has a way of grabbing folks by the tail, and they're forced to head in another direction. One they may not have planned."

"That's not really our problem, though, is it?"

Dear Lord, this woman is cold. Just like Aunt Fee said. The way she has patronized me, refusing to acknowledge all the years I've spent working here, is causing my insides to boil. But I take a deep breath. And I make a conscious decision to keep the lid on, because the pressure in my stomach wants to blow that lid right out the roof of this House. I didn't want to make this about my skin color, but I know, and she knows, that's exactly what this is about. She could bend the college-degree rule if she wanted to, and probably would if one of her friends applied for the job, but I can't modify the color of my skin.

I have a choice. I can file a lawsuit, then spend the next few years fighting it. Lose all the friends I've made and be *that person*. That black woman who sued Alpha Delta Beta sorority and won. Because I know I have a good chance of winning.

But what then? I actually get to be the House Director? Come home to find all the girls standing out on the porch welcoming me with open arms after I'd sued their sorority? I could never do that. That's not me. But it's not going to stop me from letting this woman know she's no better than I am.

I notice Miss Lilith's eyes leave mine and glance down to her booties.

I stand up so we're eye to eye. "If I were the mother of Patrick Willis, the best linebacker in Ole Miss history, or even Beyoncé's mother, how would you feel about my application then?"

"What?"

"How about if I was kin to Stevie Wonder and I could bring him here to perform at your Grove party? Then would you want me as your House Director?"

She's flustered when she answers. "Tha . . . that is irrelevant."

"This is about the color of my skin, isn't it, Lilith?"

That silk flower smile fades. I don't know what's made her madder: calling her Lilith or calling a spade a spade. She's up on her tiptoes now, thrusting a finger in my face. "Absolutely not," she responds with righteous indignation. "It's in the Alpha Delt bylaws, and I'm going to get—"

"No point in dancing around it," I say, begging God to keep me calm because I want to point my finger back at her. But I refuse to stoop to her level. So I keep my voice at an even keel. "That's exactly what this is about."

"No, it's not," she answers, taking three steps toward the door.

I step with her. "If it could be proven that this is about my skin color, you would be in a lot of trouble, Lilith. I know that and you know that."

She slowly turns back around.

I stare at her and wait for my words to stick, like bugs on flypaper. "But since I love everybody here and since Alpha Delt has been my home and my family for the last twenty-five years, I will not put the people I love in that position."

I see her shoulders relax, then her tone softens. "Again, the bylaws specifically state that the House Director . . ."

She's rambling on and on about the same ol' thing—her *only* defense. But instead of listening to her I listen to my heart, and the more I do the clearer the problem becomes. "This is not your fault."

That lady's posture stiffens like a soldier's. I have her attention now.

"It started with your great-great granddaddy and grandmama and trickled down through all the generations in your family."

"What are you talking about?" she asks with that same sharp tone.

"Generational racism. It's like a weed. In one season it can overtake the garden and choke out the beauty. It never stops reseeding itself till somebody makes the choice to pull it out by the root and destroy it once and for all."

She closes her eyes, then shakes her head like I don't know what I'm talking about.

"That goes for both sides. Black folks can't be running around talking trash about white folks. Don't get me wrong; there's been plenty of injustice, we have to stand up for what's right. But if we keep blaming every white man for all our problems, what good does that do? Progress will never happen."

"Finally you've said something that makes sense. If I hear another word about 'Black Lives Matter' I'll throw up. Don't all lives matter?"

I'm not sure how we moved on to Black Lives Matter, but even so I decide to change my tone. Add some kindness back in. See if I can help her. "May I make a suggestion?"

I notice she's lightly tapping her foot, but she does answer me. "Sure."

"You have an awesome opportunity in front of you."

"How's that?"

"You could set a beautiful example by showing every one of our well-to-do girls that a *qualified* African American"—I flick a finger at her now—"you know full well I'm qualified—can be the House Director of one of the finest white sororities in the South. You could be the one to show them that it doesn't have to be because of affirmative action or equal opportunity, but just because I'm the right person for this job."

I look up at her, thinking she might stop me, but she doesn't. So I keep on.

"The world you and I grew up in says I shouldn't have a job like this. But things are changing. Young people today don't buy that any longer. This is your chance to make a difference in Mississippi and show folks all over our state that a Caucasian woman from an old Natchez family is willing to lead her sorority down a new and better path."

She has not interrupted me one time. Not only is my face smiling, but my heart is, too. I'm certain that everything I've said to her has had an impact, and that she might be willing to pull herself out of darkness and step into the light.

But the expression on that lady's face stays the same. She's not budging.

On second thought, I don't believe one word I've said has penetrated her brain, much less her heart. All my words must have soared right over her frou-frou Barbie head and smashed into smithereens on the composite behind her.

Looks like I've got another choice. What will it be like if I choose to stay in my job as housekeeper? After the way this woman has insulted me? Aunt Fee was exactly right. I must find another job. As much as I love these girls, I don't want to work here with a ball and chain of resentment hanging from my heart. My time with Alpha Delt has come to an end.

I take a few steps toward the door, then turn back around. "Twenty-five years is a long time to work somewhere. It won't be easy to start over, but you've left me with no choice."

After looking at me like I'm crazy, she says, "You're quitting? Because you can't have the promotion?"

I shake my head slowly. "And resent working here? No thank you. I best be moving on."

"Okay. You win."

My breath catches. "Wha . . . what?"

"You can have a raise. How's does seventy-five cents more an hour sound?" By the switch in her tone, it's evident. She thinks she's saved the day.

I just look at her. Then I turn, put my hand on the doorknob.

"Fine. I'll give you a dollar extra per hour," she says to the back of my head.

I make an about-face, take a few steps toward her. "You could offer me a *hundred* more dollars an hour and I wouldn't stay. This is about my dignity, not my paycheck."

"Don't be silly. It's . . . I don't know exactly what it amounts to, but I'm offering you a big raise."

"Actually, it's right around twelve hundred dollars by the time I pay taxes and collect unemployment all summer."

Her mouth falls open. Seems she's surprised I can calculate her offer in my head. "Suit yourself."

I clasp my hands together, shake my head from side to side. "I feel sorry for you, Miss Lilith, you know that?"

Another of her big plastic grins spreads clear across her face. "Why's that?"

"You're so worried about how something looks and keeping things the way they've always been, you don't even know I'm the best, most qualified person for this job. You go on and hire another white lady. She'll have a college degree and a good sense of how things are supposed to be run around here. But there's one thing she won't be able to do. And that's show our girls how to have relationships with people of color. I love every one of them, and I care about helping them to become the best young women they can be. Kind, compassionate, and color-blind."

"The girls have their own mothers for that. But they do need a top-notch housekeeper like yourself to keep this house looking like the showplace it was built to be. The Alpha Delts take great pride in their sorority house. That's the reason your job is so important."

Sometimes you need to know when to close the window. I look around the room—every wall full of composites from years past, a few from when I first started at Alpha Delt. I can only hope and pray that as far back as twenty-five years, I may have made a difference in the girls' hearts.

My eyes travel around the room one last time, then I open and close the door softly behind me. I head straight up to my closet, grab my pocketbook, and hurry out the side door.

SIXTY-TWO

CALI

I'm in the study lounge with several of my pledge sisters, in between classes, when I see Miss Pearl rush out the side door. She's got her purse over her shoulder and I can tell by her face something's wrong. I shove my math book aside and grab my coat.

Becca, who is right across from me reading her biology book, looks up. "Where you going?"

"I just thought of something I forgot to do," I whisper. "I'll be back." I don't give her another opportunity to ask any more questions. I hurry out of the lounge.

Then I run through the side door. After looking both ways down Sorority Row I spot Miss Pearl, already two hundred feet down, walking briskly in the direction of the Union. I rush down the front steps and onto the street. "Miss Pearl," I holler. She doesn't turn around. Now I'm running behind and calling her name again. *"Miss Pearl!"*

She stops, looks over her shoulder.

I wave, then yell again, *"Wait."* By the time I catch up with her I'm out of breath. Reaching out to touch her arm, I say, "Are you okay?"

She presses her lips together, shuts her eyes. "I'm okay, baby. Just need some time to think things through."

"What things?" We've shared our most intimate struggles with each other. Surely I have the right to ask her this question.

After inhaling a deep breath, she opens her eyes. "Cali. I just quit my job."

No, *no*. She can't do that. We're . . . Eli Manning is coming to Oxford to help us change things. I want to tell her all about it, but it's not the right time. Everyone in our pledge class had decided we would tell the whole staff together. In a special way. Right before Monday Night Chapter. "Why did you quit? What happened?"

She's not crying. In fact, she's pretty calm. "Do you remember on Bid Day when I told you to keep your distance from Lilith Whitmore?"

I snicker. "Of course I remember. And a lot has happened you don't know about. Has she done something to you?" Tons of girls are walking back from class, several have their heads down in their phones, but some are looking at us curiously.

"Let's go sit," she says, pointing down the road. "In the Grove. I haven't taken a seat in the Grove in years." It's beautiful outside, crisp with a solid blue sky, but once we pass under the trees I feel a sudden drop in temperature. I stop to zip my jacket and Miss Pearl takes a moment to look up at the trees. Autumn is in its full chromatic glory. When she sees that I'm zipped up she motions for us to sit on a short wall with the James Meredith statue behind us.

What Miss Pearl tells me is shocking. I suppose I shouldn't be surprised, though. Especially when I think about the way Mrs. Whitmore treated me. But hearing about the way she just talked to Miss Pearl is outrageous. Who would say all those mean things to Miss Pearl? She's one of the nicest people I've ever known.

"She can't do that," I say. "It's discrimination. You should sue." I point my finger down the street.

"Cali." She brings my hand down, rests it on top of my thigh. "Listen to me. I am not suing anybody. If I'm not wanted somewhere that's reason enough for me to leave."

"But you are wanted. You shouldn't have to quit your job because she's a racist."

"It's more than that, baby. I do not want to work for that woman. I would hate my job. Dread coming into work every day. Right now, I might not make much, but at least I enjoy my work. With Mama Carla leaving, things will change. My time has come to an end."

"This is wrong. You would have made the best housemother." I'm conflicted about whether or not to tell her about our plan for staff benefits. "I don't know why I thought sorority life would be so important. I was dead wrong. I wish I had never rushed."

"Don't say that, Cali. You are right where you belong. You understand the important things in life. You need to be an Alpha Delt—to set an example."

"I was gonna say that about you." I sigh, imagining the thought of losing Miss Pearl before we have the chance to develop a deeper relationship. "What will you do for work?"

"I'm headed to the employment office now to apply for a job with the University."

"Aren't you already an Ole Miss employee?"

"No, baby. We all work directly for Alpha Delt. Once I get on with the University I'll get health insurance and retirement. Aunt Fee had been bugging me to do it before she died. So that's what I'm doing."

"But... we're working on something that might change all that." I just say it.

"Nothing's going to change at Alpha Delt. I've been there a long time. I know what I'm talking about."

"We're making staff benefits our pledge-class philanthropy project. We had it all planned to tell the staff on Monday night before Chapter." Then I tell her the whole story. About Eli Manning, Ellie's dad, Mrs. Whitmore. I tell her everything.

"You and Ellie did all that?"

I nod.

Tears well up in her eyes. "For all of us? Oh Lord. I don't know what to say."

"Just say you'll stay." I reach over and hug her tightly.

"Cali. I wish I could. But I'm sure you can understand. This is about my dignity. My time with Alpha Delt has come to an end. I can't work for someone who disrespects me. I'll be fine. You go ahead on with your plan. There are still six people on our staff who need to be treated fairly. They need benefits every bit as much as I do."

"I do understand. I'm just really sad right now. I don't want to lose you."

"You won't lose me. We can get together ... anytime you want."

All I can muster is a weak smile.

"There's not a single black housemama on this whole campus. Probably not one on any other SEC campus. That's the real reason Lilith Whitmore is against me. She's worried about how it would be perceived if Alpha Delt had a black House Director."

I know she's right. I've lived in Mississippi my whole life, and there are many, many people who still care about that kind of thing. "I hate that, Miss Pearl."

She pats my knee, then pushes herself up from the wall. "I better go on over there."

I stand up, look into her eyes. "I know we haven't known each other all that long. But this is my great loss. I'm actually jealous of all the girls who have known you longer."

"That's so sweet, baby. Thank you. You remember what I said. We can still get together."

"Will you come by for visits?" Honestly, I feel like crying, because I'm so very sad right now.

"Of course. That woman can't keep me from my babies." She stretches her arm around my shoulders. "You get on back now. I'll be okay." When she hugs me, I do not want to let her go. It feels like I'm losing a mother. Not just any mother. Certainly not one with rotten teeth and dreadlocks who abandons her daughter. A real one.

SIXTY-THREE

CALI

Ellie will die when I tell her. I'm pretty sure she's in class, but I text her anyway.

Me: OMG, Miss Pearl just quit.
Ellie: Wait, WHAT?
Me: Where are you?
Ellie: In class.
Me: Meet me at the House when you're done.
Ellie: Be there in fifteen minutes.

I'm in the foyer waiting on her when she hurries in the front door. She's out of breath from running the entire way from Lamar Hall to the House in ten minutes. For privacy we dash over to the side stairwell, and I fill her in on all the details. Once we've had a chance to think it through, we make a joint decision to beeline it to Selma James's room. But when we get upstairs her door is locked. So we sit down and wait.

After twenty minutes Ellie decides to go downstairs to see if Selma is somewhere else in the House. While waiting, my mind drifts back to Miss Pearl.

The way her face brightened when I told her about our pledge-class philanthropy project and how we wanted to change things. Then I think back to how forlorn she looked after telling me all the mean things Mrs. Whitmore said to her, and I get mad all over again. Joining Alpha Delta Beta sorority, with all the love among her beautiful sisterhood, has been the best thing that ever happened to me, but I never thought I'd encounter someone with the evil character of Lilith Whitmore.

The sound of Ellie's text yanks me away from my thoughts. Found her. We're in Mama Carla's apartment. Hurry!

I grab both Ellie's backpack and mine, sling them over both shoulders, and haul butt down the staircase. When I poke my head in the apartment, Selma is in tears. Mama Carla's not crying, but it sure looks like she has been. She sees me and waves me in.

There are no chairs left, so I drop both of our backpacks on the floor and sit on my knees behind the coffee table.

"I've just started filling them in," Ellie says.

"Miss Pearl called me fifteen minutes ago," Mama Carla says. "She had just left the University employment office."

"We can't let her quit. Not when we're this close to change." I hold up my fingers an inch apart, to show how close we really are.

"Change?" Mama Carla asks. "What kind of change?" Selma shifts in her seat, then goes into all the details of our plan for staff benefits. When she's done, Mama Carla presses a hand to her heart. "That's the loveliest thing I've ever heard. When were you planning on telling the rest of the staff?"

"Next Monday before chapter meeting," Selma says, then glances at Ellie. "Ellie's dad has been a rock star. He's put tons of time and research into this."

"He's a lawyer, right?" Mama Carla asks.

"Yes, ma'am." Ellie's playing with her hair the way she always does, twisting it up in a bun. "He's always looked out for the little guy. Both my parents have. They've taught my brothers and me to carry the torch, I suppose."

"Okay," Selma says, moving to the edge of her chair. "I have a new plan. I'm calling an emergency chapter meeting. Tonight."

We all look at one another. This is good news.

"I'll get it sent out in News Now." That's our Alpha Delt weekly email blast. It informs us of everything from meal menus to date parties to philanthropy happenings. "Y'all spread the word and I'll make an announcement at dinner. No one will be happy about this. We'll put our heads together and come up with a way to get Miss Pearl back."

"But what about Lilith Whitmore?" I ask.

Everyone's eyes turn to Mama Carla.

She holds her hands up. "Don't look at me. I'm just the lame duck House Director." Then she laughs. "I'm only kidding. I'd do anything for Miss Pearl even if it means a faceoff with Lilith Shitmore." Mama Carla covers her mouth. "Excuse me, girls, I couldn't help myself." All of our mouths hit the floor at the same time. We look at each other thinking the same thing, I'm sure. Mama Carla is the freaking *bomb*. Ellie whips her hand up first, then we all give Mama Carla, and each other, high fives.

"I'll call my dad. He can't stand Lilith Shitmore," Ellie says. "Plus, he'll give us great advice."

"Oh my gosh," Selma says, holding her cheeks. "As House Corp President she'll get the email blast. I'll have to find a way to remove her."

Ellie glances at all of us, crossing her arms in front of her. "If not, we'll just plant our security guard at the chapter room door."

"Have you taken a good look at the poor man?" Mama Carla asks.

We all laugh.

"We might as well put him there," Selma says. "It can't hurt."

"What about Annie Laurie?" I ask. Ever since our confrontation, she has been much nicer to me—and Ellie. She's never said she was sorry to either of us, but I sense she feels terrible about everything. Every night before bed now she stops by my room with some sort of treat and offers to share it with Jasmine and me. Ellie says she does the same thing for her.

"She's in a tough spot," Selma answers, shaking her head slowly. "Choosing to go against her mother is not easy. But this is her chance to show us what she's made of." I think back to what I said to Annie Laurie a few nights ago: *It's hard to go against your mother. But you don't have to be like her.*

"Maybe my mom could drive down," Ellie says.

Selma leans toward her. "That's a great idea, Ellie. We need an advisor with us. Especially one who thinks like we do. Would you mind calling her?"

"Of course not. I'll call her right away."

"Everyone loves your mom." Selma's phone is resting on the coffee table. She leans over and checks the time. "Okay. It's four fifteen now. You call your mom; I'll get the email going. See y'all at dinner."

SIXTY-FOUR

WILDA

"Mom! You have to get down to Oxford. *Immediately!*" Ellie's voice is high-pitched and utterly frantic. There must have been an accident.

"Oh my God. *Is someone dead?*" I yell into my cell phone, which is carelessly tucked in the crook of my neck. Then, from sheer panic, I trip over Haynes's muddy hunting boots while trying to get in the back door. Our Chinese takeout goes sprawling all over the floor, and as I'm falling down into the middle of it, my cell phone flies off my shoulder and lands in a pool of duck sauce. Frantically trying to reach it, I step on the egg foo yong and slip again. Now I'm lying in our dinner.

When the phone is back at my ear—covered in sticky goo—I hear Ellie yelling, "Mom. *MOM*. Are you there?"

"*Yes,* Ellie, I'm here! *Who's dead?*"

"It's Lilith Whitmore!"

"LILITH WHITMORE IS *DEAD?*" I scream. At the top of my lungs . . . Then I scramble up, panting like a pug.

"NO, MOM," Ellie screams back. "She's not *dead*. She made Miss Pearl quit!"

"Oh for gosh sakes, Heart. You scared the life out of me!" My heart feels like it's speeding down the Daytona 500 racetrack.

"*Sorry*. Selma James called an emergency chapter meeting for tonight after dinner, and she really wants you here. We're coming up with a plan to get Miss Pearl back and we need you. Leave right now."

I take a look at our dinner, which Daisy is quite happy about, incidentally. Kung pao chicken is one of her favorites. "All right. I'll be there. But I have to change my clothes first."

"Why? Just come as you are. No one cares what you look like."

"And show up smelling like Peking duck?"

"What are you talking about, Mom?" I can see her eyes rolling from here.

"Never mind. I'll see you as soon as I can get there."

So much for resigning from the Advisory Board—effective immediately.

SIXTY-FIVE

CALI

Time seemed to slow to a snail's pace once I left Mama Carla's apartment. It was like I was trapped inside a bad dream moving in slow-motion. I could hardly eat my dinner. All the talk about Lilith Shitmore has my nerves bouncing around like I'm playing musical chairs. One minute I'm confident, then seconds later I'm bereft over losing Miss Pearl and the fate of my beloved sorority.

Now, sitting here in the chapter room, I'm reminded of how real this whole thing is. Our security guy is guarding the door. No joke; he really is out there. And he has a gun in his holster. I thought Selma was kidding, but apparently not. It was kind of funny to watch the looks on everyone's faces when they walked past him, and then hear all the rumblings as to why he's down here.

A glance at my phone shows six thirty. Mrs. Woodcock is on her way. It's outright amazing to me that a mom would drop what she's doing and drive all the way down to Oxford at a moment's notice. Ellie and I are saving her a seat right next to us. The new members are required to sit in the back of the chapter room during meetings and from there it graduates to the front, according to year.

When the last girl has taken her seat, Selma stands before all of us on the slightly raised stage in the front of the room. As soon as she stands up a hush falls over the large crowd and everyone gives our president their undivided attention. As I look at Selma, wearing her Alpha Delt jersey and holding a microphone in her hand, I daydream about one day becoming president myself.

"So I'm sure you've all heard bits and pieces of what happened today with Miss Pearl," she begins. "I want to give you all the details so there's no misunderstanding this whatsoever." She shifts her weight from one foot to the other, glances up at the ceiling, then breathes deeply.

Mrs. Woodcock opens the chapter room door and Ellie waves her over. She slides in next to us, then waves at Selma, who smiles and waves back.

"In a nutshell," Selma continues, "Miss Pearl went to Lilith Whitmore on two separate occasions to apply for our House Director position. I'm sure everyone has heard by now that Mama Carla is leaving to be with her daughter and grandchildren, right?" She scans the crowd, looking for nods. "Okay, just checking."

"If you don't already know, Lilith Whitmore is our House Corp President. That means she's the Alpha Delt alum in charge of everything that has to do with the operation of this House, including the hiring and firing of the House Director." She shifts her weight from one foot to the other. "Our Alpha Delt bylaws state that the House Director is required to have a college degree. And because Miss Pearl doesn't have one, Lilith Whitmore told her she's not eligible for the job."

Groans are heard from many of the girls. About sixty people raise their hands.

"Oh gosh, I'm sure y'all have lots of questions, but please wait till I'm finished. There'll be plenty of time for that." She takes a step back and rests her butt against the long table behind her. "Most everyone knows this, but in case you don't, this whole thing is much more complicated because Annie Laurie Whitmore is one of our new pledge sisters, and Lilith is her mom."

Now everyone is perfectly silent. But necks are craning around the room looking for Annie Laurie.

"I gave Annie Laurie the option of attending tonight, but we mutually decided it was better that she sit this one out."

Since Ellie and I are seated in the back with our pledge sisters I can see several of the older girls whispering to one another.

"I'm betting most of you are wondering if we can bend the college-degree rule for Miss Pearl? The answer is yes and no. First, we'd have to change the bylaws, and second, Lilith Whitmore is the one who'd have to approve it. So as you can see, we are in a bit of a mess."

A loud chorus of voices fills the room.

"Hang on. Listen up," Selma says, raising her voice over the chatter. Once everyone quiets back down, she continues. "The really hard part here is Miss Pearl feels like Lilith Whitmore made her decision based on race."

A cacophony of moans and groans fills the room again, this time even louder, and I'm afraid chaos will ensue.

"Wait, y'all, please listen," she says into the mic with a commanding voice. "Please keep your voices down. This is hard enough." Now she waits till everyone is dead quiet. "Since Miss Pearl has been here twenty-five years and pretty much runs the joint, she feels like she should have the job. And to be honest, so do I. But it's not my decision. So I've called us all here to get a general consensus of what everyone thinks."

Most every girl in the room is frantically raising her hand.

Selma grabs the sides of her head and makes a crazy face. "Yikes. Okay, one at a time, please." She looks out at the crowd of over four hundred and points to a girl I don't know on the front row. "Yes, Priestley, what's your question?"

Selma hands Priestley another microphone from the table. "Is Lilith Whitmore the only one making the decision? Aren't there other alums on the Board who have a vote?"

"Yes. We have two boards. House Corp Board and Advisory Board. This situation falls under the House Corp Board, but the other eight ladies who serve on it live all over the state. They only meet once a year. To be perfectly honest, Mrs. Whitmore pretty much does what she wants, and doesn't ask for anyone's permission. Unfortunately for us, she seems hell-bent on keeping the college-degree rule the way it is."

Selma points at another girl I don't know. "Virginia."

Priestley passes Virginia the microphone and she stands up. She turns around so all of us new members in the back can see her face. "For all you pledges that haven't met me yet, I'm Virginia Kay. I'm a senior this year. To me"—she takes a deep breath and places a hand on her heart—"Miss Pearl seems like

78

the housemother anyway. I love Mama Carla, don't get me wrong, but Miss Pearl does just as much as she does around here. She's classy and smart and from what I understand, she has a year of college already. She's going back to get her degree."

"That's actually what I was going to tell y'all next," Selma says. "So thanks for mentioning that, Virginia."

Virginia adds, "I, for one, would love to see her be our next housemother. Thank you." She sits back down.

"Miss Pearl is planning on going back to school next semester," Selma says. "She made that decision after she filled in here for Mama Carla." Selma points to a girl in the middle and Virginia passes her the mic. "Huxley?"

Huxley stands up. "What's with the security guard?" Everyone laughs.

"So, Lilith Whitmore is not happy about what we're doing. I felt like it was appropriate. Y'all will just have to trust me on this," Selma says.

Mrs. Woodcock's forehead crinkles. Then I see her slowly turn her head toward Ellie like she's been told a snake is loose somewhere in the house.

Anne Florence, a girl in our pledge class, raises her hand.

"Hang on, Anne Flo." Selma asks Huxley to please pass her the mic.

When it's in her hand Anne Florence says, "Is Mrs. Whitmore's problem that there are no other black housemothers on campus?"

Selma twists her mouth out of shape. "I suppose that's part of her hesitancy. I don't know that for sure, but I'd say, yes, that's part of it."

"That needs to change," someone yells.

"Why would we care?" another girl stands up and says. "She treats us like her own children anyway."

Tons of *duh*s, *yes*es, and *Amen*s are circulating throughout the room when Selma stands up on her tiptoes. "Hang on, everybody. We need to take a vote. Since this is impromptu I haven't had a chance to make up a ballot or anything, so let's do this." She glances around the room. "I need paper. Can someone please go to the copy machine and get a ream of paper and all the pens we have."

Lizzie Jennings stands up. "I'll go, Selma." Then she heads out the door.

Selma continues. "I think it's best to take a vote—a private vote—to see where we all stand. To Anne Florence's point, having an African American

House Director would be new for Ole Miss, so I want to make sure everyone here is okay with it. I'm not saying we need every girl to vote yes for Miss Pearl to get the job, but we do need a vast majority."

Suddenly, another senior from the front row stands up and turns around to face us. Selma hands her the spare mic. "This is a tough subject to talk about, y'all. I'm not trying to be mean, but... I'm not convinced Miss Pearl is the right person for the job." All eyes are on her as she glances around the room, as if looking for someone else to agree with her. "Maybe I'm the only one brave enough to stand up, but I know others here who feel the same way I do." She keeps looking around, but it seems everyone in the room is frozen to their chairs. "Miss Pearl's a really nice person, and I love her to death, but I just think we should be dead sure it's the direction we want to take." As quickly as she got up, she plops down in her seat and crosses her arms over her chest.

Now the room is dead quiet. Unshaken, our fearless leader nods directly at the girl before commenting. "Thank you for standing up, Brooke. Every Alpha Delt here is entitled to her opinion. Let me just make sure I understand exactly what you mean. Are you saying you aren't sure Miss Pearl should get the job because she's unqualified or because she's black?"

Brooke keeps her seat when she answers. "I'm saying we are a ninety-nine-point-nine percent white sorority. Yes, we have Alberta as a black member and I'm so glad we do, but since the rest of us are white I think we should have a white housemother. Sorry, but that's how I feel." Never directly answering Selma's question, Brooke turns to the senior sitting on her right and shrugs before passing back the mic.

Selma reaches her hand toward the rest of us. "Is there anyone else here in agreement with Brooke who's willing to share her opinion?"

No one says a word.

Selma shifts her gaze to the floor, then pulls her chin up and looks at Brooke with a neutral face. "I'm sure you're right," she says in a calm voice. "There may be several others who agree with you but are afraid of confrontation. That's the Southern way." After a nervous giggle she looks out at all of us. "There's never been a black housemother on this campus. What should our response to that be in 2016? As you ponder your vote, I ask you to consider: Is the issue that Miss Pearl is black? In which case that's a terrible precedent for our sorority to take. Or do you think she's incapable of performing the job from an ability standpoint? Yes, we have a college degree requirement in our bylaws, but we are meeting here today to decide whether or not to put pressure on our board to change that rule. We are only asking them to change because the majority of us believe Miss Pearl *does* have the ability to do the job. She shouldn't be eliminated from consideration because she has yet to finish college.

"Personally, I believe she has all the necessary skills required. Our goal here is not only to end up with the best candidate, but to do the right thing. We, as a sisterhood, should be leaders and take pride in knowing that we are promoting Miss Pearl because she is the right person for the job . . . regardless of her skin color."

Instead of applause, you could hear a pin drop when Selma finished. She never told us how to vote, but she certainly took a stand for justice and for Miss Pearl. My respect for her has grown through the roof.

Once Lizzie is back with the paper and pens, she and Selma hand out stacks to the girls at the end of every row. We're asked to simply write yes or no, fold the paper in half, then send our ballots back down to them. Selma asks three more Alpha Delt officers, along with Mrs. Woodcock, to help with the counting. All six of them sit at the table in the front of the chapter room and for the next twenty minutes tally the votes. As for the rest of the girls, most everyone is whispering. There is serious tension in the room.

The whole time they're up there I'm sure the suspense will kill me. I'm hopeful, yet I'm still worried. I look over at Ellie and I can tell she's worried, too. It seems most everyone feels the way we do about Miss Pearl, but after Brooke stood up it's hard to know.

Thirty long, excruciating minutes later, Selma stands up from behind the table. Mrs. Woodcock and the other officers keep their seats. She grabs one of the microphones and holds it an inch from her mouth. "Okay, y'all." Her smile grows and she holds her head high. "There are nine Alpha Delts, besides Annie Laurie, that couldn't make it tonight. I will personally get votes from every one of them, but I don't think it will matter. Four hundred and seventeen of you voted yes. And twelve of you voted no."

It seems like everyone stands up, whooping and hollering and dancing in place. With the large crowd, it's hard to tell who's not clapping.

Once the noise dies down, Selma leans in to the mic. "If any of the people who voted no would like to speak with me about it, please come to me afterward. We can meet privately and discuss this at great length, but otherwise I think we have a vast majority."

Mrs. Woodcock leans over and taps Selma on the shoulder. Selma looks at her and they talk for a moment before Selma continues. "For all you pledges who don't know her, this is Wilda Woodcock, Ellie's mom. She's a Rush Advisor on our Advisory Board, which is different from the House Corp Board. It's fairly confusing, but she's here tonight and we're grateful." She hands Mrs. Woodcock the mic.

"Hi, girls," she says as she stands. "I'm proud of all of you. But this is only the first step. Even though y'all are in agreement, we still have to have the House Corp Board's stamp of approval. Since Lilith Whitmore is the president, and since she's opposed, we should probably come up with a backup plan. In case she holds a hard line."

Lizzie stands straight up, whispers to Mrs. Woodcock, then takes the mic. "I agree, and I think we need to do something big. Y'all think about it. If Lilith Whitmore tells us we can't have our Miss Pearl, even if the whole board says no, which I can't imagine is possible, I'm thinking we need to stage a protest and *walk out*. I'm serious. We need to take a stand here. I say … if they try to tell us no, let's turn in our pins."

Most of us stand up and clap. Once the applause dies down, Jessica Olson pops up from the middle and motions for the mic. "Y'all, think about what's happening here. It's pretty bad. Don't you agree?" She looks around to see who's on her side.

From where I'm sitting it looks like everyone is nodding.

"Right? But there are twelve of us who don't agree, so I just want to say to them: Y'all don't have to walk out with the rest of us, but I sure wish you'd change your minds. Maybe you don't know Miss Pearl yet, but I have a story to tell you. Most of you know my mom died last year." Jessica's voice cracks and she closes her eyes to fight back tears. "Miss Pearl checked on me every single morning when she got to work for, like, five months. She let me cry on her shoulder, whether it be morning, noon or night. She'd call me, text me, send me scripture verses. Whenever I needed her, she was there. She so deserves this promotion. And one more thing. Did y'all know she's a math whiz? Seriously. Give me a show of hands if Miss Pearl has helped you out with math." She looks around the room and several girls have their hands raised. "See? College degree or not, Miss Pearl is a very smart woman. I'll sit down now, but honestly, y'all. This is a no-brainer, and I agree with Lizzie, we need to stage a protest. What are they gonna do at the National office? Spank us?"

Everyone laughs and Jessica gives the mic back to Selma.

Another girl stands up. "I'm totally in favor of all this, but when? Let's get a date nailed down and do it."

"I don't think we should wait," yet another girl says. "Let's do it next weekend. We have an away game. It's the perfect time."

"Okay. That sounds great," Selma says. "Let's get back together later in the week and iron out all the details. I'm super proud of everyone for wanting to do the right thing. Y'all are difference makers. You truly are." Now she's scanning the room. "Speaking of, Ellie, will you and Cali please come up here," she says, waving us to the front. Ellie and I leave our chairs and scoot past others on our row. As I'm walking to the front I'm swelling with pride to be an Alpha Delta Beta.

Once we're next to Selma, she says, "As you know, these two girls have spearheaded our campaign for staff benefits. Ellie's dad, who's a lawyer in Memphis, has been advising us as well. And Cali is the one Miss Pearl confided in this afternoon."

My nerves have dissipated. I'm smiling inside and out. This whole plan is coming together much better than I could have ever dreamed.

"So we'll adjourn for now. Everyone put your hand over your heart. I want to see a group secret swear that you will all keep this to yourselves."

The active members place four fingers over their hearts, something we pledges don't know about yet.

"Oops, my bad!" Selma presses her palm to her forehead. "Sorry, new members. This meeting has left us no choice but to break tradition."

The handle on the chapter room door jangles. We all can hear someone fiddling with the lock. From where I'm standing in the front of the room I watch every head in front of me whirl around to the back. The door swings open. Lilith Whitmore appears in the doorway dressed in a fancy outfit and high heels, wearing a smirk on her face.

A toe-curling hush falls over the crowd. Only the slow, steady tapping of her heels breaks the deathly silence. All 430 some-odd heads turn toward the center aisle at once, as our House Corp President saunters to the front of the room. When I steal a sidelong glance at Mrs. Woodcock her entire face has gone white. Ellie reaches over to squeeze her mom's hand. Selma and Lizzie look down at their toes and gnaw on their bottom lips. Everyone seems scared of her except me. Why would I be afraid of her now? There's nothing else she can do to hurt me. So I stare right into her eyes, daring her to cross me again.

No one is moving. You could hear a kitten's breath, it's so still. When Mrs. Whitmore reaches the front of the room she turns around and makes a purposeful inspection of the crowd. The best I can figure is she's looking for Annie Laurie. When she's convinced her daughter's nowhere to be found, she simply raises her chin and struts back down the center aisle. We all watch as she passes through the chapter room door without uttering a single word.

SIXTY-SIX

WILDA

When I saw Lilith standing in the chapter room doorway sneering at us all—dressed in a light blue suit that must have come from Neiman Marcus's couture room, and that pin on her bosom—I almost wet my pants. Because I was the only advisor in the room. I would be the one who had to deal with her. All I kept thinking was: *You idiot. Why didn't you resign when you had the chance?* As she strutted toward the front, I could feel the blood draining from my face. But when I felt Ellie reaching for my hand I knew I had to be strong. I had to show her what I was made of.

But Lilith left. She saw all of us staring at her wide-eyed and did an about-face. The security guard—well, he was dressed like one—came running in the second she was out of sight. Completely devastated.

"I tried to stop her!" he announced in a panic. "I even pulled my gun. But she barged right past me and used her key. I didn't think you'd want me to shoot her."

When I recounted the entire scene to Haynes later that night, he said, "The only reason she did that was to prove she could get past the security guard. Lilith Whitmore was not about to stand up in front of those girls and admit she's a racist. She cares far too much about what people think."

Now here we are, ten days later, in a crowd of a few thousand, standing in the street in front of the Alpha Delt House with our eyes locked on Lilith and Gage, who are watching the protest from a safe distance away. Lilith has finally been outwitted. There's no way she'll embarrass herself today. Not in front of this many people. And certainly not in front of a television camera.

"I wonder who tipped off Channel Five?" I say to Haynes. Their news truck has been parked in front of the House since ten o'clock this morning.

He shoots me a sly smile.

My mouth flies open. *"Haynes Woodcock!"*

"Four hundred and thirty-eight college girls walking out on their sorority to take a stand for their beloved housekeeper who's been denied a promotion because of her skin color? That's big news."

I'm staring at him in shock.

"I figured a little help from the media couldn't hurt the cause." He winks and smiles devilishly.

"Don't you know Lilith is furious right now? I'm surprised she's even here." I can't take my eyes off of her. Several times now she's put her phone up to her ear, then hung up abruptly. Like she's calling someone who isn't answering. "How many people do you think are here today?"

Haynes scans the crowd, which has spilled into the street halfway down Sorority Row. "Looks like Bid Day to me. It's hard to tell, but I'm guessing two or three thousand?"

"It's got to be that many." The crowd is made up of students and professors, even uniformed campus workers. Seems like everyone wants to witness the historic event.

Haynes Woodcock, Esquire, could not be happier. Watching his daughter, all dressed up along with her sorority sisters, awaiting Miss Pearl's arrival—having lead the charge for staff benefits and racial equality, has him on the verge of tears. He might be fighting them back, but I'll see them any minute now.

"Look at her, Wilda," he says, gazing at Ellie, who is in her total Ellieness, chatting with several Alpha Delts on the front lawn.

I entwine my fingers with his. "What are you thinking right now?"

He looks at me—there's that tear—and says, "How lucky we are that our daughter's head is on straight and how she cares about social justice and doing the right thing for people. At such a young age."

I think back to when I was Ellie's age. Drinking, smoking pot, acting as wild as a March hare. No doubt about it, I enrolled in college to graduate with an extra degree in Fun. I don't begrudge that time. It does sadden me, though. Never once did it cross my mind to consider the needs of the ladies who worked at the Alpha Delt house. Or how little it would have taken to provide for them. We loved them, too, every bit as much as the girls love Miss Pearl, Miss Ophelia, and the other staff members.

Haynes looks at me funny. "Why the sad look? You should be happy."

"I'm so happy about Ellie. It's just . . . I can't help regretting the wasted time before today. The staff was every bit as wonderful when I was an Alpha Delt. We never even thought about them. It makes me sad."

He stretches a loving arm around me. "I never thought about it either till the night Ellie and Cali told us about their plan for change. You'd think I would have. I make my living defending less fortunate people."

"Oh well. We can't look backward."

He shrugs. "But we can damn sure focus on the future."

I happen to spot Annie Laurie's face, just beyond Ellie's. "Did you notice Annie Laurie?"

Haynes looks up. "Where?"

I point to the porch. "Third girl from the left."

"How did that happen? I thought she wasn't participating."

"Cali and her roommate helped her to see the light. From what Ellie tells me, Jasmine heard Annie Laurie in her room crying while the girls were at the emergency chapter meeting. When she went over to see if she could be of help, Annie Laurie told her she felt like everyone in Alpha Delt hated her. And that she'd been wanting to stand up to her mother for a long time, but didn't know how."

"Really?"

"Evidently so. Then that sweet Jasmine took Annie Laurie out to dinner—*paid for it*—and spent the rest of the evening consoling her. Until the girls got back to the dorm. Apparently, she's had a real change of heart. She's been a different person since."

"Do you trust her?" Haynes asks with skeptical eyes. "People don't change overnight."

"I know they don't. But Ellie thinks it's been coming for a long time, and that Annie Laurie has buried a lot of her feelings about Lilith. We all reach our tipping point." I think back to my recent come-to-Jesus moment when I had to confront who I'd become. "We have to look ourselves in the mirror, or..." I throw my hands up.

He juts his chin across the street. "Or end up like them."

Gage and Lilith have moved in closer for a better view.

"I bet she's furious at Annie Laurie," I say. "Can you believe she had the nerve to show up?"

After rubbing one of his eyes, he adjusts his glasses, then pats my shoulder. "Be assured. This is far from over."

Lilith is still frantically trying to call someone. She keeps punching in a number then waiting for an answer. But no one's picking up. I can tell she's angry. Her arms are crossed and she's tapping her foot.

"Uh-oh. Buckle your seat belt." Haynes's gaze has shifted to our front yard and, more important, toward Annie Laurie. She's left her post on the porch and is hurrying down the front steps in a long, flowing black dress. Her phone is in her right hand and now she's crossing the street. Lilith emerges from the crowd and marches out to meet her. Gage follows behind.

"Let's eavesdrop," Haynes says, taking me by the hand.

"You can't be serious."

"And miss the best show in town? Damn. I want a front row seat."

He weaves us along the edge of the crowd until he finds a spot within earshot. I hide behind him—just in case.

Annie Laurie storms up to Lilith, shoves her hands on her hips. "Stop calling me! Can't you take a hint? I don't want to talk to you."

She's turning back around when Lilith grabs her by the arm.

"Let *go*," Annie Laurie says, yanking her arm free. Then she gets up in Lilith's face. "I am *embarrassed* to be your daughter."

Gage steps between them. "Don't you talk to your mother like that, young lady."

Annie Laurie glances at him. Then her eyes travel right back to Lilith. Her arms fall to her sides and her posture slumps. Seems like something has cracked inside. "I'm so disappointed in you. You aren't the mommy I remember." A startling tenderness has crept into her voice. "We have to help Miss Pearl so her world can change."

"You'll have to trust your father and me on this, Annie Laurie. There are some issues you're still too young to understand."

The way she hangs her head tells me she feels defeated. Instead of trying to persuade her parents again, Annie Laurie takes a step back.

"Wait. We can talk about it," Lilith says desperately, moving toward her. "You've always trusted my judgment before."

"Well, not anymore." Annie Laurie takes another step back. "For the first time in my life I have friends. Nice friends who want to do the right thing for people. Unlike you two."

Lilith reaches for her, but Annie Laurie stays put. "No, I don't want to talk about it. Not tomorrow, the day after that, or the month after that. If you insist on acting this way, just leave me alone." After a heartbroken stare at Lilith, she turns around and runs back across the street, up the stairs to the House. I see Cali, who is along the walkway, reach for her. Then Ellie, who is right next to Cali, does the same. After several reassuring hugs from other Alpha Delts, Annie Laurie moves back to her place on the front porch.

Lilith stands there watching her daughter. Her lips are no longer pressed together in fury; they have softened into a straight line. For the next five minutes her eyes never leave Annie Laurie. It's hard to read her, but I'd swear on my children's lives I see more than anger. Call me crazy, but those eyes look more wounded than furious. It takes a mother to know one and I'm pretty sure I see pain all over her face. As hard as it is for me to believe Lilith Whitmore is capable of that emotion I have a sixth sense it's there. I actually think Annie Laurie may have ruptured a valve in that cold heart of Lilith's. I start to bring it to Haynes's attention, but decide to let it go. I'm not sure he'd see it. He is a man, after all.

Lilith turns around. From where I'm standing, only fifteen feet away—safely behind Haynes—our eyes happen to meet. For a second I'm afraid, thinking she might clock me, but instead her eyelids drop sadly. When she opens them again, I get the sense she's trying to tell me something. Could it be an apology? There's pleading in her eyes. I consider going over to her but, before I can make up my mind, she motions for Gage. Ever the doting husband, he extends his elbow.

"Here comes Miss Pearl!" Selma shouts through her microphone. "I see her car. Everyone get in position."

Lilith glances briefly over her shoulder before hooking an arm inside her husband's. Haynes and I watch as Lilith and Gage Whitmore slip namelessly back into the crowd.

SIXTY-SEVEN

MISS PEARL

I told myself all day yesterday there was no need for a going-away party. That it would be too sad and I couldn't keep myself from crying every time I looked into the face of one of my babies. But when Selma called and asked me to please reconsider, I felt like I had to at least think about it.

She sounded so sad. Said all the girls wanted to do something nice for me. After twenty-five years of loyal service, they felt like a going-away party was the least they could do. She said everyone understood why I was leaving, and that they supported me one thousand percent, but they still wanted to be with me one last time . . . as a family.

Mama Carla is the one who finally talked me into it. We've talked almost every day now since I walked out. When I left the University employment office, she was the first person I called. I told her every last word that she-devil had said to me. She cried when I told her I had worked my last day, and that I wasn't coming back. I heard the first crack in her voice and that made me break down, too. I was already in my car headed home when she asked me to please come back to the House so she could hold me in her arms, but I told her I couldn't do it. Especially with Miss Lilith there. Seeing that woman is not something I ever want to do again.

Now here I am, on an away-game Saturday afternoon, headed to the House. Not as a staff member, but as a guest at my own party. Selma assured me Lilith Whitmore would not be here. How she'll keep her away is anybody's guess, but Selma swears it's true.

I took the same route I've driven a thousand times. From Highway 6, I veered left onto Jackson Avenue. Instead of parking a quarter mile away in the satellite parking lot, Selma had told me to go ahead and take a right on Sorority Row. "I have a space right out front reserved especially for you today, Miss Pearl."

The only thing different about this drive is I'm not wearing my navy blue scrubs. I picked out my favorite pair of black pants and a pretty long white sweater—the one that accentuates my Mississippi pearl necklace.

The instant I turn down Sorority Row I see all kinds of commotion going on near Lenoir Hall. Folks have spilled out in the street, like it's Bid Day. I'm having to drive extra slow to avoid hitting someone. Every time I try to accelerate I have to brake again. All kinds of folks out here. Not only sorority girls, I see plenty of boys, too. Black students, white students, teachers. Must be a few thousand people here today.

Seems like there's a large white truck with a satellite dish ahead, parked near the Alpha Delt House. As I get closer I can see it's a news van. WMC Channel 5 from Memphis is all the way down here in Oxford? And WTVA in Tupelo has a van in front of the Tri Delt house? There are even two University police cars with lights on, blocking the street. What in the world is going on around here?

When I finally make it past Lenoir Hall, I see the Alpha Delts dressed in their pretty black dresses, lined up in front of the House the way they do for Pref. Some are on either side of the walkway. Others are on the front porch. More lined up on the balcony. The entire yard is full of my sweet babies.

Now that I'm closer I can see all of them wearing big white buttons on their dresses, with black letters. I can't read what they say, but when I get a few yards from the House I see they match two banners, the size of Texas, hanging from the upstairs balcony. I gasp; feel the blood draining from my face. Before God, one says, GIVE US OUR MISS PEARL! The other, hanging right next to it, says: OR WE QUIT!

Wha… What is happening here today? Oh Lord. My heart is racing so fast I feel faint. I place my hand on my chest, trying to get it to slow down, then I drive forward a few more feet. There's Selma. She's motioning for me to park. Standing on the curb in front of a space with a sign that reads: RESERVED FOR PEARL JOHNSON. I pull on up a little past her, then put my car in reverse. Parallel parking has never been my strong suit, especially with my nerves jumping all over this car, but I manage to squeeze my Honda in somehow.

Now Selma has her hand out to open my door. The second it opens I hear their voices. Soft and steady, like a choir of angels, filling the air with a song they sing on Pref. About pearls and roses. I don't know every word, but after twenty-five years I'm very familiar with the song. When I step out of my car, and turn around to face the House, I see what seems like all 438 of my Alpha Delt babies, with their hands outstretched, singing and smiling right at me. Before I have a chance to put my foot on the curb, a young black man sticks a microphone under my chin.

"What's your reaction to this altruistic show of support from the Alpha Delta Beta sorority sisters?"

I'm so choked up I can barely speak. But I manage to say, "I thought I was coming to my going-away party. I had no idea they were doing this until now." I'm talking to him, but my eyes are pinned on the girls.

"Do you feel discriminated against?" he asks. I guess my babies filled him in on what's been going on around here.

Sarah Mason, who is standing a few feet away, catches my eye. That baby loves me like a second mother. "Not by them, no, sir."

"Then from whom do you feel discrimination?"

"Sir, sir," Selma says, placing her hand out to stop him. "You'll have plenty of time to talk to Miss Pearl. Right now we want her to enjoy her moment. *Please*."

She guides me away from the reporter and up the front steps to the long walkway. With each step I take, girls reach out to touch me. I feel the love radiating from their fingers to mine. Can this be happening? Have they actually threatened to quit Alpha Delt? For me? I walk slowly up to the House, the way I've done a thousand times, and each girl turns as I pass by. When I step onto the front porch, I happen to glance to my left. Well, there's Annie Laurie Whitmore. Something told me she wouldn't be here today. Yet here she is with her hand outstretched, singing with the rest of the sisters.

Mama Carla is waiting for me when I make it inside the door. Right behind her are Mr. Marvelle, Helen, Latonya, Bernie, and Kadeesha. I'm overflowing with emotion; my entire face is covered in tears.

Someone taps me on the shoulder. When I turn around, I see Cali with her arms open wide. I knew there was something special about that sweet little redheaded girl.

SIXTY-EIGHT

CALI

The last twenty-four hours have been the best hours of my life. Yes, we totally surprised Miss Pearl, and she was blown away with the amount of love and support she received from all the Alpha Delts, and how we were willing to walk out of the sorority on her behalf, but equally as good—shock of all shocks—Annie Laurie has made a turnaround. Now she's one of us.

It must have started the night I confronted her. When Selma called the emergency chapter meeting and Annie Laurie was excused, things really turned around. At first she acted like her normal self—all haughty like she couldn't have cared less. She would hardly look at Ellie when she left for the meeting. All that had changed by the time Ellie and I got back from the House. When I opened the door to my room and saw her propped up next to Jasmine—*on Jasmine's bed*—Ellie and I had to do major double takes. Especially when we noticed her eyes were red and swollen.

"Hello, ladies," Jasmine said when we walked in. "I'd like for you to meet our new friend, Annie Laurie Whitmore." I was sure Ellie was thinking the same thing. *What the hell is going on around here?*

Annie Laurie slid off the bed, fresh tears in her eyes, and slunk over to us. She hung her head and wrung her hands before muttering, "I never meant to be so ugly to y'all. Especially you, Cali. I'm sure y'all hate my guts." She couldn't meet our eyes. Instead she looked back at Jasmine for help.

Despite the way Annie Laurie had treated her since we moved in, Jasmine came to her rescue. She crawled right off the bed and wrapped her arm snugly around Annie Laurie's shoulder. "Our friend here has been embarrassed about her mother for a long time, but she hasn't wanted to admit it. She's not sure what to do about it, either." They looked at each other like total BFFs before Jasmine added, "Now she's embarrassed to ever show her face at y'all's sorority house again."

The way Annie Laurie struggled to lift her chin was painful to watch, but she finally made eye contact with us. Fresh tears had flooded her eyes. "It was awful being here, knowing all my sorority sisters were meeting at the House . . . because of something my mom did. This time she's gone too far. I don't know everything she said to Miss Pearl, but I don't have to. I know my mother."

Tucking her hair behind her ears, she gazed at us with an emotion I know all too well—shame. She used her fingers to twist her bottom lip out of shape, as if she wasn't sure how much more to confess. "She wasn't like that when I was little. Well, if she was I never noticed it. I've been thinking about it nonstop. Ever since that night I got mad at y'all for going against her. She has a problem, y'all. So does my dad." She turned to Ellie and shrugged. "They aren't like your parents."

Although she was at a loss for words, Ellie still gave her an understanding nod.

Our new friend, as Jasmine called her, sniffled several times from all the crying she'd been doing, so I took a tissue from my desk and handed it to her. Once I did, a look of conviction replaced the apprehension she'd shown moments earlier. "They are racists. There's no way around it. And my mom is rude to people who don't come from wealthy backgrounds. She thinks she's better than they are. Honestly, for a while I thought that, too. But we're not. And my mom . . . She is a total embarrassment."

I wanted to make sure I said the right thing. First I glanced at Jasmine, who responded with a slight nod, as if to say: *Go ahead. It's okay.* So I took Annie Laurie by the hand. "I get embarrassment. I get it in a big way. Most of my life has been spent embarrassed by my mom." She already knew the basics from her mother's nosy digging into my past—I was sure of it—so there was no need to go into more gory details. But that was the icebreaker. She reached out to hug me, and when she did something inside of me cracked wide open and I cried, too. As mad as I am at my mom, I actually felt sorry for her in that moment. We all stayed up till two in the morning letting Annie Laurie talk about her mom. She is furious. When or if that will change is anyone's guess.

Ever since that night, Annie Laurie has been a real friend. She loaned me her totally awesome short black dress to wear to Miss Pearl's going-away party. Once she saw the way it looked on me she even said I could have it. I know people don't usually flip a 180 that fast, but I think Annie Laurie has been in more pain over her mother than she's ever let on. Kind of like me.

The night we all stayed up late made me realize we all have issues we'd rather not face. Everyone has her share of rotten fruit. Even Annie Laurie, a girl with all the money and all the looks in the world, is totally embarrassed by her mother. And she's been hiding that secret—only God knows how long. Granted, she hasn't handled it very well, but have I?

Ellie's grandmother drives her stark raving crazy and Jasmine's older brother, I learned a few nights later when we stayed up talking till four in the morning, is HIV positive. The gossipmongers in Martin have uncovered dirt on Bailey. Her father is rumored to have embezzled money from his company and may go to jail. Sweet Tara, at the end of our hall, has an alcoholic father. When I think about throwing everyone's dirty secrets and problems into a pile, maybe I'll still pick mine. I have the greatest grandparents who ever lived and they love me deeply. God gave me a brain that ensures I never have to worry about my grades. Who knows? Perhaps I inherited it from the dad I never knew.

I have the power to be anyone. Shame over my past doesn't have to dictate who I am or, more importantly, who I'll become. I, California Ann Watkins, from itty-bitty Blue Mountain, Mississippi, have the power to be governor of our beautiful Magnolia State, even if I am five foot two.

Thinking like this, I have to admit, is a big relief. But our pressing dilemma, the one constricting my heart, is still unresolved. Now that we've taken a stand and shown we're willing to walk out of our sorority, will Miss Pearl be able to return as House Director of Alpha Delta Beta? Or will Lilith Whitmore have the final word?

SIXTY-NINE

WILDA

Four weeks later

I decided to temporarily disconnect our home phone and change my cell phone number. Once the protest story broke on the national news, I became a celebrity. It seemed like every person I'd ever known—at least those who knew I was an Ole Miss Alpha Delt—"blew me up," as Ellie would say, dying for the inside scoop.

But as an Alpha Delta Omega, I'm sworn to secrecy. I can't publicize our dirty laundry, no matter how I feel about Lilith Whitmore. I'm terrible at telling people no, so the only way to handle it was to go off-grid. I may have come a long way in the last few weeks, but I'm still in the "work in progress" category.

The day after the protest, an emergency House Corp Board meeting was called. Something had to be done, and it had to be done fast. All but four of our girls were willing to walk out of the sorority on Miss Pearl's behalf. The eight others, who had also voted no in the chapter meeting, ended up changing their minds and supporting Miss Pearl. We had to make a decision about the college degree requirement and offer Miss Pearl the job—or not.

All of the House Corp Board members drove in, that Monday after the protest, from all over the state. Although we were merely Rush Advisors without a vote, Sallie, Gwen, and I were invited to the meeting also, and so was Selma James. Because of our commitment to Alpha Delt, they valued our opinions and felt we should, at the very least, be included in the discussions. Now, looking back on it, I should have stayed home. I'd give anything to not know what I know. And I wouldn't have had to change my phone number.

We convened at the Inn at Ole Miss for a clandestine conference—sans Lilith—in a small meeting room. Our National Alpha Delt president even called in to the meeting and was put on speakerphone as we discussed our fate. Someone had the great idea to have lunch catered in from Volta, a favored Oxford restaurant, and it saved the day. For me, anyway.

The first order of business was to address whether or not Lilith should remain as House Corp President. Even with the way she had handled everything, including her switcheroo of the Rush ballot—which no one can prove— it was still tricky business. Lilith is a volunteer. But every single House Corp Board member voted unanimously to ask for her letter of resignation. When one of the board members turned to me and suggested I break the news to her since we were close friends, I almost had to change my underwear. "Who, me?" I gasped, with a hand on my heart.

Sallie saved me with her laugh, then added, "Unless you want to pay Wilda's cardiac arrest hospital bill, y'all best let someone else do it."

Lilith's been stripped of her crowning glory, but she gets to keep her pin. Haynes, believe it or not, doesn't give her all the blame. He includes the entire Greek system.

He explained it this way: Any time an injustice is going on, more than one person knows about it. It doesn't matter if it's a sorority or a fraternity, a corporation, a media outlet, or even a law practice. People in charge know what's going on, but they choose to keep the status quo. It's more convenient that way. But when something of this nature comes to light, like our girls protesting against the way Miss Pearl was treated and the lack of staff benefits, all of a sudden it becomes public and paints the organization in an unfavorable light. He says someone has to take the fall, and this time it's Lilith. He's not saying she doesn't deserve to be ousted—he believes that wholeheartedly—but he believes the system is also to blame.

As for me, I think the whole thing is a tremendous oversight. Haynes, bless his heart, is bent toward cynicism.

Call me extra crazy, but I feel sorry for Lilith now. Her own daughter wants nothing to do with her. To say her friends have dropped her like a hot potato is putting it mildly. They've put her in the "rotten, slimy potato" category. It seems like the entire state of Mississippi is talking bad about her. When Fran from the board called to tell her she'd been asked to step down, Lilith said she'd never step foot in the Alpha Delt house again.

Surely a nice person lives in there somewhere. Surely she's not inherently mean. I've been giving it a lot of thought these last four weeks, and I've decided she's a wounded, tortured soul. Something must have happened to her in childhood or another time along the way. Childhood wounded me, but I tend to take it out on myself more than I do others. And for God's sake, I'm the last person who needs to be judging another person's mistakes.

Here's the kicker: Once the decision was made, the board members tried talking *me* into taking over Lilith's position. I politely declined, but somehow agreed to serve on an interim basis until a permanent replacement can be found—someone like Lilith with tons of free time. The ten grand I owe Mama certainly won't get repaid with volunteer hours.

I'm beginning to sound like a broken record, but I knew I should have resigned from the Advisory Board when I had the chance.

SEVENTY

MISS PEARL

Thirty minutes into *The Voice* I hear a rap on the door. I knew I shouldn't have waved at James Hardy this morning. Soon as I did it I regretted it. His chest puffed up the second I lifted my hand. That man can keep on knocking as far as I'm concerned; I am busy. Usher is on the television.

Looking at my main man with his handsome self is the best way I know to take my mind off everything that's happened. On the bright side, I've got two job offers. First, the University has a position with my name on it: a supervisor in the maintenance department making fifteen dollars an hour *plus benefits,* including health and dental insurance and retirement. I can even attend the University again at a discounted rate. I'm supposed to give them an answer by close of business Friday.

Miss Wilda came over here personally the other day to let me know the board unanimously approved my application for House Director. She even said there's a plan in the works for staff benefits. Eli Manning is on board to help the pledges with their fund-raiser. When he heard about the protest, he called Selma personally and commended her on a job well done.

The best part about the offer is Lilith Whitless will not be my boss. That lady finally got her due. I might not know everything that's going on behind closed doors over there, but I do know one thing: Before God, I will never be in the same room with that woman again. Not today, not tomorrow, not ever.

I haven't made up my mind yet. There are pros and cons for both positions. Attending the University at a discounted rate translates to quite a bit of money. When I explained that to Miss Wilda, she said it was perfectly understandable. On the other hand, having a lovely apartment to live in has value and is something I would greatly appreciate. But I have to consider my future and where I have the best opportunity for advancement. No matter the outcome, I am happy. Knowing the girls took a stand for me is something I'll cherish for the rest of my life.

Lord have mercy, here comes the knock again. I mash the pause button down so hard, I leave an imprint on my thumb. Then I drag myself off the couch and pad over to the door. Once I put my eye up to the peephole, I nearly fall out on the floor. It's not James Hardy. The Evil Queen herself is perched right outside my door.

What in the world could she want? I sigh so loud I'm quite sure she can hear me, but I do not care. She can stand there all day long if she wants to. I am *not* opening my door for her. Now I wish it was that James Hardy fool. As I'm headed back to the couch I hear her say, "Hello. Miss Pearl?" in a tone that's not harsh.

So that's what she's doing. Putting some nice in her voice. Coming over here to save face. *Go on home, lady. You're not fooling me.* I plop back down on the couch and snatch up my remote.

"It's Lilith Whitmore. I have something for you."

Something for me? Like what? A warrant for my arrest? What on earth is so important that this lady has made it her business to drive all the way out to my neck of the woods? She's crazy if she thinks I'll listen to one more word of her disrespectful bullcrap.

"It won't take long."

Why would I want to show my face to her? So she can slap it again? I may not have a college degree, *yet,* but I am no dummy. Maybe I should call the police. She's on my property now. Where's my phone?

"I'll leave it on your stoop. Please don't wait too long to get it, though. I wouldn't want it stolen."

Stolen? What makes her think anyone around here would want what she has? And who does she think is a thief? Maybe I should open this door and give her a big piece of my mind. Let her know despite what she thinks she sees on the outside, my neighborhood has more love on the inside than that Natchez mansion of hers has ever had. That I know.

"I'm leaving now. I hope it will be okay out here."

That's it. I'm fixing to let her have it. I push myself up, pad back over to the door and put my eye up to the peephole again. She's digging inside her extra large Louis Vuitton pocketbook. Probably going for her gun. Because of me, she's lost her board president position. I've read about people like her, snapping all of a sudden.

But the more I think about her coming to shoot me I reconsider. Mama Carla said she was watching everything that happened at my going-away party from a safe spot across the street. She's nothing but a chicken. With her head cut off! I have to stop myself from laughing out loud imagining her running around the House headless.

Instead of a gun she pulls out a wrapped gift in shiny light blue paper tied with a white satin bow. And here comes a card. I watch as she bends down and sets them both on my doormat. She stands back up, then turns and walks away. The echo of her clicking heels can be heard a mile off.

Once I figure she's gone for good, I creak open the door, bend down, and scoop up the gift and the card. Simply because I'm curious. Half of me is scared to see what's inside. Suppose it has some kind of deadly poison inside, set to go off when it opens? Or a small bomb ready to set me on fire?

On second thought I better not open the box, but I go ahead and take a chance on the card, open the envelope, and slide it out slowly. It's on fine ivory paper with a deckled edge, a watercolor rendering of the Alpha Delt House with our Greek letters over the front door. I'm still alive—praise Jesus—so I turn it over to see what in the world she has to say for herself.

Dear Miss Pearl,

It's never been easy for me to admit when I'm wrong. Call it control. Call it a generational curse. Call it whatever you want, but it doesn't justify the bitter truth. I treated you horribly. The bad news, for me anyway, is that you aren't the only one. To be candid, I've hurt so many people, in so many ways, I don't know how I'll ever begin to clean up the carnage.

This is for you. I'm not worthy of it. Everything it represents is the opposite of who I've become. I'm not sure what to do about that, but it's certainly not your problem. Although I don't deserve it, I can only pray that someday you may be able to forgive me.

Even though I'm no longer president, I hope you'll please return to the House as the House Director. Amending the bylaws was the easy part, I'm sure. But finding another real Mississippi Pearl would be impossible. You are our official jewel, the heart of Alpha Delta Beta.

With Love,
Lilith Turner Whitmore

I am thunderstruck. My heart, the one I thought had petrified when it came to her, cracks. These are the last—*last*—words I ever expected to hear from Lilith Whitmore. Half of me believes it must be a hoax; she couldn't have written these words if a gun were put to her head. But the other part of me says: "Open the gift, Pearl."

When I remove the bow and tear back the wrapping, I find a small black velvet box. Real slow like, I open the lid. When I see what's inside, my breath catches. It's Miss Lilith's pin. The one she wears over her heart every time she walks in the House. I'd seen plenty of them over the years, but seeing hers up close makes me think it's older than most—an antique from another generation. Someone told me her mother was an Alpha Delt. Perhaps it was hers.

"Pearl," I hear a small voice call from the stairwell. The sound of her heels fills the air as she walks toward me. I've never seen her looking so casual. Blue jeans and a short jacket. Her hair is a mess, no makeup on her face. Once she gets closer she tries looking at me, but her lids fall, like she can hardly do it.

There's a battle going on between my head and my heart. My heart wants to believe her, but my head is still telling me no, it's all for show.

Before I have a chance to put words together she says, "I am the antithesis of every symbol on that pin." Then she hangs her head. She's close enough now that I can see sprouts of gray have rooted in her part. After a long stretch of time, she finally pulls her head up. "I am ashamed of myself for ever wearing it. But that shame pales in comparison to the disgusting way I've treated you."

Confusion is swirling through me every which a way. So much of it, I can't speak. At first I thought I was crazy thinking I could hear emotion in her voice, and now, this close to her, I see real tears.

"Instead of listening to you, when you came to me about the House Director job, I insulted you. Of course you're qualified." Her shoulders crumple, like she's hiding from herself. She presses a hand against her cheek, hangs her head again. "I can't stand the sight of myself."

This woman is not the Lilith Whitmore I know.

I'm thinking of at least touching her on the shoulder, but before I can do it she says, "To think I held a hard line about the college degree requirement is . . . deplorable. Oh my God." She squeezes her head in her hands. "I'm a monster."

Now I feel like I have to say something. If I don't, I'll be the monster. So I go ahead and say exactly what's been on my mind since she started talking. "I appreciate all you're saying; I really do. I'm curious, though, what changed your mind?" It must have to do with her getting fired.

"Four weeks ago, at the House, when all the girls took a stand for you, and rightfully so, Annie Laurie—my one and only child, *the love of my life*—told me she was embarrassed to my daughter. And not to call her again." Her voice cracks. Teardrops stream down her face. "I hurt so much I can hardly breathe."

This lady is crying her heart out. And struggling for her words. After digging in her pocketbook, she pulls out a used tissue and dabs her cheeks. "I started th-thinking about what I'd already passed on to her, and I couldn't stand myself. No wonder she has no fr-friends."

"That's not true, Miss Lilith. She has friends."

"It's absolutely true. She was cut from Alpha Delt. Not a single vote."

I jerk my head back, give her a dazed look. What is she talking about?

She wipes another tear from the end of her nose. "I saw the list. Not a single vote. So I manipulated the Rush ballot. I couldn't stand for her to be hurt and rejected again. I'd tried everything I knew to buy her a set of friends, but it never worked. When I saw her at the House, with the girls actually embracing her for taking up for you, something clicked. I finally understood what a witch I'd become and worse, what I'd passed on to her." She hangs her head again and sobs.

I take a deep breath. This is a lot to hear out of someone. Especially her.

She blows her nose, looks me in the eye. "I've been thinking about what you said about generational racism. I never thought I came from a racist family. But after thinking about it for days I realized: We're all racists. Even my own mother. The woman I strove to be exactly like. I'm embarrassed to admit that, but it's true."

I start to comment, but decide to let her finish.

"Gage and I were furious when Ole Miss wanted to change the mascot to the brown bear. We rued the day we had to stop singing Dixie at the games. And we really hated it when we were forced to stop waving our little Rebel flags. I thought Ole Miss was crazy for making the change. It was all tradition, but I never thought about the real reason behind it until you said what you said. It's terribly offensive. Please know I am so, so sorry." When she pleads I see honest emotion on her face. I'm starting to believe her.

If this isn't an uncanny turn of events I don't know what is. For the last twenty-five years I've been sitting in the therapist's chair counseling hundreds of girls through whatever they've been going through and now here she is, as broken as any person I've ever seen, taking her own seat. Not in my closet, at my home. I want to be very careful what I say, because until now, she's done ninety-nine percent of the talking.

"Why don't you come inside? It's cold out here." I reach my arm across her shoulder, guide her into my apartment. After offering her my seat on the couch. I take the chair.

Before I say a word I hand her the box of tissues I keep on the end table. She removes a few and nods in thanks. I lean toward her. "Mrs. Whitmore, you have been given a special gift. Do you realize that?"

She lightly shakes her head no.

"Some people go their whole lives with their eyes closed. They live in darkness and never see light. They never see the error of their ways. And they sure don't admit it." I take a chance, put my hand on her knee. I'm half expecting her to draw away, but she leans in closer. "You have done a difficult thing. I appreciate you coming to talk with me. From the bottom of my heart I thank you."

"Will…will you please call me Lilith?"

Now we're getting somewhere. "Sure I will."

"Pearl?" She says, with her eyes on mine. "Would you allow me the honor of pinning you?"

I nod, feel my own tears stinging the backs of my eyes. Fifteen minutes ago, when I heard her knock, my heart was full of anger and resentment. Thank you, Lord, I wasn't too stubborn to open the door.

"Thank you," she says. "Let's stand up, please."

Once we've both pushed ourselves up she takes the box from my hand. She removes the pin and places it in the palm of hers. With trembling fingers she touches each of the symbols. She glances at me, tries to smile, but she can't do it. "The quill is our symbol of truth and the quest to obtain it." She hesitates, takes a deep breath. "The white rose represents our sympathy toward one another in times of need or hardship. And, finally"—she holds my gaze—"the pearls symbolize love, perfection, and purity."

I smile at her. And so does my heart.

"When an Alpha Delta Beta is pinned, it's a symbol of her love, devotion, and never-ending friendship with her sisters."

Now her hands are steady. She reaches out, pushes her tiny gold pin through a pinch of my sweater, and clasps it softly. She does the same with the quill, hanging from a small gold chain. Then that lady wraps her arms around me like I'm a member of her family. The resentment I've been harboring melts away, as if my heart has been placed in a hot oven and the dirt and grime have seeped out into the pan. But when she pulls back she hangs her head like heavy bricks of shame have been reattached to her shoulders. Her chin is quivering.

I reach out to touch her arm. "What's wrong now?"

She won't look at me, just talks to the floor. "I can't help thinking about initiation in December. I won't get to pin my own daughter. She'll never be able to forgive me."

"That's not true, Lilith. When she sees the change in you, she'll come around."

"Not after what I've done." Her sobs return.

For the first time I feel her pain. Because of a choice she has lost her only daughter, the very essence of her heart and soul. "Raise up your head, Lilith. There's something I want to tell you." As she lifts her gaze her poor little ol' face looks like she's been inside a torture chamber. Not wanting her to look away, I make sure to lock my eyes onto hers. "I've done plenty of things I'm not proud of."

"You mean you're not perfect?"

Now she's got me tickled. "No, ma'am. Far from it."

A forced grin is all she can muster.

"I'ma tell you something else I know. Your daughter *will* forgive you."

"After what I've done?" She shakes her head. "No way."

"Yes, she will."

"How do you know?"

My mind drifts back to Aunt Fee and all the times she and Mama told me those very words. Slowly I lift my arm, show her my tattoo.

"What does it mean?"

"It means: I have been forgiven."

"What have *you* done? Everyone loves you."

A lump springs in the back of my throat. When I open my mouth to answer words won't come. So I have to force myself to speak. "I gave up my own flesh and blood. An innocent baby girl—to a couple up in Memphis I didn't even know. It was selfish. But I know the good Lord forgives me and she does, too."

Lilith tilts her head to the side. A deep furrow lines her brow. "Selfish? Adoption is the most *un*selfish act I know." Her posture has stiffened; the tone in her voice is pointed. "If you couldn't raise her—no matter the reason—you did the right thing. You showed her great love. Not to mention the love you gave to a childless couple. You enriched their lives beyond their wildest dreams. You gifted them their greatest joy. You are *not* selfish, Pearl." Adamant eyes lock onto mine.

I feel my shoulders relaxing. Sharing my story with her has given me a surprising sense of relief. And her unexpected words have given me fresh encouragement. I sure do appreciate her reassurance.

Before I can tell her Lilith reaches over and gently pats my cheek. "Now I'll tell *you* something." She pauses, making sure she has my gaze. "I spent years, the best years of my life, thinking I'd never have a child of my own." The emotion in her voice is raw and bloodstained. "If it weren't for the selfless choice of another teen mom, I wouldn't have Annie Laurie."

I'm tempted to gasp, but instead I stay still. I know her pain. Although our situations were opposite, they were the same difference. "You have no idea what it means to me to hear that. I've spent my entire adult life thinking about my choice and how it has affected my child. Not a day goes by that I don't wonder what kind of woman she is today."

"I'm sure your daughter is a very lovely young lady." She leans toward me with a tender gaze. "Gage and I have friends in Memphis. We could help you find her."

I smile, feel our hearts joining together. "That's mighty sweet of you, Lilith, but I put that in God's hands a long time ago. That's her decision. If she wants to find me, I'll be waiting." Then I take her pretty manicured hand in mine. "One day soon, let's you and I go out to lunch. I hear the City Grocery is a good place. We'll sit down, order us a nice glass of wine, and really get to know each other."

"Does this mean . . . you'll be my friend?" she asks timidly.

Less than thirty minutes ago I swore before God I'd never be in the same room with this woman. It just goes to show we should always choose our words carefully because we never know what the future holds. All at once I'm confounded by the power of forgiveness. Lilith Whitmore was my least favorite person and now, thanks to God, opened secrets, and receiving hearts, we have our own bittersweet bond. "Of course I will."

"What about the House Director position? Please don't turn it down because of me."

I look at her like she's crazy. "A Mississippi tornado couldn't keep me away from the Alpha Delt House. Besides, I know a special young lady from Natchez who might just need my counsel."

For the first time since she's been here, Miss Lilith smiles.

ON A PERSONAL NOTE

Some of my best days were spent at my sorority house at the University of Alabama. I formed sincere friendships that will last for the rest of my life. Although I don't see my sorority sisters as often as I wish, when I do spend time with them it seems only weeks have passed. Not decades. We pick right up where we left off. Well, maybe not with our famed college antics, but certainly with love and camaraderie. Our bonds are special and I treasure the memories and our time together.

When I attended college back in the late seventies, my sorority sisters and I dearly loved the ladies on our House staff. I well remember mornings before class, poking my head in the kitchen and reeling off a special order to one of the cooks. My requests were always met with a "Coming right up, baby. How you doing this morning?" A weeknight or a Sunday lunch didn't go by without all 150 of us sitting down together—in our Sunday best, mind you—to enjoy a home-cooked meal made and served by the ladies in our kitchen. Our favorite dinner was fried chicken with mashed potatoes, gravy, and green beans. Zebra pudding was our favorite dessert: thin chocolate wafers stuffed with real, hand-whipped sweet cream. Our rooms and bathrooms were cleaned for us daily. I remember feeling jealous of my friends in another sorority who had a housekeeper they all considered a second mother who gave sage advice about whatever trouble they had gotten themselves into or any other personal crises they were facing.

As a college student it never once crossed my mind, and I'm betting it never crossed the minds of other sorority girls, to ask if these women had health-care or retirement benefits. After all, House business was none of our busi-ness. We were students. It was only thirty-five years later, while attending the dedication of our brand-new sorority house, that the thought actually occurred to me. (Rush is a phenomenon in the South and pledge classes have grown exponentially. In 2016, each of the eighteen Alabama sororities extended bids to approximately 155 girls. To accommodate the larger memberships, all the old University of Alabama sorority houses have been torn down and forty-thousand square foot, multimillion dollar mansions have taken their places.)

I met my college roommate in Tuscaloosa for the ribbon-cutting ceremony for our expansive new sorority house, held during the Alabama-UT football game weekend. When we walked inside the House our jaws dropped—the marbled entryway, the grand staircase, the exquisite decor—it was extraor-dinary.

Later in the day, a housekeeper pushing her dust mop down the long hallway lined with composites caught my eye. As I continued to watch her I noticed several members and alums stopping to give her heartfelt hugs. I over-heard many of the girls telling her they loved her. I became so intrigued that I moseyed over and introduced myself. We spent a great deal of time talking about how much she loved working at the sorority house. One conversation dissolved into another and when she took me by the hand, leading me to the past year's composite with tears rolling down her face, naturally I became con-cerned. Her beloved friend, the head cook, had recently passed away from can-cer, and the active members had included her picture on the composite to honor her memory and her twenty-seven-year legacy. Wiping the tears away with the back of her hand, the housekeeper went on to explain the cook had not had proper health care. When I pushed her for more details, she reluctantly admitted that the cook had no health insurance. In fact, none of them did.

After returning home I kept thinking about her story. It grabbed ahold of my heart and wouldn't let go. After a few phone calls, and quite a bit of research, I learned this was not only true at my sorority house, but at the majority of sorority and fraternity houses on campus. And not just at Alabama, but all over the South and possibly the country. A very few houses in the SEC,

I learned, do offer health insurance, but, like many jobs, the staff is required to pay a percentage of the premium, which often precludes them from participating. (In some cases the House Directors are provided health and dental insurance by the sororities or fraternities. The University of Alabama, in particular, has begun hiring House Directors as state employees to extend health and dental insurance benefits.)

Many of these men and women have worked in these opulent environments for decades for minimal compensation and have to work two jobs to make a living wage. I researched how much it would cost to provide not just health insurance, but a full gamut of benefits for everyone on the staff and was surprised to learn how little it would take. Most SEC sororities have active memberships ranging between 250 and 550 girls, with fees as high as $7,600 per semester for girls living in and eating their meals at the House. If each active member paid an additional small amount, in some cases as low as fifteen dollars per month depending on the number of active members and staff members, the house staff could be given a full benefits package.

It is my belief that the reason this is done today is due to an unintentional oversight. Often times things continue simply because of the way they have always been done in the past. Perhaps this practice will have changed by the release of this book. I am not familiar with the employment practices of every sorority on every campus, so perhaps there are chapters already on board. I hope so.

As a lifelong Southerner and a child of the sixties and seventies in Memphis, Tennessee, I grew up in a prejudiced environment. As shameful as it is for me to admit, I spent time in my younger years with the notion that I was somehow better because of my skin color, my religion, and my socioeconomic status. When I look back on my thoughtlessness now, I am filled with sorrow and deep regret. Another hard thing to concede is that my father was a blatant racist. Ironically, like most affluent families in the South, he employed African American women to care for his children. My sisters and I fell in love with these ladies like they were our second mothers. We loved them throughout our lives and grieved deeply when they passed away. Their love and concern for us had left indelible imprints on our hearts. They taught us life skills and life lessons and, most poignantly, we never once heard them complain about their situations.

Has an African American lady ever been housemother of a white sorority house? I was in the bathtub one morning—my favorite place to ponder—when that thought crossed my mind. I had heard of rare occasions when black housekeepers filled in for vacationing white House Directors but had no idea if a black lady had ever been given the full-time job. To satisfy my curiosity a friend introduced me to a former beloved housekeeper at an SEC sorority house who had substituted for her boss on several occasions. This lady gave me countless hours of her time to answer this question and many others. Although she was working on her bachelor's degree at the time, she never considered applying for a full-time House Director position at any sorority house on campus. On the days she filled in, rumblings from parents let her know she'd never get the job. Even today, to my knowledge, there are no African American House Directors of National Panhellenic Sororities anywhere in the SEC. Perhaps this, too, will change in the near future.

Why Ole Miss? Why not set my book at Alabama? The simple answer is that everyone loves Ole Miss and Oxford, Mississippi, provided a more charming and colorful backdrop for the story. But, no matter the location, it is the same story most everywhere. I spoke with housemothers at several SEC sororities and fraternities, alumnae board members, active sorority sisters, and alumnae sorority sisters. I interviewed both past and present staff members. Some people I interviewed asked to remain anonymous. Many were eager for change. I interviewed Charlotte Sands-Malus of Greek House Resource, an esteemed organization that matches House Directors with sorority houses all over the country. She remembers only placing two African American House Directors in her nineteen-year career.

Like most good Southern stories I needed a devil, in this case a she-devil, so I created Lilith. She is not based on anyone I know. She is simply a figment of my imagination. Yet, sadly, I've met people like her. It was never my intention to single out House Corporation Presidents, or board members, who give graciously of their time and money to their home sororities, but someone had to be the story's villain. I'm sure you have guessed by now, but I should probably mention that Alpha Delta Beta is a fictional sorority.

This book took me much longer than my others. Resistance threw every fiery dart in its arsenal my way, trying its best to thwart my progress. I gained weight, I got sick, I couldn't sleep. There were family issues and significant,

yet beautiful, changes to my author team—then more drastic, but more wonderful changes to my author team. My computer died, twice. I dropped my
phone in the toilet, thrice. I even quit several times, threatening to buy back
my contract and hang up my career as an author. But all the while I felt God
pushing me toward the finish line of what whould be a genuine labor of love.

Like all novelists, I asked myself the ever-important question: What if?
What if the staff's story had a different ending? What if things really could
change? What if a black lady became the House Director of a white sorority
house? (The Nashville Junior League just elected its first black president.)
What if every sorority girl or fraternity guy pitched in a little more per month
so health insurance, life insurance, dental insurance, and retirement benefits
could be available for each staff member? Wouldn't that be the right thing to
do? Wouldn't all of their lives be changed forever? It seemed not only possible, but entirely doable.

There is an old saying: "The shortest distance between the human heart
and truth is a story," so I closed my eyes and imagined one where racial equality is the norm, not the exception. I dreamed of a story where the men and
women who work for sorority and fraternity houses had a better ending. After
my eyes were opened I knew I had no other choice.

ACKNOWLEDGMENTS

I've been working on this book so long—with the help of so many wonderful people—my biggest fear is that I may leave someone off my thank-you list. If that someone happens to be you, please know it was unintentional. When I do remember, rest assured, I'll be in a codependent coma, balled into the fetal position.

There's no one more deserving of my gratitude than Stuart. For two years he'd often come home to dirty dishes, three-day-old leftovers, an unmade bed, and a wife still in her pajamas. Yet he'd listen to me read passages from the book, endure my talk about the struggles, then deal with my insecurities as a writer, all the while offering encouragement and hope. Bless your big generous heart, sweet husband. I am incredibly blessed it's mine.

Next thanks goes to my beautiful boys, Michael and Will, for boundless encouragement. You are the reason I do this. I wanted to show you how to fight for your dreams, show you what hard work can bring, and give you an example of what happens when you never, ever give up. All I ever wanted was for you to be proud of me. More importantly, I'm beside-myself-proud of you.

I'm fortunate enough to be part of a big family now, with eight lovely bonus children and ten, yes, *ten* precious grandchildren. Thank you, Shannon, Sara Beth, Sloane, Whitney, Tommy, Andy, Emily, Taylor, Rylan, Levi, Ty, Quinn, Annie, Ella, Judah, Wendy, Arie, and Boone, from the bottom of my heart, for putting up with me while I hid out and obsessed over this book.

A SHOUT of thanks to my publishing team. Vicki Lame, you are a jewel of an editor. So are you, Laurie Chittenden. How lucky am I to have had you both? Thank you for your expertise, patience, enthusiasm, and especially your kindness. I adore you both. Thank you to the rest of my team at St. Martin's. Sally Richardson, Jen Enderlin, Katie Bassel, Lesley Worrell, Kathryn Parise, Brant Janeway, Karen Masnica, Angus Johnston, Cathy Turiano, Melanie Sanders, Lisa Davis, and Lisa Bonvisuto. And Jeff Willmann from SMP sales.

Scott Miller and Sarah Phair at Trident Media Group, I feel like the coolest woman in America to have landed you. Your hard work and enthusiasm has given me a huge boost. Thank you, thank you. Conrad Rippy, you are *so* kind. Thank you for everything you've done for me. Susie Stangland, Kathy Bennett, Susan Zurenda, and Meg Walker, thank you for jumping on board and helping me get the word out about *Rush*. I adore you all.

Shannon Sheshatt Howell Perry, what can I say? You had no idea what you were getting yourself into when you agreed to meet me for dinner all those years ago in Oxford. Even though I was a stranger, you graciously let me ask you personal questions about what it was like to be a housekeeper at a Southern sorority house. Thank you for the many hours on the phone and the multitude of texts. It was a privilege to be invited to your graduation and watch you receive your Master's diploma. I am honored to be your friend.

Three young sorority women helped to reacquaint me with the Rush process, gifting me with hours of their time. From interviews and introductions, to phone calls and endless texts, I couldn't have written this book without them. Katherine Johnson, Virginia Kay, and Sydney McCarthy, you ladies are my superheroes! My heartfelt thanks to each of you. Other young friends helped me with interviews, too, and I'm equally grateful to them: Grace Bradley, Kate Farley Laws, Natalie Hardy, Hannah Mims, Mary Grace Murphey, Claudia Wilder, Amelia Brown Williamson, and Priestley Worsham.

Mary Pettey, you helped me much more than you know and I love your kind heart. Thank you for the hours of information you shared. Your keen insight helped me to shape this book. I have three secret friends who don't want to be acknowledged publicly, so out of respect for that request I'll keep their names private. They know who they are, but they don't know the deep well of respect and gratitude I have for them.

Cindy Acree Marshall, my co-activist and sorority sister at Bama, witnessed my love-fest with the housekeeper who inspired *Rush,* and grieved with me over the lack of staff benefits. Without your encouragement and reassurance I may not have attempted it. Thank you, sweet sis'tah.

I'm not sure this book would have come to fruition if not for the help of two close author buddies. Ariel Lawhon, you teach, promote, listen to, and encourage me. I'll never be able to repay you, but I know you're not keeping score. You're Faithful and I adore you. Same goes to you, J.T. Ellison. You've stretched out on so many limbs for me, and I'll *never* forget your generosity. A bear hug and thank you to you both.

In addition to the aforementioned, I have more sweet writer friends who happily encourage me and keep me sane! Laura Benedict, Anne Bogel, Jillian Cantor, Paige Crutcher, Fannie Flagg, Susan Greg Gilmore, Patti Callahan Henry, River Jordan, Amy Kerr, Joy Jordan Lake, Kerry Madden, Bren McLean, Laura Lane McNeal, Adriana Trigiani, Marybeth Whalen, and Karen White. Thank you one and all.

Blake Leyers, a treasured early independent editor, thank you for digging in deep and discovering a better twist to the story. To my dear friend Bill Barkley, a heartfelt thank-you for all your editing help on my author's note. As busy as you are you still found the time.

A heaping helping of gratitude to Victoria Pan, my brilliant intern from Belmont University. From editing (speed reading my book in four hours and still retaining it) to marketing, and every other chore in between, you're a superstar! I'm just glad I'll be able to say, "I knew you when!" The Chiaravalle family always deserves my thanks. Bernie for your wonderful web design, Gail for your dear friendship and for shouting the news on all my books, and now, Rachel. Only you could shoot a decent author photo of this old girl.

Others helped me with research, too, and I deeply appreciate their generosity. Steve Berger, Beth Hamil, Vicky Hardy, Sally Legg, Patrice Pipkin Mason, Dawn Thomas of After Five Designs, Charlotte Sands-Malus of Greek House Resource, Wanda Barton Jenkins, Vicki Taylor, Karen Churchill from Hickory Flat, Mississippi, Christy Pipkin from Blue Mountain, Elise Lake, and Ann Christiansen. I'm so grateful.

There have been a few bookstores that have made a big difference in my career. First, Novel Bookstore in Memphis—Formerly Booksellers at

Laurelwood. If not for Joann Van Zandt, and the rest of their fantastic team, I would still be in obscurity. Sundog Books in Seaside, FL, put me on the map—Linda, Laney, and Dwan, your hand-selling has made a difference! So has yours, Karen Scwettman and Jackie Tanase at FoxTale Book Shoppe. Landmark Booksellers, Square Books, and Turnrow Books deserve big thanks, as do all my friends at Parnassus Books in Nashville. Niki (one K) Coffman, Karen Hayes, and Grace Wright, thank you for your support. And to the other booksellers, SIBA and beyond, book clubs and librarians who have spoken highly of my books, I hope you can hear me shouting THANK YOU! I simply could not do this without you. Kristy Barrett, creator of "A Novel Bee," you are so good to us authors. Thank you for your "bee-utiful" support.

For those who know the real Wilda, the one and only, you know Wilda Woodcock is NOT based on her. Our Wilda is strong, confident, decisive, classically beautiful, and *the* funniest person who ever lived. She's eat-your-heart-out-Tiny-Fey funny! I begged her for years to let me use her name in one of my books; thank you, "Lizzard," for finally letting me. I totally stole "Wildebeest" from her famed vernacular. Wilda Weaver Hudson is not only my lifelong friend since the age of five, but also my college roommate and sorority sister. I've laughed harder with her than I've ever laughed in my entire life. And I'm grateful to her sweet husband, Tim. He's convinced her of how beautiful her name is. I hope I have, too.

My sister, Leslie Patton Davis, and three dear girlfriends, Becky Barkley, Anne Marie Norton, and Kathy Peabody, gave me constant encouragement and wouldn't let me quit. Be it a phone call, a text, a prayer, or a pearl of wisdom, they always showed up when I needed them most. And I have three other friends who, even though I don't deserve it, go overboard acting as my PR agents, selflessly megaphoning the news about my books to everyone they know. My oldest and dearest friend, Lisa Blakley, and my sweet friends Cathy Farrell and Vicki Olson—my deepest gratitude to you all.

To you, dear reader, and all the Facebook and Instagram friends who have tirelessly commented, read, liked, and shared...thank you. I well know it is your support that has spread the word about my books, and I owe you a HUGE debt of gratitude.

And finally, to the Master Storyteller—my Advocate, my Counselor, my Prince of Peace. I owe every single word in this book to You.